MW00789724

Praise for *The Re*

"*The Reluctant Pioneer* by Julie McDonald Zander is a gripping debut novel about the westward journey of historical figure Matilda Koontz and her family. Julie's meticulous research recreates the harrowing and heart-stopping trip. She transported me back to 1847 and put me on the trail with Matilda as she overcame heartbreaking trials to reach Oregon City. Julie is an incredible storyteller! I couldn't put The Reluctant Pioneer down until the very last word."

~Leslie Gould, #1 bestselling and award-winning author of *A Brighter Dawn* and more than three dozen other novels

"I've been fascinated by the Oregon Trail pioneers since I was a girl, and their courage continues to intrigue and inspire me. Julie McDonald Zander's debut novel captures the tumultuous journey of these pioneers through the heartbreaking trials and unwavering hope of one woman who began the walk to Oregon Territory in 1847 with her husband and four boys. *The Reluctant Pioneer* invites readers to join Matilda Koontz on the trail and experience her joy and sorrow as she perseveres in her husband's search for a new home. If you enjoy reading Jane Kirkpatrick's fiction or other historical novels about women who overcome tremendous hardship for the sake of their family, you'll love *The Reluctant Pioneer!*

~ Melanie Dobson, award-winning author of *Where the Trail Ends, Catching the Wind*, and more than two dozen other novels

"*The Reluctant Pioneer* is a heart-grabbing read about a courageous woman with incredible faith and fortitude. Based on a true story, walking alongside this woman on her journey from Missouri to the Oregon Territory grips your emotions. You find yourself cheering for her and grieving with her. I couldn't put it down. It encouraged me to keep trusting in our powerful God. He alone brings us through our trials."

~ Marilyn Rhoads, Oregon Christian Writers past-president

The Reluctant Pioneer by Julie McDonald Zander features a breathtaking thrill of a ride down a waterfall, horrible tragedies, and the drudgery and dangers of crossing the scenic west by foot on the Oregon Trail. Inspired by the true story of Matilda Koonz Jackson, this engaging historical novel brings readers to tears and, at other times, to the edge of their chairs. Zander infuses realistic detail with facts while painting the portrait of an anxious but resilient pioneer whose stabilizing influence settled the West.

~ Sandra Crowell, author of *The Land Called Lewis* and *Up the Swiftwater*

"Julie Zander is a lover of history, and it shows in this intriguing book. This fictionalized version of the true story of Oregon Trail pioneer Matilda Glover Koontz is replete with authentic detail and historical accuracy and draws a vivid picture of the difficulties those early travelers experienced on the trail to a new life. A must-read for fans of historical fiction and of strong women who will go to the ends of the earth for their families."

~ Dawn Shipman, award-winning author of the Lost Stones of Argonia series

"Ms. Zander has taken the facts of a true story and woven a heart-rending, beautiful tale inspiring us to relate to the courage, heartbreak, and joys of an amazing woman."

~ Barbara Tifft Blakey, author of the upcoming release *Angel of Second Street, Bertie's War*, and three short stories in collections.

THE
RELUCTANT
PIONEER

JULIE M^cDONALD ZANDER

The Reluctant Pioneer
Copyright © 2024
By Julie McDonald Zander

Published by St. Helens Press
Toledo, Washington
www.sthelenspress.com

ISBN 978-1-963467-00-0 print
ISBN 978-1-963467-01-7 ebook

Library of Congress Control Number: 2024917240

Cover design by Kathy Campbell

Subjects: Novel / Historical Fiction / Immigration / Nineteenth Century / Old West / Oregon Trail / Pacific Northwest / Christian Fiction

DEDICATION

To all the courageous and steadfast pioneers who ventured into the unknown to forge a path and homes in a new land. And to my children, Paul and Nora. May you hold fast to the perseverance and faith of Matilda as you face obstacles in your life.

PROLOGUE

1894, Chehalis, Washington

THE REPORTER ADJUSTED his suit jacket as he settled into a stuffed chair across from the diminutive and elderly pioneer. "Mrs. Jackson, may I ask how long you have lived here on the prairie?"

The woman, her white hair tucked beneath a faded crimson floral bonnet, shifted in her rocker a moment before replying. "It's been forty-six years since I arrived."

He nodded. "And may I ask, how old are you?"

Matilda Jackson pursed her lips. "Eighty-four, I suppose."

"I imagine you've seen a lot of changes on the prairie during your lifetime, haven't you?" the reporter asked as he jotted notes onto paper.

"I reckon I have." Matilda rubbed her hands over the worn black Bible in her lap.

"What year did you cross the trail?"

"Summer of '47."

"How long did the journey take by wagon train?"

"Let's see." The woman counted off the months on her fingers. "We left in May from Saint Charles, northwest of St. Louis, and arrived in Oregon City in November. So six months."

"Did you know you can cross the country in six days now in a railroad car?" The reporter chuckled.

Matilda nodded. "That's what I've heard."

"Have you ridden on the railroad?"

She shook her head. "I don't intend to."

"Have you even seen the railroad?"

"Once. My son drove the wagon over to Napavine to show me a train as it arrived."

He leaned forward, elbows on his knees, and gazed at her. "Tell me, was it really as dangerous on the Oregon Trail as they say?"

Matilda stared at him for a moment, then looked away as liquid filled her eyes. A lone tear escaped, trickling down her wrinkled cheek.

ONE

Saint Charles, Missouri, early April 1847

"WHY WOULD WE LEAVE?" Matilda Koontz asked her husband. "We have everything we need here in Missouri—the farm, our church, our families, my mother."

As he scrubbed lye soap over his calloused hands, Nicholas peered through the window and squinted. "Mattie ..."

Matilda set down the bowl of biscuit dough and faced her husband, hands clenched against her abdomen. "I've heard of entire families perishing on the trip to Oregon. Mountain fever. Snakebites. Accidents. Children run over by wagons."

Nicholas gazed at the billowing clouds of dust swirling above dozens of oxen as rumbling wagons shook the farmhouse walls. He turned to her. "Like I've said before, the farm isn't big enough to divide among four boys. We can have 640 free acres out west. Free! Why wouldn't we go?"

Matilda bit her lip and stepped to the wood stove. She hated arguments. Discord unsettled her, tightening her midsection. Especially when she knew they'd likely go west no matter what she said. She plopped rounds of dough into a cast-iron skillet, slid it into the oven, and stirred scrambled eggs on the stovetop while bacon sizzled in another pan.

Her stomach flipped, this time not from fear. Could it be …? She calculated backward in her mind. No, most likely just a sour belly, which was probably for the best. If she were expecting, Nicholas would worry about having to divide his farm among five sons instead of four. And she certainly didn't want to trudge thousands of miles while pregnant.

Nicholas wrapped his arms around her waist and nuzzled her ear. "I'll keep the boys safe. I'll keep you safe."

Matilda swiveled into his embrace and gazed at her husband. She loved his blue eyes, the color of a deep lake. But she didn't want to go. She didn't want to leave her mother, her brothers and sisters, their home.

"I know you'll keep us safe, but traveling into a strange land, it's almost as if we're testing God's providence. We have a good life here. The boys can share the farm. It's good land, close to the Missouri—"

Nicholas tilted her chin. "Which flooded not long ago and destroyed farm crops, including ours."

Little feet skittered overhead. The smell of bacon and biscuits filling the small clapboard farmhouse must have awakened her hungry boys.

She looked around the room that served as the kitchen, dining, and sitting area. A wall beside the stone fireplace partitioned off their simple bedroom. The three older boys slept in the loft, while their youngest, Johnny, curled in the corner on the far side of the fireplace beside the grandfather clock her father had built. It was small, but it was home.

The boys descended the ladder one at a time—first Henry, the eldest, followed by Barton, whom they called Bart, and finally Grundy, who rubbed sleep from his eyes. Nicholas tousled each boy's hair as they scrambled to the rough oak table for their morning meal.

"Pa?" Eight-year-old Henry poured milk into his cup. "Are we goin' to Oregon?"

Matilda frowned as Nicholas settled onto a sturdy handcrafted chair. He reached for his cup as she brought him the tarnished tin coffeepot and a pitcher of fresh cream.

Nicholas glanced at his eldest son. "Do you think we should follow those wagons west? Find us some free land in Oregon Territory?"

"Yes," Henry shouted. "We want to go west."

"Nicholas." Matilda shook her head slightly and dropped her voice to a whisper. "Johnny's too young to make the journey. Maybe in a few years."

"He'll be three later this month." Her husband looked at their youngest son. "What do you say, John? Can you walk two thousand miles to Oregon?"

Nodding his head, Johnny slid from the bench and dashed around the table. "I walk. I run." Kicking up his heels, he barreled into his mother's skirt.

She laughed as she steadied her towheaded son but quickly sobered. How could a tiny child survive such an arduous journey? *He complains just walking from the wagon into church.*

"Climb back up if you want breakfast," she told him.

After dishing breakfast onto tin plates, she carried two at a time to the table. She served Nicholas first and then Johnny. As she set Henry's plate before him, she thought of his eagerness for new adventures, which paralleled his father's enthusiasm. Bart took after her, a quiet homebody. Henry always dove into a lake; Bart waded in. Grundy was a mix of his two older brothers.

Judging from his morning sprint around the table, Johnny would likely follow in his father's footsteps.

Matilda perched on a padded stool at the table. "Nicholas, will you give thanks?"

Grinning at the boys, he nodded. "Almighty God, we thank you for Ma's great cooking and the many blessings you provide. And help Ma change her mind. Amen."

Matilda frowned as she helped Johnny cut his biscuit.

"So, are we going to Oregon soon, Pa?" Henry asked around a bite of biscuit.

"Yes, we're going—just as soon as your ma agrees."

Matilda shook her head, eyes lowered.

"Why not?" Henry slammed his tin cup onto the table.

"Now, that's enough." She tilted her head at him. "Eat your breakfast."

After they finished, Matilda carried the plates to the counter beside the sink. Nicholas had built it beneath the window so she could enjoy the sunshine while she washed dishes. Attached to the side wall were pegs for cooking utensils.

She gazed outside toward the woods towering behind the barn and chicken coop. Ten years they had lived here. Chopped down trees. Cleared land. Erected buildings. Why would they leave after working so hard to improve this place?

Nicholas swallowed his coffee and stood. "Time for chores."

Henry and Bart scooted away from the table.

"Can I help, Pa?" Grundy tugged on his father's flannel shirt. "Please?"

Her husband tilted his head, squinting one eye at his third son, then broke into a grin. He pointed a finger at Grundy and admonished, "You need to work, ya hear? Not play."

"I will, Pa. I promise."

"I go, too." Johnny strutted toward the door.

Matilda quickly swept him into her arms. "Hush, now. You can help Pa when you're older." Her toddler squirmed, pulling chestnut-colored hair from her bun. When the door closed tight behind the older boys, she let Johnny slide down her body to the floor.

She tucked loose strands of hair back into her bun and then scraped the plates, opened the door, and tossed the breakfast scraps to Bo, their large Chesapeake retriever. He gobbled the goodies and barked his gratitude. She stroked his brown fur and stepped back inside.

She glanced at Johnny as he played with kindling near the cold fireplace.

All those stories Nicholas heard as a boy from fur trappers and mountain men stopping at his pa's tavern and trading post on the busy Boonslick Road probably spurred his wanderlust. Or maybe that old Kentuckian Daniel Boone who lived nearby had filled Nicholas with a desire to explore. Maybe it was just in his blood. *His* blood, not hers.

Matilda preferred the security of home and nearness of family. She liked having her mother close—not thousands of miles away. She had never needed a fancy house, servants, or slaves. Never slaves. Her daddy had freed all of his before they moved west from Maryland when she was seven.

"Come on, little fellow." Matilda knelt beside her youngest son. "You want to help Ma wash clothes?"

"I help."

She smiled at his eagerness. Her boys always liked to help at this age, before the novelty of chores wore off.

Matilda carried her wicker laundry basket outside into the clear, blue skies of a perfect day. She girded herself mentally for yet another disagreement with her hardworking but headstrong husband.

The conversation about emigrating to Oregon would arise again—just as it always did.

TWO

MATILDA DREW THE SHAWL tightly over her shoulders as she stepped from the church into the crisp day. Wisps of fog lingered over the Missouri River like tendrils of angel hair. She buttoned Johnny's jacket against the chill and lifted him onto the wagon. Perhaps the clouds would disappear, but during April in Missouri, it was unlikely.

Matilda glanced over her shoulder to see Nicholas shake hands with Reverend John Ball outside the white clapboard church.

As they headed home in the wagon, the boys chattered while Matilda gazed at the gray sky and breathed deeply. Pale lavender toothwort and yellow buttercups sprouted amid the purple poppy and red blooms on rosebud shrubs. The growth smelled fresh. How she loved spring in Missouri. Did poppies and roses grow in Oregon? Nicholas was adamant that they find out.

"I invited Reverend Ball and his wife to dinner today," Nicholas said. "The Wilsons, too."

She swiveled to face him. "It might be nice to have a little forewarning."

"I gave you a full hour." He grinned.

"An hour is scarcely enough."

Nicholas draped his arm over her shoulders and pulled her close. "Now, Mattie, you know you can pull together a banquet in no time at all. You'll have a feast prepared before our guests arrive."

Matilda shook her head, furrowed her brows, and glared at him, although she secretly enjoyed how Nicholas liked to show off her cooking. Her mind flitted over the ingredients in her kitchen—the bread dough rising on the counter, apples and green beans from the root cellar and potatoes in the larder. The boys could butcher a couple of chickens.

"Tom and Freda are thinkin' of moving west to Oregon Territory," Nicholas offered. "Thought we could talk about it over dinner."

Matilda pursed her lips, again shaking her head. The extra guests posed few problems, but talk of Oregon set butterflies fluttering in her stomach like fresh laundry on the line. She bowed her head and tamped down the fear that threatened to spill over into tears. How could she leave Missouri, her home since she was seven? She had already left behind everything familiar once; why must she do so again?

Nicholas leaned toward Matilda and covered her clasped hands with one of his. "You upset about the company? I didn't figure you'd have any problem with extra guests for dinner."

"No. It's not the dinner." She searched his blue eyes for any understanding of the fear that plagued her heart at the thought of venturing west. "It's all this talk of Oregon."

"Oregon Territory is the promised land of our generation, Mattie. It's simple. We pack our belongings, travel west on the trail with a wagon train, and claim free land—a square mile, six hundred forty acres. Enough for all of the boys."

"But we'd leave our farm, our siblings, my mother …"

"Your mother has Philip and Janette and your other brothers and sisters. You stayed home with your folks longer than most." He tilted her chin toward him. "Our family can have a great future out west."

After the wagon stopped, Matilda scurried into the clapboard house they called home to swap her wool cape for an apron. "Henry! Barton!"

"Yes, Ma?" Bart wiped his hands on his britches.

"You boys change out of your Sunday clothes, then please butcher a few plump chickens for dinner."

Matilda listened through the window to her sons' banter as she rolled pie crusts. Henry chopped off the chickens' heads and handed the bodies to Bart. One slipped from their hands, the headless body flapping as it ran.

"You go get him," Henry ordered. "You dropped him."

"Did not!" Bart chased after the tottering bird and scooped it into his arms before their dog caught it.

Henry opened the door to retrieve the kettle of boiling water. "Sheesh! Sure is hot in here!" He wiped his brow with a grimy shirtsleeve. Outside, he dipped the bodies into hot water and yanked off the damp feathers. They'd save them for pillows, comforters, even fishing lures.

Her boys were only eight, six, five, and almost three. She'd heard horrific tales of children maimed by rolling wagons or dying of disease while traveling along the Oregon Trail. Blinking back tears, she slid two apple pies into the oven, smeared lard into her big black skillet, broke eggs and stirred them. The last of the lard melted just as the boys brought in the headless, now naked birds. She lit a candle and ran each chicken past the flame to burn off pinfeathers, wrinkling her nose at the stench of singed hair. She pulled out the innards, cut the chickens into pieces, then swirled the legs, wings, thighs, and breasts into an egg mixture, rolled them in seasoned flour, and placed each gently into the frying pan. Lard sizzled and sputtered around the meat.

Matilda was mashing the potatoes just as the rumble of a wagon and voices raised in greeting resounded from the yard.

She wiped her hands on her apron and opened the door. The Wilsons' half dozen children scattered with her sons in tow. After exchanging pleasantries with Freda Wilson and Emma Ball, the pastor's wife, she invited them into the tidy little house. Both brought desserts for the meal.

"What can we do to help?" Emma asked.

"Please, sit," Matilda said, happy to have prepared dinner on such short notice. "Would you like tea or coffee?"

The two nodded as Matilda poured tea from a kettle and smiled. She would miss her friends if they moved west.

Or perhaps she'd be traveling west with Freda.

"Are you indeed moving to Oregon Territory?" Emma lifted her eyebrows and her teacup at the same time.

"We haven't decided yet." Matilda turned to the cupboard and reached for glass dishes to set on the table. "Nicholas wants to go. I'd rather stay here."

"Why would you want to stay?" Freda's teacup clattered against the saucer. "We can all do much better in Oregon Territory. Why, the men can cut timber and sell it. They can farm the land and sell produce. It's a wonderful opportunity."

Matilda nodded as she set silverware next to the plates. "But don't you worry about leaving your family here? We may never see them again."

Freda waved her hand. "I'll be happy to put a thousand miles or more between my mother and me. We never did get along."

"But…what about your children? Won't they miss their grandparents?" Matilda placed cast-iron trivets on the table for the hot pans.

"Oh, they'll miss them a bit, but they'll be fine." Freda shrugged. "The adventure excites my boys more than anything, and my daughters just hope to find handsome husbands among those in the wagon train." She wriggled her eyebrows and laughed.

Matilda smiled. Nothing ever ruffled Freda. She was a woman of strong opinions and unlikely to be forced into doing something she didn't want to do. Matilda wished she could demand that Nicholas stay in Missouri and said as much.

Emma patted Matilda's hand.

"Dear, you know the verses as well as I do." She quoted from Ephesians: "'Wives, submit yourselves unto your own husbands, as unto the Lord.'."

Matilda inhaled a breath. True, but she didn't have to like it when her husband wanted to uproot her family.

"Nicholas is the head of the family." Freda lifted her teacup. "You must do as he says."

Like you do? Matilda bit back the words, though she couldn't imagine headstrong Freda ever submitting to her husband.

Emma choked on her tea, and Matilda bit her lip harder. Perhaps only fear of the unknown held her back.

"You must trust God to care for your family if He wants you to move west," Emma said with a slight smile.

"But how do I know?" Matilda asked. "How do I know it's God's will and not just Nicholas'?"

Voices drifted from outside, and boots stomped on the porch. Matilda checked the oven. A golden brown tinged the crusts and apple cinnamon wafted from the oven door. She pulled out the pies and set them on the windowsill to cool.

"Mmmm, something smells mighty good in here." Nicholas winked at Matilda as he stood back to let his guests enter the house. Reverend Ball and Tom Wilson stepped to the washbasin beneath the window.

"We were just looking over the place, trying to figure out how much it could sell for." Reverend Ball wiped his hands on a towel and pulled out a chair beside Emma. "If you start advertising soon, it might sell before you leave."

Matilda's brow furrowed. "We haven't decided if we're going." She poured coffee and set the cup before the preacher.

He laughed, a low contagious rumble, then lifted the cup and nodded to Matilda. "You might want to let your husband know that. He sure talks like you're going."

Nicholas cleared his throat, glancing at his wife as if embarrassed. "Mattie's right. We haven't settled on it for certain, but I'm doing my best to persuade her. I told her she's got brothers and sisters who can take care of her mother."

"I certainly wouldn't let worries over my parents hold me back," Freda said. "After all, they've lived their lives. It's time for us to live ours."

"Oh, my!" Emma placed her hand on her friend's arm. "That sounds a little harsh, don't you think?"

"But it's true." Freda shook her head. "I'm not saying they'll die tomorrow. But they decided where they wanted to live and raise their family. We have the right to do the same."

"And if Nicholas wants to go," Emma said, patting her husband's arm and smiling at him, "the Bible does say the man is the head of the household."

"Indeed it does," the reverend said. "Women should respect and obey their husbands."

Emma, ever the good preacher's wife, always deferred to what he said.

Freda scoffed softly. She looked at Matilda and quoted a different Bible verse. "Whither thou goest, will I go."

Matilda couldn't help herself. "I believe Ruth said those words to her mother-in-law. She promised Naomi she wouldn't leave her."

Freda's face flushed, and Emma giggled.

Matilda changed the subject. "Nicholas, will you call the children?"

Her husband stepped onto the porch. "Vittles are ready! Come get 'em while they're hot."

The children crowded into the house, and Reverend Ball raised his voice to pray a blessing over the food.

Matilda pulled out the tin plates and dished crispy fried chicken, mashed potatoes, green beans, and bread onto plates for the younger children. She handed her eldest son a plate.

"Thanks, Ma," Henry said.

Frank, the Wilsons' eldest son at fourteen, piled his plate high. "Thanks, Mrs. Koontz."

Their teenage daughters and younger sons paraded past, grabbed forks, and picked up plates to eat outside on the porch. Bart and Grundy followed. Matilda dished up a plate for Johnny and led him outside to the porch.

She then put the rest of the food into serving bowls, which she placed on the table. The couples ate, and Matilda relaxed as the conversation focused on happenings in Missouri and not the Wild West.

Nicholas worked hard, and he wanted badly to move west. Matilda had heard of other men who packed their wives and children into wagons and left, without giving the women a choice. At least Nicholas wouldn't leave her. He would keep asking until she said yes. But at least he asked. He wanted her to embrace his dream. But could she?

The next evening, Matilda sat near the fireplace, her sewing basket beside her, the boys safely sleeping on their straw beds in the loft. She sighed as her body relaxed. She loved quiet evenings when she could sew, spin wool, or read her Bible. She felt a gurgle and rubbed her palm over her stomach. Was it indigestion? Or perhaps another little one on the way?

She sorted through the basket and lifted the flannel shirt she was stitching for Bart's seventh birthday next month; she had already finished one for Johnny.

As she attached the cuff to the shirt, Nicholas opened the door and shut it quietly behind him. He washed his hands and face. Farmers worked from dawn till dusk; so did farmers' wives, for that matter. But the Good Book admonished against idle hands.

And against a rebellious wife who didn't submit to her husband's will.

More words from the Bible echoed through her mind: "Therefore shall a man leave his father and his mother and shall cleave unto his wife: and they shall be one flesh." She supposed the same held true for a woman.

Nicholas stepped to the fireplace mantel, picked up his pipe, and poured tobacco from a pouch. After tamping it down, he struck a match and inhaled deeply, lowering his lanky limbs into a wooden chair.

A few minutes passed in companionable silence. As Nicholas puffed on his pipe, his eyes stared into the blue and orange flames of the fire. He leaned forward, elbows on his knees. "We need to talk."

Matilda knotted a stitch, folded the shirt, and tucked it into the basket, her mind already prepared for the conversation. Her neck stiffened.

"We have four boys. This farm isn't large enough for one family, much less five." He sucked on his pipe and exhaled slowly, circling gray smoke rising toward the loft. "We need to go west. We can give our boys a better future in Oregon."

Matilda crossed her arms over her chest. "Their roots are in Missouri. Your roots are here."

"But the government's giving away land in Oregon, just for the taking. Many have moved west in the past six years; the best land will be gone if we don't leave soon."

Nicholas kept his voice low, but Matilda heard the scamper of feet above. Probably Henry, eager to see if she'd finally agree to leave. Or perhaps Bart, worried that she would.

Matilda sighed and looked at Nicholas briefly before gazing into the stone fireplace as flames devoured the wood.

"But Nicholas—"

"Now, Mattie …" He held up a hand and stepped to the corner desk. "I've heard what you said. But listen …" He picked up a book and flipped to where he had left a loose slip of paper. She had seen the volume: *The Emigrants' Guide to Oregon and California* by Lansford Hastings.

He struck a match, lit a candle, and knelt beside her. He began to read. "'It is a very beautiful and productive valley … well-timbered, well-watered … with a superabundance of all the grasses … it is admirably suited to agricultural and grazing purposes.' Doesn't the Willamette Valley sound grand?"

Matilda closed her eyes and pictured green meadows where the boys could farm and raise their families.

"It sounds like paradise—if we all arrive safely." She shook her head. "But I've heard so many stories …"

"It's safer all the time." Nicholas rubbed her back. "They're building military posts along the trail. Besides, it's our patriotic duty to go. In fact, President Polk said it's our manifest destiny to settle the land all the way west to the Pacific Ocean."

It was hard to dispute Nicholas' logic. Still, her stomach fluttered in misgiving.

"But what about Ma?" She whispered the words, guilt pricking her conscience at the thought of abandoning her mother, a widow since Pa died seven years ago.

Nicholas exhaled deeply, breath whistling between his teeth. "Maybe she could come along."

Matilda chuckled without humor. "Not likely. You've heard her complain about everyone moving west." She fought back tears swimming in her eyes. "She's showing her age, and she's the only grandparent our boys have left."

Nicholas stood, towering over her. "You took care of your mother for years. She can stay with Philip and Sarah, or live with Janette and Hiram, or one of the others. You have seven siblings. You're not solely responsible for your mother just because you're the youngest." He bent to grasp her hands, his thumbs caressing her palms. "Please, Mattie, say we can go."

Nicholas would keep pleading with her until she agreed.

"Please?" He knelt beside her chair and picked up her hands. "You know it's the best for our boys."

"Is it?" Her voice trembled as she posed the question. "Will they be safe on the journey?"

"I will do everything to keep them safe." Nicholas gazed into her eyes. "I promise."

She sighed. "I don't know…"

"Please say yes, Mattie. I don't ask much, but this is so important."

Her strong husband never did ask much. He thanked her often for everything she did for him and their boys. Was his request too much? It seemed like a lot, but he was her husband. And the Bible told her to submit to him.

As she nodded slightly, her heart fluttered with excitement tempered by misgivings. Truth be told, she could survive anywhere, as long as she had her husband and children. Silently, she asked God for His providence on the journey west.

The tension in her shoulders released as she stepped behind the curtain to their bed.

Nicholas smiled, blew out the candle, and wrapped his arms around her. "You're a good woman, Mattie."

THREE

Early May 1847, Saint Charles, Missouri

NICHOLAS LIFTED HER CEDAR CHEST of goods by the handles and strode out the farmhouse door. Matilda followed him to the narrow wagon. Axes, spades, and hoes dangled from the rig's outer walls, with everything else they needed for the next six months crammed inside.

When they'd told the boys about their decision to go west a few weeks ago, Henry shouted "Yee-haw!" while Bart kept his head lowered. His subdued reaction, though, was nothing compared with the histrionics of her mother.

The sapphire blue in her mother's dress reflected the shimmer in her eyes, but when she heard their news, those eyes turned to ice. She collapsed into a rocker in her son Philip's home. "My grandsons … I'll never see them again." Matilda ached with grief for her mother, for her sons, for herself, even though she knew her place was beside her husband. She and Nicholas both invited her mother to join them, but she rejected the notion.

Then, when William, Philip and Sarah's eldest son, said he and his wife were going west too, her mother left the dining room table and took to her bed for days.

Matilda sighed. They had scrambled the past month to buy all their supplies and sell their furniture, animals, and household goods. Reverend Ball and Emma loved the grandfather clock although it grieved Matilda to part with it, the last piece crafted by her father before his death. Giving it away was like saying goodbye to her father again.

Very little actually fit inside the long, narrow wagon other than the supplies needed to simply survive on the trail—crates and bags of flour, sugar, salt, bacon in brine, dried peas, fruit, coffee, tea, tobacco, plus cooking and eating utensils, tents, quilts, blankets, sheets, tools, and of course guns, knives, and gunpowder. One box contained cakes of soap, another held saleratus for baking, and a third, candles. Oh, and an extra pair of shoes for everyone as they'd be walking most of the way—and twice the amount of food they'd normally eat because of all the walking.

Nicholas slathered tar on the bottom of the wagon so it wouldn't leak while crossing rivers and linseed oil on the white canvas covering its bowed wooden strips for waterproofing.

The wagon was heavy, requiring six oxen to pull it.

Matilda glanced one last time around the now-empty farmhouse. She would miss this house filled with happy memories of baking, cooking, reading by the fire, celebrating holidays … birthing babies. She felt a flutter and rubbed her palm over her stomach. She hoped it was indigestion.

After walking outside, she offered a silent goodbye to the farm she and her husband had built over their ten years of marriage.

"You all set?" Her husband grinned as Johnny hopped toward the high seat, arms outstretched. "Here, let me give you a boost."

Nicholas swept an arm under the boy and tossed him into the air, laughing. He settled their youngest son behind the wagon seat. Matilda bit her trembling lip and clutched her *Book of Common Prayer*. She had already packed *Gunn's Domestic Medicine* into her chest of goods, hoping they wouldn't need it but prepared in case they did. And thanks to Hastings' book, she knew what emergency supplies to pack— bandages, hartshorn for snakebites, laudanum, castor oil, camphor, morphine, quinine, herbs, and citric acid to prevent scurvy.

She smiled her thanks as Nicholas lifted her to the wagon and walked in front of the oxen, patting each on the back as he did. "Pet. Baul. Browny. Duke. Old Buck. Jerry. We're depending on you to haul this heavy load to Oregon."

He climbed into the wagon, flashed a smile at Matilda, and grabbed the oxen's reins threaded through nasal rings. "Get up!" he shouted.

As the wagon rumbled forward, Matilda reflected on the excitement of her husband, a man on a new adventure. Her thoughts flitted ahead to their first stop—the home of Philip and Sarah Glover. Philip, her eldest brother, had married Nicholas' older sister, Sarah, thirty years ago. Matilda and Nicholas had been only children then. She never imagined they would marry. In fact, she didn't even like the boisterous rough-and-tumble boy who wouldn't leave her alone.

During a visit a few weeks earlier, Philip had promised to sell their farmhouse and gave Nicholas a pouch of money to tide them over until he did. He and Sarah planned to head west in two years, although their son William and his wife would leave for Independence with Matilda and her family tomorrow.

Henry and Bart rode the mare, Belle. Grundy stretched out on the mattress stroking the fur of their retriever, Bo, while talking to Millie and her heifer tethered behind the wagon. Her boys' hearts would break when they left for Independence, not so much at saying goodbye to their grandmother but at leaving Bo. But he'd be safer in Missouri. Nicholas had told her that folks on a wagon train five years ago voted to kill all the dogs to avoid problems along the trail.

Matilda reached for Johnny to cuddle him on her lap. The boy squirmed, then rested his head against her bosom. Although she would miss Missouri, it was only land; those she held most dear would go with her to Oregon.

"Mama, look at those red flowers." Johnny pointed to lush blooms.

"Aren't they pretty?" Matilda snuggled her youngest son closer as she gazed at the tree, buds opening into pink blossoms. "It's an Eastern Rosebud."

Her first kiss had come beneath an Eastern Rosebud at her parents' place outside Saint Charles. Oh, how she had loved Marcus Springer. Or imagined she did. So handsome and charming as he whispered of losing himself in her brown eyes, tangling his fingers in her chestnut hair, loving her quiet spirit. They were engaged but drifted apart, and when she heard he had married another woman, her heart shattered.

She had wondered what life would have been like with Marcus—that is, until she saw him flirting at a dance with a young girl while his pregnant wife sipped tea with the matrons. She thanked God then for sparing her the pain she saw in his wife's eyes.

"A penny for your thoughts?"

The question interrupted Matilda's reverie, and she smiled at her husband. "Oh, I was thinking of the dances in St. Louis—do you remember the one you took me to?"

"When you were still pining over your first heartbreak?" He winked at her.

Matilda felt her face flush. How could he do that? It seemed like he read her mind. "I never loved Marcus, not the way I do you, but we did attend a lot of dances together."

"Most dandies dance, but I doubt they do well as providers." He nudged her shoulder with his and laughed.

Later, she gazed at Nicholas, his square jaw, large nose, black hair, and stout build. His contagious grin and deep blue eyes captivated her.

"What?" He flicked the reins on the oxen's backs as he glanced her way.

"Nothing." Matilda smiled. "Just admiring my husband."

He barked a laugh.

Nicholas might not be as physically attractive as Marcus, but he was a good man, a hard worker, and a wonderful father to their boys. She loved his smile, twinkling eyes, and sense of humor.

The wagon rolled along, rocking, and lulled the boys to sleep. She and Nicholas spoke only occasionally, in whispers. Just before dark, they set up the tent under an oak tree and slept. As the sun peeked over the horizon the next morning, bathing the landscape in a warm blanket of red, Matilda glanced heavenward to thank God for another glorious morning.

As they traveled, the constant flapping of the canvas billowing in the wind lulled a squirming Johnny back to sleep on her lap. They stopped for sandwiches at midday and ate cold chicken for dinner. And bread, boiled eggs, and cheese sufficed for breakfast. Two days. Then three.

Finally, they arrived at the Glovers' farm in Montgomery County. Nicholas urged the slow-plodding oxen to stop next to another wagon, its canvas bulging with items protruding at odd angles. Looked like William and Jane were packed.

Philip and Sarah greeted them on the porch of the flint-rock farmhouse surrounded by bountiful orchards and fertile fields.

"You're ready to leave the great state of Missouri?" Philip clapped Nicholas on the shoulder. "I wish we were going too. Won't be far behind. A year, maybe two."

"I'll keep track of what happens." Nicholas pulled a pencil from his flannel shirt pocket and waved it before his brother-in-law. "We'll send notes back with settlers returning east. That way, you'll know what to expect."

"Hope you hook up with a good company." Philip glanced at his wife, tears streaming down her cheeks, and shook his head. "You'd think they'll never see each other again. We'll all be in Oregon soon."

Matilda rested a hand on her brother's elbow. "How is Mama doing?"

He waved dismissively. "She'll be fine. She's got us, Janette and Hiram, a lot of family left here."

Matilda removed her bonnet as she walked into the living room, wondering how her mother would survive saying goodbye again when Philip and Sarah moved to Oregon. Her mother, thin and pale, sat in a rocking chair, her wispy white hair twisted into a tight bun.

"Hello, Mama."

Her mother rose and opened her arms. Matilda rushed into the embrace and held tight, realizing this would be among their last embraces this side of heaven. "I'm going to miss you so much."

Her mother remained silent, but her shoulders trembled. Matilda didn't dare tell her mother about her suspicions; she'd write to her from Oregon.

Nicholas entered the room. "Good to see you, Mother Glover. Maybe you can join Philip and Sarah when they travel west in a few years."

"I already told you I could never survive that trip." Her blue eyes glittered as she glared at him. "I may even be gone by the time they leave."

Matilda kissed her mother's cheek. "Mama, you're healthy. Perhaps you can visit us one day in Oregon."

Her mother sniffed slightly, threw back her shoulders, and walked to a trunk beside the fireplace. She lifted the lid and gently slid her arms beneath a package wrapped in brown paper.

"This is for you, daughter, to remember us all. Janette and Sarah helped with it."

Matilda glanced at her sister-in-law, who had followed her into the room, and then at her sister, Janette. She sat on the sofa, untied the string, and carefully folded back the brown paper. On her lap sat a white Touching Stars quilt highlighted with red and green. She fingered the exquisite triple line stitches around the diamond pieces forming the large celestial body.

"It's a friendship quilt, so you'll remember us when you're gone," Janette said.

Tears swam in Matilda's eyes as she unfolded part of the quilt, watching its colorful highlights pulsate in the flickering firelight.

"Of course I'll never forget any of you." Matilda folded the quilt, placed it inside the paper again, and retied the string. She embraced each woman. "I'll keep you in my prayers—always."

She dabbed at her eyes.

"We've no time for tears," Sarah said briskly with a smile. "I'll roll out the quilts upstairs for the boys."

"Please, let me help." Matilda followed her sister-in-law through the kitchen to an upstairs bedroom.

"I do worry about Mother." Matilda flipped a quilt over the blankets on the wooden floor.

"She'll be fine." Sarah smoothed a rumple from the quilt. "She's not as ill as she puts on."

Matilda laid a faded quilt of colorful silk tumbling blocks on the floor. She had sewn it as a gift when Sarah was expecting William. Was that really twenty-four years ago? Goodness!

"Mother will object more when you leave," she told Sarah. "Her eldest son … It won't be easy."

Sarah waved her hand. "I'm not as softhearted as you. I know she'll be fine. She's a survivor. Besides, you're her baby." She sighed. "I am glad William will be traveling with you, and that he'll live near us in Oregon. I do think it would break my heart to leave any of my children behind in Missouri."

They joined the menfolk downstairs.

"Go on now." Sarah herded her younger five children toward the wooden steps leading to the second story.

"Goodnight, boys." Matilda kissed each of her sons on the forehead as they followed their cousins, laughing and jabbering about the Wild West, buffalo, and Indians.

Philip, Nicholas, and William puffed cigars in the living room and visited. She sighed as she settled on a wooden chair at the kitchen table.

Jane, whom William had married three years earlier, sipped her tea. "Your mother retired to bed."

Just as well. Matilda didn't have the energy to placate her. It had already been emotional leaving their home. Tomorrow would be more difficult when they said their final goodbyes.

Final. Most likely it would be the last time she ever saw the woman who had nurtured her from birth, tended her scraped knees, taught her to sew and cook, supported her when Marcus broke her heart. She had accepted Nicholas as another son but couldn't disguise her resentment toward him now for hauling the family so far away.

Matilda blinked back tears. Would she have the strength to say goodbye without breaking down in front of her boys?

Footsteps clattered above, followed by whispers, laughter, and a loud crash.

Matilda rushed to the staircase, lifted her long calico skirt, and scampered upstairs.

"You boys need to settle down now. Other people are trying to sleep." She struggled to keep her voice gentle after the long day. Henry, Bart, and Grundy snuggled into their blankets and closed their eyes. Johnny was already fast asleep.

Matilda returned downstairs and, after finishing her tea, helped Sarah carry the cups to the kitchen. Again they heard the patter of footsteps and another loud noise.

"I'll go," Sarah said.

"No, let me. It's probably my boys anyway." Matilda again climbed the stairs, spoke softly to her sons, and retreated. She leaned against the railing, her legs weary. Goodness. How would she survive walking all the way to the Oregon Territory when her legs hurt after only three trips up the stairs? She gingerly descended to the main floor and snuggled beneath the warm quilt, her going-away gift. She would treasure it forever.

Her excited sons finally settled into sleep, and so did she.

Morning brought the moment Matilda dreaded. Saying goodbye. Oh, if only she could fly like an eagle, soaring over the mountains and prairies, swallowing the miles between them whenever she missed home.

Philip's house slave, Ophelia, fixed her master and his guests a hearty breakfast of eggs, ham, fried potatoes, and fresh bread with peach preserves. Matilda climbed the stairs to fold and put away the quilts but found a young slave girl already doing so.

"Here, let me help." Matilda stepped forward.

"No, ma'am. It's m'job."

Matilda dropped her hands to her sides. She hated slavery, but her uncle had gifted her brother, his namesake, with more than twenty slaves when the family left Maryland for Missouri years ago.

"Thank you—what is your name?"

The teenage girl in a black dress with white apron bobbed a curtsy without dropping the quilt. "Betsy, ma'am."

"Thank you, Betsy. I appreciate you cleaning up our mess."

Retreating downstairs, she tied the strings of her bonnet and wrapped her wool cape around her shoulders. She carried the brown package to the wagon and tucked it safely beneath the bedding in her chest of goods. Back inside the house, she bundled Johnny into a warm jacket.

A few minutes later, her mother, white fingers clutching a black shawl tightly around her stooped shoulders, shuffled from the house and down the steps. Matilda spoke to her boys in a soft voice. "Say goodbye to your grandmother." She bit her lip to still its trembling. Her boys knew they were moving west but couldn't comprehend the finality of this farewell.

Henry hugged his grandmother briefly, grabbed the rope from the wagon, and hopped into the saddle on Belle's back. Bart embraced his grandmother tightly, and Matilda saw tears drip down his cheeks before he dashed them away with a swipe of his sleeve and raced toward Henry. Grundy gave a perfunctory hug and scrambled into the wagon.

Her youngest son tugged on his grandmother's plain cotton dress, then grabbed her around the legs. "Bye, Gamma."

He toddled toward Nicholas, who had nodded his goodbyes to his in-laws and stood waiting beside the team. "You take care now, Mother Glover," he said. "Mattie?"

Matilda inhaled deeply. Oh, she would miss her mother! She hugged her tightly. Tears wet both their faces. So much for looking strong in front of her boys.

Her mother held her at arm's length. "Now you write me."

Matilda nodded. "I will, Mama. And please write back. I want to know how you are. Send me all the news of Missouri."

Her voice choked on the name of the state she had adopted as a child. She hugged her mother once more, reminding herself that a wife must cleave to her husband even if it sliced her heart in half.

"Where's Bo?" Henry asked from atop Belle.

Grundy whistled and the retriever raced from around the corner of the house.

"Now, boys, you know we talked about this." Nicholas shook his head. "We're leaving Bo here with Philip and Sarah."

"But why?" Bart cried.

"You know why. He's safer here than on the trail."

"We can keep him safe." Tears swam in Bart's eyes.

Matilda rested her free arm on her son's shoulders. "We did talk about this before we left home. You remember?"

Bart kicked a rock and nodded but said nothing, his eyes cast downward.

"We'll have enough trouble keeping you boys safe along the journey," she said. "You remember what I told you—stay back from the wagons. The wheels can…"

"They'll crush you if you're too close, and the oxen don't know whether anyone's nearby," Nicholas said. "They just pull."

"Mama?" Grundy looked up at her.

She squatted before him. "We just need to walk beside the wagon but not too close." She looked at each boy in turn. "Can we remember to do that?"

Henry and Bart nodded.

"Grundy?"

"Yeah, Ma. I'll stay back from the wagon."

"Me too!" Johnny said.

"Now, say goodbye to Bo." Nicholas gestured toward the hound. "We need to move out."

Henry slid off the mare, and the boys dropped to their knees in the dirt, draping their arms around the dog, crying. Bo licked their faces, slurping up the tears, tail wagging.

"Let's go now," Nicholas ordered the boys before urging the oxen forward.

Matilda lifted her head to the lightening horizon as she brushed tears from her cheeks. She grasped Johnny's little fingers in one hand and followed the wagon. Don't look back; it'll only be worse. Matilda prayed for her mother. She prayed for their safety. She prayed to have King David's courage as he faced a battle. Trudging thousands of miles into the unknown, leaving behind everything familiar, could be considered a battle. She felt ill-equipped as a warrior. Her heart pounded erratically in her tight chest.

Johnny babbled with excitement. Hens squawked in crates beside Grundy. The older boys urged Belle to a trot. They'd need to keep Belle, Millie, and her heifer close. That writer Hastings said Indians were more likely to steal horses and cows than oxen.

"Get up," Nicholas commanded, and his oxen shuffled forward. West. To a new life. William shouted the same order from where he and Jane sat in their wagon.

This was it! They were on their way to Independence.

FOUR

Early May 1847, enroute to Independence, Missouri

LATER THAT AFTERNOON, Matilda shifted on the hard wooden bench in hopes that a new position would ease the gurgling in her stomach. She had sewn a long pillowcase and stuffed it with feathers to soften the seat, but it still jiggled as the wagon rumbled west. Nicholas had told her it would take nearly two weeks to reach Independence—if they traveled more than ten hours a day, which he wanted to do as they were already behind many of the emigrants. Perhaps her bones would grow accustomed to the constant jarring.

"Pa," Grundy called from the back of the wagon. "Can I have a turn on Belle?"

"Next stop we'll switch." Nicholas flashed a grin at his third son and snapped the reins lightly over the oxen's backs. They stepped a little livelier, but since they lumbered only two or three miles an hour, it was difficult to tell much difference.

The oxen slapped flies with their tails and tossed their heads. Matilda gulped and inhaled deeply. Urgently, she grasped her husband's forearm. "I need to stop."

Nicholas pulled back on the reins. "Whoa!" Swiveling on the bench, he turned toward her. "Are you feeling all right? You look pale."

She raised her left hand and gulped in fresh air. Her right hand rested on her gurgling stomach.

As the wagon stopped, she slid off the seat and ran to a nearby shrub. Bending at the waist, she vomited her breakfast and then wiped her mouth and inhaled deeply. A hand dropped on her shoulder.

Jane gave her a tin cup filled with water. "Has the green sickness already caught hold of you?"

Matilda shook her head, accepting the cup with thanks. "No, it's not chlorosis." She drew a deep breath as her nausea eased. "It's motherhood, although I didn't have this problem when I was pregnant with the boys…"

Matilda's voice drifted off as the younger woman's brows drew together and tears flooded her eyes. She turned away.

"Dearest, what's wrong?" Matilda drew her into her arms. "What can I do for you?"

Jane stepped back. She pulled a handkerchief from the sleeve of her dress and wiped her eyes. Her cheeks flushed and she stammered. "I'm sor—sorry. Please forgive me. What a nuisance I am. You're the one losing your breakfast and here I am crying like a ba-baby."

"I'm much better now," Matilda said. "What's troubling you?"

Jane inhaled deeply and stretched to her full height. She was a tall, regal young woman. "It's just that William and I have tried—we've wanted to start a family since we married. It's been three years already. Every time my monthly flow starts, my heart breaks."

"Oh, dear." Tears pricked Matilda's eyes. Feeling helpless, she glanced between the young woman and the two waiting wagons. She had never tried to become pregnant; it just happened. But she couldn't imagine life without her boys. Poor Jane!

"I'm happy for you and Nicholas, truly I am."

Matilda embraced the younger woman. "I'm so sorry for your struggle. Maybe it's just not the right time."

Jane nodded as the two women walked back to the wagons. "I suppose if it's meant to be, it'll happen. I pray, but it seems to do little good."

Matilda squeezed Jane's shoulder. "My boys adore you and William." She chuckled. "At least you aren't heaving breakfast in the bushes."

Jane offered a half-hearted smile as she patted her face dry. "I should count my blessings however small they may be."

"Daylight's wasting, ladies." Nicholas cinched the harness tighter around Duke and nodded at William, who was doing the same with his animals. Matilda saw Grundy behind Henry on the mare and Bart beside the wagon.

"Are you feeling better?" Nicholas surveyed her small form from head to toe.

Matilda nodded. "I think I'll walk awhile."

"I'll walk with you, Ma." Bart picked up a limb from the ground and sidled up to his mother.

"Me too! Me too!" Johnny hollered from the bench seat. He leaned forward, arms outstretched.

"Whoa there, little man!" Nicholas pulled the boy from the seat onto the grassy trail. "Watch out or you'll tumble headfirst and break your neck."

Johnny giggled and raced to his mother and brother. He ran circles around them before collapsing onto the grass where he wiggled his arms and legs as if making a snow angel. Matilda smiled. It must be tough for a toddler to sit still.

Nicholas hopped onto the wagon seat, lifted the reins, and shouted at the oxen. They jerked forward and settled into their steady plodding. On to Independence.

Matilda tucked away her sewing as the sun dipped toward the horizon and daylight faded to gray. She had stowed her bag containing cloth, needles, thimble, and thread behind the seat. As they traveled, she planned to sew shirts for trade with natives as Nicholas had suggested.

"Time to set up camp." Her husband reined in the oxen, halted the wagon, and gestured toward a grassy meadow. "What do you think, William? This look good?"

"Whoa!" His nephew pulled on the reins to slow his rig. "Jane and I will be mighty glad to stay put for the night."

Nicholas pulled the long harnesses from the six oxen.

"Grundy, come here." He gestured toward his third son, the only redhead in the bunch. "I have an important job for you to do on this here trip to Oregon."

"What is it?" Grundy slithered over the chicken cages, dropped through the rear of the wagon, and raced to his father's side.

"Grab yourself one of those rags your ma packed."

Matilda dug through the rectangular box beside her chest, pulled out a long canvas flour sack, and handed it to her son.

"Now, here's what you need to do." Nicholas dipped the cloth into a basin of water and wrapped it around Grundy's small fingers. "These oxen have their heads down in the dirt all day pulling this heavy wagon, and they're breathing in all that dust and dirt and weeds. Your job is to clean each ox's nose with this cloth. Gently swab around inside the nostrils and wipe them clean. Then rinse it out and do the same for each animal."

Nicholas rubbed his hand over Duke's rough hair and swatted a horsefly from his back. "These beasts are mighty important. We can't pull the wagon without them."

Grundy petted Duke's forehead as he thrust his cloth-wrapped fingers up one nostril and swiped it in a circle. When he yanked it out, the once-white cloth was striped with brown slime and speckled with debris. He repeated the steps and showed the dirty cloth to his father.

"That's right. When you're done, you need to wash that rag with lye soap, rinse it well in the basin, and hang it on a nail on the wagon's side so it'll dry." Nicholas nodded to Grundy. "You'll do that every night without me asking, ya hear?"

When the five-year-old nodded, Nicholas chuckled. "That's my boy."

He gestured to Henry and pointed toward a pine tree. "You take Belle to the creek for a drink and then hobble her next to that tree."

"Sure, Pa." Henry sat atop the mare.

Matilda smiled at her husband before she climbed into the wagon and retrieved her Dutch oven, coffeepot, wooden bowl, and kettle.

"What's tickled you?" Nicholas wrapped an arm around her waist. She set down her load and turned to him. "You." She smoothed his flannel shirt over his chest. "I love the way you teach our boys. They adore their pa."

He laughed. "They're good boys and good workers. Now I have a question for you." He tucked his hands in his pockets and tipped back on his heels. "Mattie, are you nestin'?"

Matilda nodded slightly as she bent to retrieve her cooking utensils. "I'm going to warm the stew and bake corn bread."

He squinted at her. "Why didn't you tell me?"

"I wasn't sure." Matilda shrugged, cast her eyes upward, and spoke a silent prayer. "And ... I didn't know if ... whether ... I knew you didn't want to postpone the trip."

"But Mattie ... are you going to be able to walk all that way, heavy with child?"

She gazed into her husband's eyes. "I'll do what I have to do ... with the good Lord's help."

Nicholas rubbed his hand over his scruffy chin, shifted his glance away, and pursed his lips. Liquid shimmered in his eyes. Were those tears?

"I'm sorry," she whispered.

"What?" He looked at Matilda "Oh, no, Mattie. No." He stretched out his strong arms to embrace her and then caressed her abdomen with one hand, her back with the other. "I'm happy about the baby." He tilted her chin to gaze into her eyes. "Maybe this time we'll have a daughter, a girl just as pretty as her ma. She'll be a true pioneer, born on the western frontier."

Matilda rested her cheek against his warm chest, listening to the strong pounding of his heart. She felt so safe in his embrace. She smiled, but her lips trembled. Her first four pregnancies caused her little nausea or discomfort. Why should this one be different? But what kind of life awaited this baby in Oregon? The knowledge that her child would never know his or her grandmother pierced her heart. Bracing herself, she inhaled deeply. "Other women cross the plains in the family way. I can do it too. Besides, I won't even show for a few months, and we should be settled in Oregon before the baby's born."

"That's my girl." He winked. "I'll take care of the oxen."

As Nicholas strode away, Matilda pulled out cornmeal, flour, sugar, saleratus, salt, buttermilk, and molasses. After stirring the ingredients, she poured the mixture into the Dutch oven.

Their oldest son returned to camp.

"Henry, will you please take Bart and gather dry wood for a fire?"

"Sure, Ma." He grabbed his younger brother by the elbow. "Race ya!"

"Stay together, boys!" Matilda shouted. "And don't wander too far from the wagons."

Matilda arched her back as she watched the two boys scamper into the brush, kicking up dust. Grundy started to follow.

"No, Grundy, stay here." Matilda waved at him. "Did you wash up after working with the oxen?"

Grundy shook his head. Dropping an arm on his shoulder, Matilda drew him toward the back of the wagon, handed him a bar of lye soap, opened the spigot on a wooden water barrel, and held a small bowl beneath it to catch the water.

"Scrub well. I need you to watch John for me while I prepare dinner." She brushed the tousled red hair from his eyes, then bent down to kiss his freckled forehead.

"Okay, Ma." Grundy dried his hands on his pants. "Come here, Johnny."

He pulled his three-year-old brother onto his tiny lap, and they proceeded to draw pictures in the soft dirt.

When the two older boys returned, arms loaded with twigs and dry limbs, she gestured toward the kettle and Dutch oven.

"You can set them there."

"You want me to start the fire?" Henry rubbed his palms together.

Matilda glanced at her eldest boy, only eight yet so responsible. "Yes, please do. We have matches inside the wagon next to my sewing basket."

Later, after she settled the boys in their tent, Matilda sat by the firelight reading her Bible. Nicholas and William stood near the creek, smoking pipes.

Jane approached. "May I ask you a question?"

"Of course," Matilda closed the Good Book.

"Are you scared? I mean, leaving your home and family. Walking alongside a wagon for thousands of miles." The young woman shivered and crossed her arms over her chest. "Aren't you worried about your boys?"

Matilda paused, gazing at the towering trees overhead. So peaceful. Turning to Jane, who was thirteen years her junior, she smiled and wrapped an arm around the younger woman. "Yes ... and no," she responded. "I try not to worry, but to be honest, I do. I want to heed the admonitions in the Bible. Isaiah says, Trust ye in the Lord for ever: for in the Lord Jehovah is everlasting strength.' And I pray every day, asking God to help us reach Oregon safely."

FIVE

MATILDA POURED STEW into the kettle, just as she would have done in their cozy, little cabin at home. Nicholas spread a tarp on the ground, erected poles in the center, and draped their canvas tent over the top. The pungent odor of linseed oil wafted in the air. Matilda stood erect and pulled back her shoulders. This rig and tent would be their home for the next six months. As long as she had her husband and her boys, she was home.

Nicholas pounded the last tent stake into the ground. He glanced across the clearing at William setting up his tent. "Where's your wife?"

William glanced toward his wagon. "She's not feeling well tonight. She's lying down."

"Is she in the family way?"

William shook his head. "No, nothing like that. Mayhap it's the motion that unsettled her stomach."

Nicholas guffawed. "Well, she'll have plenty of time to grow accustomed to it." He strode to his wagon, retrieved a wooden bucket, and scrambled down the hillside to the creek.

"You're both welcome to join us for stew." Matilda set the three-legged cast iron trivet over the flames and hung the Dutch oven from the hook in the center. Bart had filled the coffeepot with water from the creek, and she nestled it and the kettle of stew into the fire as well.

Jane climbed down from the wagon and wandered to the campfire.

"Something smells mighty good." The younger woman reached for the lid of the Dutch oven.

"No!" Matilda grabbed her hand. "Don't let the heat out or the corn bread won't finish cooking."

"Oh." Jane shrugged, poured herself a cup of coffee, and sat on a log. "Smells better than what Ophelia cooked us at home. ... Still, I wish we could have brought her with us."

"I don't think they allow slavery in Oregon." Matilda pulled the tin plates and spoons from her wagon. "Do you have eating utensils for you and William?"

"Somewhere." Jane stepped to her wagon and crawled inside.

"Time for dinner!"

The boys rushed toward the campfire. Matilda poured thick stew onto tin plates and added a chunk of corn bread to each. "Wash your hands before you eat." She scrubbed Johnny's dirty fingers with a clean damp cloth and handed it to Henry.

She gave each boy a plate with a spoon. Arms encircled her waist as Nicholas leaned forward and sniffed. "Smells first rate. I'm hungry enough to eat a horse."

Matilda dished a double portion and handed him the plate, then ladled less onto one for herself.

"Next time Jane's going to help you with the meal, right?" Nicholas eyed the younger woman.

"I'm not a very good cook." Jane swallowed another spoonful of stew. "We had slaves to prepare our meals."

"Well, you'd better learn quick." Nicholas said before taking a bite. "Everyone needs to pitch in. You can wash the dishes after dinner."

Matilda placed her hand gently on her husband's arm and shook her head.

When the meal ended, she stood and tucked a wayward lock of hair into the bun beneath her bonnet before storing the leftovers inside the wagon for the next day's noonday meal. She looked for Jane, who had once again disappeared. Matilda poured hot water into a basin and scrubbed with baking soda and abrasive sugar sand. She dried the dishes herself and set Jane and William's utensils on their wagon seat. Maybe Jane would help tomorrow.

When Matilda reached for the short-handled broomstick, her husband gently moved her aside, then pulled a rocker from the wagon and set it on the packed dirt.

"Woman! Sit!" he ordered. "You swept out the wagon when we stopped."

"Maybe for a minute." Matilda smiled and sank into the rocker with a sigh. Johnny climbed onto her lap. She was exhausted, and the trip had only begun. She counted the months and reckoned they'd arrive by October, a month before the baby was due.

She lit the kerosene lantern and reached for her sewing basket. Then, settling again in the rocker, she picked up the cotton cloth to stitch a shirt.

Nicholas lounged against a log, packing a pipe with tobacco. Scratching a match against a rock, he lit the pipe, inhaled deeply, then blew smoke into the air, where it joined curling gray swirls from the campfire.

"Pa, tell us a story about Grandpa," Henry begged.

"Yeah, Pa." Grundy scooted closer to his father's feet. "Maybe one about the fort."

Bart glowered at his younger brother. "No, I wanna hear 'bout a hunting trip."

"Grandpa. Grandpa." Johnny repeated, joining the chorus of voices.

Nicholas puckered his lips, then beamed as he rubbed a hand over his chin, his bushy black brows lifted above his blue eyes. He drew deeply on his pipe and glanced toward the stars just beginning to dot the night sky like chips of ice. His eyes twinkled in the firelight.

"Well, my pa was quite the trapper," he began. "His father taught him and his five brothers to hunt—duck, pheasants, deer, elk, bear—anything they could kill to feed that big family of theirs. They'd go huntin' all through Missouri."

"Great-grandpa—he's the one captured by Indians when he was little, ain't he, Pa?" Henry nodded toward his younger brothers.

"Yep, he sure was. But that's another story. We're talking about my pa tonight."

Matilda smiled as she drew her shawl tighter around her shoulders to ward off the chill in the night air. She loved listening to the deep timbre of her husband's voice in storytelling mode.

"My pa, he was the fifth boy, so his big brothers taught him too. But he was always tryin' to outdo them, so he'd be stronger, braver, and better at everything. He was fearless, leastways that's what my uncles said.

"When he was huntin', he always killed his bear—a big 'un too. Know how he could tell it was a big 'un?"

Matilda knotted the end of the thread as her sons shook their heads.

"Why, my pa, he was just a boy, but brave as they come. He'd sneak right up to a hollow tree or a cave where a bear was sleepin', crawl right in on his belly, and touch the fur to see if it was fat enough to kill."

The boys held still, scarcely seeming to breathe. As Nicholas relit his pipe and inhaled, Bart asked, "Did he ever get bit?"

"Well, he didn't get bit, but he nearly lost an arm one time when a big ol' bear felt somethin' a'pryin' his fur and swatted at it. Pa rushed outta that cave, holdin' his arm tight against his side, blood dripping down his shirt. Turned out it just cut the skin. He was lucky … that time."

The boys sat around the fire, wide-eyed. Although they had heard the story before, they kept still, as if unwilling to do anything that might break the magic of the tale.

Silence fell as the story ended, punctuated only by the crackle and spark of the fire.

A moment later, Henry whispered, "Boy, I wish I'd met Grandpa."

"Me too." Bart looked up at his father. "How old were you when that horse threw off your pa and kilt him?"

Matilda sighed. Their swashbuckling grandfather, a tavern owner, had died years before she and Nicholas married. Only Henry had met their grandmother who passed away six years ago.

"I was just a young'un—about eight, I guess. Just a little older than you. I missed him somethin' terrible, but I survived. That was nigh on thirty years ago now."

"I'd sure miss you if'n something happened, Pa." Bart bit his lower lip.

Matilda raised her head at his comment and looked at her husband. How would her boys survive if something happened to their father? How would she survive? She shuddered. No sense begging trouble. All the same, she gnawed at the inside of her cheek as she resumed sewing.

"I know, Bart, but ain't nothin' going to happen to me. But if it did, you boys would survive, just like I did. And you'd take care of your ma and Johnny, wouldn't you?"

His sons nodded solemnly. Grundy pulled Johnny onto his lap, encircling him with his arms.

"Stop squeezing!" the youngster bellowed. "I can't breathe."

"Shhh, John Nicholas." Matilda admonished her youngest and beckoned to her other sons. "It's time you boys grabbed your bedrolls and spread them in the tent."

Matilda tucked away her sewing as Nicholas hauled out the straw tick and a blanket. He placed them underneath the wagon. He drew her down onto the mattress.

Bone tired after a long day, Matilda struggled to shut off her mind and its worries. Where was her faith? The words from Matthew 6:34 flowed into her mind: "Take therefore no thought for the morrow: for the morrow shall take thought for the things of itself. Sufficient unto the day is the evil thereof." Good advice but hard to do.

She reached for her husband's hand in the darkness and held it tight. When they married a decade ago, she had thought of herself as "settling" for Nicholas, an old friend but definitely not the romantic hero of folklore. Oh, how she loved this man now. What would she do if she lost him? Nicholas rolled over and wrapped his arms around her.

Voices rose from the wagon next to them.

"You're going to need to learn then," William shouted.

"But how? Slaves always cooked. I never paid attention." Jane's voice rose. "Whyever would I?"

"You heard Nicholas," William said. "We're not at home anymore. You'll need to learn. I'm sure Aunt Matilda will show you."

Nicholas nudged her and grinned. "More work for you now, less in the long run."

She smiled. "I can teach her … if she's willing to learn."

Eventually, she drifted off to the rustling of the oxen as they grazed in the grass.

Six

THEY HEADED OUT soon after dawn, Nicholas leading the team, the older boys on Belle, and Matilda walking with Grundy and Johnny.

A crack suddenly resounded as wood splintered sharply. The wagon shuddered. Matilda grasped Johnny into her arms, rushing away as the wagon lurched to the left, and jerked to a stop. Bart yanked back on Belle's reins as she whinnied. Nicholas, who had been teaching Henry to handle the oxen, cursed as he climbed down from the bench.

"Now what?" Exasperation tinged his voice as he strode around the wagon and bent to examine it underneath. "We're still a day out of Independence." He squatted and peered up at Matilda. "Hit a hole. Looks like we broke an axle."

Matilda shuffled forward and stooped to peer beneath the wagon. She wasn't entirely sure what to look for, but from her husband's cursing, it spelled trouble. Would they be stranded? Miss the wagon trains, left to travel the trail alone?

"See that wooden beam?" Nicholas pointed to the splintered wood. "It's split."

"What are we going to do?" Her voice rose as her mind filled with pictures of dangers they'd face on the trail magnified by going alone, without others to help them cross rivers and prairies, ward off dangers from predatory animals and people.

He stood silent, arms crossed, and lips pursed. "Well, I brought along a spare. It's tied under the wagon." He pounded his fist on the bench. "I never thought I'd need it this soon."

They hadn't even reached Independence. Would they spend their little savings on another axle? Or delay their trip to make one? This didn't bode well for the journey as they hadn't yet reached the start of the Oregon Trail.

William pulled his rig to a stop. "What's happened?"

Nicholas kicked a clump of dirt. "Broke an axle. But I've got a spare. I'd appreciate a hand replacing it."

"Sure enough." William handed the reins to Jane and clambered down.

With help from Henry and Bart, William finagled the wagon toward one side and then the other to reduce pressure as Nicholas slid the round wooden axle tree through the hubs of each wheel.

Nicholas glanced toward the fast-moving sun. He dropped his voice, but she heard his words to William. "I'm worried we might not make it to Independence in time to hook up with a train. We're late as it is, and now this."

Matilda certainly didn't want to travel in a train of two across the plains and mountains. She shivered as chills of fear shot through her.

It took all day to replace the axle. Finally, Nicholas slathered a mix of animal fat and tar from the grease bucket onto the axle and wheels.

He stood. "It's done."

Matilda had prepared dinner while the men worked. As usual, Jane remained in her wagon until she heard the words, "Dinner's ready."

Matilda shook her head. Although she felt bad for Jane, she didn't think it healthy to dwell on her barrenness. Putting idle hands to work usually helped shift her focus from problems to blessings. Maybe she'd ask Jane to help with the cleanup. She dished up potato cakes and scrambled eggs sprinkled with cheese.

Nicholas sniffed the food on his plate and a grin spread across his face. "You know how to turn a bad day good."

"I figured we should use the eggs while we have them. The hens won't lay long with all that jostling in the wagon."

She dished up second helpings for Nicholas and William. "We have molasses stack cake for dessert."

After they finished, Nicholas struck a match to a pipe.

Jane stood and strode toward her wagon, leaving her dishes on a log.

"Jane." The younger woman stopped and turned as Matilda cleared her throat. "Would you like to help with the dishes?"

After hesitating for a moment, the younger woman nodded.

"I'd be pleased if you could collect the dirty ones for me." Matilda poured warm water from a pot on the fire into a bucket. "I'll wash and you can dry."

She handed Jane a towel and bent at the waist to scrub the tin dishes, pots, and pans. After dipping each into cool water for rinsing, she gave it to Jane.

"How'd you fare on the trail today?" Matilda handed the younger woman a plate.

Jane shrugged.

"Were you able to do any sewing?"

She shook her head as she dried and stacked the dishes.

"Did you sleep then?"

"How could anyone sleep in that?" Jane glared at her wagon.

"Perhaps you'll sleep well tonight." Matilda finished rinsing the last pot. "Walking wears me out by the end of the day."

"I didn't walk." Jane tossed the towel onto the stack of dishes.

Matilda smiled. "Nonetheless, I hope you sleep well. Thank you for drying the dishes."

Jane nodded and shuffled toward her rig. Matilda draped the towel over a rope on the wagon's side to dry, then settled the boys in the tent. Nicholas lit the oil lamp and pulled out a long sheet of paper. With pencil in hand, he wrote. Matilda, holding her Bible, pulled her chair next to the stump where Nicholas perched and glanced over his shoulder.

He leaned backward to nuzzle her cheek. "Philip asked me to keep track of hazards we find on our trip, so they'll know better what to expect when they come out in a few years."

She smiled. "How will you send that to Philip from Oregon?"

"I'll find folks returning east and give it to them." Nicholas faced the paper again. She knew he hated writing and struggled to spell. But it was kind of him to share insights with Philip and Sarah so they could be better prepared for their trip west.

He nibbled the end of his pencil and then wrote.

Make your cupling pole stout and your axel tree four inches at the big end of the hub. Have your timbers of the best and wel seasond.

He noted that most of the road so far had been good, except for a sixty-mile stretch.

The road from tharon is first-rate except sum places they are very bad.

"Do you want me to check your spelling?" Matilda offered help without looking up. Nicholas would never admit it, but she knew he found his lack of education embarrassing.

"Naw. He can figure it out." Nicholas folded the paper, tucked it into his shirt pocket, and stood. "That's enough writin' for now. I'm ready to sleep."

"I'll finish shortly." Matilda bent to read the holy words on the page before her, praying their last axle would hold until they reached the Willamette Valley.

SEVEN

Mid-May, Independence, Missouri

WHAT IF THEY MISSED the last company headed to Oregon Territory? Would they return home? Matilda knew that faint hope to be vain. Nicholas was moving west, with a wagon train or on his own. And she and the boys were going, too.

He urged the oxen to a faster pace as they neared Independence, where clapboard houses dotted the side of the road.

The homes gave way to fairly new storefronts. Independence was only twenty years old, younger than she was. She remembered hearing about the town when it first started as a trade hub with Santa Fe. Now it served as a launching point for Oregon.

Matilda marveled at all the storefronts and proprietors hawking wares to passersby amid the noise and clamor of the busy street. Wagon wheels squeaked. Horses neighed. Oxen bellowed. Her nose tingled, filled with smells of manure mixed with coffee and sweet pastries. Men, women, and children jostled past each other on the street, darting in and out of buildings. Wagons pulled to the side so the drivers could hop off and purchase supplies.

"Tools—you'll need an ax on the trail!" a loud voice called.

"Flour, beans, bacon! Lady, don't let your children starve on the trail!"

Matilda turned to her husband. "Nicholas?"

"We bought all we needed in Saint Charles," he said. "I'm glad we did, too. Look at those prices. That's three times what I paid back home. Of course, if Jane doesn't learn to cook for William, our supplies will give out long before we planned."

Although they'd been traveling for hours, it was still early morning.

Matilda eyed the people hurrying from one shop to another in what Nicolas told her was the courthouse square. "I'm surprised the stores are already open."

He shrugged. "Probably don't want to miss any customers."

She grasped her husband's arm as a man shouted, "Watch out!" Arms laden with packages, the older fellow glared at them as he shuffled in front of the oxen.

"I see him." Nicholas pulled back on the reins, then scrambled to the dirt street to lead the agitated team and heavy wagon past the courthouse square. Matilda looked for Belle, who skittered behind the wagon with Henry and Bart on her back. Henry's hands were white where he clenched the reins.

They passed hotels, wagon shops, grocers, general merchandise stores, blacksmith shops, and livery stables. Wagons rolled ahead of them; others followed behind William and Jane. With so many rigs clogging the road, they'd have enough to form a wagon train.

One woman rode her pony astride rather than sidesaddle. Another held a parasol over her head. As they left the town behind, lurching six miles along a rough road to the Missouri River, they found dozens of wagons encamped in a jumble, their occupants waiting for a turn to cross. As the buildings grew sparse, Nicholas returned to the wagon seat, reins in both hands. They followed other wagons toward a muddied pasture. Indians drifted among the tents, some with torn blankets draped over their shoulders, others wearing colorful calicoes, offering goods for sale. Some had shaved heads and painted faces.

"Pa, look!" Henry pointed toward the warriors.

"Hush now." Matilda swiveled to face her boys. She stared at their blond and chestnut hair, trying to erase the horrifying image of their scalps dangling from a belt.

"They're friendly." Nicholas caressed her leg. "Likely as not, Missouri and Osage. Maybe Kansas."

"How do you know, Pa?" Henry tilted his head and glanced left and right as the mare trotted along the road.

"Get up!" Nicholas bellowed to the oxen. Nodding to Henry, he said, "I read those are the tribes who hang around Independence."

"What about the unfriendly Indians?" Bart asked, a tremor in his voice. "Where we going to see them?"

"Never you mind, boy." Nicholas laughed and rubbed his second son's head. "Indians. Non-Indians. Bears. Buffalo. They're no match for you and me."

Nicholas fretted over how long it took to cover each well-worn mile west. "We're going too slow."

Most folks had left for Oregon a month ago. They needed to reach the clearing at Elm Grove before the last train left or they'd travel alone and risk a harsh winter. He relaxed a bit when they arrived in the early evening at a clearing filled with wagons, oxen, tents, and people. He guided his team through a gap to a patch of vacant trampled grass.

After hopping off the wagon, Nicholas grabbed a bucket of water, strode to the front of the team, and lowered each beast's head in turn to drink. "You boys wait with your ma."

"Do we have to?" Henry slid from Belle's back. "Can't we go with you, Pa?"

"You heard me: stay with your ma. I need to check out the surroundings." He beckoned to his nephew and William followed. They tromped past wagons and stopped along the bank of the Missouri River. Upstream, a steamboat docked near the bend at West Port. Muscles rippled on the arms and chests of two shirtless black men who plunged long poles into the deep water to guide a flat-bottomed ferry diagonally across the shimmering blue expanse. Passengers stood beside wagons on the boat. Downstream, a bearded man led two horses into the water, but a shout startled the beasts, and they backed away, splashing.

Nicholas raised a hand to block the setting sun's glare. "Looks like he's got his horses tangled in their ropes."

An older man beside him wearing a black felt hat nodded.

They watched the bearded man urge his animals forward. One stumbled while the other swam forward. Yanking a knife from a sheath on his belt, the young man sawed at the harness while following the horse into deeper water.

Nicholas peered closer. "He's cutting his harness?"

"He'd better if he wants to save the animals."

Nicholas saw the lead horse go under again. "You're right."

Freed from the ropes, the horses surfaced and clambered up the bank.

Nicholas released a breath. "Other than needing a new harness, looks like the fellow made it." He crossed his arms. He'd take care crossing rivers. "They've got quite the setup here."

A tall man with dark hair and spectacles tipped his hat back. "Look-ee there."

Nicholas followed his gaze. Oxen strained against their yokes as a wagon tipped to one side. "Looks like his team's restless." He gestured. "I heard that could happen."

As they watched, the wagon toppled on its side, barrels and furniture floating into the river.

A scream pierced the air as the young man leading the oxen scrambled in vain to right the rig.

The other man laughed. "That's one emigrant who won't be heading west anytime soon."

Nicholas started down the bank.

"Where do you think you're going?" The fellow grabbed his arm. "Nothin' you can do. Look at those natives racing down the far bank. His loss is their gain. Land across the river belongs to the Indians."

Nicholas yanked his arm loose. He scrambled down the riverbank, dove into the water, and swam toward the wagon. Finding footing in the mucky sand, he nodded toward the young man who cursed as he tried to settle his oxen.

"You got your family in the wagon?" Nicholas shouted.

"No, my wife and daughter are riding the ferry. Thank God!" he said with a hitch in his voice. He cleared his throat.

"Let me give you a hand." Nicholas turned as William and several others swam up. "We can use our backs to right the wagon as you lead your team toward the shore."

The young fellow nodded. Nicholas and the others pushed against the wagon as it lurched forward and hefted it upright. As the owner led his team, Nicholas and the others pushed from behind, freeing the rig from the sand and up onto the rock landing at the river's edge.

As the wagon lurched forward, the men swam back to the east bank. Nicholas retrieved his hat from the shore and strode back up the rise, where the tall, thin man stood bent over, heaving with laughter. "That's the funniest thing I've ever seen."

"You think that's funny?" Nicholas squeezed water from his shirtsleeves. "Coulda just as easily been your wagon."

"Naw." An older man jostled the lanky fellow in the arm. "Jimmy's just trying to look at the lighter side. 'Tweren't funny."

"I imagine it's pretty rough for the fellow and his family to lose so much." Nicholas set his hands on his hips.

The older man held out his hand. "Name's Samuel Rawlins." He nodded toward the younger man. "This here's my younger brother, Jim. We're from South Carolina. Lived mostly in Missouri."

Nicholas shook the older man's hand and introduced himself. He nodded at the tall skinny fellow, Jim. A sandlapper, or more like a lanky loon. He shifted his gaze back to the older man. "So do we line up here to cross?"

Samuel nodded downstream. "Those wagons are crossing with the oxen." Pointing upstream, he gestured to another ferry. "Passengers can ride on that one."

"You know the cost of the ferry?"

"Think it's about two dollars for a loaded wagon and team, maybe a little more. Mayhap two bits per passenger."

Nicholas nodded. "Sounds like the safest way to get the wagon across."

Jim Rawlins scoffed. "That fellow didn't know how to handle his team."

Nicholas clenched his teeth, tipped his hat to Samuel, and strode back to his wagon. *Sure hope I don't have to deal with that Jim fellow on the trail.*

Matilda herded her boys onto the flat-bottomed ferry and out of the way as Nicholas led their team and wagon, holding the lead yoke tight.

"Good boys. Keep calm." He uttered the names of the oxen as he patted their haunches. "Good boys."

When they reached the shore, William and Nicholas led the team and rumbling wagon up the bank and onto the Santa Fe Trail, which they'd follow for a bit before turning north. They did the same with William and Jane's wagon.

The two women walked behind and gazed at the natives, a few with shaved heads and painted faces, many on shaggy ponies, hovering on the hillside, watching the emigrants.

"Yeaww!" An Indian on a pony raced past and downstream, then hopped off his mount and dove into the water. He surfaced and retrieved a barrel that had fallen from a wagon.

Jane shuddered. "Savages."

Matilda pushed back her bonnet to look closer at the bare-chested men and the women in calico dresses. Some wrapped themselves in old blankets. "I wonder if they're the friendly Indians Nicholas mentioned, the Osage or Missouri tribes. Or Kansas."

"What does it matter?" Jane leaned toward Matilda and dropped her voice. "It's like they were trying to see what we have in our wagons so they can steal it."

Matilda touched Jane's hand. "I think they just enjoy watching men swim their livestock across the river."

Jane shivered. "I felt like they were undressing me."

"I'm sure our clothing covers anything of interest to the braves." She chuckled. "Besides, they'd need mighty fine eyesight to see through all these layers."

EIGHT

Mid-May 1847, Elm Grove outside of Independence, Missouri

NICHOLAS LOOKED at the clustered wagons, relieved they would have company on the trail, and pulled out his tent posts. "Better set up camp."

Matilda glanced right and left. "Here?"

Wagons crowded beside one another. People built fires next to their wagons. Men pounded tent stakes into the ground. Animals grunted. Women called for young ones. Smoke swirled above the huddled wagons like a cloud covering a stockyard. A fiddler's music floated through the camps.

"There's no privacy," she said.

"Might as well get used to it now." Nicholas spread the tent beside the wagon. "We're not likely to have much privacy for the next five or six months, not until we're in our own place in Oregon Territory."

"Boys, stay close to camp." Matilda gestured to her sons. "Grundy, when you've finished with the oxen, will you watch Johnny?"

The boy squeezed water from the damp rag and nodded.

After erecting the tent, Nicholas touched Matilda's shoulder. "I'm going to find out about how to join the company." Raising his voice, he called their nephew. "William! Want to join me?"

"I want to go, Pa!" Henry grabbed his father's shirt. "Please?"

"Me too, Pa. Can we go?" Bart's plea joined his brother's.

Nodding, Nicholas left with William beside him, his two older sons trailing behind as they navigated through people, oxen, cattle, horses, and wagons.

"Never seen so many wagons and livestock in one place." William shook his head. "It's going to be a crowded road."

"Likely so." Nicholas chuckled. "You know what they say—the more the merrier."

William raised his brows. "If you say so."

"Just hope they left enough grass for our animals." Nicholas clapped the younger man on the back as they moved around the wagons. A group of men gathered near a pasture fence. He and William joined them. Nicholas thrust out his hand toward a younger clean-shaven man of small stature.

"Name's Nicholas Koontz." He tilted his head toward his nephew. "This here's William Glover."

"James Jory." The young man shook their hands.

"You British?" Nicholas asked. "Bit of an accent is why I ask."

"We've been living in Illinois, my wife and I, but yes, my folks brought us over from England back in '37." He glanced toward the nearly one hundred wagons cluttering the pasture. "We planned to meet my father and brothers here but haven't seen them."

"Hard to find people in all this. You heard anything about them forming a company?" Nicholas had no intention of crossing the trail alone. Most everyone joined a company to provide safety in numbers and help during difficult times. If they broke an axle or found themselves lagging behind, they'd do their darnedest to catch up.

Jory ran a hand over his chin, but before he could answer, a voice boomed.

"They're meeting here tomorrow morning to elect a captain."

Nicholas groaned. Not Rawlins again. He looked toward the tall, thin man with spectacles, the know-it-all he already disliked. The annoying man was at it again.

"We're just outside of Elm Grove. Ferry crossing is to the east, and that there is the Kaw River." Jim Rawlins pointed as he stepped into the circle of men. "Since it's May 12th, we're already behind the other companies. We'll need to elect a wagon leader tomorrow."

Nicholas pursed his lips as he glanced at William and shook his head. Although he knew most trains picked one man as leader, he hoped Rawlins wouldn't seek the position. He couldn't imagine answering to that irksome dunderhead for the next six months, much less pooling money to pay him for making life miserable.

"It's also known as McKinney's pasture." Jory said softly. "I met the reverend who owned it, but he's going west with us. Reverend John McKinney, a man about fifty or so."

Nicholas gazed in the direction Jory indicated but couldn't see anyone dressed in black robes like a preacher in the growing darkness. "Got any ideas for who'll lead us?"

"I've heard others speak highly of a young fellow named Joseph Magone." Jory nodded toward a tall man leaning against the fence, eyes scanning the crowd. "They say he has a good head on his shoulders. Not quite sure what to make of that American expression, but I understand he's studied the route quite thoroughly."

"Why do they think he'd make a good captain?"

Another man beside Jory answered. "Good sense of direction. Strong presence. Carries himself well. Humble but confident. Seems like one of those natural leaders. He's already organized the trains a bit to make room for latecomers."

Nicholas nodded. That's why they'd found a spot to camp so easily. "We'll see you at sunup then. Glad to meet you."

When they returned to camp, Matilda handed each a chunk of cured bacon and a biscuit slathered with butter and molasses. After they ate, Nicholas gestured toward the tent. "You boys go on now. Get some shuteye."

"How we s'posed to sleep with all this noise?" Henry waved his arm at the wagons and tents. Laughter and fiddle music echoed and mingled with the buzzing of insects and lowing of cattle and oxen. Campfire smoke almost overpowered the putrid smell of manure in the growing darkness.

"You get on in there, close your eyes, and sleep." Nicholas pushed his eldest son toward the tent. "Once we get to Oregon, it will be as quiet as snowflakes blanketing the ground."

"Say your prayers." Matilda kissed Henry's forehead and then Bart's. "Focus on the Almighty and you'll drift to sleep. All of you boys say your prayers now."

Nicholas plopped onto the grass and leaned against the wagon wheel. He lit his pipe and inhaled deeply as he listened to Bart's voice praying, "Almighty God, protect us. Don't let us get killed on the way to Oregon Territory."

oⅤᴑ

Dawn brought a flurry of activity to McKinney's pasture as Nicholas and the other men hustled to the trailhead for the organizational meeting. Nicholas had read that every company needed a strong leader to break up fights and keep laggards from slowing the train. Henry begged his father to let him and Bart tag along so they could see how a wagon train was organized.

"All right then." Nicholas placed an arm around the shoulders of each boy. "Let's go. We don't want to be late. Might be left behind."

He chuckled. William joined them as they gathered at the center of the field.

"Looks to be nigh on a hundred rigs here." William gestured to the wagons. "Mighty big train."

"Last one going west. Nobody wants to be left behind."

"Now I've heard that we line up behind whichever man we'd like to elect captain." The irritating voice belonged to that Rawlins fellow. Thin wisps of hair lifted off his head in the light breeze.

"I don't see why we need to do that." It was the man who had spoken highly of Magone the previous night. "How many people want to serve as captain? I think we've got a great leader right here in Joseph Magone."

Magone stepped forward, twirling his broad-brimmed hat between his fingers.

"I'm willing to lead, but I'm also fine with stepping back if another man would like to do it." He swept a lock of hair from his eyes and gazed at each man in turn. "I'm Joseph Magone. I was born back east in St. Lawrence County, New York. I'm twenty-six, a miller, never married. I figured I'd work cattle, so I don't have a wagon, but I'm happy to serve as captain if you'd like. I promise to remain alert and vigilant, ride up and down the line of wagons, and do my best to see that all you folks arrive safely in the Willamette Valley."

"Sounds good to me," Nicholas said. A chorus of assents ran through the crowd as men dropped coins and cash into a hat passed among them to pay the young man for his work.

"But what about the election?" Rawlins piped up again.

"All in favor of electing Magone as captain, raise your hand." Jory's friend lifted his arm. All the others did the same, except for Rawlins. "It's settled then. When do we move out, Captain Magone?"

"Let's plan on leaving by eleven. We'll line up the wagons before we go." Magone set his hat on his head and strode toward the livestock.

"But we didn't have a proper election." Rawlins bellowed the words as the men dispersed.

"Quit your whining." Nicholas threw both hands into the air. "You think you should have been captain?"

"Well, perhaps …"

Nicholas leaned forward, his nose inches from Rawlins. "You're sure actin' like you know it all, Rawlins, but that ain't the case. You'll follow Magone like the rest of us, or you can find another train."

Rawlins' eyes widened as he stepped back. "Why…what a bouncer you are!" He cursed and stormed through the cluster of wagons.

Nicholas snorted and rolled his eyes. He wasn't going to like traveling with that man.

As the crowd dispersed, Nicholas lingered with the boys and William.

"I'm happy to be in Magone's company," Nicholas said. "Heard that young man's got a good head on his shoulders. It's sure somethin' to see how he handles all these different folks. Some are mighty irritating."

William chuckled. "I think I know who you're thinking of."

Nicholas laughed and clapped him on the back. "But we have some mighty good folks in our group too, so we'll do fine."

NINE

WITH A CAPTAIN ELECTED, Nicholas, his boys, and William veered around campsites to reach their rigs and pack up. Henry darted ahead, Bart on his heels, and then shouted, "Look, isn't that Frank Wilson?"

"Where?" Bart's gaze followed his brother's finger.

A gangly, blond boy loped toward them.

"Hey, Frank!" Henry ran toward his friend. "When'd ya get here?"

"Two days ago." The taller boy nudged Henry, grinned at Bart, and turned toward Nicholas. "Pa and Ma said we were waiting for you."

"Where's your wagon, Son?"

When Frank pointed, Nicholas headed in that direction with William at his side. The three boys followed. The family hadn't seen the Wilsons since dinner with the reverend and his wife in Saint Charles. As they approached, Frank ran ahead, shouting, "Pa! I found 'em. The Koontzes."

Tom Wilson stepped around the rig and shook hands with Nicholas. His wife, Freda, peered out from the canvas covering, her blond hair twisted into a knot.

"Well, look who it is!" she exclaimed. "Where's Matilda?"

"Over that away." Nicholas tilted his head over his left shoulder. "This here is our nephew, William Glover. He and his wife, Jane, are traveling with us. William, this is Freda and Tom Wilson. They were neighbors in Saint Charles. Attended our church too."

Tom and William shook hands.

Nicholas pursed his lips. "Didn't see you when we elected the captain."

"They've done that already?" Tom shook his head. "See there, Freda, I missed it. I told you I should have followed those fellows instead of eating breakfast."

"Never you mind, Tom. What difference did it make whether you were there or not?"

He rolled his eyes. "Who'd they pick?"

"Young fellow named Magone." Nicholas pulled off his hat and wiped his brow. "Seems like a good sort." He put it back on and said, "We're pulling out within the hour, so we ought to pack up."

"Glad we connected." Tom moved toward his wagon. "I wondered how we'd ever find you in this crowd."

"Leave it to the boys." Freda laughed. "They're like magnets—drawn to one another wherever they are."

"True enough." Nicholas headed back toward his wagon. "Come on, boys. We need to hook up the oxen."

Racing into their camp, Henry and Bart spoke over each other. Henry shoved his younger brother. "Ma, we found the Wilsons."

"They're here," Bart added. "We found Frank's wagon."

Matilda turned to glance at her boys. "Nicholas?"

He nodded. "Tom and Freda are over yonder. Frank said they waited for us."

"That was kind." Matilda lifted the iron spider for cooking over fires into the wagon. "It'll be nice to travel west with people we know."

Nicholas laughed and whispered in her ear. "You sure you're going to like spending the next five months with Freda? I thought that bossy Swede drove you nuts after an hour."

His wife lifted a hand to her mouth, but Nicholas grasped it, kissing the palm. "I see that grin."

She swiveled in his arms. "You know Freda and I are friends."

"Even though she likes to tell you what to do." Nicholas guffawed. "You can always introduce her to Jane."

Matilda chuckled. "I will. Perhaps they'll forge a friendship."

"Ha. I'll believe that when I see it." Nicholas strode to where Henry and Bart led the oxen toward the rig.

Finally, amid the lowing of cattle and clamor of voices, the train moved west—or at least northwest. More than ninety wagons rumbled out of the pasture along the rutted trail. Men and boys on horses herded cattle behind the train so the oxen wouldn't step in so much dung.

Matilda inhaled a deep breath. This was it! She walked beside their rig, holding Johnny's hand, worried about him darting in front of a rolling wagon. Nicholas guided the oxen into one of the lines and then pulled back on the reins to create distance. Matilda figured he probably didn't want their animals swallowing too much of the billowing dust. Grundy walked on her other side.

"Shall we sing a hymn?" she asked.

Grundy shrugged. "Pa told me to count how many times the wagon wheels rotate so we can track how far we've gone." He kept his eyes peeled to the painted spoke of a wheel. "Bart's doing it too, on the other side from the horse."

"While you're counting, then, I'll sing." Matilda draped her arm over his shoulder and lifted her soprano voice to sing.

"My hope is built on nothing less
Than Jesus' blood and righteousness;
I dare not trust the sweetest frame,
But wholly lean on Jesus' name."

From the wagon, Nicholas joined in with his deep baritone.

"On Christ, the solid Rock, I stand;
All other ground is sinking sand,
All other ground is sinking sand."

Matilda smiled at her husband and nudged Grundy, who added his voice to the hymn. The assurance offered by the words brought peace to Matilda's heart as she and her family passed farms without fences, across a treeless plain, rolling into the unknown.

Nicholas poured himself coffee as he watched Matilda bent over the campfire, stirring stew in a kettle, pushing back a strand of her long chestnut hair. She toiled from dawn to dark.

As William crossed the camp to his wagon, Nicholas asked, "Where's Jane?"

"Not sure…maybe inside."

When Nicholas started toward the Glover wagon, Matilda stood and grabbed his arm. "Nicholas…"

"She needs to help you with the cooking and cleaning." He faced her. "You are not her slave."

"I realize that, but I don't want to anger her. We have months of traveling together."

"All the more reason we need to settle this now. She needs to help." He shrugged her off his arm.

Outside the Glovers' wagon, Nicholas bellowed. "William. Jane." He crossed his arms over his chest. "We need to talk."

"What is it?" William clambered from the wagon. "Jane's dressing."

"She's just now waking up? Great guns!"

"Nicholas!" Matilda admonished him. She hated conflict, which often followed her husband's outbursts.

"Well, we're not on holiday here. Everybody needs to work. You hear me, Jane?"

The cinched canvas at the back of the wagon opened and Jane stepped gingerly onto the ground. "I wasn't feeling well this morning."

"Seems to me you aren't feeling well most mornings." Nicholas glared at the young woman. "You in the family way?"

Jane shook her head, liquid swimming in her eyes.

Nicholas ignored her tears. "Matilda's been sick too, what with that young'un growing inside her. She's got a husband and four boys to watch after, but she's doing all the cooking and cleanup—for us and you."

"Nicholas ..." William stepped between his wife and his uncle. "Jane will help. I think she just doesn't know what to do. She's never cooked before. Slaves did all the cooking at home."

Nicholas gestured toward where his wife dished beans onto tin plates. "We left slavery back in Missouri—ain't nobody going to wait on your wife hand and foot." He shook his head, inhaled deeply, and let out his breath slowly. "Look, Jane. Just because you've never cooked doesn't mean you can't learn. I'm sure Mattie would teach you. Now get on over here and eat, and then you wash up those dishes. No more layin' about like a princess—or plantation mistress."

Matilda's head remained bowed over the kettle, but her cheeks flamed, and her stomach churned at the conflict. She didn't like waiting on Jane, but she'd rather not create a scene. Perhaps she should tell Nicholas about Jane, but would he understand?

"What are we having?" Bart sniffed the air.

"Beans with salt pork."

"Again?"

"We'll be eating lots of it on this trip," she said. "Remember, the Good Book says we need to do all things without complaint or grumbling. Even if it means eating beans with bacon for five months, which in our case it does."

Bart nodded. "Yeah, Ma. It's just—"

"I do have a surprise in the oven for tonight, though, if you'd like to take a peek."

Bart pulled his shirtsleeve over his hand and lifted the hot lid to peer inside. He inhaled deeply. "Apple cobbler?" He rubbed his stomach. "Mmm...."

The next morning, Matilda pulled the steel grinder from the two-drawer spice cabinet and handed it to Grundy. "Will you grind the coffee beans, please?"

After mixing flour, salt, water, and lard, she put the soda biscuits into the Dutch oven dangling from the cast-iron spider over the campfire.

Her third son twisted the handle to grind the beans, releasing a rich aroma into the air. Then he scooped water from the keg attached to the wagon, filled the coffeepot, and handed it to his mother to put over the flames.

Bacon sizzled on the cast-iron griddle, and she cracked the last of the eggs into the grease. Although the hens had provided eggs initially, the wagon's jostling upset them, so they quit laying. It looked like the family would enjoy fried chicken dinners before long. Matilda rotated her breakfast fare—biscuits, johnnycakes, and cornmeal mush—but figured her boys would tire of all of it long before they reached Oregon. The Wilsons had already joined them, and Freda stirred the eggs.

"Smells good." William sauntered toward the campfire. Jane climbed out of the wagon and glanced around the camp.

As Matilda and Freda set out the meal they had prepared—eggs, bacon, and beans with bacon cooked in molasses—Jane walked over from her wagon and picked up a plate.

"Who are you and why are you preparing to eat our meal?" Freda demanded, hands on her hips.

"Oh, dear." Matilda grasped her friend's forearm. "This is William's wife, Jane." Turning to the younger woman, she said, "Jane, this is Freda Wilson, a friend from Saint Charles."

Freda nodded but furrowed her brows. "Question remains, why is she eating food her hands haven't prepared?"

Jane dropped the dish and backed away.

Matilda winced at the shimmer of tears in her eyes. "Jane, you're welcome to eat with us as always."

Jane backed away, then turned and fled toward her wagon, scrambling inside.

"Freda." Matilda shook her head. "Jane's …"

"She's what? Lazy? Spoiled?"

"No, she's experiencing emotional troubles."

Freda scoffed. "So? Who isn't? Life on the trail is hard. Buck up or go home. And everyone must do her share."

"She helps with the dishes," Matilda said.

The older woman rolled her eyes. "Isn't there something in the Bible about not eating if you don't work?"

"In Thessalonians, 'if any would not work, neither should he eat,'" Matilda recited automatically while dishing food onto the plates.

"Ha! There you go. I knew it." Freda laughed and then squinted toward the Glover wagon. "She's not fat enough to last five months without eating, so she'd better get to working."

Matilda cringed at the harsh words. Her friend seemed to thrive on creating conflict.

"Wash up before you eat," Freda shouted as her brood of five raced into the camp with Henry, Bart, and Grundy. Matilda's boys adored Frank, the Wilsons' oldest boy.

Matilda handed a plate to Nicholas and then turned toward William. With her back to Freda, she offered her nephew two plates and tipped her head toward his wagon. His eyebrows shot up as he glanced around the camp. He nodded and carried their food to his rig.

Freda, busy doling out food to her children, hadn't noticed. Matilda exhaled in relief.

In the early dawn the next morning, Matilda examined Jane as she shuffled forward, clenching a blanket around her shoulders, knuckles white, eyes red-rimmed and swollen.

"I'm sorry about Freda." Matilda reached to embrace the younger woman. "She's not one to mind her tongue. Here, sit and enjoy your breakfast."

Jane perched on the log and nibbled on bacon and a biscuit. William sat close, an arm wrapped around her waist. She shuddered as if holding back sobs.

The boys pelted their father with questions about the journey as they gobbled the morning meal. He answered patiently, then stood. "Gotta pack up. Looks like Magone's lining up the wagons."

Jane quickly stood, dropping the blanket as she collected the dishes for washing without being asked. As Matilda poured hot water into a basin, Jane moved to her side, a dry towel in her hand.

"I wondered..." Jane's voice shook as she dried a plate. "Can you show me how to bake corn bread over the campfire?"

"I'd love to." Matilda smiled.

As she packed away the cooking gear, she whispered a prayer of thanksgiving. Praise God for small blessings.

TEN

May, Elm Grove to Big Blue in Kansas

MATILDA, HOLDING JOHNNY'S HAND, walked beside the wagon as it rolled along a rutted trail. Henry and Bart rode Belle and kept track of Millie and the heifer roped to the back of the wagon.

A black and brown foxhound pranced beside Johnny and licked the toddler's hand occasionally. When it did, Johnny giggled, and the dog's tail wagged. Matilda smiled, grateful to the friendly mutt for keeping her little one entertained. It had been so hard for the boys to leave Bo behind with her brother. She wasn't sure who owned this dog, but it often wandered into their camp at night to play with her boys.

Exhaustion threatened as the sun beat down. She wiped sweat from her brow. How much farther would they need to walk?

"Perhaps we should sing a song or memorize a verse of Scripture." Matilda glanced at Grundy, who walked on her other side, staring at the wagon wheel.

"I can't. I'm counting." He kept his eyes peeled to the red bandana on the back left wheel.

"I imagine you can do that and praise the Lord at the same time." Matilda draped her arm over his shoulder and kissed the top of his head. "Let's see … how about Psalm 146? Now repeat each line after me."

As the boys repeated her words, Matilda gazed ahead at the never-ending prairie dotted with sparse brush and brown weeds swaying in the breeze. They crunched the miles beneath their shoes as the afternoon wore on, praising the Lord in song and verse. Matilda yanked her calico skirt free of thistles.

As she walked with Johnny and Grundy, she created a game to see how many twigs and light branches they could collect for the fire. She tucked them into the pockets of the white apron covering her calico dress and, when the wagon slowed, tossed them into a basket hooked to the side.

"Oh, look, Johnny. Do you see that fuzzy flower? Feel it."

Johnny squatted beside the white and green plant and rubbed his palm over the bud.

"Isn't it soft?" Matilda stroked another bud. "It has a funny name. Grundy, do you know what it's called?"

Her third son glanced away from the wagon wheel and laughed. "Pussytoes!"

"Pussy?" Johnny plucked the bud from the plant. "Toes?"

He looked down at his own shoes. Matilda could imagine him trying to figure out how his toes looked like the furry bud in his hand.

At dusk, when the company halted, Matilda and the other women unpacked cooking utensils, gathered wood, and cooked over an open fire.

"I'm so tired of this routine." Jane wiped a stray hair from her brow. "Pull out the utensils, cook the meals, wash the dishes, pack it all away again. And we still have months ahead of us!"

"I know." Matilda opened the drawer of the spice cabinet below and handed the steel grinder to Johnny, knowing he liked to twist and turn the handle and watch coffee beans magically change to ground coffee. "Although I'd be doing much the same at home—cooking, cleaning, washing dishes—it would be nice to have a roof over our heads and a comfortable bed to sleep in at night."

"I wouldn't be working!" Jane grimaced. "I never realized how much I'd miss our house slaves. Delilah did all the cooking and cleaning."

"But Jane." Matilda lifted her head to gaze at the younger woman. "You don't agree with slavery, do you? I mean, it's not right to own another person."

"What do you mean? It talks about slavery right there in the Good Book you're always reading."

Matilda bit her lower lip. "My father insisted God created all men equal—black or white. That's why he freed our slaves in Maryland before we moved to Missouri."

"Your brother kept his slaves." Jane shrugged. "I imagine it's simply a matter of opinion. I guess that's why they have slave states and free states."

Matilda handed the Dutch oven to Jane. "Add the water to the cornmeal and mix it together. Then put the lid on tight and set it on the fire, please."

"As I said, I sure do miss Delilah." Jane grabbed the pan, measured out the cornmeal, and added a cup of water. Matilda placed the black coffeepot on the fire. She stirred the beans and added wood to the campfire, mulling over the conversation with William's wife.

The Good Book did mention slaves, but she held firmly to the words in Galatians. "There is neither Jew nor Greek, there is neither bond nor free, there is neither male nor female: for ye are all one in Christ Jesus."

Besides, the Bible admonished against idle hands, too.

Rain blasted the company one day. Wind billowed the canvases the next. But for the most part, they enjoyed good weather, and the days merged into one another as they settled into the routine.

Breakfast most every morning consisted of fried bacon and soda biscuits but no longer fried or scrambled eggs.

"Bacon again?" Henry groaned.

"Be glad you've got something to eat." Nicholas nudged his eldest son. "Besides, your ma's a good cook. She makes tasty soda biscuits."

Matilda smiled as she stirred together the ingredients. Nicholas always bragged about her cooking.

"Jane's becoming quite a good cook too." Matilda handed the bowl of dough to Jane, who rolled it out and cut it into circles to bake in the Dutch oven. They always baked enough for lunch too.

"We'll have johnnycakes for breakfast tomorrow." She ruffled Henry's hair.

After she dished up the plates, Matilda sat on a stump to eat, gazing into the fire.

"What are you smiling about, Ma?" Bart gestured toward her with his piece of bacon.

"Oh, just remembering." Matilda nibbled her food. "When I was a little girl in Maryland, I once carried a basket of eggs to the Potomac and tossed them in."

"What?" Bart dropped his plate to the ground—face-up, fortunately. "Why would you do that?"

"Just for amusement. Sometimes they'd plunk into the water whole; other times I'd see the shell crack and the yellow yolk stretch downstream. We had plenty of extra eggs then."

"Boy, what I wouldn't give for some of those eggs now." Henry popped the last of his biscuit into his mouth and stood. "I'll go saddle Belle."

"Please don't talk with your mouth full." Matilda dropped her voice as she realized Henry had scrambled out of earshot.

She gathered the rest of the dishes and put them away after washing and drying them. They packed everything else into the wagon and moved out.

At midafternoon, the wagons slowed. Nicholas stood and peered ahead. "Looks like a river up there we need to cross. Hop on up here."

He gestured to Matilda and the younger boys. "No need to get your shoes wet if you don't need to."

She lifted Johnny to her husband and watched Grundy climb into the wagon bed before she hefted herself onto the seat. Matilda watched the wagons ahead to see if they had trouble, tipping or sticking in the mud. She trusted Nicholas, but she also prayed silently for a safe crossing.

The water looked placid enough despite occasional ripples. As they approached the bank, the dry dirt turned to mud. Water splashed from the oxen's hooves as the wagon lurched into the river. Matilda grasped Johnny around the waist and held onto the bench as the rig tilted before righting itself. She grasped her son in one arm, the side of the wagon with the other. Water splashed from the wheels as they turned, drawn through the mucky river bottom by the six oxen.

"I think this here's Cow Creek." Nicholas gestured toward the water.

"Cows?" Johnny squirmed on his seat and scrambled to the edge. "Are there cows in it?"

Nicholas laughed. "Naw. That's just what they call it. Maybe 'cause cows drink from it."

Johnny looked at the water on either side of the wagon and laughed.

Once they reached the other bank, the oxen pulled the heavy load back onto the trail and Matilda and the boys slid to the ground. The less weight those burdened beasts needed to haul, the better. Matilda preferred walking anyway; it eased her morning sickness and even refreshed her in the afternoons. When fatigue hit, she could climb into the wagon and card wool.

ELEVEN

FOUR MILES BEYOND THE CREEK, the company set up camp.

"Why we stopping so early?" Nicholas asked when Captain Magone rode past their wagon on his stallion. "I hate wasting daylight, especially when we're already behind. We need to make it to Oregon before the snow falls."

Magone reined in his steed. "We've got to gather for a meeting tonight."

"What about?" Nicholas unhitched the team.

"Jim Rawlins is insisting we need to corral the horses and calves inside the circle at night."

"What? He's just a blowhard." Nicholas waved his hand dismissively.

"Well, some of the women have been grumbling about it, and now Jim's taken up their cause, so we'll need to talk about it tonight."

Nicholas shook his head. "William and I will be there to speak for a quiet night's sleep. The last thing we need is a bunch of calves mewling all night next to our pillows."

The wagons spread into a circle. The older boys hobbled the mare and led the oxen into the field for grazing. Grundy followed to clean their nostrils while Matilda unloaded supplies.

After dinner, Nicholas stood and dropped his plate in the basin. "Gotta go. Captain called a meeting tonight."

"Another meeting?" Matilda asked. "Why?"

"Can we come, Pa?" Henry asked.

"Not this time." He glanced at Matilda. "Hey, why don't you boys wash those dishes to give your ma a rest? She can come with me."

"Nicholas, I—"

"Come on, Mattie." He wrapped his arm around her waist. "Walk with me." Over his shoulder, he hollered, "Henry, you're in charge."

"Yes, Pa."

Bart groaned.

Nicholas led Matilda from the camp, clasping her hand in his. As they reached the center of the clustered wagons, Captain Magone raised his hat in the air for quiet.

"We've heard complaints from some of the folks worried about losing their horses and cattle to Indians." Magone kicked a clump of dried prairie grass. "It's true that the farther west we go, the more likely we are to lose animals."

"We need to keep them inside the wagon circle," a woman said. "We'll lose them otherwise—they'll wander off or ..." She shook her head. "Or worse."

"But they'd be runnin' wild and makin' a mess where we need to cook our meals," Freda insisted, hands on hips. "They keep the young'uns awake with their bellowing, endanger the little ones with their hooves. They need to be kept outside with the other cattle."

"No, you're wrong. We need to keep them inside the circle at night." Jim Rawlins raised his voice and faced Magone. "We've got to keep them safe. Otherwise, they'll die. Wolves or ruffians or bears will kill them."

"You worry like an old woman." Nicholas waved his hand dismissively. "We need to keep the calves outside."

Rawlins glared at him.

"We don't need the mess and the noise inside the circle." Nicholas shook his head. "It's tough enough to sleep with all the noise from you yahoos!" The men chuckled. Many nodded.

"Not to mention the stench from all that manure." Tom Wilson placed his finger over his nostrils, his face skewing into a grimace.

Laughter erupted. Murmurs of assent followed.

"That's settled then," Magone said.

"What?" Rawlins whined. "How is that settled? We didn't take a vote."

"Okay, Jim, we'll do that." Magone glanced around the circle. "Let's see a show of hands by all those who want the calves and horses inside the circle."

Rawlins and a handful of women raised their hands.

"Everyone against it?"

A majority raised their hands.

"It's settled then. We'll continue to keep the cattle outside the circle with the oxen. Those who are worried about losing their animals can tie them to the far side of their wagons." Magone replaced his hat on his head. "Get some sleep, folks. Sun'll be up soon enough."

As they walked toward their wagon, Nicholas shook his head. "That Rawlins…"

"Hush now."

"What a ninnyhammer!" He rolled his eyes. "We just ain't cut from the same cloth, him and me."

When they returned to camp, he strode to the dwindling campfire.

"How'd it go, Pa?"

Nicholas glared at the dying embers, silent.

"It was fine, Henry." Matilda pulled him toward her in a quick hug. "Time for bed now."

"But Ma—"

"You heard her, Son," Nicholas grumbled, wiping a hand over his scruffy whiskers. "Get some shuteye."

"Yes, Pa."

They settled in for the night. As Matilda sidled next to him on the mattress beneath the wagon, Nicholas continued the conversation, still in a dither over Jim Rawlins. "We have plenty of serious concerns without worrying over a couple of calves among a herd of a hundred. I'll bet Captain Magone wishes Rawlins had gone with one of the other companies, too."

Matilda rubbed the tight muscles in his shoulders.

He pulled her close. "You always have a way of making me feel better."

Matilda smiled. "You know we must make peace and never let the sun go down on our anger."

Nicholas twisted his lips into a grimace. "Can't say as I feel peace toward Rawlins, and I'm not apologizing, but I suppose it does no good to be angry."

As the sun rose, Matilda crawled from beneath the wagon. She was pulling out cold biscuits and cured bacon for breakfast when Nicholas appeared. He stretched, yawned, and hollered for the boys.

"Henry! Bart!" Nicholas rattled the tent. "Time to round up Belle, Millie, and the oxen."

With no time to build a campfire, Matilda handed cold food to the boys as they raced after their father.

Matilda filled a basket with soiled clothing and turned to Grundy. "Will you watch Johnny while I wash these in the creek?"

"I want go!" Johnny jumped up and down. "Creek!"

Grundy held his younger brother by the shoulders. "Let's play a game with twigs. Can you help me find some?"

"Twigs!" Johnny took Grundy's proffered hand and followed him to the brush.

Matilda tossed a bar of lye soap into the basket and, at the creek, bent over the cold water, angling the washboard and scrubbing the clothes to loosen dirt. She wrung out the excess water and draped them over nearby bushes.

"Ma! Ma!" Grundy's voice echoed down the hillside. "Fire!"

Matilda dropped the bucket and raced up the path.

Not their wagon. Please, God. Her boys!

Smoke shot into the air as she ran uphill to the campsite. Orange flames licked their wagon's canvas covering.

She rushed toward the fire, but hands grasped her and held her back.

"No!" Sarah Jory shouted. "There's nothing you can do."

Her husband, James, swatted at the flames with a damp woolen blanket. Smoke swirled into the sky as Matilda's knees buckled. Johnny and Grundy grabbed her skirts, eyes wide.

Their wagon! Everything they owned, their future and survival, lay inside. Nicholas would die if they lost their wagon. At least his dreams would die.

Suddenly, Matilda remembered. "Mr. Jory! The gunpowder!" she shouted. "It's behind the seat." What if the fire reaches the ammunition? Everything would explode. She scrambled backward, drawing her boys and Sarah with her.

"James!" Sarah jerked away as flames snaked up his shirtsleeve.

He batted the fire with his hand.

"Looks like it's all out." Jory lifted the frayed wagon flap and ashes showered to the ground from the charred fabric "I think it just damaged the top layer of the sheet, and only this corner."

"Let me see your arm." Sarah examined his scarlet limb and wrapped a damp cloth around it.

"It's nothing, dear. Might have singed the hair but didn't burn my skin." James smiled. "But it looks like I'll need a new shirt."

Matilda brushed the blackened edges from the canvas. Her legs trembled, heart pounding like a galloping steed.

"Thank you—" Matilda choked back tears, inhaled deeply, and tried again. "Thank you for your quick action. I don't know what we would have done ..." Her mind swirled with what ifs—what if the gunpowder had exploded? Killed one of her boys? She couldn't bear to lose one of her children. "Thank you."

Matilda turned to Sarah. "Thank you, too. Here—let me wash that blanket."

She reached for the soiled cloth draped over Jory's arm.

"There's no need." He shook his head.

"Please. I was washing at the creek anyway. I'll just clean this too. We owe you that, and so much more."

"What—?" She swallowed and tried again. "How did this happen?"

"I'm not certain." Jory glanced at his wife. "A stray ember perhaps?"

She glanced around the camp where a few fires burned. "Thank you for your quick action. I don't know what we would have done …"

The Jorys returned to their wagon, and Matilda sent Grundy to the creek for the bucket. She cuddled Johnny on her lap, her mind flitting to possible causes of the nearly tragic blaze … and then to how her husband would react when he and the older boys returned with the oxen.

Grundy tottered up the trail, water sloshing from the bucket. He set it down beside her.

"Honey…" Matilda gazed into his eyes. "Did you see anyone… did anyone come to the wagon while I was at the creek?"

Grundy shook his head. "I don't think so. But I was playing with Johnny."

She embraced him. "Just as I asked you to do."

As she packed their belongings into the wagon, Nicholas stomped into camp.

"What's this I hear about a fire?" Stepping toward the rig, he lifted the frayed canvas. He hopped onto the wagon seat and crawled inside. Boxes scraped against wood. Pans rattled. He jumped down and glared around the camp, hands on hips, jaw clenched.

"I don't know how it happened, but James Jory quickly put it out." Matilda reached inside the wagon for her sewing kit. "I can stitch that to the bottom cloth to keep it from flapping."

"That's not the point," he barked. "You didn't start a campfire this morning. Neither did anyone else." Nicholas squinted as he looked at the circled wagons and peered at the one owned by Jim Rawlins. The tall thin man caught his gaze and quickly turned to cinch an ox's harness strap. "Yep. It's him. Gotta be."

"Now Nicholas, you don't know that. Nobody saw what happened."

"I'll just bet he struck the match." Nicholas strode to the wagon. "If Jory hadn't noticed it and doused the flames, our entire wagon could have blown. My gunpowder was right here. All our provisions."

He swallowed, shook his head. "What if you or the boys had been inside?"

"We weren't, thank God." Her voice shook.

Nicholas draped an arm over her shoulder but glared at the man across the way. "I'm going to confront him."

As he started to storm across the circle, Matilda grasped his arm. "We can't accuse anyone. It could just be an accident. Perhaps someone lit a pipe or cigar and tossed the match too close to the wagon."

Nicholas shifted his gaze to Matilda. "Could be." He grabbed the team's harness. "But I have my doubts."

That night, William sauntered into the Koontz camp. Matilda stood to pack utensils into the wagon and gestured for her nephew to take the camp chair beside Nicholas.

"Heard about the fire this morning." William glanced at his uncle. "Any idea how it started?"

Nicholas lit his pipe and inhaled. "I have my suspicions." He offered his tobacco pouch to William.

The younger man pulled out his own already-filled pipe. As he tamped it down, he glanced at Nicholas. "Rawlins?"

"If I had to guess."

"Might have been an accident."

"Maybe." Nicholas followed the smoke as it swirled into the dark sky.

William changed the subject. "You meet that Luelling fellow we passed when we were catching up to the train?"

Nicholas shook his head. "Not sure that I did. What's he look like?"

"You can't miss him." William laughed. "He's the man hauling two wagons west—one with his provisions and another filled with trees and shrubs."

Nicholas sat forward. "What's that you say?"

"Sure enough." William grinned. "The fellow's one of those Quakers from Iowa—you know, the church meeting folks with long beards. Long face, too. Henderson Luelling. Appears he has a green thumb. Can make anything grow. He's determined to haul fruit trees and nut trees to plant in Oregon. Seven hundred."

Nicholas whistled. "Hard enough to get one wagon through, but two? And with trees, that must be one heavy wagon. How's he gonna keep those plants alive?"

"Well, he says he's got sixty different types—apples, pears, plums, peaches, currants, gooseberries, grapes, hickory nuts, and black walnut. He put charcoal on the bottom of his wagon, then soil and manure, and finally compost and seedlings."

"Are they growing?" Nicholas asked.

"Sure enough. Looks like they're pretty healthy from what I saw. Of course, he's got plenty of help with that big family of his—wife and eight kids—not to mention those other Quaker families he's traveling with."

"Glad he's not with our train. We're slow enough as it is." Nicholas mumbled as he puffed his pipe anchored in the corner of his mouth "Looks like we've got about ninety wagons in our company now."

"That's plenty." William rose. "I'd better get back to Jane. She's not feeling too well."

"Is she ill?" Matilda asked.

William shook his head. "She'll be fine."

Matilda embraced her nephew quickly before he left. Nicholas draped his arm across her shoulders and guided her toward their mattress.

TWELVE

AFTER A WEARY DAY OF WALKING, the company halted near a stream, and the wagons fanned out near the cool water.

"Time to do a little wash," Matilda told Jane who'd been walking beside her for the past hour. "Would you like to join me?"

"I don't know if I can walk another step."

"The captain says that we may not be close to water again for two or three more days."

"Guess we should wash and fill up our barrels too."

Jane climbed into her wagon and returned with a basket containing a washboard, lye soap, and dirty laundry. They trudged to the riverbank, where they found a dozen other women already at work.

Bent over the cold water, her abdomen protruding more each day, Matilda angled the wooden washboard, scrubbed, and rinsed the clothes. She glanced up to see a familiar face trudging down the trail.

"Hello, Sarah." Matilda paused, rubbing her back. "How are you feeling?"

"Just fine, Matilda." Sarah Jory held her basket on one hip to avoid bumping the stomach protruding in front of her.

Jane looked up at the woman, but when her eyes fell upon Mrs. Jory's swollen abdomen, her smile faded. She murmured a greeting and set to scrubbing her clothes.

"It's a pleasure to see you, Mrs. Glover."

Jane nodded, but Matilda noticed a tear sliding down her cheeks, mixing in with the creek.

Poor Jane. How hard it must be to hunger so much for a child. Matilda glanced at the bulge growing beneath her apron, wondering what Jane thought of her. Maybe that's why she and William weren't camping beside them as often.

Matilda returned to her scrubbing. Well, it couldn't be helped. She was pregnant, and so was Sarah. Jane would have to grow accustomed to working alongside pregnant women.

"Seems everyone around here is with child." Jane whispered the words. "Like a contagion or something."

Matilda stretched out a hand to cover the younger woman's. "Perhaps God wants to wait until you're settled in your new home before He gives you a babe." She squeezed excess water from her clean clothes. "Safer that way."

"But …" Jane swiped a hand over her damp cheek. "What if it never happens?"

"God's timing is always right." Matilda gazed across the stream, choosing her words carefully as she wondered if He had put her beside Jane to shore up the younger woman's faith during disappointment. "And sometimes He does tell us no." She stood, swinging the basket onto her hip. "But in the meantime, our boys love you and William, and we can pray for His blessings—on this trip and on your womb."

Jane lifted her lips in a wan smile before they returned to camp and hung their clothes to dry.

The following morning, as they walked beside the wagon, Matilda inhaled deep breaths of the sweet, spring air. How she enjoyed God's handiwork along the trail—whippoorwills singing in a hickory tree; strawberries growing wild, ripe for the eating; shrubby timber providing twigs and limbs for firewood. As long as she had her family close, she could endure the hardships of this trip west, sweeping dust from inside the wagon, kneading dough outside, baking bread, and cooking meals over an open fire.

"Ma." Johnny dragged his feet in the dirt and dropped onto his knees. "My legs tired."

Matilda lifted her little one onto her hip and stroked his blond hair as he nestled his head onto her shoulder. Soon, the rhythmic breathing of a slumbering babe kept time with her stride. Thinking of babies brought her thoughts to the child growing inside her womb. She always felt energized when carrying a baby, perhaps because she felt called by God to this precious role of motherhood.

Her thoughts settled on Jane. She glanced at the younger woman, trudging beside the wagons, head down. Jane had hastened away after her introduction to Sarah and a pain-filled glance at the woman's bulge of budding life. She sighed. All in God's timing.

Her mind shifted to Nicholas, the father of her baby. Oh, my, she loved him dearly, but he could be stubborn at times. She shook her head and shifted Johnny gently to her other arm. He squirmed. "Down!"

She let him slide to the ground and he darted forward to pick a deep red and purple flower. "No, Johnny! Don't!" Matilda ran to catch him, but he had already grasped the pretty flowers. He wailed and cradled his hand. Matilda bent to see where thistles pricked his tiny palm. Swiping a corner of her apron over a dab of blood, she pulled out the sharp protrusions, then wiped away his tears. "Oh, honey, I think those are bull thistles. Pretty but prickly."

He nodded. She grasped his other hand and drew him back toward the trail. "We'll just admire their colors from afar; what do you say?"

She smiled at him as he dropped her hand to run to Grundy. He lifted his hand.

"I help count!"

Grundy shook his head. "You don't know how to count!"

"Uh-huh. One…two…free…"

"Grundy, why don't we help Johnny learn to count?" Matilda

plucked a handful of dry weeds from the ground. She held each one up and added to the count: "One weed, two weeds, three weeds, four weeds…"

As they reached the Big Blue River, the wagons rolled to a stop. Nicholas unhitched the oxen and Grundy grabbed his stick. Matilda unloaded the utensils and walked with Johnny to the river. At the foot of a tree, she spied a large stone with etching. She stopped to read the words.

"Mrs. Sara Keyes, 70, deceased May 1846."

Johnny yanked her arm to draw her toward the water. As she walked, she thought about the family who had buried their mother alongside the Oregon Trail. Had Mrs. Keyes been eager to see Oregon? Or had she gone west only to avoid being left without her family? Matilda thought of her own mother. As difficult as their parting had been, she much preferred leaving her mother safe at home in Missouri than burying her in the middle of nowhere.

"Stay back from the water's edge," Matilda admonished her youngest while she dipped her bucket into the river. "Can you help Ma carry this bucket?"

Johnny grabbed the handle just below Matilda's hand. She smiled. Such joy these children brought her every day, just by being themselves. *Thank you, Lord, for entrusting them to us.*

As she entered the camp, Matilda spotted Sarah Jory. "How are you feeling, Sarah?"

"Oh, fine. I've just heard the most disturbing news, though, from James." She dropped her voice to a whisper. "A man passing through shared news about a family we started west with. The Wilcoxes."

Sarah dabbed at her eyes with a handkerchief she pulled from her sleeve. "It seems most of the family died of measles. James said they spent many hours in the rain looking for their cattle. The whole family died—all except two girls and a little boy."

"Oh, those poor children. What happened to them?"

Sarah lifted her eyes heavenward as if in silent prayer. "I imagine another family took them in. But … what if that happens to this wagon train?"

So many dangers. Matilda couldn't imagine losing one child, much less all of them. The flames licking the wagon's canvas paled in comparison to the loss of life. Why did they ever leave Missouri? Her teeth clenched in anger and fear. They faced so many perils—accidents, illnesses, unfriendly Indians, and if Nicholas' suspicions were true, even fellow travelers. She could end up burying one of her boys along this cursed trail. *Oh, please God, no!* Panic pounded in her chest. Stop! *Where was her faith?*

She inhaled a deep breath. No time for worries. What does the Good Book say? Matilda whispered Isaiah 41:13 aloud: "For I the Lord thy God will hold thy right hand, saying unto thee, Fear not; I will help thee."

Louder, she said, "We must seek God's providence on the journey and pray nobody perishes." She stepped forward. "I need to start dinner. Take care of yourself, Sarah, and the little one."

Sarah nodded. "You too."

Matilda watched as the woman walked toward her camp. She prayed for the safety of the people under Magone's care as she set the bucket near the wagon and poured water into the coffeepot.

Her mind flitted over preparations for supper and tomorrow's breakfast. She had plenty of time to plan out her evenings as she walked each day but little time before darkness fell to accomplish all those things she needed to do.

Thirteen

May, Big Blue River in Kansas to North Platte

MATILDA GLANCED UP as Bart set down an empty bucket. "Millie's gone and dried up."

"Are you sure?"

Her seven-year-old son nodded and led the way to where he had tethered the milk cow after capturing her in the field that morning. It was his job to catch Millie and milk her while his pa and Henry rounded up the oxen. He'd learned to milk when he was only five—two whole years ago.

He squatted before Millie, massaged the udder, and then squeezed the teats with his small strong hands, encouraging the reliable old cow to let loose her milk. Nothing.

Matilda knelt but teetered for a second. Balancing on bended knees grew a little more precarious each day as the baby swelled her belly at nearly five months along. She steadied herself with a hand on Bart's shoulder and tried to milk Millie. "Come on, old girl. We love your milk, Millie. We need your milk."

Soft touches. Kind words. Massages and tugs. Nothing worked when the udder ran dry.

"Oh, Millie." Matilda stood and rubbed the Guernsey's roan and white fur. "I imagine Nicholas will want to butcher you now."

"No, Ma." Tears filled Bart's eyes.

"Now weren't you complaining just the other day about always having to eat beans and bacon?"

"But Ma ... Millie?" Bart cast a glance at the beloved bovine he had milked morning and evening for two years. "I—I don't think I could eat her."

Matilda nodded. "I know it's hard, Bart, but on this trail, we need to be thankful for any food God provides. Even if it's steak and roast from Millie."

Bart nodded, but he still looked unconvinced.

"You did eat the fried chicken after the hens quit laying a while ago." Matilda nudged him. "Remember?"

Bart shrugged. "That's different. Those were old hens, and you cook great fried chicken, Ma. This is Millie. She's like ... one of the family."

"We'll make sure Pa doesn't butcher her and salt the meat where you'll have to watch. You'll never even know it's Millie when I've cooked the meat."

"Don't tell Henry. Please? He'll call me a baby."

"I won't say a word." Matilda held a finger in front of her lips. Then, bending to kiss her son's cheek, she added, "I love your tender heart, Bart."

When she told her husband about Millie, he reached for his rifle. Matilda herded the boys to the riverbank to skip rocks. But Bart was right about how tough it was to eat the meat, knowing the beef they chewed belonged to their beloved cow. They cut the rest into thin strips and salted it before letting it dry into jerky. She told Nicholas to give the hide to someone else.

After a quick breakfast and rounding up the livestock, they left camp about seven each morning. They stopped briefly at midday for lunch and set up camp around five o'clock. They usually traveled between eight and eighteen miles a day—sometimes more, sometimes less.

They were traveling toward the North Platte River in Nebraska. The landscape began to change, flat prairie replaced by limestone bluffs visible in all directions. Unfamiliar shrubs and red, blue, and yellow flowers sprouted from the sandy soil.

The wagons spread out across the open prairie, a long line of white canvases flapping in the breeze as far as Matilda could see. Most wagons stayed in the ruts carved by earlier emigrants; others created their own ruts by driving their wagons side by side across the land.

Jim Rawlins liked to carve his own path. At least he and Nicholas hadn't engaged in any further confrontations. But she could tell when Nicholas had bumped into the lanky man. He let his dislike for Rawlins sour his mood.

They hadn't seen much of Tom and Freda Wilson, whose wagon was closer to the back. Matilda would make a point to visit Freda to see how she and her children were doing.

On a particularly dreary afternoon, Captain Magone halted the wagons. Nicholas reined in the oxen and Matilda stopped, hands resting on her hips, looking ahead at the wide river meandering through the valley. Was that the Platte?

The captain stood at the river's bank, hand in the air to make sure all the wagons stopped. He ruffled the brown fur of his water spaniel, Ring, then straightened, mounted his stallion again, and bellowed an order. "Dash in, Ring!"

The canine careened into the water, his master following on horseback with a long pole in hand. He measured the depth of the shallow water as he crossed. On the opposite bank, Magone dismounted and hollered for the lead wagon to cross.

The wagons, their wheels sloshing, followed Magone across the river and onto the prairie.

That night, the wind picked up and drops of rain fell. Matilda helped as the older boys struggled to set up the tent in the blustery breeze. After they snuggled into their bedrolls, the heavens opened.

Rain pelted the tent. She strode to their rig and crawled inside as lightning grew closer with every clap of thunder.

A few hours later, Matilda sat up inside the wagon, where they had slept to stay dry. Nicholas stirred beside her. "I'm going to check on the boys," she said.

"They'll be fine." He rolled over.

Matilda draped a cloak over herself as she rushed to the tent and peered inside. Flashes of lightning pierced the dark sky overhead, lighting the tent.

Bart sat up straight in his bed, eyes wide. "What if that river floods?"

"It won't flood, honey." Matilda squatted beside him.

Henry rolled over. "What's all the yammering about?"

"Do you suppose lightning could strike the tent?" Bart's voice rose. "Or the wagon?"

"Million to one chance," Henry mumbled as he collapsed back to the ground. "Go back to sleep, chowderhead."

Bart lay down and curled tightly into his bedroll. Matilda pulled the blanket closer and rubbed his temples until he relaxed. As his breathing slowed, she crept from the tent and crawled into the wagon.

By morning, all three boys were soaked, along with their sopping bedrolls.

Rain fell all day. The only highlight proved to be the sighting of antelope. Matilda had never seen one of the graceful pronghorn animals.

After dinner, with the boys tucked into their still-damp tent and the sun waning in the sky, Nicholas shared news about travelers from other trains. "A fellow today spoke about his wagon train—quarrels and fistfights and more." Her husband inhaled and watched smoke curl from the fire into the black night sky. "Guess my tiff with Rawlins ain't so bad after all."

"Probably be best to forget about it." Matilda tied a knot and bit the end of the thread on the shirt she had sewn.

"Huh." Nicholas grunted. "Heard that train had men drawing guns on each other. A woman even pulled a knife."

Matilda shook her head in disbelief. "I can't imagine women embroiled in fisticuffs."

"I guess they didn't draw blood, but the captain expelled that family from the train." Nicholas puffed on his pipe. "Hope they don't join us. Magone wouldn't put up with any of that ruckus."

He laughed and stroked Matilda's leg. He shifted his hand up to the small mound at her abdomen.

"How's that little Koontz doing?" He patted her stomach. "Moving around yet?"

"Quiet as can be while I'm walking or riding in the wagon, but when I'm ready to rest, the baby kicks and turns." She laughed as a small foot or elbow rolled past both their palms.

"She's a strong one, that's for sure!" her husband said. "She probably takes after her mother."

"How do you know it's a girl? We have four boys, and this little one could easily be our fifth."

"No, I'm sure of it. This little darling is the spittin' image of her beautiful mother."

Matilda smiled. Perhaps so. They'd know after they settled in Oregon.

The next morning, as Matilda prepared breakfast, Nicholas strode over to William's wagon. "Hey there, Son," he said. "Your wife going to help Mattie fix the grub?"

William popped his head through the opening in the canvas. "Uncle Nick."

Shuffling sounded from within the rig.

"I'm thinking Mattie could use a bit of help fixing all these vittles for our crew." Nicolas cleared his throat. "Her being in the family way and all."

A sob sounded from behind the canvas.

Nicholas crossed his arms. "Well, see, Mattie's never one to complain. She'd work her fingers to the bone, but I won't have it." He sighed. "Fair is fair."

"I understand," William said. "We'll be over in a few minutes to help."

Nicholas nodded, his lips pursed. Then, hearing hushed voices inside the rig, he strode back to the campfire. "Jane'll be over to help."

Matilda glanced up from where she knelt before the fire. "Nicholas, you didn't …"

"Mattie, it even says it in the Good Book—you need to be willing to work if you want to eat."

At the sound of footsteps, Matilda rose, placing her hands on her hips as she stretched her back. "Good morning, Jane. William."

The younger woman dropped her head but not before Nicholas saw her red-rimmed eyes. "What can I do to help?" she murmured.

Matilda drew her toward the fire, picked up a bowl of dough, and stirred it. She plopped dough in piles onto the griddle. "Would you flip the johnnycakes for me when they're ready? I'll fry the bacon."

"How will I know when to flip them?" she asked.

"When bubbles pop on the surface and the edges brown, flip them over with that spatula." Matilda leaned forward. "See that little one? It's ready." She flipped it over. "Just like that." She handed her the spatula and dropped her voice. "Thank you for helping me this morning."

Jane gripped the spatula and offered a tremulous smile. "Thank you for teaching me."

❧

The sun beat mercilessly on the emigrants that afternoon as they trudged through the endless prairie grass.

"I tired," Johnny wailed. "Mama, carry me."

So was she. Matilda hefted the toddler onto her hip and gazed at the pine trees covering the nearby bluffs. Once resigned to the trip west, she determined she would gain worldly experience no matter the cost—or as people called it, see the elephant. Learn what she could despite the risks. She admired God's handiwork as the brilliant sun shone off rocks and light green brush dotted hillsides.

Four miles beyond the river, the company set up camp.

"Why we stopping so soon?" Nicholas asked when Captain Magone rode past on his stallion.

"We've got to wait for the wagons behind us," the captain answered. "Ninety wagons are too many—more than twice as many as most companies. We need to break into smaller groups for easier traveling."

Nicholas nodded. "Makes a lot of sense. I hate wasting daylight, especially when we're one of the last companies traveling west."

Magone nodded. "We'll need to have a company meeting and divide. Pass the word, and I'll do the same."

He spurred his stallion to a trot.

As they walked toward the men gathered around Magone, Nicholas told his nephew, "I sure hope we don't get stuck in a train with that Rawlins character."

William glanced at his uncle. "Might be rather entertaining to see you two go at it."

Nicholas guffawed. "Think I'll stick with Magone."

The young captain gestured to the circle of billowing canvas around him. "This train's just too big with more'n eighty wagons. That's too many to keep track of. Some folks sit and wait for wagons in back to catch up. We don't have time to waste if we're going to cross the Blue Mountains before the snow falls."

Magone nodded toward Reverend John McKinney, who stepped forward wrapped in a big blue Army blanket with a hole in the middle for his head, which was topped by a wide, gray hat.

"What I'm proposing is that we divide into two or three groups. McKinney, you could lead one group, maybe the back half."

"Wait a minute." Rawlins strode forward. "My wagon's back there and I want to stay with you."

Nicholas groaned audibly, ignoring his nephew's grin. The last thing he wanted was to keep traveling with Rawlins.

McKinney, a man of about fifty, spoke to Magone but looked at the men in the circle. "I've got my son and his wife, along with Luelling and his trees, which travel about as fast as a turtle with a limp."

Men laughed. A few snickered. Nicholas grinned. How the Quaker fellow was ever going to manage two wagons Nicholas had no idea. He was only glad the traveling nursery wouldn't be in Magone's company.

"Some of us want to keep going on Sundays rather than stopping," a man blurted.

"Heathens." Nicholas whispered beneath his breath. Tom Wilson chuckled.

Magone looked around. "Anyone else here willing to serve as captain? Someone who doesn't mind traveling Sundays?"

A tall fellow with blond hair curling at his shoulders stepped forward. "I can do it." He reached forward to shake Magone's hand. "Elijah Patterson." He gestured toward his friend, a fellow in his twenties. "And this here is William Powell. We led our crew down from Iowa."

"Good. We'll have you lead a passel of wagons too," Magone said. "Now, John, you stand here on my left so folks who want to go with you can line up there. Elijah, you stand here on my right. If you want to travel Sundays, line up behind him."

Men shuffled forward, some to the right, others to the left. Nicholas stayed put.

"Okay." Magone counted the men in the rows. "That's twenty-seven in McKinney's train and sixteen in Patterson's company. The rest of you can stay with me." He counted again. "That leaves me with thirty-seven and anyone who hasn't showed up for the meeting."

Nicholas, who with William and Tom remained in Magone's train, glanced at Jim Rawlins. "Too bad he's not a heathen as well as a blowhard."

"Tsk. Tsk." Tom jostled his shoulder. "Remember, it's Sunday. What would Matilda say?"

"What a lickspittle!" Nicholas laughed and clapped him on the back. "Long as he stays out of my way, I'll be fine."

Leastways with smaller groups, they should travel faster without stopping every time a wagon broke a coupling, which they'd had to do several times. Yet they'd still be traveling in a train for safety.

Nicholas returned to their campsite and found Matilda in a clean dress, a shawl draped over her auburn hair she had twisted into a bun.

He washed his hands and wrapped an arm around her shoulders. "We're staying with Captain Magone. He'll have nearly forty wagons. Reverend McKinney will lead twenty-seven, and Elijah Patterson sixteen."

Matilda stood and stretched her back. "The reverend is such a nice man."

Nicholas looked at his wife. "You ready for church services?"

She brushed dirt from her husband's shirt. "Yes, the Lord knows we need His help crossing this country."

"He's smiling down on us now." Nicholas squinted into the setting sun. "Can't you feel it?"

Matilda smiled, but inside, her confidence wavered. "Boys, are you ready?"

She clutched her Bible in one hand, which she linked through her husband's arm, and grasped Johnny's with the other. The older three boys traipsed behind to the gathering in the meadow. Reverend McKinney stood at the center in a black suit and preached from a large Bible cradled in both hands.

"That Methodist preacher was wearing a blue Army blanket earlier." Nicholas whispered in Matilda's ear. "Dresses up real nice."

Freda frowned at them across the circle. "Shhh…"

Most of the pioneers attended the service. A few watched the stock.

"The wagons following Elijah Patterson are pulling out this morning." Nicholas whispered again. "They don't want to stop for the Sabbath."

Matilda pursed her lips. "Not everyone believes as we do, but most seem to be strong Christians, like William and Jane, and Freda and Tom. It's nice to travel with people we know."

They glanced up to see Freda lift a finger to her lips with a scowl.

"Then again …" Nicholas chuckled.

The reverend prayed and admonished everyone to praise God for His blessings. "Shall we sing?"

As they raised their voices in a familiar Lutheran hymn, they heard the rumble of wagons pulling out.

Nicholas looked at Matilda and his boys. God had blessed him mightily. His eyes dropped to his wife's abdomen. And more on the way. What with a new home in Oregon Territory, a land flowing with milk and honey, he couldn't ask for anything more.

Later that evening, as Matilda sewed, Bart stopped beside her, his lips pursed.

"What is it, Son?" Matilda bit off the thread and knotted it.

"I heard some men talking at the meeting." Bart glanced quickly around. "They said Reverend McKinney left his wife and six children at home to come west with his oldest son."

Matilda pulled him close and looked into his eyes. "We know better than to listen to gossip. The reverend's business is none of ours."

"I know, Ma—it's just …" He glanced at the dirt beneath his feet before looking up. "If you hadn't agreed to come, do you think Pa would have left us behind?"

"Oh, no, honey." Matilda embraced her sensitive son. "Of course not. He loves his family too much to ever leave us."

Bart's head moved against her shoulder. Stepping back, he swiped a fist across the dampness on his cheeks. "It's just that Pa wanted to come west so bad, I wondered…"

"We are a family. All of us. Pa. Me. All four of you boys. And the little one growing inside me. We will stick together, come what may."

She tucked her sewing into her basket and rose. "Time to wash up and crawl into your bedroll."

"Yes, Ma." Bart turned and scampered to the tent, ducking inside the canvas.

Matilda sighed. She thought of the McKinneys and Nicholas' insistence on moving west. Despite her strong words to Bart, a doubt lingered. Would the lure of adventure have drawn her husband west if she had refused to go?

FOURTEEN

June 1847, Following North Platte River to Courthouse Rock

THAT NIGHT, as they set up camp, a howling wind ripped the canvas from their sons' hands. They chased after it and erected the tent with help from their father and then crawled inside to snuggle into their bedrolls.

Then the heavens opened. Again, rain pelted the wagon and the tent. Matilda and Nicholas curled in the wagon beneath the canvas as flashes of lightning pierced the dark sky.

They rose in the morning, groggy and soaked, to pack up and slog west.

It rained all day, and the loose sandy soil changed into an uneven muck that slowed progress even more. Nicholas led the team through the mud. "Hop off, boys." He gestured to Henry and Bart. "Tough enough for Belle to wallow through that mud without carrying passengers."

He squinted at the dark clouds. They'd already traveled a month, which left another four before they arrived in Oregon Territory. Leastways they were heading west with the first chunk behind them.

The next day, the train met a French-Canadian bishop and seven Catholic priests traveling south with a guide they hired to hunt and lead their animals as far as Fort Hall. They asked to join Captain Magone's train heading west, bringing the number of rigs in the company to forty-four.

That night, Nicholas sat beside William and puffed his pipe while discussing events of the day. "By the way, what do you think about those priests?"

"Catholics? Looks like they're set up pretty good with a guide to hunt for them. How many are there?"

"Think seven or eight. French Canadians. One's going to be bishop at Walla Walla, name of Blanchet—Augustin Magloire Alexandre Blanchet. Looks like his older brother's a priest too. Magone invited them to join our company."

"Maybe they'll do some marrying of folks around here. I've seen a lot of young men courting girls from other wagons." Nicholas glanced toward his wagon where Matilda had settled Johnny in for the night.

In a soft voice, Matilda said, "Let's just hope they don't end up doing funerals."

They followed the North Platte River in Nebraska, a long line of white canvases flapping in the breeze as they crossed the land.

Nicholas grumbled and shook his head, gesturing at the wagon to his right. While most wagons followed ruts carved by earlier emigrants, Jim Rawlins carved his own path. As if trying to avoid the extra dust, their team snorted and veered to the left.

"Whoa, there, boys." Nicholas jumped to the ground and stroked the backs of his beasts as Rawlins' rig passed. "Dad-burned scalawag," he muttered.

William hopped off his wagon and strode forward toward his uncle. "Something break?"

Nicholas grimaced. "Naw. The team choked up eatin' Rawlins' dust." He returned to the wagon bench. "Sorry to slow you up."

He let his dislike for Rawlins sour his mood. He shouted, perhaps louder than necessary, "Get up."

As his team sloshed across the wide low North Platte River to the opposite bank, Nicholas recalled the young buck at Independence who had lost all his belongings. Even in shallow water, crossings could be treacherous.

After they tucked in the boys that night, Nicholas pulled his wife onto his lap as he perched on a log and smoked his pipe, watching as the smoke swirled upward. Then he tapped the ashes from his pipe into the remnants of the campfire and led Matilda to the wagon. They crawled underneath and cuddled together on their straw mattress.

He rubbed his calloused palm over her stomach. "When do you reckon she'll make an appearance?"

"She?" Matilda chuckled. "You're certain it's a girl?"

"Pretty as her ma." Nicholas kissed her. "And doted on by her big brothers. So when will we meet her?"

"Late October maybe. Or early November." She glanced at her husband. "We'll be settled then?"

"Sure hope so." Nicholas tightened his embrace. "Snow'll be flying by the mountains then."

Matilda wiped her brow and noticed the gray tinge of dirt-stained sweat on her sleeve. She readjusted her bonnet and dropped the brim to keep the glare from piercing her eyes. During the morning, she could lift her collar to keep the heat from burning her neck, but as evening approached the pioneers walked directly into the setting sun on the western horizon.

She squinted ahead. Was that water shimmering in the distance? A cool, clear lake? What she wouldn't give for a plunge into the water to wash the dust and grime from her body. As she peered closer, the shimmering faded to brown dirt and golden weeds at the base of a rocky cliff. Nicholas had told her some travelers see mirages when they're thirsty and tired. She understood now how the brushy thickets below the cliffs could look cool and inviting.

She bent to adjust Johnny's cap over his eyes.

"I can't see!" He yanked off the hat.

"No, Johnny. You mustn't remove the cap." Matilda grasped it from his hand and tugged it over his blond curls. "You need to shade your eyes from the sun. Look at Grundy. He's kept the front of his hat low."

Johnny glanced at his older brother. Then he put on his cap and tipped the front even lower.

Matilda chuckled. She didn't know how he could see where he was going, but at least his eyes would be protected. Once again thistles clawed her skirt like kittens, ripping the fabric. She'd need to mend it tonight. She mended the tears and patched the holes, but this calico dress looked like a tattered rag. She had only her Sunday dress, which she dared not wear along the trail or it would look the same.

Despite the throngs of emigrants who had already passed this way, the campsites provided plenty of fodder for cattle and horses.

"Mama. Carry me." Johnny held up his arms.

Matilda hefted him up, but he was certainly growing heavy, and those little legs didn't wrap around her quite as well now. "I'll carry you for a bit, but you're a big boy. You're a pioneer!"

"Pineer." He tucked his chin into her collarbone.

"Aye—aye—Johnny." Matilda shifted him to her other shoulder. "Move your pointy chin, please."

He shifted positions again, his leg kicking her stomach. An elbow pushed back from inside her womb. A little fighter. Perhaps another boy ... or a feisty girl. She set Johnny on the ground. "You can walk." Matilda swung his hand in hers. "Let me hear your letters."

"A, B, C, D...." When he stumbled, Matilda asked Grundy to provide the answer. He swiveled his eyes away from the wheel-counting long enough to help, but he certainly took his responsibility seriously. They were good boys, all of them.

Johnny pointed to birds and flowers and babbled about bugs and insects. He and Grundy both helped her collect firewood, but twigs and trees were sparser now. She'd soon have to resort to dried dung for fuel. She'd read it took three bushels of buffalo chips to make a good cookfire.

Clouds darkened the sky, blotting out the sun. Winds blew in cooler air. Rain soon pelted the ground. When the weather turned, it slowed the oxen as they plodded through muck and hauled the wagon. Passengers trying to keep dry inside their wagons added extra weight, but they couldn't afford to catch a cold. Not on the trail.

As if he had read her mind, Nicholas leaned close so she could hear him over the howling wind. "It's too early to stop for the night, but I'm worried about the oxen. Those wet yokes could chafe their necks. I'll need to rub salve on them when we stop."

Two miles later, Magone's company of 172 people stopped to set up camp. True to his word, Nicholas asked for salve, which he and Henry massaged onto the necks of their six oxen while Grundy did his nightly duty wiping out their nostrils. Bart hobbled their mare, Belle, nearby.

They hadn't seen much of the Jorys, whose wagon was closer to the back. Matilda would make a point of visiting them this evening. Freda too.

A few days later, Captain Magone halted the train at the wide bluish-green waters of the North Platte River meandering through the valley. He pointed to wood on islands in the middle of the river, but even the heartiest swimmer didn't dare brave rain-swollen waters to gather wood.

It looked like the moment had arrived: Tonight's dinner would be cooked over a fire of sun-dried buffalo dung. Matilda grabbed a basket and called to Johnny and Grundy.

"Boys, we need to go on a hunt."

"A hunt?" Grundy tilted his head to look her in the eye. "Ma? What are we hunting?"

"Buffalo chips." Matilda spotted a dried cake of gray dung and lifted it gingerly from the ground. She hated to slip it into the basket but plastered a smile on her face as she did.

"Since there aren't as many trees around, we need to gather these to fuel our campfire."

"What are they?" Grundy looked at her askance.

Matilda sighed. Somehow, she knew he would ask. "Truth to tell, they're dried buffalo droppings."

"Buffalo poop?" Grundy wrinkled his nose.

"Or dried cow manure. Come on, boys. It'll be fun. And we need to find a lot of these for our fire." Matilda picked up another dusty cow pie. "If we're careful to stay back from the wagon, we can take turns tossing them into the basket."

Grundy grinned. "Well, if that don't take the rag off." He nudged his little brother. "We'll have a hog-killin' time."

"Hog-kiln." Johnny echoed, toddling after him.

Grundy skipped ahead on the trail, picked up a buffalo chip, and tossed it toward a basket hooked on the side of the wagon as it rumbled past. He lifted his arm behind his head and let fly. The chip hit the wooden side and slid into the basket below.

"Well done." Matilda tossed the buffalo chip in her hand. It hit the side of the basket and dropped to the ground. "Looks like I need more practice."

The afternoon passed quickly as the boys gathered the chips and flung them toward the wagon.

Johnny wound up his arm and let fly. The buffalo chip, still damp inside and thrown wildly askew, splatted on the side of his father's face.

Johnny's eyes grew wide. "Uh-oh."

Nicholas glanced with furrowed brows at the dried dung on the wagon seat. He pulled off his hat, wiped his sleeve over the side of his face, and wrinkled his nose. Looking at Matilda, he spied Johnny with his little hands splayed over his face, as if trying to hide in plain sight.

Nicholas grinned. "Try again, Johnny. Try again."

The next evening, Captain Magone called the men to a camp meeting.

"We're entering Indian country," he said. "Most of the tribes are friendly—the Arapahoe, Cheyenne, Crow, Kiowas, Pawnee, Shoshone, and others. Only thing is, it's more likely we'll have horses and cattle stolen during the night by renegades—Indian or white."

"Pa?" Bart tugged on his father's sleeve. "Belle? Is she gonna be okay?"

"Sh-sh now," Nicholas said. "We need to listen to the captain."

"We're going to organize shifts of guards to watch the livestock at night. We'll have six groups of ten men each, supervised by a sergeant. One shift will stand guard half the night, and then we'll have another group stand guard."

"Some of us don't have horses." Jim Rawlins pushed the spectacles up on his nose. "What about us? If it's the horses they're after, not my cattle, why should we have to stand guard?"

Nicholas tightened his lips. Oh, but he wanted to give that scallywag a tongue-lashing.

"Now, Jim, we're all in this together," the captain said. "If they can steal horses, they can do the same to your steers or oxen."

The men nodded in agreement. Nicholas clenched his fists.

One of the Catholic priests raised his hand.

The captain nodded to him. "Father, I know you're not fond of shooting guns. You and the other priests will be exempted from the guard duty."

Rawlins swept his hat from his head, mouth open, and stepped forward.

"Hold on." The captain raised a hand. "You know the priests have hired a guide who's an expert hunter. Jacob Bernier's brought back plenty of antelopes to share with the rest of us in camp. They're doing their part. And Bernier can stand guard for them."

Rawlins' face reddened, but he held his tongue.

"With that settled, we'll form into groups."

As the men shuffled forward, Captain Magone raised his hands. "One more thing. We have one rule above all other rules: Don't pull the trigger unless you're certain you know what you're aiming at—and what's behind it."

Nicholas nodded. "Don't want any accidents, right Joe?"

The captain agreed. "I've heard too many tales of trigger-happy men shooting other folks in their company."

Nicholas was assigned to take the first shift. Henry wanted to help too, so he let him come, but he sent Bart back to camp.

"Someone needs to watch over your ma and the younger boys." Nicholas rubbed his hand over Bart's short hair, cropped with scissors by Matilda the previous evening. "I'm depending on you, Son. You're the man of the family while Henry and I stand guard duty."

Nicholas smiled as he saw his son's chest puff a little before he scampered toward their camp to tell his mother about his new role.

FIFTEEN

THE FOLLOWING DAY, Matilda woke to the wide, bluish green waters of the Platte River, which they would follow west. Although they had traveled five hundred miles from home, more than three hundred from Independence, they still had more than a thousand to go. Daunting. But at least the smooth trail in the sandy soil enabled the wagons to move more quickly than through mud and muck of wet clay after a rainfall.

Matilda finished cleaning the dishes and lifted a second apple cobbler from the Dutch oven.

"I'm going to take this to Freda and see how the Wilsons are doing."

"I'll go with you." Nicholas packed tobacco into his pipe and tucked it into his shirt pocket. "Henry. Bart. You boys watch your brothers, ya hear?"

"Yeah, Pa."

Nicholas slipped his arm around Matilda's waist and guided her past the wagons. Men gathered around the campfires, laughing and telling tales. A couple of them passed a flask. They stepped around a wagon and spotted Tom pouring the dregs of the coffeepot onto the ground.

"Hey there, Tom. How you doin'?"

"Nicholas! Here we're traveling in the same company but seldom see each other. Too busy moving during the day, too exhausted to visit at night."

Matilda slipped around her husband to the rear of the wagon. "Freda?"

"Who is it?" The voice of her friend sounded rather harried. "Matilda? Is that you finally coming to call?"

Freda climbed out the front of the wagon, so Matilda walked forward. Before Matilda could say hello, small faces peered from inside the canvas. Freda turned back to her children and shouted. "You shut those eyes—now! I don't want to hear about any more fighting."

She climbed down from the wagon and opened her arms wide. Matilda embraced her quickly. "I've brought you a cobbler."

"What? You have food to spare?"

Matilda shrugged. "Not exactly. But I wanted to use the last of these apples before they spoiled, and I figured your family would enjoy a treat. My boys devoured it."

Freda took the tin plate with the cobbler from Matilda and nodded. "Appreciate it."

Matilda wiped her now empty hands on her skirt. "With forty-some wagons, it's hard to keep up with everyone. I trust your trip has been without trouble."

"Scarcely. Broken axletree. Blisters on Jenny's feet. Little Timmy caught a cold. And Frank, well, I hardly see him. He's taken a shift of guard duty. That leaves him so tired in the morning that I'm left with the oxen reins, guiding the wagon through mud and rivers, while Tom herds the cattle. And the older girls, why, Grace and Bethy are always running off with Mary Ann Thompkins, looking for husbands." Freda laughed as she brushed her hair back. "They can't get enough of that handsome young captain of ours."

She looked closer at Matilda. Her brows furrowed. "You're in the family way? How did I not know that?"

"Ah, yes." Matilda said. "But I feel fine."'

"How far along?" Freda set her hand on Matilda's abdomen. "I'd say maybe four or five months already. Now that doesn't seem like a smart thing to do before setting out on a two-thousand-mile journey."

Matilda felt heat in her cheeks. "It wasn't exactly something we planned. God is the one in control, remember?"

"Pshaw. You can feign a headache as easy as the next woman. I did plenty of times before we set out. I had no desire to cross the plains with children tugging my skirts and filling them out too."

"How are you feeling? Are your supplies holding out well?" Matilda wanted desperately to change the subject.

Freda listed foodstuffs her family was running through as Matilda listened and nodded.

"I hear nothing but complaints from the children about the menu—'not beans with bacon again!'" Freda threw her hands into the air. "What's a woman to do?"

Matilda chuckled. "I've heard the same complaint from my boys. I tell them to just be thankful we have food to eat."

"Truth be told, I'm a wee bit tired of the same meal too but don't let the young'uns know."

Matilda reached forward to embrace Freda. "I need to return to our camp. It's good to see you."

"Don't be a stranger." Freda climbed back into her wagon as Matilda sidled up to Nicholas.

"—and he's hunting antelope for the priests." Tom glanced at Matilda. "Looks like your woman is ready to leave. Good to see you."

Nicholas slapped Tom on the back and waved toward the wagon, but Freda had already disappeared.

"You survived your encounter with Freda, I see." Nicholas again placed an arm around her waist to guide her past the other wagons as a fiddler played a mournful tune.

"I did." Matilda replied. She rubbed her hands over the protruding mound on her belly. "For the most part."

The next morning, thinking of her discussion with Freda, Matilda examined the food in the wagon. They had enough stores for the trip, didn't they? Had she been foolish to give away the cobbler? She glanced at the part-empty bags of cornmeal, flour, and sugar. They still had smoked jerky from Millie, but the slab of cured bacon was shrinking. Coffee beans were disappearing fast. She'd be more careful going forward. They didn't have much money to spend on restocking supplies along the trail.

Hands on hips, she planned. They could have mush or johnnycakes again tomorrow. Of course, hardtack for snacks and dinner of beans, bacon, and soda biscuits. Matilda added different spices at times to change the flavor, but the food remained the same. Except when she splurged and cooked molasses pudding, apple dumpling soup, or berry pie.

They packed up and moved west again, Matilda on foot with the younger boys, Henry learning from his pa how to guide the oxen and Bart on Belle.

Suddenly, Nicholas grabbed the reins and pulled back as the wagons in front of him slowed. "Looks like someone's stuck."

Giving the reins to Henry, he hopped off the wagon and strutted forward.

Captain Magone rode back to the stuck wagon. It was Tom and Freda Wilson's rig. Freda herded her children to the side as Nicholas and the captain joined Tom behind the wagon. They dug in their heels, leaned forward, and shoved.

The rig didn't budge.

"What are we going to do?" Nicholas wiped his brow. "That wagon's wheels are mired in mud."

Tom pursed his lips as Freda shouted advice from the side of the trail.

"We shouldn't have packed so much. I knew it," Tom grumbled, climbing inside. He hefted a piece of furniture through the opening in the canvas onto the dirt. "Maybe this will help."

"My dresser!" Freda screamed, storming forward. "What do you think you're doing?"

"It's too heavy." Tom faced the inside of the rig again. "We need to lighten it."

"We're not leaving my dresser here." Freda shooed her younger children away from her skirts. "You hear me, Tom Wilson?"

"Freda …" He sighed. "We aren't going anywhere if we don't get this wagon unstuck."

"Push it!"

"What do you think we've been doing?" Tom shouted.

"Whoa, folks." Magone stepped between them. "Let's think about this a minute. Might help to lighten the load." He glanced at the men who had gathered near the back of the wagon. "Any ideas?"

"Perhaps we could wedge a limb under each wheel," Jory offered. "A few of us can lean on those while you fellows push from behind."

"Might work." Magone headed toward scrubby trees and busted off a limb. Others followed his lead, some using saws to cut through the wood. They returned and wedged the limbs beneath the wheels.

Tom's son Frank took a position at a front wheel, Jory at a back one. Two other men grasped the limbs under the wheels on the other side, prepared to push down with their weight.

"Now those of you leaning on those limbs, be sure you hop out of the way if the wagon moves," Magone shouted. "Don't need anyone run over."

Nicholas, Magone, and Tom pushed from behind as the others leaned against the limbs.

"Giddyup!" Mr. Nelson led the oxen. "Get up!"

The beasts pulled against the mud, hooves slipping, as Nicholas pushed with all his might. The wagon lurched.

Frank yelped and slipped in the mud beneath the wagon.

Freda's scream pierced the air. "Frank!"

Jory ran to the front of the wagon as it teetered to the side and then righted.

The captain and Nicholas raced forward but not before the heavy wagon's wheel lumbered over the boy's torso and clipped his head.

"Oh, God, no!" Tom rushed to his son's side. "Frank! Speak to me."

The boy moaned and gasped, his breath a wheeze. "I'm okay ... Pa." His head listed to the side, chest still.

"No, no, no!" Tom lifted his son's battered and bloodied body. "Frank." His shoulders shook with sobs as he gently carried the fourteen-year-old to the side of the trail and laid him on the grass.

Freda fell to her knees and rocked back and forth, arms across her chest. "My son. Not my boy." Their other children wailed.

Jory stood, wiping mud from his vest and pants, smearing more than he cleared. He gasped an explanation. "His hat fell off. When he leaned over to grab it, a limb snapped and knocked him to the ground. Wheel rolled right over him." He gulped, cleared his throat. "What … Is he …?"

Magone nodded, lips pursed.

"You did what you could." Nicholas squeezed the younger man's shoulder. "I'll fetch Matilda, see if she can help Freda."

Nicholas strode from the wagon, wiping a hand over his eyes. Frank, such a good strong lad, a great help to his pa. Henry would be devastated to learn of his friend's death.

"Pa?" Bart stood on the wagon bench. "What happened?"

Nicholas gestured for him to sit. "Where's your ma?"

Bart pointed toward the other side of the trail. Nicholas strode to her. "Freda…" He swallowed, started again. "Freda's in need of your help now. Frank, he … a wagon rolled over him."

"Oh, dear God. Is he injured?"

Nicholas lowered his gaze. He didn't want to see the fear in his wife's eyes. "Worse than that. He's … he didn't make it."

"Oh, no!" Matilda grasped her skirts in her hand and ran toward the Wilsons' rig ahead of them on the trail.

Nicholas picked up Johnny and strode toward their wagon. Handing the younger boy to Bart, he said, "Stay put and keep an eye on your brothers." He glanced around. "Henry!"

His eldest son rode forward atop Belle. "Yeah, Pa?"

"There's been an accident, up at the Wilsons' rig."

"What happened?" Henry lifted his body in his saddle to look ahead of the wagons before them. "Everyone okay?"

"No, Son, they aren't." He took Belle's reins from Henry. "Young Frank, well, he got run over by a wagon."

"He's hurt?"

"No, Son." Nicholas looked him in the eye. "He died."

Shock sprang to Henry's eyes. "What?"

"I'm sorry, Son." He laid a hand on his eldest boy's thin thigh. "You're gonna need to be strong now. I need you to watch the boys while I help Tom."

Tears flowed down Henry's cheeks, but he nodded. "I will, Pa." He slid off Belle and hitched the reins to the wagon. He climbed inside and cradled Johnny on his lap, burying his face in the toddler's neck.

Nicholas reached into the wagon, pulled out a bottle, and trudged back to the Wilson wagon. He didn't know how he could help, but he'd try.

The sun had long set when Matilda and Nicholas returned to their wagon, which William had pulled off the trail near his. He had set up the tent for the boys, and Jane had cooked them dinner.

"Thank you," Matilda said.

"It's the least we could do," Jane responded. "How is Freda?"

Jane and Freda hadn't gotten along well, but Matilda knew the younger woman would never wish ill on her outspoken friend. Matilda's shoulders drooped. "She's strong, but ... losing a child ..."

"Such a tragedy." Jane patted Matilda's shoulder. "I'll leave you and Nicholas now. We just wanted to wait until you returned before retiring."

"We appreciate it."

Nicholas pulled out the straw tick and shoved it beneath the wagon, then yanked out blankets. He curled onto the mattress, the blanket over his shoulders.

Matilda slid in beside him. They'd scarcely spoken all evening. She comforted Freda, although her friend could find no solace after the loss of her son, while Nicholas stayed with Tom. Captain Magone planned to say a few words before the grave in the morning. They'd bury Frank on the trail so wagons could pack down the dirt over his grave.

Oh, dear Lord, please comfort Freda and Tom and their children. Matilda's thoughts drifted. That could have been one of her boys run over by the wagon. Johnny. Or Henry. Bart. Grundy. How could she survive such a loss? She knew Freda would rally, stuff her grief beneath her rough exterior, so deep perhaps she'd never find it again.

Beside her, the mattress shook. Her stolid husband, always so strong, gave in to his grief.

Loud pounding jolted Matilda awake in the wee hours of the morning.

Nicholas rolled over. "What in tarnation?"

A shout pierced the air. "Freda!"

Matilda scrambled from beneath the wagon followed by Nicholas. They rushed toward the Wilson wagon in pouring rain. Was it thunder?

Smash!

More harsh pounding.

"Please, Freda, stop!" Tom's voice sounded frantic.

They reached the wagon to see Freda wielding an axe over the abandoned dresser, slamming it into the polished wood. Tears streamed down her face.

When Tom reached for the axe, Freda shoved him aside. "Leave me be. My baby … My baby needs a coffin!" She ground out the heartrending words and choked back a sob. "I'm not leaving him in the cold earth."

She pounded again. "I hate this dresser!"

Grace and Beth did their best to comfort the younger children who stood wide-eyed beside the wagon, wailing. "Mama!"

Magone rode up on his horse. "What's going on here?"

Nicholas answered the captain's question while Matilda scurried forward to her friend's side and wrapped an arm around her waist.

Freda whirled, axe raised above her head, shoulders shaking with stifled sobs.

"Oh, my dear Freda." Matilda hugged her friend. "Cry. Let it out."

"No!" She struggled against Matilda's embrace. "I have to…I must…"

"Tom and Nicholas can make a fine coffin for Frank." She reached for the arm holding the axe. "Here, why don't we let them use this?"

Freda hesitated, then let the axe drop into the mud. She plunged to her knees, her body shaken by wracking sobs, tears mingling with the rain as if angels mourned with this heartbroken mother over the loss of her eldest son. Matilda knelt beside her, arms rubbing her back, trying to comfort a friend suffering an unfathomable loss. She had no words, only a shoulder to offer, a loving embrace.

Tom's shoulders shook too as he strode toward the younger children. "Your ma's going to be all right. Let's get back in the tent and try to sleep."

Nicholas kicked the splintered oak of the varnished dresser. He pulled apart the top and laid it on a grassy spot out of the mud. He yanked another piece from the side. Magone slid off his horse and helped him disassemble the furniture Freda had attacked with such vengeance. They spoke in low voices.

"I can hammer the pieces together first thing in the morning," Nicholas said.

"Where do they have Frank?"

Nicholas nodded toward the wagon. "Tom said he's inside, rolled up in a quilt."

"We'll bury him at daybreak." Magone replaced his hat. "I'll head back for a bit of shuteye."

Nicholas nodded at the younger man. "Mattie and I can take care of the Wilsons. I hope we can persuade them to sleep at least a bit."

Matilda lifted Freda from the mud and, with one arm encircling her friend's back, trudged toward the tent. "You need to sleep, Freda."

She shook her head. "I can't sleep."

"Then just cuddle your little ones." Matilda said. "They're going to need your strength in the coming weeks."

"Strength?" Freda scoffed. "I have nothing left."

"You do." Matilda shifted to face her friend. "Look at me. You still have five children. They need you. Frank would want you to be strong—for them."

Freda dropped her head as tears filled her eyes again. She shuffled forward.

Tom held back the tent flap for his wife to enter. "Thanks," he whispered.

Matilda left her friend in her husband's care and strode to Nicholas. "Can I help?"

He shook his head. "I'm done till daylight. I'll be back early to pound together a coffin—after most of the company is awake."

He draped an arm over Matilda's shoulders. "How's Freda?"

Matilda shrugged. "I don't have words to comfort her. How can anyone endure the loss of a child?"

Nicholas pursed his lips, silent as he gazed toward the cloud-filled night sky. "Mother Mary did it, so I guess a mother can survive. But I wouldn't wish that heartbreak on my worst enemy."

Mary, the Virgin Mother, had indeed watched her son suffer and die. How had she gone on? Perhaps if she knew the answer to that question, she could help Freda look ahead to tomorrow. The finality of death had lost its sting because of Jesus. He promised eternal life for all believers. Frank. And Freda and Tom. They'd all be united again one day because of His sacrifice on that cross.

When the sun rose, the company gathered near the rear of the train where a few men had dug a grave in the rain-softened dirt.

The sun glinted off the coffin Nicholas and Tom had created from the dresser. Tom lowered his son's body, wrapped in a wedding ring quilt, into the box. Freda leaned forward and kissed her boy's forehead before tucking the quilt over his face.

Matilda held Johnny on her hip, rested an arm over Bart's shoulders, while Grundy leaned against her legs. Henry stood beside her, lips trembling. Nicholas draped both arms over his eldest son's shoulders, drawing the eight-year-old against his body, as if bracing the boy for the turmoil he'd feel when that first clump of dirt covered his friend. Saying goodbye was never easy, but this—a death of one so young, the older friend their son had so admired.

"Lord, we give You back this boy, Frank Wilson, a beloved son, a big brother, a fellow far too young to pass away," Magone said. "Care for him as You do and comfort his family as best You can. Amen."

"Amen." The crowd gathered around the grave echoed the words in the early dawn and then drifted back to their wagons as birds chirped in nearby bushes.

Life goes on, even after such a tragedy. Matilda glanced at Freda, held in her husband's arms, their children beside them. She'd rally and march forward; that was Freda's way. But inside, a part of her friend's heart would lay forever buried beneath the hard-packed dirt of this godforsaken trail.

Matilda put away the clean supper dishes. "I'm going to visit Mrs. Jory and see how she's doing. Her baby should arrive soon."

"I'll go with you." Nicholas didn't have guard duty again until early morning. He packed tobacco into his pipe and tucked it into his shirt pocket. "Henry. Bart. You boys watch your brothers, ya hear?"

"Aw, Pa. Do we have to?" Henry looked wistfully toward a nearby wagon. "I wanted to play with William and Andrew."

"And Sadie too," Bart added, never one to forget their friends' sister.

"You can see the Browns after we return."

Henry kicked a clod of dirt. "All right."

Nicholas slipped his arm around Matilda's waist and guided her past the wagons.

"How are you holding up?" Nicholas glanced at her.

"Tired is all. Sore feet. But the blisters have turned to callouses so it's not as painful."

Nicholas chuckled. "It's not as bad as you feared, is it?"

Matilda glanced at the wagons, the oxen grazing nearby, the setting sun's fiery orange reflection on the clouds. "We still have more than a thousand miles to go. I pray nothing will happen, that God will keep everyone on this train safe during the journey."

"You worry too much." Nicholas hugged her tight. "Before you know it, we'll be building a cabin in the Northwest forest."

She smiled. Her husband's jolly attitude seldom slipped, except for those occasions when he ran into Jim Rawlins. She glanced at the men gathered around campfires, laughing and telling tales. A couple of them passed a flask. She didn't imagine her husband imbibed.

Matilda and Nicholas spotted James Jory.

"Hey there, James. How you doin'?"

"Nicholas! Fine, just fine. And you?"

Matilda slipped around her husband to the rear of the wagon.

"Sarah?"

"Who is it?" The young woman's voice sounded harried.

"It's me, Matilda."

Sarah Jory hefted her swollen body through the canvas hole at the front of the wagon and onto the seat. As she turned to step to the dirt, her husband rushed to her side.

"You must let me help you down." He held his arms outstretched, and she leaned into them as he swept her to the ground.

She thanked him with a smile and faced Matilda. "He fusses ever-so-much over me."

"I imagine so, especially with the first baby." Matilda glanced at her husband. "Nicholas did too—with the first one. He scarcely let me open the door by myself or lift a skillet." She chuckled and rubbed her abdomen, which was smaller than Sarah's. "With this one, our fifth, he's fairly sure bearing a baby won't break me ... at least, it hasn't yet."

Sarah smiled.

Matilda raised her hand. "I do know a growing baby in the womb triggers my sweet tooth, so I've brought you dessert."

Sarah looked at the container in Matilda's hand and lifted the white cloth. Inhaling, she closed her eyes. "It smells divine. How kind of you."

"Just molasses pudding." She glanced at Sarah's protruding belly, about the size Matilda's would be in a month. "And I realize it's not as easy to bend over and cook in your condition."

"We appreciate your kindness."

"How are you feeling?" Matilda asked.

"Beyond exhausted, but I'm doing well." Sarah rubbed her palms over her swollen abdomen. "I miss my mother though."

"Plenty of women in the company are happy to help when the time comes. Just send James to our wagon, and I'll be here."

"Thank you," Sarah's eyes watered. "You are a blessing to me and so many others."

Matilda waved aside the praise and wiped her now-empty hands on her skirt, pulling it over her swelling abdomen.

Sarah bit her lip. "I'm a bit worried it might happen while James is on guard duty."

"Oh, I understand why. Would it help to have Bart sleep under your wagon when James is standing guard? He could alert me if you need help."

"I don't want to put him out."

Matilda reached for the younger woman's free hand. "You've met Bart. He's happy to help wherever he can. I'm sure he'd be pleased to do it."

"What a relief that would be for me and James. We've talked about what to do."

"Now that's one less thing for you to worry over." Matilda embraced the younger woman. They ambled over to their husbands where Nicholas again spoke about the priests' guide.

"Who's hunting antelope?" Sarah asked.

"The priests' guide." James wrapped an arm around his wife's disappearing waist and glanced at Matilda. "Thanks for the food."

Nicholas slapped James on the back and dipped his head toward Sarah.

He and Matilda walked hand in hand past the wagons and listened to the soft strings of a fiddle playing a mournful tune that lulled the emigrants to sleep.

The next morning, as she fried bacon for breakfast and boiled a little rice with butter and sweetened it with sugar, Matilda worried about Sarah Jory's pregnancy. Would she recognize the signs of labor? Did anyone tell her what to expect?

"Bart," she said. "Would you mind sleeping under the Jorys' wagon when Mr. Jory stands guard duty?"

He shrugged. "Sure, if it'll help." Bart responded exactly the way she knew he would.

"You be sure to run back here and tell me if she needs anything or if her time comes."

He nodded. "I will, Ma."

She rubbed his shoulder. "You're a fine boy."

"What's for breakfast?" Jane sauntered over to the fire.

"Tomorrow you can help me make cornmeal mush or johnnycakes." Matilda flipped the bacon and stirred the rice. "Do you remember how to make it?"

Jane shrugged. "I think so."

"Did you soak your beans in the pot?" Matilda dished rice and bacon onto a plate and handed it to Bart. "We can have beans, bacon, and soda biscuits this evening."

"I just let them soak, don't I?" Jane shrugged again. "It's not as hard as I thought it would be to cook."

Matilda smiled. Nicholas complained for what seemed like hours about Jane's burnt biscuits the other night, but sometimes you had to burn to learn. He wouldn't let Matilda do all the cooking for both families anymore, but she felt a bit sorry for William. Her nephew looked like he had lost a few more pounds than the rest of the folks in the company. At least they always had hardtack. And it's hard to ruin beans with bacon.

Sixteen

MATILDA YAWNED as she moseyed along the trail, regretting her restless sleep but holding tight to Johnny's hand. Lifting her head toward the early afternoon sun, she spotted a large cloud of billowing dust against the hills. She hurried closer to the wagon.

"What do you suppose that is?" She pointed to the cloud.

Nicholas rose from the wagon bench. "Hard to tell. I imagine the captain will let us know if it's anything dangerous. But maybe you and the boys ought to ride in the wagon for now."

She nodded. "Grundy. Johnny. We're going to ride for a bit."

Nicholas slowed the wagon as the boys approached. Matilda lifted Johnny onto the seat.

"You sure you should be lifting him?" Nicholas took the boy from her. "He's a sturdy little fellow."

Matilda smiled. "I'm fine." She moved aside to let Grundy climb onto the moving wagon and followed him.

Captain Magone rode ahead of the company, a spyglass in one hand. He straightened his legs, stretching in his saddle, peering through the glass, then slipped it into his saddlebag and wheeled around.

"Buffalo!" he shouted. The captain halted the wagons as he rode the length of the train. "Looks to be several thousand heading our way. Stay in your wagons until they pass."

"Buffalo." Grundy poked his head through the opening in the canvas. "Real live buffalo."

The ground trembled beneath pounding hooves. Matilda gripped the wagon as it started to shake. "What about Henry and Bart?"

"They'll be okay if they stay by the wagon." Nicholas leaned around to peer at the mare. "Boys, bring Belle up here close to the wagon. She might be skittish when those buffalo stampede past. Tie her up here and stay put."

Henry guided the mare forward and handed Nicholas the reins.

"I think you boys should climb into the wagon." Matilda gestured to Henry and Bart.

"Oh, Ma. Do we have to?" Henry looked at Nicholas. "Pa? We can hold real tight to Belle. We wanna see the buffalo."

Nicholas placed his right hand on Matilda's. "They'll be fine on the mare. She's tied to the wagon."

"But what if she bolts?" Matilda twisted on her seat to look at the wide-eyed mare. Noise drowned out any response Nicholas gave.

Matilda's body swayed as the wagon shook when the huge furry beasts thundered past a dozen yards from the company, shaking the ground like an earthquake. Snorts, bellows, and walloping hoofbeats filled the air. Johnny clapped both palms over his ears.

Belle skittered, prancing as she pulled against the reins.

"Hold on!" Henry held tight to her mane, but Bart, gazing open-mouthed at the buffalo herd, lost his balance and toppled off.

"Bart!"

Nicholas swiveled beside her and dove off the seat. He covered Bart's body with his as the earth rumbled from pounding hooves.

"Oh, God help them!" Matilda shouted, pulling Grundy and Johnny tighter, shutting her eyes. "Oh, dear Lord!" Tears streamed down her cheeks.

"Mama?" Johnny's hand wiped her damp face. "Why you crying?"

After most of the buffalo passed the wagon, she opened her eyes, terrified to gaze upon the crumpled bodies of her husband and son.

"Ma—they're okay." Henry shouted at her from his seat atop Belle. He grasped the reins tight, trying to still the fidgety mare.

Nicholas rose to his feet and lifted Bart onto the wagon.

"I told you—" Matilda began.

"He's fine, Mattie." Nicholas brushed dirt from his pants. "Bit of a scare, though, wasn't it, Bart?" He flicked his second son beneath the chin. "Make a man of you."

"Nicholas…" Matilda hugged Bart and glared at her husband, though relief at their safety left her muscles weak.

A gunshot fired. Matilda glanced ahead at Magone, smoke circling above his rifle.

After the last of the herd passed, the captain rode to the wagons and ordered everyone to set up camp, even though they still had daylight left. The captain led three oxen from a wagon and climbed a slight rise.

Matilda and the other women pulled out their cooking utensils, although it was a bit early for supper. Grundy cleaned the oxen's nostrils while Henry and Nicholas wiped them down before setting them out to graze. Bart rubbed down Belle and hobbled her nearby.

As they finished, Captain Magone led the three oxen into the circle of wagons, dragging behind them the carcass of what looked like a year-old cow. Everyone gathered around to see a buffalo up close. Bernier, the priest's guide and hunter, stepped forward to slit the beast's hide down the center and pull out the entrails.

"Men." Magone looked around the circle. "Take a chunk of buffalo meat."

Nobody moved. Matilda knew Nicholas wanted to try the buffalo. But she figured he didn't want to look greedy. Neither did anyone else.

"Come, come," Magone said. "Don't be bashful; the best-looking man start first."

Still nobody moved.

"Well, then," the captain said. "The man with the best-looking wife come first."

Matilda smiled as Nicholas and the other men rushed forward, each carving a chunk of the beast's meat. Nicholas handed the bloody mess to her. She held it out from her skirts as they returned to their wagon. She sliced the chunk into smaller slabs and braised it slowly in the Dutch oven. They had enough for everybody to try.

Nicholas bit into the brown meat and rolled his eyes upward. "Nice change from salt pork and beef jerky, don't you think so, boys?"

His sons, gnawing on their steaks, simply nodded.

Later that night, the Englishman, James Jory, wandered past their camp.

"How did you like that buffalo, Jory?" Nicholas gestured toward the campfire.

"Best meat I've tasted on the trip," he replied. Mr. Jory seemed a quiet man compared with Nicholas, who was always jovial—except around Rawlins. "What did you think?"

"Mighty tasty." Nicholas smacked his lips. "That bishop fellow, Blanchet, said it tasted like Canadian beef. Of course, I've never eaten Canadian beef, so I wouldn't know."

"I've tasted Canadian beef," Jory said. "This was better."

"Coffee?" Nicholas handed Jory an empty cup.

Matilda filled the tin cup with steaming coffee. "How's Sarah?"

"As good as can be expected, I suppose." He touched her second son's shoulder. "We do appreciate Bart here sleeping under the wagon while I'm on guard duty." He took a sip. "Her time's coming soon—before we make Oregon, I expect."

"You heard anything about your parents and the rest of your family?" Nicholas gestured toward a barrel set up as a makeshift chair. Jory sat but shook his head.

"I'm uncertain how we could have missed them at Independence," he said. "Perhaps they left later than they had planned."

"Were they in Missouri?" Nicholas tapped tobacco into his pipe.

"No, Illinois." Jory shifted on the barrel. "When we left England, we landed at New Brunswick, up in Canada and then headed to New York. But we wanted to go west. We planned to buy a farm in

Missouri—until my father discovered in St. Louis that slavery's legal there. He detests slavery."

Matilda nodded. She hated slavery too, the very idea of owning a person, like a dog or an ox.

Jory sipped his coffee and continued. "After working a winter on a large plantation, my father moved us north to the free state of Illinois and purchased land. That was a decade ago."

"They're farmers, you say?" Nicholas lit his pipe.

Jory nodded. "Carpenters and wheelwrights, too. My father's an excellent woodworker."

"What brought you west?" Nicholas asked the younger man.

"Cholera." Jory said. "After I married Sarah last year, I heard about so many young married women in Illinois dying from the cholera. I didn't want that to happen to Sarah."

Nicholas glanced at Matilda. "I can certainly understand that. The rest of your family wanted to go west too?"

Jory nodded. "We talked about it, and all decided the west offered a healthier climate. I'm sure we'll connect somewhere along the trail."

"Likely so. Nice to have kin on the trail." He nodded toward William's wagon. "Nice to know family can step in if need be."

Jory glanced at Matilda and then Nicholas. "Sarah and I would be happy to help if you ever need anything—either of you."

"Same here," Nicholas said. "I reckon your kin will come by soon. We certainly see a lot of wagons. Seventy in one day, I counted."

As Nicholas swallowed the last of his coffee, Jory stood and bid them goodnight.

SEVENTEEN

"PLEASE, PA…"

"You're not old enough yet, Son."

Bart pleaded with his eyes. "But you showed Henry how to drive a team of oxen when he was eight."

"You just turned seven in April."

"Close enough."

Nicholas grinned, pleased with Bart's tenacity. He tousled his hair. "I suppose you just might be old enough at that."

Bart scrambled onto the wagon seat and held out his hands.

"Now you don't want to hold these here reins too tight." Nicholas handed the leather straps to Bart. "Or too loose. Call the oxen by name to urge them forward."

Bart held the reins as the six oxen slogged through the mud and kicked up sticky brown chunks with their hooves. It had poured down rain the past three days. The wagon slid through the slippery ruts, hauled by the sturdy beasts. In his young voice, Bart called encouragement to the beasts as they traveled, echoing words Nicholas used daily. "Go, Duke! Yo, Pet. Attaboy, Jerry. Yo, Baul. Come on, Browny. Giddyup there, old Buck."

The mighty oxen were steady, strong, and slow but not invincible. They had passed sun-bleached skulls of several oxen along the trail. Nicholas checked their hooves every night to keep the animals in good shape.

"We've got to take care of 'em if we want to haul this load all the way to Oregon." Nicholas glanced at Bart. "That's why I rub each one down before letting them loose to graze."

"Pa?" Bart glanced at his father.

"Hmmm?"

"How much farther is it to Oregon?"

"Well, now, we've got to pass through Nebraska, Wyoming territory, the Snake River, and then we'll be in Oregon." Nicholas reached back into the wagon and pulled out a piece of paper on which he had drawn a map. "We've got to cross a couple of mountain ranges. We ought to arrive by the middle of October."

"But it's only June." Bart looked up from the map. "That's gonna take forever."

Nicholas laughed. "Might seem like forever to you, but it'll be behind us in a few months. Then we'll build our homestead. Nice and warm for the winter." He grabbed the reins from his son's hands as the wagons in front of him slowed. "Looks like someone ahead is stuck." He handed the reins back to Bart and strode forward to help.

When Nicholas returned, he nodded to Bart. "They've moving again. Let's head out."

An hour later, the company passed a circle of wagons off to the side of the trail.

"Why do you suppose they stopped?" Bart asked.

"The captain told me a group was camped because one of their folks died of mountain fever. Fellow was only thirty-one, with a wife and little girl." Nicholas counted the wagons as they passed. "Forty. A few less than we have."

"What's mountain fever?"

"Sickness, sometimes called black fever because the teeth turn all black." Nicholas pursed his lips. "They're burying him today near those willows. But don't you worry none. We're healthy as our oxen, and you can see they're doing well."

They finally camped near the high water of Plum Creek and crossed a canyon the next day, stopping after thirteen miles. Some days they made good time and traveled eighteen miles, but mud slowed them down. While rain proved refreshing, it hindered their progress—and they were already behind other companies, perhaps the last on the trail. They couldn't afford any delays.

Matilda and Grundy—and sometimes Johnny—picked up buffalo chips for fuel and tossed them in the basket tied to the wagon. Matilda kept Johnny on the far side away from the wagon. She didn't want another close call.

Captain Magone rode back to where a wagon listed to one side and dismounted.

Nicholas eyed the loaded prairie schooner, its wheels buried past the hubs in mud. "How are we going to move it?"

Magone looked toward the rig's owner. "Mr. Brown, anyone inside?"

Solomon Kelly "S.K." Brown nodded. "My missus and little Sadie, who's feeling poorly." He reached inside to help his wife out and lifted her onto drier ground. Then he leaned inside to cradle the six-year-old girl. He strode to his wife and handed her the unresponsive child, whose cheeks flared red while a pink rash covered her limp arms.

"We'll need as many men as possible shoving the back," Magone said to the wagon's owner. "You and your boy jerk hard on those harnesses. We need those beasts to pull with all their might."

"You stay here," Nicholas told Bart.

"I can help too." Bart dropped the reins to climb down.

"No!" Nicholas raised his voice. "You stay here and keep our oxen steady." He saw moisture in the boy's eyes and swallowed. "Now, I'm depending on you, hear?"

Bart nodded.

Nicholas strode to the back of the wagon as Brown grabbed the harness on the left side while his eldest son did the same on the right.

"Now!" Magone hollered. "But be careful! Think about Frank."

A dozen men heaved their shoulders and backs against the wagon. When his feet slipped, Nicholas shifted position to burrow his boots deeper.

"Again!" Magone shouted the order just as the wagon nudged forward. "Keep at it!"

The wagon broke free with a loud slurp and rolled forward, mud clinging to the wheels.

Nicholas rested his hands on his knees, breathing deeply. The other men did too.

Magone strode over to Mrs. Brown. "How's your girl?"

"Sadie's running a fever." Anne Brown looked toward her husband, the father of her four stepchildren. "I'm not sure what to do for her."

Nicholas overheard the conversation. "I'll ask Matilda to stop by this evening. Maybe she can help. She's nursed our four boys back to health plenty of times."

"I'd appreciate it, Mr. Koontz." Anne Brown handed Sadie to her husband, who lifted the child inside the wagon.

Nicholas strode back and swung onto his rig's seat. He took the reins from Bart. "Let's veer to the right to avoid that slick spot." He shook his head. "We'll never cross the Blue Mountains before the snow flies if we keep getting stuck on flatland."

"You mean we might not reach Oregon till November?" Bart asked.

"I figure the captain will give everyone a talking to tonight so's we don't have more delays." Nicholas sighed. "I hope so, anyway."

"Pa?" Bart asked.

"Yeah?"

"Did Sadie have that mountain fever?"

Nicholas pressed his lips together and frowned. "I'm not sure, Son."

Maybe Matilda would know what to do to help the girl. Then again, maybe they should all keep their distance from the Browns, so their boys wouldn't get sick.

After they set up camp on the Nebraska prairie, Matilda cooked dinner and fed her family before taking a pan of beans with bacon to the Browns. Henry begged to join her. He admired the older Brown boys, William and Andrew. Bart and Grundy liked to play games with little Sadie when the older boys ran off without them.

Matilda stopped beside the wagon as Henry ducked into the tent to chat with the boys.

"Mrs. Brown?" she whispered. "It's Matilda Koontz."

"Thank you so much for coming." Anne spoke quietly as she crawled through the front canvas onto the bench seat. "I'm at my wit's end. I don't know what to do for little Sadie."

"When did she take sick?" Matilda asked.

Anne, stray hairs escaping from her disheveled bun, beckoned Matilda to enter the wagon. "She's been tired for a week or more and told me her head hurt, especially in daylight. She had a fever too. After she vomited, I couldn't get her to eat or drink anything." Anne's voice quavered. "Now I can scarcely wake her."

Matilda crouched beside the girl and placed a hand on her forehead. "Oh, my! She's burning up." She pulled up the sleeves of her nightgown. Small, flat pink pustules covered both wrists and forearms. She glanced at the thin legs, where the rash spread upward from the ankles.

"I don't know what to do," Anne whispered. "I've never had any children. I just married Solomon—Sadie's father—last year. Sadie is such a sweet girl. My husband is beside himself with worry."

Matilda nodded as she lifted the girl's arm slightly and let it drop. No response. She placed her ear on the girl's chest. She was scarcely breathing. "I'm not a doctor," Matilda said. "But a damp cloth to her brow might help. Unwrap the blankets slightly to cool her body. We might want to move her outside the wagon so she can breathe fresh air."

Anne scrambled from the wagon, a clean dry cloth in hand. Murmured voices sounded in the camp, and soon her husband clambered onto the seat. "I'll take her outside. We've put a bedroll beside the wagon. We didn't want the boys—" His voice caught, and he cleared his throat. "To get what Sadie has."

"That's probably a wise decision." Matilda followed him to where Anne bent over the girl, pressing a wet cloth to her brow. "I'm so sorry." Matilda clasped her hands together. "I—I don't know what else to do. Except pray."

Anne twisted her hands together, then nodded. "Thank you for your help. I know you need to care for your own children. Goodnight, Mrs. Koontz."

Matilda bit her lower lip, holding back tears as she glanced again at the unresponsive child.

"Henry." She stood outside the Browns' tent. "Would you go ask the priests if they can pray for little Sadie?" He nodded and stepped toward the circle of wagons. "Then come right back to our camp."

"Yes, Ma."

Matilda returned to her family, washed her hands and face with lye soap to remove the grime she had picked up between the wagons, and settled the younger children into their bedrolls. "Let's say a special prayer for the health of little Sadie Brown." They each bowed their heads as Matilda prayed.

She heard footsteps and whispers outside. She opened the canvas and left the tent. Veiled by the smoke of the campfire, Henry spoke to his father in urgent whispers.

"What is it?" Matilda asked.

Henry whipped around to face his mother. He quickly brushed his cheeks to remove any traces of tears.

"We were too late, Ma." He looked at his pa, who gazed at the ground. "When we got to the wagon, the priest ... he said Sadie was dead."

Pain etched across Henry's features as Matilda pulled him into a tight embrace. He struggled at first but then wrapped his arms around her waist. "Oh, Ma! They were all crying."

Matilda stroked his back as tears flowed down her cheeks. Oh, that poor family. Solomon lost Sadie's mother and now their daughter. How heartbreaking.

Nicholas cleared his throat. "It's about time we got some sleep. Looks like a rough start tomorrow with a funeral." He threw an arm across Henry's shoulders as he led him to the tent. "Try not to dwell on what happened. Nothing anyone could do about it."

As she washed the dishes, Matilda shook her head at Nicholas, pragmatic as always. What if that was their child lying cold and lifeless? It could happen—*Oh, God, may it never be!* This trail posed so many threats to their safety. Had Henry been infected with whatever Sadie had? Would Matilda catch whatever it was and give it to her boys? How could they all make it to Oregon alive?

Nicholas stepped to Matilda's side and cleared his throat. "It's not going to happen to our boys."

"How can you know that?" She whirled on him, fists pounding his chest. "How can anyone know? I'm sure Sadie's parents never figured their little girl would die. Oh, Nicholas. Why did we leave Missouri?"

He caught her fists in his calloused hands and brought them to his lips. "Now, Matilda, you're letting your worries get the best of you." He braced his wife, a hand on each of her shoulders. "You know moving west is the right thing for our family. Our boys have a better future in Oregon. They could never own and farm as much land in Missouri as they can out west. We'll have a grand future in Oregon."

"If we make it there." Matilda brushed away her tears. What would the future matter without her family?

"Where's that steadfast wife of mine?" Nicholas pulled her close. "Doesn't the Good Book say something about worrying? Seems I've heard you quote that to me more than a few times."

Matilda sighed. "Yes, it does." She recited the words from the gospel of Matthew. "Take therefore no thought for the morrow: for the morrow shall take thought for the things of itself. Sufficient unto the day is the evil thereof."

"See there, even God says don't worry." Nicholas gobbled the last piece of biscuit and dropped his dirty plate into her bucket. "Our boys will be fine. You take good care of them, Mattie. Stop worrying."

Matilda bit her lip. It was always easier to say you need to stop worrying than to actually do it. She whispered prayers to the Lord as she finished drying the dishes.

"You always see the good in everything. This is our dream, Mattie—our family's dream."

Matilda inhaled a shaky breath.

"You ready to sleep?" Nicholas drew her toward the wagon.

"Not just yet. You go ahead. I'll be along in a bit."

As Nicholas strode to the wagon and sprawled out on the bedroll, Matilda crossed her arms over her chest as if to keep her heart from shattering into millions of pieces. Our dream? Or his? Our future. Our lives ... but please, Lord, not our deaths.

At dawn when they awakened, a dark cloud hovered over the camp in keeping with the somber mood blanketing the men, women, and children as they prepared to bury little Sadie Brown.

Matilda heated beans and cured bacon for Nicholas and the boys and baked fresh biscuits. As she filled the plates, she felt a presence behind her and turned to see her nephew's wife.

Jane's lower lip trembled.

"Is something wrong?" Matilda draped an arm over the younger woman's shoulder.

"It's terrible—and it makes me angry too." Jane shifted forward and then back, pacing.

"What is it?" Matilda's heart raced. "Is William all right?"

She waved her hand. "William's fine. It's those priests."

"What about them?"

Jane tugged on the ties of her bonnet. "Sadie's parents wanted a proper burial, but the bishop refused her father's request to say words over her grave this morning. It just makes no sense to me."

"What? Why would he refuse?" Matilda kneaded the crease between her brows.

"They say she hasn't been baptized, so they can't pray the words over her grave." Jane gave her a baffled look. "The priests are urging all the parents to have their children baptized to avoid having to refuse more requests for funerals."

"But we're not Roman Catholics." Matilda shook her head, lifting the lid from the pot of beans. "We won't have the boys baptized into a faith we don't follow."

"No, I wouldn't either ... if ... well ..." Jane's voice trailed off.

Matilda rubbed her hand over the young woman's back. "All in good time, Jane. All in God's time."

Jane lifted her skirts. "I need to go back to the wagon. William will want his breakfast."

"It's too bad Reverend McKinney's in a company ahead of ours, or he could perform the graveside service."

When Nicholas and the boys gathered for breakfast, Matilda caught her husband's eye. After he sat beside her, she recounted in low tones Jane's news.

"What? Those black-robed bigots!"

"Nicholas." She hushed him. "The children."

Nicholas swiped his biscuit over the empty plate to capture any leftovers and popped it into his mouth. "I'll have a talk with Magone." Setting down the tin plate, he stormed from the camp.

Within ten minutes, Nicholas returned to camp. "Funeral's about to start." He lowered his voice. "They're burying her on the trail, so animals don't dig her up. Other wagons following will pack down the earth."

"Oh, my. Her poor parents."

"Let's go pay our respects. The captain's saying the words since those priests won't do it."

Prairie grass swayed in a soft breeze as members of the company gathered in a circle on the side of the trail. Captain Magone, hands crossed, tapped his hat against his legs. He prayed a few words over the little girl's grave. Someone had chiseled Sadie's name and age into a stone and placed it beside the trail to mark her final resting place. Mr. Brown clenched his lips as if holding back tears. His sons did the same while their stepmother cried freely and leaned heavily on her husband's arm.

Matilda wept at the heartache on Mrs. Brown's face as the woman crumpled onto the fresh brown dirt, wailing goodbye to little Sadie. She dabbed a handkerchief to stem the flow of her tears.

Suddenly, a hand swept past her bulging belly as someone grasped Matilda's elbow and drew her away from the crowd. "How's that little one doing?" Freda whispered.

Matilda flashed a half-hearted smile. "Fine."

"You hear what those priests did?" Freda's voice rose an octave.

Matilda sighed and nodded, looking around to see if they were disturbing others.

"Mighty holier-than-thou, don't you think?" Freda harrumphed. "Can't even pray over that poor little girl's remains."

"I suppose they have rules they must follow." Matilda glanced at her boys. "Are you planning to have your children baptized?"

Freda guffawed. "Like that would happen. Maybe if it freezes in hell. You?

Matilda shook her head. "We're not Roman Catholics."

"Besides ..." Freda dropped her gaze to the grass. "Frank wasn't baptized Catholic, and we all want to end up together again someday. Who knows if Catholics wind up in the same place as us Protestants?" Freda watched Mr. Brown lead his wife away from the grave. "Hmm. Wasn't even her child yet she's carrying on so."

"Oh, but she loved that little girl." Matilda wiped a tear from her cheek. "How could she help but love her? Sadie was such a sweet little darling. And to leave her behind, buried on the trail...I can't imagine the heartache."

"She only knew her a year," Freda murmured before herding her brood back to camp.

That afternoon, the company reached Ash Hollow. Broken hills, high sand banks, and ragged rocks sprouted ancient cedars. The company halted, the menfolk staring at the steep bluff they needed to descend.

"We're ten days out of Fort Laramie," Magone announced. "But we need to lower our wagons down this slope."

Nicholas listened intently as the captain explained how they would work together to control the heavy rigs and prevent them from plummeting to the rocks below.

"We'll run a chain through the back wheels and unyoke all but one pair of oxen." Magone glanced between the men and the slope. "We'll need to weigh down the chain to slow the wagon, so each man will stand on the chain to dig the metal into the rock and act as a brake."

"Stand on the chain?" Jim Rawlins' voice rose to a higher pitch. "Are you insane? We could die if that wagon rolled forward too fast."

"We're just going to take it slow, so nobody does die." Magone pushed his hat back from his furrowed brow. "We don't want to kill our oxen either. If we don't slow the wagons, they'll roll over the beasts."

Nicholas shook his head. "Rawlins, you want to sit with the women while we lower your wagon?"

"Never you mind, Koontz. I'll handle my own rig."

Magone raised his hands. "Let's start with yours, Nicholas. You game to stand on the chain?"

"My weight will slow it down." Nicholas slapped his palms on either side of his belly and laughed. "William, you want to lead Old Buck and Jerry? Then I'll do the same for you."

His nephew nodded. Nicholas grabbed the length of chain from Magone and looped it through the back wheels. He unyoked two pairs of oxen, leaving only Old Buck and Jerry. "You boys take it nice and slow now, y'hear?" He slapped each ox on the rump before striding to the rear of the wagon.

"Can we help, Pa?" Henry ran beside his father.

"Henry, you lead Pet and Baul down the hill." Nicholas eyed Bart's small frame. "Can you lead Duke and Browny? You'll need to be quick on your feet. You don't want them running over you."

"I can do it, Pa," Bart said, eyes wide.

"Here we go then." Nicholas pulled on the chain to make sure it held tight.

Matilda, her face pale and hands clenched together, stood to the side with the younger boys and watched. "Be careful."

"Woman, if I was born to be drowned, I won't be hanged." He laughed. "And if born to be hanged, I'll never be drowned." He winked to remove the sting from his familiar words. "And I will never be killed by a runaway wagon going down this hill."

Matilda held Johnny on one hip and rested her free arm on Grundy's shoulders. Nicholas saw her lips moving silently. Praying again. There was his faithful girl.

"Here goes. Nice and easy, William." Nicholas stood on the chain, grasped both sides of the wagon tightly, and shouted. "Giddyup!"

Old Buck and Jerry hesitated a moment before trudging down the steep hillside. As the wagon moved forward, he leaned back, digging the chain into the ground. Dust spewed into the air from the metal scraping the rocks. He grasped the rear of his rig, leaned back, and grimaced. Dirt plastered his face, mixing with sweat.

When Jerry stumbled, the wagon lurched forward, kicking him off the chain.

"Nicholas!" Matilda screamed.

He scrambled back onto the chain as William grasped the harness to hold back the oxen. Dropping his bottom lower, Nicholas dug in with his work boots, shoving the chain deeper into the dirt. Harsh tones of metal scraping rock pierced the air. "Whoa, there!"

It took only minutes to finish the wild ride down the hill, but Nicholas knew his wife probably held her breath the entire time— except when she let loose that scream.

Finally, the wagon rolled to a stop. Nicholas hopped off the chain, unhooked it from the wheels, and dangled it from his hands. "Next?"

William took the chain from his uncle and headed up the hill.

"Good boys." Nicholas examined Jerry's legs before he petted both him and Old Buck on the haunches. "You done good."

He followed William to the top of Ash Hollow for another adventurous downhill ride. But with so many wagons to ferry down the rock, and the captain's urging to take it slow, they were bound to lose at least one day, maybe two. Nicholas closed his eyes, envisioning the even more dangerous trek through the snowy Blue Mountains to Oregon Territory if they were delayed any longer.

After the arduous descent, the company found a freshwater spring. Nicholas splashed water over his blackened face and scrubbed with soap. His skin resumed its normal suntanned bronze. His wet hair curled at the ends.

"Bart, you and Henry bring down those barrels. We need to fill them."

The boys raced to the wagon and pulled out the nearly empty wooden barrels. Nicholas followed his sons as they ran to the water. When Bart tripped on a root and fell, his barrel flew forward and rammed Henry in the heels.

"Bart!" Henry yelled. His face switched from anger to concern. "You all right?"

Bart staggered to his feet and leaned his forearms on his knees. "Just knocked the wind outta me."

"You boys playing or working?" Nicholas laughed.

He filled both barrels with the clear spring water, hefted one between his strong arms, and trudged up the path. "I'll be back for the other one. It's too heavy for you boys."

"We can carry it, Pa."

Nicholas paused and looked over his shoulder.

"Here, help me," Henry said, slipping his fingers beneath the wood. "We can carry this if both of us do it. On three. One. Two. Three."

Both boys straightened their legs and hefted the filled barrel between them. It teetered but Henry edged around to keep it straight.

"I'll walk backward." Henry gasped. "Tell me if you see anything in my way."

He shuffled his feet backward, and Bart inched forward, grunting.

"What ... what if we spill it?" Bart's voice quavered.

"Ain't gonna happen." Henry backed up farther, feet sliding over the dirt.

Nicholas hurried to the camp and retraced his steps. "Whoa! You boys are going to break your backs." He leaned over, lifted the barrel into his arms, and smiled. "Good job. You'll be stronger'n an ox before we reach Oregon." He led the way to the campsite and roped the barrel back into place. By then Matilda had finished making dinner.

When the wagons crossed the Platte River's Lawrence Fork, Nicholas, his family, and the other weary travelers stopped briefly to gulp down cool water.

The next few days passed in grueling exhaustion as the oxen dragged their heavy loads across soft sand.

Then they caught up with another company of fifty-two wagons.

"Halt!" Captain Magone ordered, raising his hand as he rode back along the train.

"What now?" Nicholas asked.

"We need to wait for this company to move ahead," Magone said. "Otherwise, we're likely to mix our animals with theirs."

Nicholas shook his head. "We still going to reach Oregon before it snows?"

"I hope so," Magone responded. "That's the plan."

"Lookee there!" Henry pointed in the distance. "What's that off to the right?"

Nicholas followed the direction of Henry's finger as Bart squinted ahead.

EIGHTEEN

Mid-June 1847, Courthouse Rock to Fort Laramie

"THIS MIGHT HELP." Captain Magone handed his spyglass to Nicholas. "You see it now?"

"Sure do. That's Courthouse Rock, isn't it? And the smaller one is what they call Jail Rock." Nicholas raised his eyebrows toward the captain and tilted his head toward his sons."

"Go ahead," the captain said. "They can look."

Nicholas handed the spyglass to his eldest son.

"Come on." Bart nudged his brother. "Let me see."

"I will. Just wait."

After a minute, Henry handed the glass to Bart, who closed one eye and peered through it. "That pointed rock?"

"Yep," Nicholas said. "That's Courthouse Rock."

"Why's it called that, Pa?" Bart handed the spyglass back to the captain. "Thank you."

Magone latched it onto his trousers. "When we get closer, you'll see. It looks like a building you'd find in the city.... or a castle. Some even call it Castle Rock."

"Remember the courthouse in St. Louis?" Nicholas asked the boys. "Maybe they named this here rock after that courthouse."

Henry nodded.

Bart frowned.

"It's doesn't look like the courthouse in St. Louis," Bart said. "Does it, Pa?"

Nicholas guffawed. "Maybe to weary travelers it looked like a building back home. At least enough to keep them going west." It certainly encouraged him, not that he needed much motivation to keep moving west. He couldn't wait to reach Oregon Territory. He chafed at any and all delays.

"It's a good landmark," Magone said. "Means we've traveled six hundred miles from Independence."

"Twelve hundred miles more?" Nicholas shook his head. "It's June 18th. Sure hope we do make it through the mountains before it snows."

Magone shrugged. "That's the reason we can't linger long."

Two days later, Nicholas and his boys watched a tall spire protruding into the sky grow larger as they crossed the last of the flat Nebraska prairie and approached yet another landmark—Chimney Rock—a dozen miles west of Courthouse Rock. From a distance it had looked like a small stub on the landscape, but as they drew nearer, they saw the bank of clay and rock tower like an ancient round castle or fort with a large flagstaff.

"It looks like a pointed haystack," Bart said.

"Sure does." Nicholas gazed at the spiked rock, rising more than three hundred feet from its base. The company stopped for a midday meal across from the rounded hill with its chimney.

"Tomorrow we should reach Scotts Bluff, which means we're one third of the way to Oregon," Nicholas said. "Magone says we have only another twelve hundred miles to go."

Both boys groaned. "When will we get there?"

"By late October, I reckon." Nicholas tamped tobacco into his pipe.

"October?" Henry gripped his head between both hands. "It ain't even July yet. That's … forever."

Nicholas chuckled. "We'll be there before you know it." Then he pointed to foothills in the distance. The rolling treed hills didn't look daunting, but jagged peaks beyond loomed menacingly. Yet, it was nothing they couldn't master. "From here on out, boys, the trail grows steeper. We're heading into mountains. Cooler. Steeper. But closer to Oregon."

The sky darkened. A small storm brewed overhead as they passed Scotts Bluff, a sandstone rock that rose eight hundred feet from the prairie and towered above the North Platte River. Few trees or shrubs marred the smooth light brown surface.

Matilda and the boys welcomed the storm's cooler temperatures, and the boys pranced around the wagon until the heavens opened up and dropped hail as big as hazelnuts. Then they hunkered beneath the wagon until the storm passed.

Smoke curled on the horizon. Lightning had sparked a fire, scorching dry summer grasses on the prairie. The smoke appeared far enough away to pose no hazard to the company—at least Matilda hoped so. The captain would warn them if they needed to move.

She ventured to the creek to fill a water bucket, passing a ravine lush with green shrubs dotted with red berries. Wild currants? Or perhaps chokecherries. Either way, perhaps she and the boys could pick berries in the morning before they left. Jane might even accompany them. She returned to her camp with the barrel on her hip.

Shouts erupted. One voice sounded like her husband's. Matilda grasped her eldest son by the shoulder. "Henry, you watch the boys for me."

"I want to see what all the shoutin's about!" he protested.

"You stay here." Matilda prided herself on remaining calm, but as she heard Nicholas again, her volume rose. "Now!"

She clutched her skirts in one hand and hurried across the opening to where a group of men had gathered.

"Course there's not going to be much grass here for the oxen and cattle. We're following almost two dozen other companies who herded hundreds of head of cattle west." Nicholas glared at Jim Rawlins, whose thin face was mottled red.

"Well, just how do you figure we're going to feed our animals?" Rawlins set both fists on his hips and swiveled his head between Nicholas and Magone.

"We'll just have to let the cattle look for food farther afield." Magone tipped back his hat.

"Somebody's going to steal them if they're far from camp!" Rawlins' voice rose to a high pitch.

"Then the fellows on guard duty will have to follow the animals and stay close." Nicholas shifted closer to the tall man. "You on guard duty tonight, Rawlins?"

Rawlins pursed his lips. "You know I am. But I don't want to leave my wagon unguarded if I'm that far from camp."

"What—you think we're gonna steal from you?" Nicholas waved his palm in a gesture of dismissal. "You don't have anything we'd want."

"Then why don't you pull guard duty instead?"

Nicholas chuckled. "You'll do anything to get out of it, won't you?"

Matilda sidled up to her husband and placed a gentle hand on his forearm. When he glanced at her, she shook her head slightly. He sighed.

"Fine. I'll pull your guard duty if that's what it'll take for you to shut your trap and stop whining."

"Nicholas." Matilda whispered his name. Exhaustion seeped through her body. What next?

He glared at Rawlins. "You take my shift tomorrow night and do your own the next night." He glanced at Matilda and wrapped an arm around her waist. "Best get me and Henry some grub so we can follow the cattle afield." He led the way back to their wagon.

"What happened, Pa?" Henry rushed to his father's side. "What's all the shouting about?"

"Nothing to worry about. The two of us are standing guard tonight."

"Thought we didn't have duty till tomorrow."

"We're taking Rawlins' shift. That crybaby—"

"Nicholas." Matilda admonished her husband and handed Henry a plate. "Just eat your supper so you can help your father tonight."

After setting up the tent for the boys, Nicholas and Henry strode from the camp.

Matilda cleaned the dishes and pulled her sewing basket from the wagon. In dim light from a kerosene lantern, she stitched the buttons on another flannel shirt to trade at the fort or with the natives. She could sew on buttons with her eyes closed.

Footsteps shuffled in the dirt just beyond the wagon. She squinted into the dark. "May I help you?"

Jim Rawlins stepped around the side of the white canvas.

"Mrs. Koontz." He slid closer to the fire. "I wanted to apologize for what you saw this evening."

Matilda stood, tucking her sewing into the basket. "There's no need, Mr. Rawlins."

"I don't know how you put up with that husband of yours."

Matilda glanced at the tent, where she knew the boys were settling down but doubted they were asleep yet. "I'm sure I don't know what you mean." She moved toward the wagon. "But as you know, Nicholas is standing guard duty over the cattle tonight so—"

He reached out and grasped her upper arm. "You're a fine woman, Mrs. Koontz."

Matilda clenched her jaw. She looked at his hand and pointedly raised her gaze to his eyes. "I'll thank you to unhand me, Mr. Rawlins."

He released his grasp. "I'm just saying you deserve to be treated well."

"Excuse me." She lifted the basket into the wagon. "It's time for you to leave now, Mr. Rawlins. Goodnight."

She climbed inside the wagon and drew the canvas closed. Leaning back, she heaved a deep sigh. Her hands trembled as she lifted them to her damp cheeks.

Oh, God, protect us all.

Matilda rose before dawn when Nicholas and Henry stumbled into camp.

"Do you want to catch some shuteye before we leave?" She nodded toward the wagon with the bedrolls underneath.

"Maybe a few winks." Nicholas stifled a yawn as he set his rifle inside the wagon.

"I'm going to look in the ravine for berries before we leave. I'll take the younger boys with me."

Nicholas nodded and planted a warm kiss on her lips before he crawled beneath the wagon. Henry followed him as Matilda opened the tent canvas to rouse the boys.

"Wake up, now. We're going to look for berries."

As Grundy turned away from Matilda, Johnny opened both eyes wide and jumped up. Bart sat up, scrubbing sleep from his eyes with both palms.

"Who were you talking to last night, Ma?" Bart opened his eyes wide. "I heard voices."

"It was nothing. Mr. Rawlins just stopped by for a minute."

"What'd he want?"

"It wasn't important." She shook the heel of Grundy's foot. "Wake up, sleepyhead. We're going to look for berries. If we find some, perhaps we can have pie or cobbler."

She ducked out of the tent to find Nicholas standing in front of her, lips in a tight line.

"What's that I heard?" He nodded toward the tent. "Rawlins was here last night?"

She nodded. "He said he wanted to apologize for his behavior."

"Apologize? Bah! He knew full well I'd be gone." Nicholas scanned Matilda from head to toe. "Did he hurt you?"

She shook her head.

"What did that gullyfluff do?" Nicholas demanded.

"Nothing." She stepped toward the wagon and picked up an empty basket. "He just—he just wanted to apologize." Matilda dropped her gaze.

"Did he touch you?"

Matilda's eyes flew to her husband's face. Warmth burned her cheeks.

Nicholas strode to her and set both hands on her shoulders. "Did … he … touch … you?"

"He—he just—" Matilda stammered and stopped. She drew a deep breath. "He just grabbed my arm when I walked to the wagon."

"That son of a—"

"Nicholas!"

"I'll kill him. That mealy-mouthed pansy will be eating my fist."

"No, Nicholas." Although she wanted Rawlins to stay away, Matilda didn't want Nicholas engaging in a fistfight. She had no doubt her husband could take down the lanky man, but if he angered Rawlins, there was no telling the trouble he might cause. "Please."

Nicholas shook his head and stormed across the circle toward Rawlins' wagon. She heard voices raised and gathered the younger boys to her skirts. Henry, curled up beneath the wagon, slept through the ruckus.

Matilda saw Captain Magone stride toward where Nicholas held Rawlins pinned against his wagon's canvas, shouting in his face. The thin man's lip dribbled blood down his chin.

She couldn't hear the words, but she saw Nicholas gesture toward Rawlins and then back at her and the boys. Magone spoke quietly for a few minutes and gestured toward the front of the train. He then looked at Rawlins and pointed toward the rear.

Nicholas released his hold and Rawlins sagged. Matilda saw her husband point a finger in Rawlins' face and then shove him. Magone grabbed Nicholas by the arm and drew him away from Rawlins toward her.

"Mrs. Koontz." Captain Magone tipped his hat. "I'm real sorry Rawlins bothered you last night."

Matilda nodded. "Thank you, Captain. We're fine."

"He won't make more trouble for you." Magone shook his head and turned to Nicholas. "It's hard to believe he did that after you volunteered to take his shift."

"The little sh—" Nicholas glanced at Matilda and stopped the curse word.

"We'll be going into the fort shortly. I suggest you steer clear of him as best you can." Magone swiveled to leave and then turned back. "I'll make you both a promise, though. From here on out, I'll keep an eye on you and the boys whenever Nicholas is gone."

Tears of gratitude pricked her eyes as Matilda smiled at the young captain. The emigrants of this wagon train had certainly chosen well when they picked him.

"Thanks, Joe." Nicholas shook his hand. "I'm mighty grateful to you."

⚬❦⚬

Nicholas packed the tent into their wagon. "Sure could use some of that buffalo about now," he told Matilda.

She shrugged. "Finished it a week ago. Bacon's running low, too."

Just then, Jim Rawlins stormed into the camp, shouting. "Somebody's stealing the cattle!"

Magone strode to the thin man. "What's this?"

"James Gibson says three cattle are missing, including one of mine!" Rawlins gestured to the teenager following behind him.

"Were they there last night?" Magone asked the boy.

He shrugged. "Think so. Ain't sure though."

"Mine was!" Rawlins insisted. "I had just unhitched them."

"Jory, you were on guard duty last night." Magone addressed the British gentleman. "You see anyone? Hear anything?"

"Nothing at all." Jory shook his head. "Quiet all night."

Nicholas shook his head in disgust. "That's just nonsense," he complained. "We need to start early. If Rawlins can't keep track of his oxen, that's his problem."

"Now, Nicholas." Matilda touched his shoulder. "Anybody's cattle could have wandered off as easily as his."

Nicholas shook his head and grumbled to Matilda. "I've got six oxen, four boys, and a horse to keep track of, and I always know where they are."

She raised her brows at him. "I'm glad you didn't add me to your list."

Nicholas guffawed, grabbed her around the waist, and kissed her. "No, you're the one who keeps track of me."

The captain cleared his throat. "Nicholas, you want to help find the missing cattle?"

"Sure, Joe. I'll be right there," he said, glancing at his wife and winking.

The men strode from the camp of parked wagons and climbed a nearby hill. Magone pulled out his spyglass.

"You see them anywhere?" Nicholas asked the captain.

"Nope." He jogged down a trail through the brown grass. "Guess we'll have to keep looking."

"This is a waste of time." Nicholas growled the words. "We need to be leaving earlier each day, not hunting down wandering cows."

"I agree." Magone lifted his spyglass again. "We'll need to discuss this tonight." He nudged Nicholas and pointed. "There, in the shadow of that brush."

"I see them." Nicholas ran toward the grazing cattle, arms waving as he shooed them back toward camp so they could leave.

The company traveled five hours before breaking for the midday meal. The captain called a meeting.

"We're starting too late in the mornings." Magone, once again twirling the brim of his hat, gazed at the three dozen men in the circle. "We're wasting time in the mornings searching for stray cattle. The guards can make sure nobody steals the animals but rounding up strays each morning is frustrating a lot of folks. We cannot fall behind schedule—the snowfall in the Blue Mountains won't wait for us."

Silence followed.

"We need to come up with a solution," the captain said. "I'm open to suggestions."

Nicholas had only six oxen. But some emigrants had several dozen head of beef cattle.

"If someone offers a suggestion you like, line up behind that man," the captain said. "We'll let majority opinion prevail."

"We could leave and let the people missing cattle catch up later," one man piped up.

"What about having some of the boys rise early to look for the cattle?"

Nobody lined up behind either man.

"We don't even know if these cattle went missing overnight," another man said. "They could have been lost days ago."

"What if each stock owner counts his cattle at night before allowing them free to graze?" Jory suggested. "Then he can count them again in the morning. We'll search for any animals missing in the morning that were there the previous night. That way, we won't waste time searching for animals that might have disappeared days ago."

Two dozen men shuffled to stand behind the quiet Englishman.

The company moved forward again at two-thirty and traveled another eight miles before stopping for the night. The Laramie range in the Rocky Mountains towered in the distance, a menace looming before them. After they crossed South Pass, they still had another six hundred miles or more to reach the Blue Mountains. Nicholas sighed in frustration. How would they make it before the snow at this slow pace, wasting time looking for stray cattle? Not to mention staying put for a day each time a baby is born, which the captain said they'd do.

Then again, Nicholas figured his wife would be happy for a rest if she gave birth to their baby on the trail.

He strode forward toward Magone.

"Hey, Joe." He pointed toward a weathered wooden board attached to a stake pounded into the ground beside the trail. "You need to carve your name here."

Captain Magone strode forward and peered at the words engraved in the sign. *Train Captains since June 1st.*

Captain Jordan Sawyer
Captain Joel Palmer
Captain Nathaniel Bowen
Captain Albert Davidson
Captain John Bonser
Captain Wylie Chapman
Captain James Curl
Captain William Wiggins

He scanned the list of eight names reverently before pulling out his pocketknife.

The next morning, the company moved out an hour earlier than it had the day before, in large part because Jory's plan worked. Three cattle counted the night before were missing but rounded up quickly in the morning.

After a long day of travel, Magone rode up to the Koontz wagon. "Nicholas, you and your boys want to help Bernier, the guide for the priests? He shot some antelope and offered to share meat with the company, but we need to butcher and clean it."

"Sure." Nicholas pulled back on the reins to stop the rig. Then, he lifted Matilda onto the seat and handed her the reins. He gestured toward Henry and Bart. "C'mon boys, let's go cut up the kill."

He followed Magone over the rise of a hill where he saw the priests' guide, Jacob Bernier, gutting one of the lithe, long-legged animals with the bodies of three others nearby.

Nicholas handed a knife to Henry. "You and Bart take this knife and work on that antelope." He gestured to a nearby carcass. "I'll butcher this one, so you just follow what I do."

Henry gripped the long knife in his small hand, shoulders back. Nicholas loved seeing his boys take pride in their work. They'd be grown before he knew it.

Bart, however, hung back. "Come on, Bart. You can hold it while Henry cuts." The young boy gripped the antelope but looked away from it toward camp while Henry carved the meat.

Nicholas gripped the antelope by the horns with one hand as he slid the knife lengthwise through the carcass. Henry did the same. He hefted the kill to drain the blood, which seeped into the ground, then did the same for the boys' antelope. Nicholas and Henry sliced the meat from the bones and stuffed it into burlap bags.

Magone hefted the bags over his saddle, galloped back to the camp, and returned for more. Each animal provided nearly forty pounds of meat. The idea of roasting the meat left Nicholas' mouth watering.

He chatted with the guide, who said his cousin was a trapper for the Hudson's Bay Company north of Fort Vancouver.

As they strode into camp, a dog barked in greeting. Matilda handed Nicholas a cloth, soap, and a bucket of water warmed over the campfire. "I figured you'd need to do a bit of cleaning."

A few minutes later, he wiped his clean hands on the towel and inhaled deeply as he glanced toward the campfire. "That meat smells mighty tasty." He handed the towel to Henry. "What do you think, boys? Ready to eat the meat we cut?"

Henry nodded, but Bart's cheeks paled. Matilda drew the younger boy into her skirts. "Are you thinking about Millie?" she asked.

He nodded. "I didn't …" Tears filled his eyes.

"Come on, Bart." Nicholas ruffled his hair. "Buck up, boyo. We're farmers. We eat the meat we raise."

"I know, Pa." Bart swallowed and dropped his gaze "It's just … I'm not hungry."

"Don't worry," Matilda said. "We have beans and corn bread, too."

As they settled onto overturned buckets near the campfire, Jane and William joined them.

"Did you cook the antelope meat?" Matilda asked.

Jane shook her head. "I didn't know how to prepare it." She gave an exaggerated shudder. "Ophelia did all that dirty work."

Nicholas rolled his eyes. "Those slaves never prepared you for life on the trail. I suppose you want to try ours then."

William's cheeks flushed. "No, we don't want to be a bother."

"Nonsense," Matilda handed each of them a plate with antelope, beans, and corn bread. "You're welcome to join us." She smiled at Jane. "We'll eat some of yours tomorrow night—after I've shown you how to prepare it."

William bit into the meat and smacked his lips. "Now that's good game. Lean and tender and tastes a bit like sage."

"Glad you enjoyed it," Nicholas mumbled between bites of dinner. "Tomorrow, we'll see if Jane can cook it the same."

"Nicholas!" Matilda admonished her husband.

Jane stormed off toward her wagon. William finished his meal, set down his plate, and followed.

Later that night, two men on horses stopped at the camp. People gathered around to hear the news from other wagon trains.

"Couple of men strayed too far from their camp, exploring or some such nonsense," one of the men said. "They were robbed and stripped of their clothes. Returned to camp buck naked."

"Who robbed them?" Nicholas asked.

The men shook their heads. "Could've been Indians. Might have been fellows from another company. It was too dark for them to tell."

Matilda shook her head and whispered to Jane. "I can't imagine their humiliation. We'd best keep the boys and Nicholas and William close to camp."

NINETEEN

Late June 1847, Fort Laramie to Independence Rock

FOUR DAYS LATER, amid barking prairie dogs, Captain Magone called the company to halt and circle the wagons on the banks of the Laramie River. They saw the whitewashed mud walls of Fort Laramie about a mile from the Laramie River's confluence with the North Platte.

"We've come more than seven hundred miles from Missouri," Nicholas said as he unyoked the oxen. "Less than twice that much left to go to our new home."

Matilda shook her head. All that walking, and they hadn't even reached the halfway mark? How would they survive going twice as far? Her feet hurt. Her back ached. Her boys bickered. Everyone was so weary of this long journey. At least they could replenish supplies at the fort, although Nicholas warned that the prices would be high.

"We need to buy only what's necessary," he said. "Prices will be sky-high this far from civilization. Anything we can do without, we should."

Matilda sighed. "Maybe we can make our flour and sugar stretch till we arrive, but we must have coffee."

Nicholas retrieved his small money pouch from inside folded clothing in her chest of goods. They didn't have much more than perseverance and persistence to start their new life in Oregon Territory.

"Boys, we're going to visit a fort tomorrow." Nicholas told the family at supper. "We won't buy much, but we can have a good time looking at the people. We're likely to see trappers and Indians and other emigrants."

"What's the fort like, Pa?" Grundy asked.

"Never seen it, but I've heard plenty. Started as a fur trading post called Fort William—after William Sublette—and later Fort John. Don't know who John was. Now it's called Fort Laramie."

"How long will we be there?" Bart asked.

"We'll just walk inside and look around, but mostly we'll give our cattle a day to rest up before they start pulling that heavy wagon into the mountains over South Pass."

"I'll spend the time washing these filthy clothes we've been living in for six weeks." Matilda gathered the dirty dishes and carried them to the bucket. A breeze wafted fresh air over the river, and she inhaled deeply.

Captain Magone stepped into the flickering firelight.

"Nicholas. Mrs. Koontz." He nodded at them both. "We're all excited about visiting the fort, but we want to keep some people posted with the company to look after things. I've assigned a half dozen men to stay here tomorrow and hoped you'd be willing to watch things the next day so they can visit the fort."

"Sure thing," Nicholas said. "I've got some antsy boys ready to race out of here at dawn to see what's inside that fort. It'd likely kill them if they had to wait a day."

Magone laughed. "That's why I asked you to stand guard the next day. The single men will be here tomorrow."

"Rawlins?" Nicholas furrowed his brow.

Magone nodded. But Mr. and Mrs. Jory will be here too, and they've promised to keep an eye on your rig."

Nicholas pursed his lips. "Good enough. James is a quiet man, but he's as sturdy and steady as an ox."

"That he is." Magone tipped his hat toward Matilda. "Goodnight, ma'am."

As they prepared for bed, Matilda wondered if her boys would sleep at all. She had to hush them several times before they quieted.

"Ma! Pa!" Henry shouted as dawn broke. "Can we visit the fort now?"

"Can we?" Grundy echoed. "Can we go now?"

Matilda brushed back her auburn locks and twisted them into a tight bun after she crawled from beneath the wagon in her Sunday dress. "Breakfast first." She pulled out cold biscuits and cured bacon. "We'll go after we eat."

After the meal, she addressed Nicholas. "I imagine Jane and William might like to go with us?"

"I'll ask." He wandered to the Glovers' wagon.

"Line up, boys." Matilda examined each of her sons in turn. She ran her fingers through Henry's wild hair and wiped dirt from Grundy's face, although one spot proved to be a freckle darkened by the sun. Bart looked clean as could be, but Johnny? She picked him up, brushed off the dirt from his trousers, and combed his hair with her fingers. This is the first time they'd have time to interact with strangers since leaving Missouri.

Nicholas returned. "They're coming with us. They'll be here in a minute."

The Glovers and the Koontzes walked together toward the rectangular mud fort encircled by a tall wooden fence hewn of cottonwood logs. Near the gate opening into the fort, a tower with windows offered a clear view of the surrounding countryside. Sioux Indians camped nearby with their ponies and half-wolf dogs. Matilda dropped her eyes as she spied an Indian man who wore little more than a loincloth, exposing most of his naked body to full view.

"Oh, my! Did you see that savage?" Jane nudged Matilda with her elbow. "He's practically naked."

"Keep your eyes down, Jane. No point in seeing what might offend you."

"Look, Pa." Henry raced ahead to stop before a man wrapped in a blanket displaying furs, spears, bows, and arrows. "I wonder if he has a tomahawk."

"We don't need a tomahawk." Nicholas pulled Henry away from the display. "We've got our rifle and gunpowder."

Matilda paused before a table filled with colorful light blue, red, and green beaded necklaces, tanned leather, and decorated moccasins. She lifted the flat leather footwear, felt the fur lining inside. She handed it to Nicholas. "These might actually be comfortable for walking."

"Look mighty soft to me." He stroked the leather on the bottom, then handed it back to the native woman. "Sturdy?"

The woman's brows pulled together. "Strong!" She pointed toward her feet beneath a faded calico dress. "Good feet." She pointed at Matilda and gestured toward her booted feet. "Try?"

Matilda smiled, shook her head, and set down the moccasins.

"Go ahead." Nicholas nodded toward an overturned bucket. "Sit there. It can't hurt to try them."

"We can't afford them," Matilda said as she perched on the bucket. She removed a laced but worn boot and slid her stockinged foot inside the soft leather. Fur engulfed her feet. "Oh…." She couldn't stop the sigh from escaping her lips. She removed the moccasin and laced up her boot, then handed the moccasin to the woman. "Thank you."

Nicholas stroked his beard and shrugged. "How much?"

"Nicholas. No." She grasped his arm and pulled him toward the entrance to the fort. "We don't need them."

Jane's voice stopped her. "Aren't those necklaces gorgeous?" Jane lifted the beads to her neck. "How does it look?"

"Very pretty." Matilda laughed. "Though I don't know where you'd wear them on the trail."

"You're right." Jane returned the necklace to the table. "Maybe when we're settled in Oregon Territory, I can buy jewelry."

Holding Johnny's hand, Matilda looped her other arm through Jane's and followed Nicholas and William toward the wooden stockade where a guardhouse with windows protruded above the gate. Inside, a building with thick adobe walls surrounded a central courtyard. Small rooms dotted the interior of the adobe building where vendors sold wares and a blacksmith shoed a horse.

Nicholas ducked through a doorway, carrying the shirts Matilda had sewn. He hoped to trade them for flour and sugar. Matilda followed and glanced at the supplies—fabric, ribbon, bars of soap, dishes, teakettles, bookshelves, a rocking chair. Emigrants must have traded or sold those items after deciding necessities mattered more than family keepsakes. Her jaw dropped when she saw the food prices—more than ten times what they had paid for sugar, flour, and coffee in Missouri.

"Look at those prices." Matilda whispered the words.

"William said they've got to pay a lot to have those supplies hauled out here."

Just then a woman squeezed past her, an elbow jabbing into her abdomen. Matilda instinctively covered her stomach to protect her unborn babe.

"I've seen enough of the fort." She moved toward the door. "Let's go back. It's a great day to wash the clothes while we're camped near the river."

"Oh, but I need to buy some things." Jane held back. "You go on. I'll return with William."

"Very well then." Matilda scooped Johnny into her arms and approached Nicholas. She whispered in his ear. "The prices—we can't afford to restock."

"I'm trading your shirts for a little flour and sugar, but otherwise, we'll make do with what we have." Nicholas dug into his pocket for his money pouch. "Except for coffee. We need coffee."

"I'll go back to the wagon with the boys." Matilda herded her wide-eyed sons out the door of the sutler's store, glancing at the other small doors housing a blacksmith shop and other trades, and then swept through the fort's gates. The boys chased each other through the dry buffalo grass and prickly pear cactus. Blue-gray sagebrush covered the prairie, void of trees except near the rivers. The stench of manure mingled with smoke from campfires and the putrid smell of unwashed bodies. Tugging her sunbonnet lower on her head to cover her face, she leaned against the wagon.

"I want down." Johnny squirmed in her arms as he watched his brothers playing in the dried grass.

She lowered him to the ground. "Stay where I can see you."

Nicholas finished buying the flour, coffee, and sugar and left the store. With six small rooms on the east and west side, three to the north and south, the fort looked more like a small town than a trading post. A blacksmith forged a metal rim for a wheel.

Arms filled with three bags, he headed toward the wagons but stopped outside the fort. He picked up the flat moccasins Matilda had tried. "How much?"

"One dollar."

Nicholas whistled through his teeth. He picked up both light tan moccasins, running his rough hands against the soft fur. Blue beads adorned the sides while a puckered seam pulled the top and bottom together with fringed leather for tightening on top. A dollar. He shook his head and replaced the footwear.

"That's mighty pricey." He glanced at the moccasins again and then at the woman. The storekeeper, Mr. Barlow, had cut the price of the goods he bought in exchange for the shirts Matilda had sewn, so he had a bit extra. He pictured Matilda carrying that babe in her womb—and Johnny half the time—as she trudged along in those worn boots, never complaining.

He dug three bits from his pocket and raised an eyebrow at the woman.

The woman nodded. "You hide?"

He grinned. "Yeah. I'll surprise her."

She glanced behind her to a small woven mat, grabbed the moccasins from his hands, and wrapped them inside. She thrust the packet into his hands. "Happy wife?"

Nicholas laughed. "You betcha she'll be happy."

He sauntered toward the wagon, where he saw the boys playing tag. Matilda visited with Sarah and James Jory. He snuck inside the wagon and buried the package beneath clothing in the bottom drawer. He'd give it to her soon.

153

He tucked the bags of coffee, flour, and sugar beside the other foodstuffs before joining Matilda and the Jorys. "Thanks for watching our rigs while we were at the fort," Nicholas said.

"Nice place," Jory said. "Tom Wilson just came back. The sutler told him many Frenchmen work around here. They married Sioux women and live at the fort."

Matilda lifted her head, breathed in through her nose, and smiled. "What is that heavenly smell?"

"Think it's a bakery yonder." Jory glanced toward the fort. "Did you see a bakery inside?"

Both Matilda and Nicholas shook their heads.

"I'd love to have an oven for baking again." Matilda sighed.

"Soon enough you'll be baking pies, cakes, and cinnamon rolls for all the neighbors again." He glanced up as William and Jane left the fort and chuckled. "I imagine William will be returning with a much smaller pocketbook if he buys everything Jane has piled in her arms."

As they packed up to begin the arduous journey through the mountain pass the next morning, James Jory stopped by to chat. He and Sarah had visited the fort earlier.

"How'd it go today?" Nicholas asked.

Jory chuckled, shaking his head. "To be sure, it's an interesting place. Watched a man greasing his wagon, but when he reached the front, he noticed the hammer was gone." Jory sipped his tea. "When he looked up, he saw an Indian scurrying away with a blanket wrapped tightly around his body.

"'Stop right there!' the fellow ordered. 'Bring back that wagon hammer!' The native stopped, turned around, and shook his head. He denied taking anything, and to prove his point, spread his blanket wide and shook it. Then he hurried away. The fellow walked to where the man had stood and found the hammer on the ground."

Nicholas guffawed. "Good for him!"

After Jory left, Matilda sat in her rocking chair and pulled off her boots. She rubbed her aching feet as the little one began somersaulting in her womb.

Nicholas glanced at her stocking feet, strode to the wagon, and returned to wrap his arms around her. "I have a surprise for you," he whispered in her ear.

She smiled. "Let me guess … another day on the trail tomorrow?"

He laughed. "Better." He pulled a small packet from behind his back and handed it to her.

"Nicholas?" She lifted it toward the fading firelight. "What is it?"

"Open it," he said as he perched on a log and pulled her onto his lap.

Matilda unrolled the woven mat and gasped. "The moccasins?" She looked into his eyes. "You bought them for me? We don't have the money to spend on anything that isn't essential."

"Wish I could buy you more, Mattie." He nuzzled her neck. "I'm so grateful you agreed to come west. Walking all those miles, and you in the family way." He kissed her. "How did I ever get so lucky to have a wife like you?"

She wrapped her arms around his neck.

"Try 'em on." He jostled around to set her on the log. He knelt and slipped the soft leather moccasins onto her stocking feet. He glanced up at her.

She wiggled her toes and smiled. "Heavenly."

After eating, they packed up and headed west again, Matilda on foot in her comfortable moccasins with the younger boys, Bart astride Belle, and Henry learning from his pa how to guide the oxen. She smiled thinking of her husband. How she loved that man, the father of her children, her lover and protector.

"Get up!" Nicholas yelled.

The oxen heaved forward behind a trail of billowing dust from the wagons ahead of them, a cacophony of pounding hooves and rumbling wagons filling the air.

"What's that, Ma?" Grundy pointed to a small rodent darting through the dry grass.

"I'm not sure." Matilda looked closer. "It might be what they call a prairie dog. Look, it's got a black tail."

"Can I look closer?"

"Don't touch it. But you can look."

Grundy dropped Johnny's hand and raced forward. Matilda watched the prairie dog halt, sniff, scurry deeper into the brush, and dive into a hole in the ground. She laughed.

"What do you think of that critter, Johnny?"

She looked down but didn't see Johnny beside her. She quickly glanced toward the train and saw the toddler running toward the rear of their wagon, stick in hand.

"Johnny!" Matilda picked up her skirts and raced after him. "Stop!"

He looked at her. "Throw stick."

Of course they'd thrown sticks into the bucket latched to the side of the wagon on the open prairie when collecting kindling and cow pies but not with the prairie schooners moving so quickly and close together.

"Stay back from the wagon." Panic rose in her throat as William's rig bore down on her son. "Nicholas!"

She didn't know if her husband could hear her over the rumbling of the wagon and plodding of the oxen. She ran as fast as she could and tried to block images of Frank from her mind. Oh, God, not Johnny! Please, God, help!

"William!" Matilda shouted. "Stop!"

William and Jane followed directly behind the Koontz wagon. Would he see Johnny? If he did, could he pull back the oxen in time?

"Stop!" she bellowed.

Johnny tottered toward their wagon—three feet, two feet, one foot—and tossed the stick toward the basket latched to its side. He missed. As he bent forward to pick it up, their wheel crunched the wood and shot a shaft toward her son, missing his head by inches. He plopped onto his bottom, crying.

"Johnny!" Matilda hollered.

Henry glanced at her, then saw Johnny inches from their wagon's back wheel. He hurtled off the seat and dashed toward his brother as William's oxen bore down on them. He grabbed the toddler under both arms and rolled.

"Ow," Johnny yelled.

An oxen's hoof plopped onto Henry.

Matilda screamed. Her knees buckled. She fell to the ground, arms tight across her abdomen as she stared in horror.

Her eldest son jumped to his feet, grabbing Johnny again under both arms, and sprinted. Off the trail, he plopped onto the ground. Matilda scrambled toward them.

She hugged both boys tight. Henry squirmed and stood, shaking off her embrace. She lifted Johnny into her arms.

"Henry, you're bleeding." Matilda pulled out the kerchief tucked in her sleeve. She lifted the torn fabric of his shirt and paled as she saw the deep bruise already spreading over his thin arm. She ran her trembling hands up and down his body, checking for crushed bones. Perhaps the beast's hooves had missed him, although she couldn't fathom how.

"Aw, Ma." Henry wiped his arm across his shirt. "It's nothing. Just a scratch."

Turning, he pressed his nose into Johnny's face. "Don't you be running to the wagon again, hear? You almost kilt yourself!"

Johnny pushed out his lower lip. It trembled.

"Aw, go on, now." Henry patted his brother's head awkwardly with his good arm but kept the injured one close to his waist as he strode back to the wagon.

Henry's bone hadn't felt broken, but perhaps she'd need to rig up a sling to relieve pressure on the arm. Not that he'd wear it.

Grundy ran to his mother. "I'm sorry, Ma. I didn't mean to let go of Johnny—"

"It's fine." Matilda rubbed his shoulder as she inhaled a shaky breath. "We just need to keep a close eye on this little scamp. Let's all three hold hands."

She grasped her sons' warm hands and squeezed tight, trying to quell the trembling in her heart. What if they suffer a more severe injury—or worse?

Matilda's hands still trembled later as she dished the beans with bacon onto the plates and gave one to each of her sons.

"You missed all the excitement, Bart, by riding on Belle." Henry scooped a spoonful of beans into his mouth and bit into a biscuit. "Johnny almost got himself run over."

Johnny's brows drew together in a frown, his lower lip protruding.

"What happened?" Bart looked at Henry, who recounted the near tragedy without too much embellishment.

"Is that true?" Bart looked at her.

Matilda nodded.

"What? You think I'd fib about something like that?" Henry finished the last of his beans and set his plate next to the bucket Matilda used for washing dishes. Then he rolled up his shirtsleeve to show off the black bruise encircling his arm like a spreading plague.

Nicholas raised his brows. "Now that's a mighty colorful arm, Son. Does it hurt?"

"Naw." Henry buttoned his cuff again and shrugged. "A little, maybe."

Tears pricked Matilda's eyes as she imagined what could have happened. They'd avoided a tragedy by inches.

Nicholas glanced at her. "I heard some of the folks are gathering for fiddling and dancing tonight."

Dancing. Matilda hadn't danced in a long time. But after walking eighteen miles today? Her feet didn't feel like moving.

"Come on." Nicholas winked at her. "We can still dance a jig."

"I don't know." Matilda scrubbed the plates in warm soapy water then rinsed and dried them. "It's been a long day."

"I need a dance partner, and you're it." Nicholas slid his hand beneath her elbow. "Come on, boys."

Nicholas led the way into the center of the circled wagons where a bonfire spewed glowing orange sparks into the black sky. Families mingled and visited beyond the flames. Henry and Bart spotted boys they'd met along the trail. They both ran over to them, digging into their front right pockets and pulling out small cloth bags containing marbles. Matilda knew they'd be entertained for a while.

"Ma, can I watch them play marbles?" Grundy's eyes pleaded with her.

"Will you take Johnny and watch him too?"

Grundy nodded.

Matilda smiled. "You can always play catch like those other boys are doing."

Grundy grabbed Johnny by the hand and dragged him toward the older boys shooting marbles.

A fellow tuned up his fiddle. Another man strummed a banjo. A voice soon belted out the words to a tune that set even the most tired toes to tapping.

Old Dan Tucker was a fine old man
He washed his face in a frying pan
He combed his hair with a wagon wheel
And died of a toothache in his heel.

Other voices joined in for the chorus as Nicholas grabbed Matilda around the waist and led her in a polka around the bonfire. Men and women young and old joined in the dancing.

Get out the way for old Dan Tucker
You're too late to git your supper
Supper's gone and dinner cookin'
Old Dan Tucker's just a-standin' there lookin'.

More couples took to the makeshift dirt dance floor to kick up their heels as the song continued. Voices grew louder when more people joined in the chorus and faded a bit with the verses.

I come to town the other night
To hear a noise and see the fight
The watchman feet was a-running around
Crying "Old Dan Tucker's come to town."

Matilda laughed as they danced, breathless but happy as her husband's strong arms guided her between the couples. When the song ended, he placed his wide palms on her hips, lifted her high, and planted a kiss on her lips.

"Nicholas." Blood rushed to her face. "Put me down."

He did as she ordered but kept hold of her as the musicians cranked out more songs—"Skip to my Lou," "Oh, Susanna," and a dozen other tunes. As the hours passed, the music slowed, and the families bid one another goodnight. They returned to their wagons to sleep before another long day on the trail.

"Hope you all had fun while we were standing guard," Rawlins shouted.

"You can be sure we did," Nicholas hollered. Then, lowering his voice, he added, "More fun with you out there."

"Nicholas." Matilda wrapped her arm around his.

"It's true, though, isn't it?" he whispered.

She smiled. Indeed, it was a fun evening, one of the most pleasant they had passed on the trail. As she snuggled beneath the wagon beside her husband, Matilda prayed for a good night's sleep, an uneventful day tomorrow, and—oh, how she wished she could fly like a bird to Oregon—fewer blisters.

Three hours later, Matilda jarred awake, reliving the nightmare of watching her boys scramble beneath the oxen's hooves. Her heart pounded, and she sat up.

"Mattie?" Nicholas mumbled.

"Shhh…go back to sleep." She inhaled a deep breath, trying to calm her heartbeat.

Nicholas rolled over and pulled her to his side, holding her tight.

The terror subsided with the reassurance of his even breathing. But her mind couldn't stop thinking of what might have been.

TWENTY

THE NEXT NIGHT, the company set up camp near Register Cliff, a sandstone landmark where westward-bound emigrants chiseled names into the rock with axes and knives. Nicholas, glancing at Rawlins, told the boys they'd wait to carve their names on Independence Rock.

"But how far away is that?" Bart asked.

"We're nearly there. It's the end of June, and most trains make it to the rock by the Fourth of July. We'll likely be a day or two late."

"Four more days?"

"Naw, chowderhead." Henry nudged his younger brother. "Pa said it's the end of June—not June 30th. That could be any day toward the end of the month. Right, Pa?"

"Less than two weeks." Nicholas ruffled Bart's hair. "We'll climb that rock and let folks know the Koontzes passed by. What do you say?"

The boys beamed at their pa.

They reached the Bitter Fork, named for the bitter black poplars nearby, and saw oxen carcasses strewn along the trail, some eaten by wolves, others simply white bones drying in the sun. Had the emigrants before them butchered the oxen to eat? Or had they fallen sick from bad water and died? This land, so beautiful, proved fraught with peril for man and beast. How could she keep her family safe when so many dangers waited around each new bend of the road? Wild animals? Illnesses? God help her, she needed to rely on His protection for her family because she couldn't do it herself.

The wagon train headed toward Laramie Mountain, also known as Ice Peak, and passed another herd of buffalo. "Must be three thousand of them," Magone said. "Why don't you ask Bernier to join us, and we'll hunt us some meat for dinner?"

Nicholas spoke with Jacob Bernier, the priests' guide, but he hesitated as he passed Rawlins' wagon. If he hunted with the captain, would Rawlins bother Matilda again? He asked James Jory to keep an eye on his wife and then grabbed his rifle.

"Nicholas?" Matilda glanced at the gun.

"Buffalo. Captain and Bernier are hunting, so I'll go too."

"Can I come, Pa?" Henry begged.

"Not this time, Son. Too dangerous with so many buffalo. But we'll have fresh meat for dinner tonight."

He packed ammunition into his pockets and hopped onto Belle's back. "You all stay close to the wagon while I'm gone, just in case that herd veers this way."

Nicholas joined Magone and Bernier, then all three rode toward the cloud of dust. They slowed their horses as they drew closer and dismounted.

"Let's go to the top of that hill and find the best place to set up." Bernier gestured and both Nicholas and the captain followed.

In the valley below roamed hundreds of bison, large and small, with patchy spots of shaggy fur over their humped shoulders and darker hide on their haunches. Horns curled upward over their ears. His stomach rumbled at the sight. Fear? Or excitement?

Bernier whispered. "Koontz, you go to the left, Magone right. When you're in place, I'll come down the center. Wait until I fire. That way the herd moves away from us."

Both men nodded then scurried low to the ground, leading their horses.

Nicholas squatted to take aim at a huge beast and caught movement to his left. Two Indians, most likely Sioux, crouched low to the ground with arrows notched in their bows. Nicholas waved toward Bernier, but the guide didn't see him.

Swoosh!

An arrow found its mark in the haunches of a huge buffalo. As several more arrows struck their marks, the animal bellowed and stomped forward—directly toward Nicholas. A hundred other beasts followed his lead.

Nicholas fell back on the dry weeds as the herd pounded toward him. Thunder pummeled his ears from the beating hooves. Dust filled his nose and mouth as he scrambled to his feet.

A rifle crack sounded. Then another.

Bernier's bullet struck another buffalo stampeding toward Nicholas and it stumbled. He fired again and it toppled onto its side. The herd veered left—away from Nicholas but toward the wagons.

Nicholas inhaled a deep shaky breath and aimed his rifle. Bang! He missed. He dug deep into his pocket for ammunition, reloaded, and fired again. A hit. Not the largest buffalo but a good-sized animal all the same. Three more shots rang out and the herd turned again, rumbling through the valley away from the wagons and hunters.

Nicholas scurried away as the Sioux men approached the buffalo downed by arrows. He ran to the animal he had killed. An arrow lay on the ground nearby. Uh-oh. He glanced at the Sioux warriors who glared at him. He raised the arrow and gestured in question. "You want?"

A warrior stormed toward him. Nicholas inhaled deeply. Stay calm. You shot this beast. His arrow missed.

The native grabbed the arrow from his hand and swiveled without a word, running back to the animals they had already started carving up.

Nicholas pulled out his hunting knife, cut the buffalo down the center, and began dressing the meat. He packed it in burlap and hefted it over Belle's saddle. He stripped every bit of meat from the bones and then cleaned the hide as best as he could.

Magone and the French-Canadian guide had each killed a buffalo. They dressed the meat together as the sun dropped over the horizon.

Hours later, they rode into camp. Men and women gathered around.

"We can divvy up the meat from these among the company," Magone said. "Everyone should eat well for days."

The women rushed to their wagons for pans.

"They'll keep the hides." Magone gestured toward Nicholas and Bernier. "To help you stay warm on cold nights—which we're likely to find in the Blues if we don't hurry."

A hundred miles west of Fort Laramie, the company needed to cross the Platte again. A group of Mormons had erected a blacksmith shop for wagon repairs and a ferry to help rigs cross to the river's north side for a dollar apiece.

"Do we have a dollar to spare?" Matilda asked Nicholas.

He shook his head. "Not much point in paying someone to do what we can do ourselves. I'll take the rig upstream and ford the river there."

Most emigrants paid the ferry toll, while Nicholas and a few others drove their wagons upstream. Matilda sat inside, cuddling Johnny on her lap with Grundy behind her, as Nicholas led the oxen across the placid river.

Henry and Bart rode Belle.

Midstream, the wagon stalled. Nicholas waded to the rear of the rig.

"We'll lighten the load and see if that helps." He reached inside. "Johnny, you grab on to my neck while I lift your ma out of the wagon."

"I can walk, Nicholas." Matilda glanced at her husband as he cradled her body in his arms.

He shifted to jostle Johnny higher on his back. "I don't want you slipping on a rock or catching a chill."

Grundy scrambled out. Matilda watched over Nicholas' shoulder as her son plunged into the water. "Grundy!"

The freckle-faced redhead fell to his knees, scrambled forward, and raced his father up the bank. "I'm fine, Ma," he shouted as he plopped onto his bottom in dry grass.

"You need help, Pa?" Henry slid off Belle.

"Let me check it first. I'll holler if I need you."

Nicholas returned to the water and stepped behind the rig to push.

"Be careful," Matilda shouted from the shore.

"Now, don't you fret, woman." Nicholas leaned his shoulder against the wagon. "You know these beasts can do anything. Giddyup!"

The team shuffled forward, but the wagon didn't move.

"Henry. You grab the lead yoke and pull those oxen forward."

"Yes, Pa." Henry scrambled down the bank and into the water. He grabbed the yoke between Pet and Baul. "C'mon, you old brutes. Giddyup!"

Henry yanked on the yoke and Nicholas shoved. The wagon lurched free of the muck and rolled up the bank.

"Henry. Hurry! Don't let them run you over." Matilda twisted her hands together as she stood with Johnny and Grundy.

Nicholas led the oxen down the trail on the far side of the river.

"See how easy that was?" Nicholas said. "And we have that dollar to spend when we reach Oregon."

As they rejoined the company, Matilda heard Captain Magone speaking to the Mormons.

"You folks make it about four thousand who crossed the trail this year," the ferry operator said.

"That many?" Magone rubbed his whiskers.

"No wonder so much of the grass was eaten to the nub," Nicholas inserted, laughing.

"About right, that." Magone turned to the ferry operator. "Yeah, I'll see the list of captains and wagons gets to the newspaper in Oregon City. I'm sure folks will be interested to know how many rigs crossed the trail this year." He tipped his hat and left.

Later that night, eight men on horseback, accompanied by mules carrying their provisions, trotted toward the company from the west. They pulled up to speak to Magone.

"Left Oregon City the fifth of May," one fellow said. "Took the new Barlow Road that opened last year. Horrible. Rough and so steep we were glad to be on horses and mules rather than in a wagon. Toll road too."

"That's good to know." Magone thanked the men. "How many wagons you pass?"

"We saw seven hundred eighty-nine prairie schooners. How many wagons do you have in your train? We'll add that to the total."

"Started out large, broke into smaller groups, but since then we've had people join us." Magone tapped his fingers as he counted. "We've got forty-four now."

"Heard some disturbing news from down California way." A clean-shaven man glanced around the circle of people. "May not be good to share in mixed company."

"Go ahead," Nicholas said. "These women are as hardy as they come."

The man cleared his throat.

"Seems like a group left the California trail last fall and took what they figured was a shortcut. The Donner party. Got lost and most of them froze to death." The crowd gasped, and the man's eyes fell to the ground. "That's not the worst of it. Those that made it out—"

He paused and shook his head. Another man picked up the tale.

"They ate their dead."

"What?" Jim Rawlins nearly screeched the question. "What did you say?"

"Oh, dear Lord!" The words escaped Jane's mouth, and she swayed.

Matilda wrapped her arm around Jane's waist to brace her, but just then the baby flipped inside her womb. Thinking she might vomit, she led the younger woman back to camp. Eating human flesh! Oh, what an abhorrent and unimaginable sin. How desperate must someone be to eat another person? She would rather die. Then her gaze fell on her sons. But would she let them die? If it came to watching her children starve or feeding them flesh of a dead companion—oh, my! She couldn't even think of it.

A subdued group traveled away from the North Platte River for the final time, stocked with filled barrels to water the animals and quench their thirst over the next several days until they reached the Sweetwater River more than fifty miles away.

So many dangers. So many horrors. What if their train wandered onto a wrong path? If it happened to the Donners, could it happen to them?

With each passing day, new life fluttered inside Matilda's abdomen. The babe grew despite her rather monotonous diet of biscuits, beans, and bacon, with occasional fresh antelope or buffalo. She rubbed her stomach. Eight hundred miles, she'd already walked with this baby. They still had more than a thousand miles to travel, much of it uphill through mountains.

"We'll be halfway to Oregon in a week or two." Nicholas walked beside her. "You still mad at me for uprooting you from Missouri?"

Matilda smiled slightly but said nothing.

"You'll see. Life will be so much better there for our sons."

A fight broke out between the boys.

"Henry," she shouted. "Grundy." She quickened her pace, and Johnny ran to keep up as she still clutched his hand. "What's this all about?"

"It's my turn to ride Belle." Grundy thrust his chin at his older brother. "But Henry won't let me."

"Henry?" Matilda stared at her eldest son. "Is that true? Is it Grundy's turn?"

"But Ma, my feet hurt. I've got blisters on my toes."

"We all have blisters," Nicholas said. "They'll be callouses soon and won't hurt a bit."

Matilda started to help Grundy onto Belle's back behind Bart, but Nicholas stopped her.

"You let me lift him." He hefted his third son onto the mare.

"Henry, climb into the wagon," Matilda said. "Let me see your feet."

Henry shook his head. "Never mind. It's nothing."

"I can bandage your toes if they're blistered."

Henry waved his hand and raced ahead to the Browns' wagon where he walked between William and Andrew, chatting. The boys started this grand adventure with eager enthusiasm, but the novelty wore off with each mile they traveled.

They would reach Independence Rock shortly after the Fourth of July, behind all other companies. Leaving Missouri so late in May left them scrambling to beat cold weather in the Blue Mountains of Oregon Territory. Magone pushed them to move faster every day.

Before dinner, a couple of men stopped by from a wagon company up ahead after chasing missing cattle. Magone's travelers gathered round, eager for news.

"A few days ago, this here man in our company, Smith Dunlap, was hunting with a few other fellows." The speaker rubbed a hand over gray stubble on his chin. "Seems his gun misfired or something. Somehow, he wound up killing himself. Buried him along the Platte."

The man glanced around.

"Only about thirty years old. Left a wife and six young children."

Matilda gasped. "What will his widow do?"

"She's still going to Oregon. Our company can help her. She'd be alone if she tried to go back east."

"Oh, that poor woman." Matilda whispered. Others murmured.

"She'll probably find another husband." The man finished his coffee. "Men are eager for wives out west." He glanced at the women in the crowd. "Not many women have the courage to do what you ladies are doing."

Nicholas wrapped an arm around Matilda's waist as they walked back to their wagon. She silently prayed for Smith Dunlap's widow and children. They must be heartbroken.

"Now don't you go fretting again," Nicholas admonished her with a flick to her nose. "We're going to be fine."

"God willing." She whispered a prayer for her family too.

Settling beneath the wagon to sleep, Matilda rubbed her stomach. Her body ached after all the walking, and her mind yearned for rest, but as she lay there, her little babe—about five months along now, she calculated—chose tonight to tumble like a circus clown after sleeping all day, lulled by Matilda's walking.

Thinking of the Widow Dunlap, she embraced Nicholas tighter that night. What would she do without him? Lord willing, she'd never have to find out. Pregnant with four boys? She could never survive alone on the trail. Poor Mrs. Dunlap, alone with six young children. Matilda drifted to sleep, gunfire, blood, and orphaned children invading her dreams.

Independence Day fell on a Sunday. Matilda combed the hair of each boy as they joined others in the morning.

"We can stay in camp today, give the oxen a rest." Magone looked around the crowd. "Or we can keep moving. The choice is yours. All in favor of resting, raise your hands."

Matilda's aching joints screamed for a rest. Most in the crowd raised their hands as weariness over the two hundred miles they'd traveled since Fort Laramie prevailed over persistence—at least for one day. Matilda welcomed the reprieve.

"As today's the Sabbath, what say we celebrate the nation's birthday tomorrow morning?" Magone acknowledged the nods in the crowd. "All right. Let's move the cattle to the southern side of the Platte where the pasture's better."

The men left to herd the animals while the women returned to their wagons to cook breakfast. The bishop held a Sunday morning service—a Roman Catholic Mass. Matilda took her boys but stood near the back to focus on God and the Sabbath rather than the priests.

Early the next morning, celebratory gunshots rang out as everyone gathered for a morning feast of buffalo to recognize the nation's emancipation from British rule. As a man played the clarinet, voices rose in patriotic songs, including "The Star-Spangled Banner" and "Columbia the Gem of the Ocean." Captain Magone read the Declaration of Independence and spoke about the great United States of America.

"We're doing our part against the British," one man shouted. "We'll claim Oregon Territory for America. That's our Manifest Destiny!"

"Hurrah!" Everyone cheered. A few toasted with flasks; others with coffee.

As the celebration ended, people repacked their wagons, and the wagons rolled out by eight.

Independence from the British was well worth celebrating, but how Matilda longed for the other Independence—the one in

Missouri or another civilized town back home. She was so weary of the constant unpacking, cooking, packing, walking, and trudging.

"Mrs. Koontz?" A girl's voice whispered into the wagon. "Mrs. Koontz?"

Matilda roused herself and pulled a dress over her head. She scrambled over a sleeping Johnny and peered out the canvas. It wasn't quite dawn yet.

"Yes?" She recognized the girl before her but couldn't quite place the name. "May I help you?"

"My ma sent me to fetch you. It's Mrs. Nelson. It's her time."

"What?" Nicholas grumbled. "What time is it?"

"Shhh…." Matilda rubbed his shoulder. "Go back to sleep now. Freda's sent for me to help Mrs. Nelson birth her baby."

"Oh," he mumbled. "Guess we can sleep in tomorrow since we'll be staying put."

Nicholas rolled over, pulling the quilt around his head, as Matilda reached into a box for an armful of rags. He was right. When she assisted Mrs. Knighten's birthing of a son in June, a boy they named Sagarlin Columbia, Captain Magone kept the wagon train in place for a day to allow her to recover. She climbed out and followed the young lady to a nearby rig, where Freda knelt outside stoking a campfire.

"Good morning, Freda." Matilda kept her voice low. "I've brought rags. How's Louisa?"

Freda shook her head. "She's carrying on like this is her first baby, but it's her second. She should just push it out and be done with it."

"Hush, now," Matilda admonished her. "She's young and scared without her family near, I'm sure." Matilda smiled at Henry Nelson as she climbed inside the wagon where eighteen-year-old Louisa lay nestled on a blanket surrounded by furniture, pots and utensils hanging from the canvas overhead. Matilda dipped a cloth into cool water and spread it over the young woman's perspiring forehead. "You'll be fine, Louisa. You just breathe deep when the pains come and relax in between."

"I'm scared." She grasped Matilda's hand. "Oh, I wish my mother was here."

"Shhh, now. You'll be fine. Mrs. Wilson and I have both birthed our share of babies. We'll be with you until this little one pops out." Matilda smiled and wiped the young woman's sweaty brow again.

"It hurts so much," Louisa groaned between clenched teeth.

"I know it does. But when you hold that baby in your arms like you did with Billy, you'll forget all about the pains and simply marvel at that new life."

"That's bull—"

"Freda!" Matilda glared at her.

"It's true." Freda put both hands on her hips and glared back. "Think I don't know it after birthing six babies?" Her voice hitched on the number six.

Freda must be thinking of Frank. Matilda couldn't imagine her friend's pain, which she hid beneath her gruff exterior.

"Aargh!" Louisa cried out, thrashing on the blanket.

"Breathe, now. Don't forget to breathe." Matilda rubbed the woman's back as she leaned forward. Freda was right. This would be a long day. And their train would lose more time staying in camp rather than moving west.

"Did you see those small roses growing near the river?" Matilda tried to shift Louisa's focus off the pain. "Weren't they beautiful?"

"I did, but then our oxen slipped—" Louisa gasped. "Oh."

"Yes, it's so difficult for oxen to cross rivers with sandy bottoms," Matilda said in a soothing voice as she wiped sweat from Louisa's brow. "The poor animals pull and pull until you think they're going to collapse. But they managed to haul our rigs through the muck."

"Freda, what's the news from your wagon?"

"Mary Ann Thompkins is talking to Grace and Bethy about how she's going to marry our good-looking captain one of these days." Freda sat back on her heels. "She's already planning the wedding with my girls."

"They would make a handsome couple." Matilda mopped Louisa's sweaty brow. "Don't you think so, Louisa?"

"Mama!" Matilda glanced through the canvas opening to see little Billy Nelson toddling toward the tent. "Mama!"

She touched Louisa's shoulder. "I'll take care of him."

Matilda swept outside the tent and scooped Billy into her arms. She twirled him in a circle, and he giggled. "Your mama's having your baby brother or sister now, so you need to stay with your pa. Can you do that?"

Billy's face scrunched as if gearing up for a loud wail. Matilda tickled his tummy. He giggled. She glanced at Louisa's husband, hovering near the wagon, and bent down to whisper to the boy. "Can you keep your papa out of trouble for me?"

He nodded as she handed him to Henry Nelson.

"Louisa will be fine, but it'd be best if you and Billy can watch the cattle or feed the horses, so she needn't fret about you."

"Thank you, ma'am." The burly man heaved a sigh of relief as he swung Billy onto his shoulders and strode from the camp.

"I need to check on my boys," Matilda told Freda. "I'll be right back."

After peering inside her tent to check on her sleeping boys, she stopped by William and Jane's wagon.

"Jane?" Matilda said softly. After a rustling from inside, the younger woman emerged.

"Matilda? What's wrong?"

She drew in a breath, knowing the news might be hard for her to hear.

"Mrs. Nelson's time has arrived. I need to help her give birth to the baby. I wondered if you'd keep an eye on the boys for me today."

Jane nodded. "Of course I will. Is there anything I can do for Louisa?"

Matilda shook her head. "Freda's there now, and I'll be going back after I speak with Nicholas, even though he knows we'll stay in place until the baby is born."

"I'll come with you." Jane whispered to William briefly before climbing out of the wagon.

After explaining the situation to Nicholas, Matilda hurried back to the Nelsons' wagon, leaving Jane to tend to the boys.

"Now don't be going on about how you can't do this." Impatience laced Freda's voice. "Women have been giving birth to babies for eons. If they can do it, you can do it. No need for whining and complaining."

Oh, my. Matilda bit back a comment as she climbed into the wagon. "I'll spell you."

Freda rolled her eyes heavenward and mumbled as she left the crowded wagon.

"How are you?" Matilda wiped the laboring mother's brow again.

"Oh, thank goodness you're back." Tears streamed from Louisa's eyes. "That woman—I thought she was going to beat me if I screamed. Oh—no!"

Matilda chuckled while rubbing the woman's back before feeling her abdomen for the baby.

"Looks like your little one is lined up properly, ready to greet the world." Matilda smiled at the soon-to-be mother. "You'll need to start pushing now."

Louisa grunted. Grimaced. Pushed. And collapsed back onto her blankets. Over and over again, as the sun climbed, blazing onto the canvas, warming the interior. An occasional scream escaped Louisa's lips as Matilda wiped her brow, rinsed the cloth, wrung out excess water, and placed it again on the back of her neck. She heard voices raised outside the tent.

"Stop that pacing," Freda admonished. "You'll wear a rut in the dirt before your wife bears you a babe."

"But how is she?" Henry Nelson asked.

"Fine."

"But the screams…"

"Men," she scoffed. "That's normal. Can you imagine trying to push a babe out …?"

"Never mind." Mr. Nelson coughed. "What can I do?"

"Fetch more water from the creek," Freda ordered. "Then go tend to the stock until I send someone for you."

Freda climbed into the wagon with more damp rags. Matilda seated herself where she could catch the little one.

"Push hard now, Louisa."

She pushed, screamed, and collapsed onto her back.

Matilda caught the slippery infant, wiped a creamy-colored slime from the tiny mouth and body, then swatted the bottom. A wail echoed through the camp. "A boy. Louisa, you have a handsome son." As she wiped the infant clean and wrapped him in a blanket, Matilda envisioned cradling her own little one in only a few months. She clipped the baby's umbilical cord, then handed the bundle to his exhausted mother.

Louisa cradled her son against her chest, where he eagerly rooted for food. All three women laughed.

"He's a hungry one, that's for sure." Freda wiped her palms on her dress and moved toward the wagon entrance. "I'll be fetching Mr. Nelson so he can meet his son."

"What will you name him?"

"We've decided on George." Louisa smiled, her soft gaze embracing the infant.

Matilda's mind flitted through the names she'd been considering for her babe. She spent most of that early July day with Louisa, caring for the infant while his mother slept and recovered her strength. While most in the company understood, Jim Rawlins' voice rose in a whine nearby. "We need to keep this train moving. Why do we have to stop for an entire day just so a woman can give birth?"

He ought to try giving birth and see how he feels. Matilda nipped the thought before it festered in her mind.

TWENTY-ONE

Early July 1847, Independence Rock to South Pass

AFTER TRAVELING OVER STEEP, rocky ground bordered by red cliffs, the wagons reached the Sweetwater River and Nicholas spied what looked like a giant turtle in the distance—Independence Rock. Fur trappers who passed by the granite rock gave the landmark its name when they passed by it on July 4, 1824. That Hastings fellow had described the rock in his book, saying it was nearly two thousand feet in length, seven hundred feet wide, and nearly 130 feet high.

"We should have been here by July Fourth." Rawlins confronted Magone. "We're running too far behind."

"We need to leave earlier in the morning," an older man said. "We're taking too long to move each day. We could travel another couple of miles each day if we started earlier."

Nicholas couldn't argue with his logic. He wanted to leave earlier each day and travel longer.

"I agree." Magone tilted his head. "Problem is, some folks like to wait until after breakfast to go." He gestured toward the priests' guide, Jacob Bernier, who strode toward them.

"Bickel here and some of the others want to start earlier in the morning, but I know the priests prefer to wait until after morning prayers and breakfast. Is that right?"

Bernier nodded. "They don't want to leave at the crack of dawn."

"How about we divide up the company, and you lead those folks who want to start later?" Magone raised an eyebrow. "Are you willing?"

Bernier shrugged. "I can do that."

Magone called a camp meeting and looked at the gathered men. "We need to divide the company again. Some of you folks want to leave earlier each morning. The priests and some of the rest of you want to wait until after breakfast." He shrugged. "I'll take the wagons that want to start earlier. Bernier agreed to lead those who desire to leave later. Line up behind the man whose group you want to join."

Nicholas stood behind Magone. The earlier they left each morning, the sooner they could reach Oregon—and build a home for themselves. And the less likely they were to have to battle snow in the Blue Mountains.

"Nobody wants to be stuck hauling wagons up and down a slick trail," Magone said.

Bernier looked at him. "We'll make it, even starting later."

Rawlins looked at the captain and then at the shorter line behind Bernier. He shuffled over to stand behind Magone.

"Thought you'd prefer to travel with a different captain," Magone chided the tall thin man.

"Changed my mind." He glanced at Nicholas and then at the Koontz wagon.

Nicholas clenched his teeth. *Can't seem to rid myself of this chucklehead.*

"What say you go with Bernier, Rawlins?" Nicholas suggested. "You've been complaining about our train every day." He tucked both hands in his pockets, fists clenched. "Makes sense for you to go with Bernier if you're so all-fired sick of our company."

"I'll do whatever I want." Rawlins hooked his thumbs into his belt.

Nicholas pursed his lips. "Think you just want to tag along so's you can ogle my wife some more."

Rawlins sputtered and cursed. "You overbearing bootlicker. I can't stand to be around you."

Nicholas tipped his head toward the priests' guide. "There's the other line."

Rawlins started over to Bernier's line but turned around. Through gritted teeth, he cursed Nicholas. "I hope an Indian scalps you or a bear eats you."

"Why?" Nicholas shook his head. "So's you can have Matilda all to yourself?" He shook his head and sobered. "Hate to tell you this, Rawlins, but Matilda wouldn't have you if you were the last man on earth."

Rawlins' face reddened.

Magone stepped between the two men. "Now let's all get some sleep."

Nicholas spied William standing behind Bernier.

"You dividing up, William?" Nicholas nodded at his nephew.

"Jane's complaining about the toll the trip is taking." He dusted off his hat. "She's worried about the snows but says she's exhausted. She needs more rest." He dropped his voice and shook his head. "And all the babies ... every time they cry, she does too."

Nicholas shook his head and then shrugged. "I understand that. But you'd best take care of yourselves, though, or Philip and Sarah will tan my hide. As your uncle, I'm supposed to be watching out for you."

"My folks will understand. You can send them news about our delay when you arrive in Oregon City. Besides, we'll be fine." He headed toward his wagon. "I'd best check on Jane and let her know."

Nicholas watched William's retreating back, knowing full well Matilda wouldn't be happy to leave her nephew behind. But he was a grown man, free to make his own choices.

Nicholas spied Tom Wilson standing in line behind Magone. It'd be nice to have Freda in their company if Mattie's babe decided to arrive early. He dropped his gaze. After Frank's death, both Tom and Freda seemed subdued...and much less eager to reach the Willamette Valley. His own boys were suffering from the loss of their friend; he couldn't imagine how much harder it must be for Tom and Freda.

As the men departed, Nicholas slapped William on the back. "Sure you won't starve without Matilda around to cook for you?"

William grinned. "Jane's coming along as a cook, thanks to Aunt Matilda." He looked down at his waist. "Though I must admit, I've lost a few pounds on the trail. Perhaps all that walking."

"Maybe all that burnt food too." Nicholas laughed. "I'll let Matilda know. She'll probably stop by tonight with grub for your journey."

At their camp, he shared the news with Matilda. Magone kept thirty wagons; the other fourteen would leave later each morning under the leadership of Jacob Bernier, including William and Jane.

"But what if something happens to them?" Matilda placed both hands on her hips. "I could never face Philip and Sarah if William had trouble, and we weren't there."

"He's a grown man, plenty old enough to make his own decisions." He wrapped her in his arms. "He assured me they'll be careful. Not to worry. They'll catch up with us in Oregon City."

Matilda bit her lower lip. "Maybe we should leave with the later group, too."

"Now, don't you worry none." Nicholas winked at her. "I trust Magone to see us through safely. We don't want to get caught in the mountains when it snows." He lifted her chin. "Besides, won't it be nice for them to know someone in Oregon when they arrive?" He started toward the wagon and stopped. "Bad news, though—Rawlins is still with us. He complained about wanting to leave earlier, but when it came time to line up, he stuck with Magone." Returning to Matilda, he wrapped her in his arms. "But don't you worry none. I'm going to keep him far from you and the boys. Speaking of which, I want to take them to the rock so we can carve our names on it. You want to come along?"

"No. I'll fix supper while you're gone." She moved toward the wagon to pull out the oven. "Are you taking Johnny?"

"Yeah. I wouldn't want him to miss the chance to make history." He tilted his head toward the next wagon. "Jory's right yonder if you need anything."

"Boys!" Nicholas hollered as he reached inside the wagon for his chisel. "Time for us to leave our mark on the rock."

With his sons gathered around him, Nicholas hefted Johnny into one arm and carried the chisel and hammer in the other. He strode toward the rock, round like a turtle shell, so he could let the world know that Nicholas Koontz and his boys had passed by on the Oregon Trail.

As Matilda stirred the beans with bacon, her mind shifted to the stories of the Donner party who faced starvation and ate the corpses of their fellow travelers to survive. Thank God for the beans and bacon. She'd never complain about them again.

After dinner, Matilda filled her arms with corn bread and biscuits and walked with Nicholas and the boys to the Glover wagon to say goodbye.

"I'm going to miss seeing you." She hugged both Jane and William. "You be careful."

Jane stepped back from the embrace. "We'll be fine." She glanced at her husband. "We'll be there just after you arrive."

"That's true." Matilda nodded. "Nicholas said we'll scout the best land and let you know where to settle."

"That's great." William rubbed his knuckles over Henry's head and pulled Bart close to his side for a quick hug. "You boys take care of your ma and pa, you hear?"

They nodded. Matilda knew they'd miss their uncle, and William was likely to miss her sons. He would make a wonderful father someday.

Jane packed the food into her wagon.

"Is there anything I can do to help?" Matilda asked.

The younger woman glanced at the bulge of Matilda's pregnant stomach and then quickly away. She pursed her lips. "We're ready to leave. Just need a bit of sleep and we'll roll on west."

Matilda embraced her nephew's wife again. Nicholas was right. William and Jane were old enough to make their own decisions. Perhaps it was just too hard for Jane to see her, Mrs. Watts, Mrs. Knighten, and Mrs. Jory with pregnant bellies and Mrs. Nelson with her newborn when she hadn't been able to conceive. Maybe someday she would give birth or reconcile herself to life without children.

"I'll pray for you to have a safe journey." Matilda gathered her boys to return to their camp.

"Matilda …" Jane glanced up from her packing. "Thank you for teaching me to cook."

"You're a quick learner." Matilda smiled. "You'll keep William well-fed on the journey, although I do wish you were going with us."

"I know but … William and I just need to find our own way, together, with or without children."

"God has blessed you with a good man in my nephew, and he loves you so much."

Jane shrugged. "I wish I could be sure. If I can't give him children…"

"You know he loves you." Matilda embraced the younger woman. "Just look in his eyes. They follow you everywhere you go. He's truly besotted."

Jane leaned back with a smile. "Thank you, Auntie. I needed to hear those words."

"We will see you both in the Willamette Valley."

The company stopped early the following evening. While Nicholas took care of the oxen, Matilda grabbed a couple of baskets and herded her boys back along the trail to a shrubby hillside covered in spiky bushes dotted by dark berries—currants, by the look of them. A berry pie would prove a welcome treat for her weary family. She and the boys spread out to pick the ruby red and dark purple berries.

As the sun dipped toward the western peaks, Matilda felt a presence, stopped, and swiveled. Rawlins stood behind her.

"Oh, my!" She lifted a hand to still her pounding heart. "You startled me."

She looked toward the left to see her sons a few dozen feet away, picking berries. Johnny played with rocks at Bart's feet. What would he do to her out here so far from the camp? But in front of the boys?

Or would he harm her sons? Tension gripped her stomach. She pursed her lips.

"Mrs. Koontz." Rawlins drawled her name as if he liked the sound of it.

"What can I do for you?" Matilda laced the words with ice.

"Now isn't that a leading question?" Rawlins chuckled.

She ignored him and returned to picking berries. But she quickened her movements, the evening calm destroyed.

"I thought perhaps you'd like help." Rawlins tipped back his hat. "Lord knows that husband of yours isn't likely to assist you."

"I have plenty of helpers with my boys." Matilda pulled her skirts away from the prickly bush and moved toward her sons.

The tall man reached out a hand as if to stop her. "Wait, now. I just want to talk."

"Don't touch me!" She jerked her arm away and marched toward Bart. "I thought you'd have learned your lesson last time you encountered Nicholas."

Facing her sons, she tried to keep her tone casual. "Boys, it's time we returned to the wagon. We have enough berries for a pie."

Rawlins laughed and sauntered back toward the camp. Oh, why did that man bother her so? She shivered and rubbed her arm against her side, as if wiping away a print he never left.

As the company followed the Sweetwater, they passed an elderly Indian woman on the trail beside a makeshift shelter.

"I wonder why she's out here all by herself." Matilda directed her comment to her husband as he stood beside the captain.

"I'll find out." Captain Magone approached the woman, hunched over with a blanket wrapped around her, and spoke briefly. She gestured. Shrugged. He nodded and walked back.

"She's says she's from the Snake tribe," he told them. "Most likely Shoshone. Up north a ways. Seems she's old and sickly, so they cobbled together a hut from branches and left her here to die."

"That's awful!" Matilda gasped. She hurried to her wagon and unwrapped a cloth containing biscuits. Nicholas accompanied her as she held out the food to the woman, though they had little extra to spare.

The woman grasped the food close to her chest. She bowed at the waist and quickly stuffed an entire biscuit into her toothless mouth. Matilda hoped she wouldn't choke.

As word spread about the woman's fate, others brought food too. Nobody had much extra food, but their compassion won out when they saw the thin, elderly woman.

When the company moved forward, Matilda kept looking over her shoulder at the woman in her ramshackle makeshift hut. How could anyone leave an elderly woman alone to fend for herself until she died? But as quickly as the thought flitted through her mind, conviction hit. After all, she had left her mother. Not alone, but … she pressed a hand against her chest, trying to ease the pang of guilt.

She had left her mother in Missouri. Sure, Philip and Sarah would look after her, and Jane and Hiram too. But when Philip and Sarah traveled west in a year or two, what then? Mother's care would fall entirely on her sister. Matilda sighed. What else could she have done? She couldn't abandon her husband, either.

The wagon rolled past shortcuts along the way, but Magone opted for the well-worn route, which had carried earlier emigrants safely to Oregon. Matilda was glad, especially after hearing the disastrous results of the shortcut taken to California by the Donner party.

A few days later, the emigrants were setting up camp when Rawlins shouted.

"Indians!" He pointed to an approaching group of about thirty riders on horseback. "They're coming this way!"

"Don't panic." Magone cautioned everyone to keep quiet and follow his lead. "Men, form a half circle with the wagons. Women and children, stay inside the circle and set up camp. I suggest you women cook some extra supper. We may need to feed them as a gesture of friendship."

Nicholas stood beside the captain. "What kind of Indians are they?"

"I think they're Sioux, like we saw at Fort Laramie, or maybe Shoshone," Magone responded before addressing the company. "Men, you cluster those animals near the opening of the half circle. I want twenty-five armed men lined up on the other side, guarding the animals, wagons, women, and children."

Everyone rushed to follow the captain's orders. Nicholas retrieved his loaded rifle from the wagon. Matilda's hands shook as she tried to start a fire. What if the Indians were hostile? Would they attack and slaughter her children?

"Henry." Nicholas gestured toward Matilda. "Help your ma with the fire."

"But Pa, I want to stay with you."

"You heard me. No arguing."

Henry raced to Matilda's side and grabbed the matches from her. He lit the campfire. Once it ignited, he ran back to his father.

As the natives neared, Magone signaled the chief to halt. He gestured for him to dismount and sit.

The chief, a quiver of arrows looped over his shoulder, slid off his horse and strode toward the captain. After they sat in the dry grass, the chief reached into a pocket. He pulled out a long-stemmed pipe and filled the bowl. Matilda didn't know whether he stuffed it with tobacco or something else. The chief lit the pipe, inhaled, and blew smoke into the air. Then he handed it to Magone.

A younger Sioux beside the chief served as interpreter. "It's peace pipe." He gestured toward the smoke.

Magone inhaled and handed the pipe back to the chief. He raised his hand to his lips to mimic eating. The chief nodded.

"Ladies!" Magone shouted toward the women. "Bring food for our guests."

Matilda and the other women shuffled forward tentatively, arms loaded with bread, biscuits, and bacon, which they set beside the captain before scurrying back to their wagons. She took stock of their remaining supplies. Would they run out before they reached a fort? But they had little choice. They needed to keep the peace, and if food would do it, they'd scrimp a bit on their rations.

Magone gestured to the food and then to the chief and his tribe behind him. The interpreter spoke in another language. Several stepped forward to collect the food. After they ate, the chief stood. The natives mounted their horses and rode away.

Matilda released a pent-up breath she didn't realize she'd been holding.

Hours later, Matilda found herself still shaking.

Nicholas wrapped his arms tight around her. "Are you cold?" He pulled up the quilt covering their bedroll. "I could grab that buffalo hide."

"I keep thinking what could have happened today if those Indians hadn't accepted the food." Matilda shivered.

Nicholas stayed silent as he caressed her shoulder and rubbed his other hand over the whiskers on his chin. "I'll admit I was a mite worried myself, but it worked out fine. Captain handled it well, didn't he?"

"Yes, he did. But what if—"

"Now there you go fretting again over what might have been. It didn't happen. It won't happen."

As she started to question him, Nicholas rested his chin on the top of her head, rubbed the mound of her belly with his rough calloused hands, and changed the subject. "What are we going to name this little one? It's a girl I'm sure of it."

Matilda rolled over to face him and rested her hands on her husband's. She chuckled. "How can you know? That's just wishful thinking on your part."

"We could call her Matilda. Little Mattie. Pretty as her ma."

"Or Nicholas, after his pa."

"I told you I don't want a son of mine called Little Nicky." He shook his head. "I had to grow a head taller than everyone before I could shake that nickname."

He kissed her before rolling onto his back to sleep.

Matilda struggled to quiet the "what ifs" running through her mind. She prayed the words from Isaiah 41:10. "Fear thou not; for I am with thee: be not dismayed; for I am thy God: I will strengthen thee; yea, I will help thee; yea, I will uphold thee with the right hand of my righteousness."

Finally, she drifted off.

As they neared South Pass, they met a lone wagon heading east along the Oregon Trail. Matilda shook her head, baffled. Why would anyone who struggled so hard to reach the promised land in Oregon Territory return east?

"Name's Grant." The patriarch of the family of six introduced himself.

"You realize you're heading the wrong direction?" Nicholas laughed. "Think you might want to turn around."

"Oh, no." Grant said. "We've had our fill of Oregon Territory."

"What do you mean?" Magone asked.

"In the first place," Grant said, "they have no bees there so we can't have any honey; and in the second place, they can't raise corn, and whar they can't raise corn, they can't raise hogs, and whar they can't raise hogs, they can't have bacon, so I'm going back to old Missouri whar I can have corn bread, bacon, and honey."

The response prompted laughter, but for Matilda, it sparked uncertainty. She glanced at the man's wife who looked exhausted. She shuffled to her side. "I imagine the trip out west was hard enough," she said. "But coming back? Is that what you want to do?"

The woman gazed at Matilda and sighed. "Yes, I do. I miss my family."

A military colonel carrying orders east accompanied Grant and his family. He talked about the cost of goods in Oregon City, higher than back home but not exorbitant.

"For a dollar you can buy a bushel of wheat or ten pounds of sugar or a ready-made shirt," he said. "Coffee costs two dollars for ten pounds, and salt is seventy-five cents a bushel. But you can eat all the fish and speckled trout you can catch."

Later that night, Matilda questioned her husband. "Nicholas, what if Mr. Grant is right? What if this promised land isn't all it's supposed to be?"

"I think that fellow just wound up homesick." Nicholas stuffed another spoonful of beans into his mouth. "He probably couldn't make a go of it because he didn't try hard enough. That won't happen to us."

Twenty-Two

July 1847, South Pass to Fort Bridger

JUST BEFORE THEY REACHED SOUTH PASS, a gently sloping route through a valley of sagebrush, Matilda picked up a bucket and grabbed Johnny's hand. "Henry. Bart. Grundy. Let's go pick berries again." She had spotted what looked like gooseberry bushes growing among the thickets and rocks.

"I want to help Pa with the cattle." Henry turned pleading eyes toward his father. "Can I, Pa?"

Nicholas glanced at Matilda, and she smiled. He nodded at his oldest son.

"You other boys go with your ma and help pick those berries. I'm hankering after another one of her delicious pies."

Matilda handed a tin bowl to Bart and, looking over her shoulder to ensure they weren't being followed by Rawlins or anyone else, led the boys toward the rocky hillside. They trudged toward an incline.

"We'll need to be careful," Matilda said. "The branches have sharp spines."

She spotted a bush and drew the boys to it. "These small red berries will taste good in a pie. I thought they were gooseberries, but I believe they're called currants."

Bart plucked a berry from the bush but jerked back. He examined a scratch on his hand, wiped it on his trousers, and then reached for another.

"I'll look over there." Grundy climbed a few feet uphill.

Matilda hummed as she picked berries. Johnny plucked one berry, scratched his arm on a thorn, and wailed. After examining his injury, Matilda kissed the scratch. "Perhaps you should play in the dirt while I pick." She set him in the dry grass near her feet.

With dusk fast approaching, Matilda called to her boys.

Grundy, who had climbed uphill to an overhanging rock, hopped from one boulder to another, holding the tail of his shirt in both hands to cradle his berries. When he landed on a pointed boulder, it flipped over. The rock slid down the slope into sagebrush, toppling Grundy into the dry grass.

"Snake!" Grundy grabbed his right leg. "I think it bit me."

"Grundy!" Matilda dropped her bucket, lifted her skirts, and raced up the hill. She struggled to keep her face calm as terror shot through her body when she heard the telltale rattle. A yellowish-brown serpent slithered toward a large rock.

She knelt beside her son. "Where? Where did it bite you?" She rolled up his pants and searched in vain for telltale fang marks.

"Ma?" Bart asked. "Was it a rattler?"

"I think so. Run find your pa. Hurry! Johnny, you come sit beside me."

Bart raced toward the camp, hollering as he ran. "Pa! Help!"

"Where did it bite you, Grundy?"

Her five-year-old pulled his leg toward his chest. "I think it was … here." He whimpered as he pointed toward a tiny red mark, then to a scratch below it. "Or here."

Matilda pulled out the handkerchief tucked in her sleeve. She wrapped it around her son's thin lower leg, just above the marks, and cinched it tight. *God, please don't let Grundy die. Oh, God. Please.*

She glanced up to see Nicholas tearing through the grass and hurdling rocks as he raced to her side. He plunged to the ground and pulled out a knife.

"Where?" he gasped. "Where did it bite?"

"Here." Matilda pointed to the red mark on her son's rapidly swelling leg. "He's not entirely sure it bit him. I packed hartshorn in the wagon as Hastings advised."

Nicholas gripped his knife in his right hand and sliced an X over the spot. Grundy screamed and squirmed as his father bent forward and sucked, then spit. Nicholas repeated the maneuver. Again. And again. Then he swiped the back of his hand over his mouth, smearing blood.

Matilda cradled Grundy's head as he sobbed and caressed his quaking shoulders, praying all the while, grateful for her husband's quick actions.

"I don't want to die, Mama!" Grundy cried.

Johnny began to wail.

Bart, who had reached them, bent at the waist, palms on his knees as he inhaled deep breaths. He picked up his littlest brother. "It's okay, Johnny. Don't cry." Tears streamed down his face as he spoke.

Captain Magone darted from the camp followed by Henry.

"What's happened, Nicholas?" The captain bent beside him. "Is Grundy all right?"

Nicholas sat back on his heels. "I think so—if I got out all the venom. I've sucked enough blood out of his leg to feed a whole passel of leeches."

Grundy's sobs soared into a high-pitched scream. "I don't want to die! I don't want to die!"

Nicholas lifted Grundy from the grass. "Come on, where's my brave boy? You're not going to die. I've sucked out everything short of your bones. You'll be fine lickety-split."

He nuzzled Grundy's head with his chin as he carried him toward the wagon, speaking in a reassuring voice. Bart followed, Johnny's hand clasped in his.

Matilda sat among the rocks. Tears pricked her eyes as she tried to stand on trembling legs. The captain cupped her elbow and helped her up.

"Mrs. Koontz, I think he'll be fine. Nicholas cut right over the marks." He gave her a sober look. "Leg's swollen, and it might bruise, but I believe he drew out most of the venom."

"I don't—" Matilda's voice caught, and she swallowed. "I don't know how I would survive if…"

She collapsed into sobs.

The man ten years her junior lifted an arm but then dropped it. Instead, he let her weep.

That evening, after the boys had fallen asleep, Matilda tidied up the camp, lips pursed. She reflected on the harrowing events of the day, the snakebite, her husband's quick action, how close she had come to burying Grundy along the trail.

Nicholas squeezed her hand. "Time to go to bed, don't you think?"

She shook her head.

"What is it? You mad at me?"

"We could have lost our son today." She glared at him. "We uprooted our family and traveled months along this dusty trail—for what? So we can bury our babies along the route?"

Nicholas circled her waist with one arm. She struggled to free herself.

"Now, Mattie, the same thing could have happened at home. Grundy could've been bit by a copperhead or water moccasin, same as a rattler here, but he's just fine, and he'll have a good story to tell when we land in Oregon."

"Sure, if he makes it to Oregon." She untangled herself from his arm. "And did you see Bart's hand? That scratch looks like it's festering."

"You cleaned it with whiskey and vinegar, didn't you?"

"Of course I did, but that's no guarantee it won't worsen."

Nicholas caressed her cheek. "It'll heal." He wrapped both arms around Matilda and drew her to his chest.

She cried, stifling sobs so as not to wake the boys. "Grundy could have died. What's next? Who's next?" How could they ever survive this treacherous journey—all of them, alive and healthy? "Why did we even leave Missouri? Pointless. It's all pointless if anyone dies."

"Grundy's fine. I doubt that snake even bit him deep. You put enough hartshorn on his leg to kill a mountain lion. Just a flesh wound from what I could see." Nicholas stroked her back. "We'll be all right, soon as we get to Oregon."

"If we get to Oregon!" She shifted away from him.

"Aw, Mattie, you know I'll take care of you and the boys." He tipped her chin up to gaze into her eyes. "Let's get some sleep."

Later that night, Matilda sat beside Grundy as he slept in the wagon. He tossed and kicked off his blanket. Sweat poured from his tiny body. He jerked awake and sat up, panting.

Matilda placed a cool cloth on his forehead. "What is it, Son?"

Grundy shook his head. He stared at her, terror in his wide eyes. She embraced his quivering body and drew him onto her lap.

"Oh, Ma. I had a terrible dream." He clutched her cotton bodice in his small fists. "Snakes, hundreds of them, chasing me down the mountain."

"Hush now. You're safe." She rubbed his back.

"I ... I think I'm..."

Grundy clutched his stomach and hurled vomit onto the wagon bed. "I'm sorry, Ma."

He collapsed back onto the bedroll, his thin body trembling.

"Oh, Grundy ..." Matilda bit back tears. "I can clean that up easy enough. Let me look at your leg." She lifted the blanket and examined his wounded leg, twice the size of his other one. Bruising spread up the leg from the bandage she had placed on the cut. She placed a hand on the reddened leg. It was warm to the touch.

"Am I gonna die?" Grundy gasped the words.

She lifted the bandage, gently holding the leg so it wouldn't pull. A blister formed above the cut. She pressed gently on the bubble. Liquid shifted beneath her fingers.

"Ma?"

"Hmmm…"

"Am I gonna die?" Grundy asked again.

"Oh, honey, no." She pulled his warm body to her chest in a tight hug. Was he feverish? "Your father sucked out all that snake venom." She looked him in the eye. "Remember, he told you?"

Grundy nodded.

"Do you want some water?"

He shook his head. "I don't want anything in my stomach."

She gently laid him back on the bedroll as his leg muscles twitched. He relaxed, his breath returning to an even cadence. *God, please preserve this precious boy's life.*

After Nicholas returned to the hillside with Bart in the morning to retrieve their baskets, he handed the red berries to her. "Here you go." He rubbed his stomach. "I'm looking forward to that pie you promised. Think you intended it for Henry's ninth birthday, but it's three days past July 16th."

She had forgotten Henry's birthday? She sighed. He hadn't said a word. Days on the trail just ran together. But she was his mother. How could she forget?

That night, Matilda baked the currants into a large crumbly cobbler. She lifted the Dutch oven from the fire and placed it in front of her eldest son so he could have the first serving.

"I'm sorry we're a little late celebrating your ninth birthday."

"It's okay, Ma." He glanced at her. "I knew you didn't forget."

Oh, the faith her sons had in her. She had forgotten, but she hugged him and kissed his cheek.

"Let's celebrate!" Nicholas lifted his eldest son from the log where he perched and tossed him over his shoulder.

"Pa!" Henry shouted.

Nicholas swung around in a circle, then pretended to drop his eldest boy but caught him before he hit the ground. Henry's scream morphed into laughter.

"Me too, Pa!" Johnny wailed. "I want to swing."

Nicholas bent to look their youngest in the eye. "It's Henry's birthday, not yours." He slid the older boy onto the ground and glanced at him. "What do you say? Should I swing Johnny on your birthday?"

Henry grinned. "Yeah. Throw him high!"

Nicholas grabbed the three-year-old and tossed him into the air, catching him as he plummeted toward the ground, screaming and laughing. "What about you, Bart?"

"Naw, that's okay." Bart backed away, but Nicholas lowered his head like a ram and ran toward him. He locked his large hands around the boy's waist and twirled as Bart laughed.

"What about me?" Grundy asked from the wagon, where Matilda insisted he lie with his leg elevated after consulting *Gunn's Domestic Medicine*. "I want to swing, too."

Nicholas let Bart slide to the dirt and strode to the wagon.

"Nicholas." Matilda shook her head.

"I'm not going to swing him, Mattie." Nicholas ducked into the wagon. "But a few tickles won't hurt his leg."

Grundy burst into peals of laughter. "Oh, it hurts!"

Matilda rushed to the wagon. "Your leg?"

"No, my stomach!" Grundy gasped for breath. "I need to go."

Nicholas guffawed and backed away. "He needed to laugh on Henry's birthday, too, right?"

She grinned at her hardworking playful bear of a husband. Their boys loved wrestling with their father.

Nicholas lifted Grundy from the wagon and headed into the woods.

Matilda watched Grundy with care to see if he exhibited any more snakebite symptoms. He vomited again and complained of aching muscles. Her normally rambunctious third son was so weak. She wrapped a salve of hartshorn and honey on the swollen red lacerations left by her husband's knife.

As they entered the mountains at more than seven thousand feet elevation, temperatures dropped, with patches of white on shaded ground even in July. Snow-covered peaks melted into the Sweetwater River. Temperatures dipped so low at night that water nearly froze. The heavy wagons rolled past a small mountain lake surrounded by pine trees and crossed several streams emptying into the Sweetwater.

"Why are we fording this river three times?" Bart asked his father.

Nicholas swallowed a spoonful of beans. "Cap'n said we'll be fording it six more times before we leave it."

"Nine times?" Bart asked, eyes wide. "Pshaw!"

Nicholas nodded and tousled his second son's hair. "That's right. Nine times."

"Oh, my," Matilda said. "Will our things stay dry?"

"Tar's holding good underneath the wagon. We'll be fine."

After they forded the Sweetwater the ninth time, Matilda stared in wonder as she beheld for the first time water flowing west instead of east. "Nicholas?" She pointed to the stream flowing away from the Sweetwater.

Nicholas followed her gaze then guffawed. "There's your proof, Mattie! We've just crossed over the Continental Divide—water's flowing toward the Pacific now." He winked at her. "Oregon Territory—here we come!"

Shortly thereafter, they finally found good pasture for the stock near the beautiful mountain-fed Blacks Fork of the Green River, bordered by quaking aspen.

They also faced a shock.

As they rolled past a place where earlier travelers had camped, they spotted a freshly dug gravesite and stopped to read the inscription: "William Powell, 1820–1847."

The company paused for a moment. Matilda remembered the young man who had been a close friend of one the captains, Elijah Patterson, who led the group that was willing to travel on Sundays when they divided the company.

"What could have happened?" Matilda whispered to Nicholas.

He shook his head. "Hard telling. Maybe some sort of disease." Nicholas plopped his hat back on his head.

If the man died of illness, had it spread to others in their company? And what about William and Jane traveling behind them? Would her nephew wind up in a grave along the trail? Or his wife?

"If it was disease—what if …" Matilda whispered a prayer. "Oh, dear God, protect them."

"Now don't go fretting again. I can see it on your face." Nicholas strode to the lead team of oxen and urged them forward. "Worrying won't do anyone any good." He called over his shoulder. "William and Jane are fine."

Matilda and Johnny walked beside the wagon; Bart sat on the wagon seat with the reins in his hands while Nicholas plodded beside the animals; and Henry rode Belle. Grundy lay inside.

"When we going to reach Fort Bridger?" Bart asked.

"I'm guessing five more days," Nicholas said. "We might even see the mountain man himself."

"What's he like?"

Nicholas laughed. "I've never met him. But I've heard stories about the Virginian." As they walked, he spoke of Jim Bridger's prowess as a mountain man and trapper, an Army scout, and guide. "He learned to speak to the Indians in their languages so he could trade with them. I hear tell he speaks French and Spanish, too."

"What's the fort like?"

"Probably about like Fort Laramie—the one that used to be called Fort John, right Johnny boy?" He grinned at his youngest son. "Bridger named it Rocky Mountain Fur Company, but that's too big a mouthful, so folks shortened it to Fort Bridger."

"Mama, I'm tired." Johnny pulled against Matilda's hand. "Can I sleep with Grundy?"

"Let's check on your brother." She climbed onto the wagon seat, Johnny clutched in one arm.

"Ma?" Grundy poked his head out the hole in the canvas. "Can I walk now? My leg's better, and I'm tired of staying in here."

"Let me see." Matilda pulled up the bottom of his trousers and examined the leg, no longer inflamed and nearly the size of the other one. "Come on down for a bit. But don't overdo it."

He scrambled to the edge of the wagon seat and jumped.

"Grundy!" Matilda shook her head. Incorrigible. Her boys healed fast. Bart's scratch faded completely, and Grundy ... well, he raced ahead of her toward the Browns' wagon. She gently stepped from the wagon and pulled Johnny with her. "What do you say we play a game?" Matilda bent at the waist, hands on her knees, and gazed into her baby's eyes. "How about a guessing game? You guess what I'm looking at, and I'll try to find out what you see."

TWENTY-THREE

Late July and Early August 1847, Fort Bridger to Fort Hall

WHEN THE COMPANY FINALLY rolled up to Fort Bridger on the Blacks Fork of the Green River, nearly four hundred miles from Fort Laramie, Nicholas noted the contrasts between the two forts. Unlike Fort Laramie's large well-stocked structure of thick adobe walls, Fort Bridger consisted of two rough-hewn log buildings with a few smaller ones inside a wooden fence. A pen between the large buildings held horses. A blacksmith shop offered axles, and oxen grazed in the grassy valley inside a corral.

Nicholas joined Magone and the other men entering the largest building.

A grizzly-looking man who appeared to be in his forties introduced himself. "Jim Bridger," the legendary mountain man said. "Look around, stock up on supplies, rest awhile."

"It's a true pleasure to meet you, sir." Nicholas stepped forward to shake his hand. "I've heard plenty about you."

Bridger waved a hand and chuckled. "Half of it's sure to be lies."

Magone gestured toward the women who had followed the men inside. As they spread out to examine the goods, he addressed Bridger again. "I wondered if you could show us the route going forward."

The famous Army scout removed his hat, pulled down a rolled map, and spread it before them. A native approached and Bridger spoke to him in another language. When the man left, he tilted his head. "Shoshone."

"How many languages do you speak?" Nicholas asked.

"Shoshone. Sioux. Bit of Arikara and Cheyenne. Some Kiowa. Spanish. French." He shrugged as he counted them off on his fingers. "Of course, English. I guess that's eight."

Nicholas let out a low whistle. "Well, I'll be. That's mighty impressive."

"Met a lot of people exploring this wilderness." He squinted at the map, deepening the lines on his weathered face. "Lot of mountain men, Canadians, and Creoles from St. Louis living here. All of them wanting to trade."

Nicholas caught his wife's eye. She shook her head and left. Prices must be mighty high here too.

Magone, Nicholas, and a couple of other men leaned over the rough map before them.

"Mormon trains are heading south toward the Great Salt Lake," Bridger pointed to a spot on the map. "But if you're going to Oregon or California, you've got to go north to Muddy Creek and cross the Bear River Mountains."

Nicholas looked at the two routes drawn on the rough parchment, one leading north and west, the other due west.

"You hear about that Donner party?" Nicholas asked.

Bridger grimaced. "Terrible business."

"Do you know where they went wrong?"

Bridger chewed on the wad of tobacco in his mouth before aiming spittle in the general direction of a spittoon. He squinted at the map and drew a line with his finger. "Those folks started late and took a shortcut, that there Hastings Cutoff, and wound up stranded in winter." Bridger pointed to an unmarked westward route. "Snow fell early and hard."

"They stop here?" Nicholas asked.

"Sure enough. Late July, I figure—they must have left later than you folks. Stayed about four days." Bridger scratched the stubble on his chin. "Since they were late, a fellow here, James Clyman, thought that cutoff might save them four hundred miles. Would have, too, but they cut through a new route to the Wasatch Mountains to avoid Weber Canyon, and it took them too long. They were already about a month late reaching Truckee Lake when a snowstorm hit, dumped twenty-five feet of snow, and blocked the path." He shook his head. "Shame what happened."

"But what they did …" Magone said.

"Can't say as I blame 'em."

Audible gasps greeted his statement.

At the incredulous look on the men's faces, Bridger asked, "You ever been so hungry you feared you might die?"

Nicholas pondered the question. He might joke about dying, but he'd never been hungry enough to truly perish.

"I'm not saying it's right, what they did." Bridger rocked back on his heels. "I'm saying I can understand why they did it."

"But eating folks?" Nicholas wasn't sure he'd heard right.

Bridger held up both hands. "Now, don't get me wrong. I ain't never eaten a person, but I've found myself mighty hungry at times. If it's a choice between dying and eating a dead friend, well, I guess it won't bother the dead friend none."

Nicholas gulped.

"Don't let the women hear you talk like that." Magone shook his head. "They're worried already."

"Stick to the worn path and you'll be fine, long as you don't linger too long any one place." Bridger leaned to the side again to spit, this time hitting his mark. "You'll want to pass through the Blue Mountains before it snows—and it looks like you might just have enough time to do it."

By August, even Nicholas' rambunctious boys tired of the continuous travel.

"How much longer will it take?" at least one of the boys asked daily so Matilda didn't need to do so.

"We're closer all the time," he responded. "We've already come nearly two-thirds of the way. Only five hundred miles to go."

"Five hundred miles?" Bart repeated.

Matilda repeated the words in her mind too. The journey seemed endless.

"We'll be there before you know it." Nicholas tousled his son's hair. But his words rang hollow as dust swirled, covering everything inside and outside the wagon.

When skies darkened and thunder rumbled, Matilda relished the cool rains washing dirt from her face and clothing.

"Look boys," she said, twirling in the rain. "It's bath time— straight from the heavens."

"No soap though," Henry said.

"I can remedy that." Matilda climbed into the wagon for a cloth and the bar of lye soap and tucked them into her pocket. As the warm rain poured, she scrubbed her face and hands before turning to each of the boys.

"Oh, no you don't!" Henry scrambled away from her. "I like being dirty."

"Me too," Grundy echoed.

Matilda simply laughed. As long as the rain fell, her boys would be cleaner than they were this morning.

Each mile brought them closer to Oregon, but she couldn't help worrying about what danger lay around the next bend.

Whenever boredom set in, Matilda entertained the boys by clipping long pieces of string and tying them into loops.

"Who can make Jacob's ladder?" she asked.

"I can," Bart responded. He twisted the string around his fingers until they formed what resembled a ladder. "Let's play Cat's Cradle, Grundy."

His younger brother moved closer and stuck his fingers between the string, twisting until he held the cradle.

Henry swung a ball tied to a string, trying to catch it in a cup, but even that proved tiresome after three months on the trail. Matilda shared Bible stories, sang hymns, and pointed out birds, flowers, and plants, but the farther west they ventured, the fewer names she knew.

The oxen hauled the Koontz wagon over the Rocky Mountains, trudging slowly uphill but much faster on the descent into beautiful valleys with cool mountain streams and grassland upon which the cattle could graze.

Nicholas hopped off the wagon and walked back to where Matilda hiked up the trail with the boys.

"Soda Springs up ahead," he said. "We'll make camp there. Joe wants to hold a meeting to talk about dividing again."

"Why are we dividing again?" Matilda asked.

"Some folks want to cut off to California, while the rest of us will head to Oregon." Nicholas shrugged. "Maybe we'll be fortunate and Rawlins will leave."

"Nicholas." Matilda lowered her voice but couldn't quite hide the hint of a smile on her face. Her husband was still convinced his nemesis set the wagon canvas afire when they first started the journey. Maybe he had.

As the sun dipped behind a ridge, she strode to the wagon and pulled out the cooking utensils to cook dinner. "Henry, will you fill the bucket with water?"

"From the springs?"

"Yes," Matilda said.

He left to do as she asked but returned with a sour look on his face. "Ma, this don't taste like water."

Matilda frowned and picked up a tin cup, then dipped it into the bucket. She swallowed a sip of water and grimaced.

Nicholas laughed. "That's why they call it Soda Springs," he said. "Tastes like soda water." He pointed to the cattle licking the ground near scrubby cedars and pines. "That salt's a treat for the oxen."

"But what do we do for drinking water?" Matilda asked.

"Captain said we can add sugar to make it taste okay."

"Sugar?" Matilda looked inside the wagon. "We're running low on sugar. How far until we can buy some more?"

"Think the next place is Fort Hall." Nicholas ran a hand down his beard. "Think about seventy miles or so. Not quite a week. Will it hold out until then?"

Matilda nodded. "I imagine so. But the price of sugar is likely to be quite dear at the fort."

"You let me worry about that, Mattie. We still have a few coins."

He settled in for dinner with the boys around him.

"Tell us another frontier story, Pa." Henry loved adventure, and his father's stories of childhood misadventures the most.

"Well…" Nicholas swallowed a bit of stew and gnawed on his biscuit. "Let's see. Did I tell you about the time I tried to break a horse, and it broke my arm instead?"

The boys gazed at their father, waiting for him to continue.

"I must have been about your age, Bart, maybe eight." Nicholas recounted the story, perhaps embellishing the size of the horse or its wildness, but he stretched out his arm to show the scar where bone had broken through his skin.

"Did it hurt?" Grundy asked, absentmindedly rubbing his snakebit leg.

"Sure did." Nicholas finished his dinner. "But it hurt even more when the old doctor shoved that bone back where it belonged. Eee-yii! I'll tell you it hurt. I screamed loud enough to wake the dead."

"Nicholas?" Captain Magone stepped into their camp. "You ready for our meeting?"

"Sure, Joe." He swallowed the rest of his coffee, rose, and walked away with the young captain.

Matilda washed, dried, and put away the dishes, then settled down to sew clothes for the new baby before the firelight faded. Wolves and coyotes howled in the distance.

Twenty-Four

"MEN," THE CAPTAIN RAISED HIS VOICE and his arms to quiet the crowd. "We're approaching Fort Hall, so anyone who wants to go to California can cut off on the southern trail." He asked for a show of hands, but nobody responded.

"California?" Rawlins scoffed. "Who in their right mind would go there? Bunch of Spaniards. And Catholics to boot."

"Is there anyone you do like, Rawlins?" Nicholas shook his head. "Besides my wife, that is."

"Your wife is far too good for the likes of you."

"She'd never look twice at you, Rawlins. I doubt any woman would."

Magone stepped between the two men, arms raised, and Nicholas scowled. They'd been on the trail for too long—punching Rawlins in the face would certainly raise his spirits.

"I guess we'll all be going north to Fort Hall and on to Oregon Territory. Let's rise earlier tomorrow. We've got to make better time. We're falling behind. Snow will fly in the Blues before we know it."

Back at their camp, Nicholas watched Matilda as she sewed. "Do you need something?" she asked, tying a knot and biting off the end of her thread.

"Nope. Just thinking how lucky I am to have such a handsome woman for my wife."

When her face flushed red, he laughed aloud. He wrapped his arms around her waist and nuzzled her neck. "Every man who meets you wants you for his wife."

"Now that's just silly." Matilda returned to her sewing.

"That Marcus threw away the best woman in the world when he broke your engagement."

"Nicholas!" She flushed a deeper red. "Hush now. The boys will hear."

"Think they don't know I'm crazy about their ma?" He swatted her on the behind. "I need to talk to Joe a minute before guard duty. By the way, the captain said we're leaving earlier tomorrow morning."

She nodded as she put her sewing basket inside the wagon.

Nicholas tramped across the clearing to where Magone sat beside his fire, straddling an empty barrel.

"Sorry about getting in Rawlins' face earlier." Nicholas pulled out his pipe. "Guy opens his mouth, and I want to punch him."

Magone chuckled. "Think he has that effect on others too."

"But at least you don't have a wife he wants. The way he looks at Matilda, I just want to pluck his eyes out and feed them to the buzzards."

Magone laughed. "Better not do that. I promised I'd get everyone to the Willamette Valley safely. That probably means with both eyes, too."

Nicholas chuckled but then sobered. "Appreciate you and Jory keeping an eye on Matilda on nights when I'm standing guard."

"Sure enough." Magone sipped his coffee. "You've got a nice family. Good boys."

"That I do." Nicholas blew smoke from his lungs. "I'd better go relieve Jory."

⚜

"Lookee-there, boys!" Nicholas pointed in the distance. "Three Buttes! That Hastings fellow said it means we're almost to Fort Hall."

The boys cheered and pranced.

"How long until we arrive?" Matilda lugged Johnny on her hip as they walked beside the wagon.

"A few more days, maybe."

Sure enough, three days later, they rolled into Fort Hall and camped just beyond it. They set up in the midafternoon and the women washed clothes, watched the children, and relaxed.

Nicholas strode to the fort beside Joseph Magone and James Jory, his money pouch lightweight in his hip pocket. He wanted coffee and more pipe tobacco. Matilda asked for sugar too. Knowing frontier prices, it might take all the coins he had left. He stepped inside a long square building of sunbaked clay bricks and gazed at the supplies stacked on shelves. He whistled. "Would you look at those prices?" Back home, he could buy ten or twelve pounds of coffee and sugar for a dollar. Here they cost a dollar for one pound!

Magone opened his eyes wide. "Guess they can charge what they want. Not much competition hereabouts. If you need something, this is the only place to buy it."

"Don't need it that bad. Oregon's only a month or so away, right?"

"Let's see. It's August 23rd. I reckon six or seven weeks, based on what I've read." Magone glanced out a window. "We'll connect with the Snake River to the west and follow it to the Columbia, and then we'll follow that nigh on to Fort Vancouver."

The captain stepped to the counter to speak to the proprietor, Captain Grant. A corporal who stopped at their camp a few weeks ago had mentioned that this British fellow, Grant, liked French Canadians but wasn't fond of Americans. That was another reason Nicholas preferred to keep his money firmly in his pocket and out of Hudson's Bay Company's hands.

But they needed coffee and sugar. He wanted tobacco, but he could ration himself till they reached Oregon City. He pulled out a pouch to pay for the goods when his gaze stopped at a crimson bonnet that hung from a peg, pink and blue flowers dancing across it. A matching infant bonnet was nestled beside it.

"How much?" he asked, nodding toward the head coverings.

"Four bits for each."

Nicholas grimaced. "Too rich for my blood."

The proprietor halted him as he started to leave. "Give me four bits; you can have both."

Fifty cents? But wouldn't Mattie be surprised when he gave it to her after the birth of their baby girl? He handed over the coins. "Can you wrap it for me? I want to surprise the missus."

After Grant folded paper around the bonnets, Nicholas grabbed the package along with his coffee and sugar, then wandered to a table where a couple of grizzled men sat swapping stories. Jory followed. Sounded like hunters or trappers. They spoke in a mixture of English and French. A couple of natives stood beside the table, leaning against the wall.

"Headed to Oregon?" one of the mountain men asked Nicholas.

"Sure enough. My wife, four sons, a company headed by that young man." Nicholas tilted his head in Magone's direction.

"Lose anyone on the trail?"

Nicholas thought a moment. "A little girl. Then the son of a friend—wagon ran him over." He cleared his throat at the thought of Frank's death. "Broke up into smaller companies a couple of times. Been a good group." Just then Rawlins skulked into the store. "For the most part."

Jory swiped a hand before his face in a failed attempt to hide his grin.

"What can we expect up ahead?" Nicholas glanced at the Indians. "Friendly?"

"Oh, yes. They're friendly. Give you the shirt off their backs, the Nez Perce. Even trade you for salmon and camas roots, kind of like onions or potatoes."

"The Cayuse, though—" Another man inserted. "Not too happy 'bout all the white folks coming and bringing diseases. Measles. Cholera. Diphtheria. Don't like fences none either."

"Cayuse?" Nicholas asked. "I can't keep one tribe straight from the others. But most of 'em are friendly, eh?"

The men at the table concurred.

"Won't see them till you arrive at Waiilatpu."

"Waiilatpu? What's that?"

"Whitman's Mission. A doctor and his wife set up an outpost near the mighty Columbia River about a decade back. Missionaries. Might want to rest up there on the trip west."

"That close to Oregon? After traveling this far?" Nicholas laughed. "Not a chance. I'll be heading west as fast as I can go. Don't want to wait to start building my cabin."

Nicholas chuckled as he shook hands with the men at the table. "Thank you kindly." He and Jory headed out the door.

"We're likely to have a few more delays," Jory offered. "Sarah may be giving birth any day, and Mrs. Watts, too."

Nicholas rolled his eyes. "Can't be helped, I suppose. But do they need an entire day to recover?"

"I imagine so." Jory said.

"You've never been through it before. After Johnny was born, Mattie climbed out of bed and fixed dinner." Nicholas laughed. "Of course, he was her fourth, so he arrived pretty fast." He glanced at the clouds forming in the sky. "Just wish I knew how to make the others birth quickly, so we hit the trail faster."

TWENTY-FIVE

August to Early September 1847, Fort Hall to Three Island Crossing

MATILDA SLAPPED HER NECK. Yet another mosquito bite. "These skeeters are huge." Henry smacked his bare arm. "They're like to eat me alive."

"Put on a shirt with longer sleeves," Matilda said. "That'll give them less skin to gnaw on."

John Watts, who was about Henry's age, ran into their camp.

"Mrs. Koontz," he said, breathless. "Ma asked me to fetch you. It's her time."

"I'll be there right away." Matilda retrieved clean cloths from the wagon. "Henry, I need you and Bart to watch the younger boys while I help Mrs. Watts. Your pa should be back soon."

"Yes, ma'am," Bart asserted.

"Want to play marbles?" Henry nudged John Watts toward a flat area near the wagon.

"Sure." The other boy followed, pulling a bag from his pocket.

"Did you hear me, Henry?"

"Yes, Ma." Henry pulled out his own bag of marbles. "We'll watch 'em."

Matilda hustled to the Watts' wagon, arms laden with cloth, soap, and a butcher knife to cut the umbilical cord. As she arrived, she spotted Mrs. Knighten, nearly ready to burst with a baby herself.

"Are you feeling better after your scare?" Matilda asked.

"Oh, thank you, yes." Louisa "Lou" Knighten clutched her hands to her heart. "I thought sure this baby and I would die when our wagon sped toward that cliff." She wiped a tear. "Might well have, too, if not for the quick thinking of our captain."

"Nicholas told me about it. Joseph raced before the oxen and grabbed their reins, didn't he?" Matilda asked. "Veered them away from the drop-off?"

"Just in time, too." Lou rubbed her swollen belly. "I never could have jumped from the wagon quick enough if he hadn't stopped the beasts."

"He's a fine young man." Matilda heard a groan from inside the wagon. "I'd better check on Johanna. Do you think Sarah might like to help?" Matilda asked. "She's pregnant with her first, and perhaps it'll ease her mind if she knows a bit more what to expect."

"Probably. I won't need help when my time comes. Plenty of womenfolk in our family. But I'll fetch Sarah now," Lou Knighten sighed. "Big as I am, I won't leave much room in the wagon if I'm in there. I've put on a kettle of water to boil."

Matilda smiled and climbed onto the wagon seat. Peering inside, she spied Johanna sitting with her back against a dresser.

"Thanks for coming. I'm more than ready for this little one to arrive." She panted a bit and then laughed. "Tired of trying to lace my boots without being able to see my feet."

"I do know the feeling." Matilda chuckled.

"Ah, but you've still got a few months to go, and you're carrying it close. Not like this whale. Ohhh—"

Matilda set down her armload. She dipped a cloth into a basin of water and placed it behind Johanna's neck. "Would you like me to rub your back?"

She assented with a nod, her teeth clenched.

Sarah Jory peered inside the wagon. "May I do something to help?"

"We're going to need that hot water soon, it looks like." Matilda wiped Johanna's brow again.

Between groans, she ground out words. "Susan. Where is she?"

"Mrs. Knighten's watching your little one," Sarah assured her. "They're playing pat-a-cake."

"Oh, she loves that one—un—un!"

"Mr. Watts just returned from the fort." Sarah set down the kettle of hot water. "Do you want me to fetch him?"

"Whatever for?" Johanna laughed. "He'd be absolutely no use to me now." She rubbed her tight abdomen. "He's already done his part."

Matilda knew the feeling. She loved Johanna's sense of humor.

"I see the head," she told Johanna. "Your baby will be here any minute."

Matilda handed the wet cloth to Sarah and motioned for her to wipe Johanna's brow. The young woman's eyes widened. It was good for her to see the birthing, so she'd know what to expect when her time came. Within a month, from the looks of it.

As she sat back on her heels, she prayed Johanna's would be a simple birth. She dipped a cloth in the hot water and waited for it to cool.

Johanna tightened her legs and groaned.

"It's time to push now." Matilda saw the dark hair as the baby's head crowned. "Push, Johanna! Push."

Johanna groaned and writhed. "Something's wrong," she panted. "He's stuck."

Matilda slid her fingers inside, checking the baby's position. All was well. What could be wrong?

Johanna screamed.

"Hold on, Johanna." Matilda shifted her position to check the baby's neck. Oh, no! The umbilical cord was wrapped snug around it. She tugged but couldn't free it.

"Argh!" Johanna sat up. "I've got to…." Another scream and a push.

The baby's head slipped through the opening followed by the shoulders. His skin was purple.

Matilda gripped the wee boy in one hand and, with the other, slit the cord around his neck.

She paddled his bottom. Nothing.

"What's wrong?" Johanna gasped. "My baby ..."

Oh, dear God. Matilda pried open his tiny mouth and wiped her little finger inside, pulling out mucous. She puffed into the thin lips. Come, little one. Breathe.

The infant whimpered. Matilda sagged in relief. Thank You, God.

After a thin wail, he sucked in air, and the purple tinge faded to red. She wiped the blood from the baby's body. "It's a boy. A big boy."

Johanna gave a soft laugh. "Boy. Girl. Boy."

"Sure enough. John and Susan have a little brother. Do you have a name yet?"

"Lewis. Lewis Wesley."

"Welcome to the world, little Lewis Wesley Watts." Matilda whispered softly to the baby and then passed him into Sarah's arms. Her eyes filled with tears as she handed the baby to his mother.

"How long we gonna stay here?" asked Henry.

"It's only been nine hours since Johanna had her baby," Matilda answered. "Rest is important after giving birth. We'll probably be back on the trail by tomorrow morning."

Sure enough, the next morning, the company moved out, following the path where heavy wagon traffic ground the earth into fine powder. As the oxen shuffled through it, dust shrouded animals, wagons, and people.

The more stories they heard, the more Matilda thanked the Lord for the camaraderie of folks on their wagon train. Some companies experienced fights, bickering, and constant criticism. She credited the cheerful young captain for keeping everyone working together toward the common goal.

Matilda couldn't abide riding in the wagon as the constant jolting and lurching made her wonder if that baby might jostle right out of her womb. Instead, she walked beside the wagon, but not too close after the scare earlier on the trail with Johnny and Henry. She held Johnny's hand as often as possible.

Although bruised, Henry's arm seemed to have healed well. It looked like Grundy escaped permanent repercussions from his encounter with the snake too. What next? Illness could sweep through the company at any time and claim the lives of her boys.

A shrieking wail pierced the air. Lewis Watts had a good set of lungs—truly a blessing since she wondered if he'd ever breathe at all. She smiled and massaged her abdomen, wondering about the baby inside. Perhaps Nicholas was right. Maybe they'd have a daughter this time. She loved her boys so much, but she would cherish a little girl.

The company followed the Snake River. Squinting through a dust cloud, she could scarcely see the oxen's horns. Although she swept the wagon every night, dust covered everything—clothes, bonnets, barrels, and the wagon's canvas. Grundy washed his cloth frequently while clearing the oxen's nostrils each evening. Grit coated even the biscuits and their teeth as they ate.

When they settled into camp, Matilda prepared the same meal she'd cooked most days. The fare remained simple and plain.

"Beans and biscuits again?" Henry asked in a voice just shy of a whine.

"Now, Henry," his father admonished. "We have to make do with what we have while on the trail."

"How long till we get to the Willa—Willa—Oregon Territory?" six-year-old Grundy asked.

"Willamette Valley," Nicholas answered. "About six weeks."

"Six weeks?" Grundy asked. "How long is that?"

"More than a month, ya coot." Henry jostled his younger brother.

Borrowing the stick in Grundy's hand, Nicholas drew a map in the dry dirt. "See here, this is our house in Missouri. We've crossed the plains and South Pass; we've been going through the Rocky Mountains and passed Soda Springs and Fort Hall…"

"The place with all the skeeters," Bart said, scratching his arms and swatting his face.

"Yep, that's Fort Hall." Nicholas nodded. "Then we crossed through that gap in the rocks to that flat prairie above Raft River. Remember? We saw a few wagons from other companies headed south to California."

The boys nodded again. Matilda smiled at her husband as she watched him earnestly explaining their journey yet again to their sons.

"Now we're here at Rock Creek—finally a place to water the livestock. We can jump in the water tomorrow and clean some of that grime off you." He lifted the chins of both Henry and Bart, squinting as he brushed dirt from their faces. They laughed.

"So, see, we've come all this way already—over the mountains, across the desert, up and down hills. We're on an adventure, boys, to our new home. Where are we going?"

"Willamette Valley!" the boys shouted in unison.

"You bet," Nicholas said. "Next, we'll cross the Snake River. We'll stop at Fort Boise for a spell. Then we'll reach Oregon Territory."

Henry raised his fist in the air and shouted, "Oregon!" His younger brothers did the same.

Nicholas looked back to the drawing.

"Then we have one more set of mountains to cross before we follow the mighty Columbia River to the Willamette Valley where we'll build our new home."

The boys jumped up, prancing around the fire.

Matilda sighed. A new life away from the dusty trail sounded wonderful.

"Now we're all tuckered out so crawl into that tent and close your eyes." Nicholas stood and tapped his pipe against a rock to dump the ashes. He started to refill it but instead tucked it into his pocket. "Joe's holding a meeting to talk about crossing the Snake. I'll be back shortly." He kissed Matilda's cheek before striding past more than a dozen wagons toward the captain's rig.

She sat on a log, relishing the coolness of the coming darkness. A rustling sounded in the brush, likely a rodent. An owl hooted. The pale moon darkened to golden in the sky as the sun dropped below the horizon.

Thank You, God, for blessings in my life. My husband, a good strong man whose dream of reaching Oregon will be fulfilled soon. My four boys, each one precious and precocious. She smiled and pressed against the little foot or elbow poking into her rib. And this little one.

If she peered closely above, she could almost see the face of God smiling down on her family.

The company reached the Portneuf River, a tributary of the Snake, and traveled a mile farther to find a better place to ford. The advent of September brought freezing temperatures at night and fearful dread of crossing the Blue Mountains in a snowstorm.

They met a group of Nez Perce who spread blankets before them with beaded necklaces, berries, some sort of bulbs or tubers, and smoked salmon as what they called gifts for their new neighbors. They didn't beg for food as the Sioux and Kaw had earlier on the trail.

Matilda found the native women friendly as they cradled babies at their breasts and pointed at her protruding stomach.

When one older woman patted her belly, Matilda stood still, startled. Nicholas frowned, but Matilda simply smiled at the woman and nodded. She gathered her boys to her skirts and gestured that they were all hers.

The woman held up four fingers. Then she added her thumb, pointed again at Matilda's stomach, and laughed.

"What's she crowing about?" Freda shuffled up beside Matilda.

"She's just being friendly." Matilda rubbed her abdomen. "Counting my children. Mothers' talk is rather universal, isn't it?"

Freda's brow rose. "I suppose." She shrugged. "We're all the same if it comes down to it. We eat. We sleep. We birth babies. We …"

"Yes, we do." Matilda glanced at her boys, eyeing the jewelry, moccasins, and food on the blankets. "Come on, boys. Back to the wagon."

"Aren't you going to take some of this?" Freda lifted a chunk of salmon. "They're not even charging for it."

"I'm sure some other family is in greater need of it than we are." But she licked her lips as she eyed the berries.

"Free?" Freda rolled her eyes. "You're passing up free food? Not me. Not with my hungry crew."

Young Nez Perce boys and girls, all barefoot, raced behind the adults, playing in the dirt.

"Ma?" Henry tugged Matilda's arm. "Please? Can't we at least try the fish?"

The Nez Perce mother who had touched her abdomen stood with berries in one hand, salmon in the other. She thrust it toward Matilda. "You eat." She nodded toward her bulging belly. "For baby." She smiled at Henry. "Big boys."

Matilda smiled as she accepted the gifts. "Thank you." She reached inside her pockets, but they were empty. She had nothing to offer in exchange. Passing a hand over her head, she smiled. Yes, she did have a gift. She handed the food to Henry before untying her bonnet and holding it out.

"Are you crazy?" Freda asked. "You'll perish from the heat with the sun beating down on your head without a bonnet."

"Hush now." Matilda admonished Freda but kept her eyes on her new friend. "I have another bonnet in the wagon."

Freda harrumphed. "Well, I'm keeping mine right on my head— where it belongs."

The Nez Perce woman reached for the light blue calico and placed it atop her coal-black hair. It slipped to one side, askew.

Matilda moved forward to adjust the cloth.

The woman jerked back.

Mimicking the tying of a bonnet, Matilda shuffled closer. The woman stood still as Matilda positioned the cotton bonnet over the dark locks, shifting the brim to shield her eyes from the sun and lifting the long dark braids to the back before tying the laces. "You look lovely," she said.

"Ridiculous, more like," Freda mumbled as she shook her head.

Matilda pursed her lips, then smiled at the woman. Retrieving the food from Henry, she lifted her hands. "Thank you."

"Qe'ci'yew'yew." The woman tipped her head. *"Qe'ci'yew'yew."*

Freda grabbed Matilda's arm. "Let's get on back. Next thing I know you'll be giving her your skirt."

Matilda herded her boys back to the wagon, sighing as she parted ways with Freda. She loved her spunky friend, but that woman could try the patience of a saint—and the good Lord knew she was no saint.

"We need to pack up now." Matilda placed the food inside the wagon.

As the oxen plodded uphill again, hauling the heavy rigs to the summit of the Portneuf Range and down again, a roar rumbled in the distance.

"Hear that, boys?" Nicholas grinned. "Twin Falls. We'll reach the Willamette Valley in a month."

When the boys groaned, he added, "We'll be there before you know it."

The company reached the foaming falls later that afternoon. Lush green trees on either side of the rocky bluffs created a gorgeous backdrop to the powerful force of the Snake River spewing through a canyon and splitting around jagged rock. Whitewater cascaded upward as the two waterfalls forked and dropped several hundred feet before the river blended, flowing northwestward to the Columbia River and then the Pacific Ocean. A prism of color glistened as the sun touched the riffling mist.

"Whoa—look at that waterfall!" Henry dashed forward and stopped near the edge of the roaring river.

"Henry!" Matilda hollered. "Stand back from the edge."

"I can feel the water spraying me!" Henry giggled and wiped the moisture from his face.

Bart and Grundy ran to join him. Matilda held tight to Johnny as he tried to follow. "You stay right here, young man." Matilda watched her older boys. "Step back from the edge. Now!"

Her heart raced as she envisioned them toppling into the river, tiny heads and bodies broken as they dashed against the rocks, torn and twisted by the raging water. She turned to her husband. "Nicholas. Make them move back from the edge."

"Woman, you worry too much." He winked at her.

She glared at him as the boys shuffled closer to look over the rocks where the frothy water tumbled into a pool below.

He sighed. "All right, boys. You heard your ma. Step back from the edge. We'll have plenty of time to swim later where it's not so rocky."

That night, the burbling rumble of the falls lulled her to sleep.

But in the wee hours of the morning, Matilda awakened to the sound of a baby's cry. She heard whispered voices and knew Lou Knighten had given birth. She thanked God for a new life in the camp—and added her gratitude that she wouldn't give birth until after they had settled in the Willamette Valley.

When they rose the morning of September 4, everyone gathered near the center of camp. Lou's husband, Wiley Knighten, stood to the side of Captain Magone, his infant son in a blanket cuddled in his arms.

"Just want to introduce you all to the newest member of our company," he said, raising the bundle.

"Maybe we ought to stay an extra day, given what you named that young'un." Magone chuckled as he grinned at the bundle in Wiley's arms.

"What'd you name him?" Nicholas asked. "Not Ammon after your father?"

Everyone knew that their seven-year-old daughter bore the name of Wiley's mother, Frances "Fannie" Knighten.

"Joseph Magone Knighten." Wiley said, announcing each word with pride. "After our brave captain."

Cheers erupted.

TWENTY-SIX

September 7, 1847, Three Island Crossing

THE SNAKE RIVER SLITHERED like a serpent around rock formations and dove over lava rock into a deep pool below the canyon.

Matilda longed to plunge into that cool lake and rinse the trail's dust from her body, especially after the last couple of days rolling across thirty miles of dry land, eying the river below but unable to reach the water without descending steep, stony paths suited only to mountain goats.

Rubbing her hand over her rounding middle, Matilda knew better than to try. Instead, she thanked God for His beautiful creation and took solace in the warm evening rain that washed her body and clothes.

The smooth water of the Snake River rippled as salmon leapt to the surface and dove below again. At Salmon Falls, Indians with nets caught the slippery fish and traded for shirts, bacon, and other goods. At night, the emigrants used sagebrush as fuel for fires, having left buffalo chips behind on the Nebraska prairies.

Finally, the company arrived at one of the few spots where the river left the canyons and spread out enough for wagons and cattle to cross.

Captain Magone called the men together that Tuesday morning, September 7th, to discuss whether to cross the river.

"Grassland's better on the north side, from what I've read," Magone said. "We'll have easier access to water, too."

"Let's cross then," Rawlins shouted. "What are we waiting for?"

Magone held up his hands. "Whoa, wait a minute. I'm not finished." He gazed at those around him. "This here crossing at the Three Islands can be dangerous. The river looks calm enough, but they say the current is strong." He wiped a forearm across his brow. "Deep holes, too, might injure some of the stock. Whirlpools could suck under an ox or tip a wagon."

Matilda glanced at Nicholas. Danger, they didn't need. She tugged his arm and shook her head.

He pursed his lips. "What's the alternative?"

"Stay on the south side," Magone answered. "Though since it's so high above the river, finding water might be difficult."

"Maybe we should just keep going on this side," Rawlins said.

"More reliable water from mountain streams on the north side." Magone shrugged. "I'll do whatever the majority decides. Raise your hand if you want to cross here?"

"Looks quite tame to me," Wiley Knighten said, lifting his hand as he gazed at the wide expanse of placid river.

Matilda looked around. Nicholas kept his hands at his sides, along with a couple of other men, but more than three dozen others raised theirs, including Rawlins. That decided it. They would ford the Snake to the north side at Three Island Crossing.

Matilda groaned as the baby kicked. "I don't feel good about this," she said, rubbing her stomach. "Maybe ..."

Nicholas rested his hands on her shoulders and pulled her close. "We'll be fine." Striding toward their camp, he hollered for the boys to help him set the yokes on the oxen and hook them to the wagon. "We'll be at Fort Boise before you know it. Then the Blue Mountains, the Columbia River and—"

"The Willamette Valley!" Henry and Bart shouted the words nearly in unison.

The oxen dragged the wagons toward the water's edge.

Magone, seated as usual on his stallion, shouted at his dog. "Dash in, Ring!"

The hound jumped into the water and paddled, floating downstream before reaching the other shore. Magone nosed his horse from the shore into the river. Water flowed up to his haunches as the stallion stepped lightly across the first two islands and sandbars. At the third island, the horse lost his footing and stumbled. Magone held tight to the reins as the stallion lunged forward and swam across and up the other side.

"We'll stretch a rope across to guide the animals," Magone shouted. He looped one end around a tree trunk and stretched the rest behind like a long tail as he rode his stallion back across the river to the waiting wagons.

On the other side, he pulled the rope taut and tied it to another trunk.

"We've got underwater holes just past that third island." Magone gestured toward the small shrub-covered islands. "It's fine for horses, but the oxen may have trouble. We'll need to keep them heading straight across, even if they swim, but as you can see by where Ring climbed out, the downstream current's strong."

Matilda stood beside the wagon and eyed the river with skepticism, a sense of foreboding filling her. "It looks dangerous."

"No more so than any other," Nicholas said. "All those rivers we've crossed, and we never so much as tipped our heavy load off-kilter."

Matilda tried again. "Nicholas, maybe we should—"

"Woman, I've said it before," he added with a chuckle, "If I was born to be drowned, I won't be hanged—and if born to be hanged, I'll never be drowned."

"I don't want to see you hanged or drowned," Matilda said, her voice somber.

"The water looks calm." He gestured toward Magone. "Besides, the majority voted to cross, and we need to stay with the captain and the company."

They watched lighter wagons ford the river, a few tilting as the current rushed against the wooden wagon sides before the oxen hauled the waterlogged rigs up the bank on the far side.

Then Wiley Knighten led his oxen into the water. One ox bobbed beneath the surface, and the wagon lurched sideways, its rear drifting downstream with the current.

Matilda bit her lower lip. Would it topple? Were Lou and the baby inside?

Water pulled the rear of the wagon down and two barrels spilled into the river, floating downstream, before the rig righted itself.

James Jory stopped his wagon beside the Koontz rig. "Looks a mite dangerous, I'd say." He looked at Sarah, whose baby was due any day, and drew her closer. "Wish us luck."

The Jorys' oxen lugged their wagon through the deep water. Just past the second island, the wagon drifted downstream.

Matilda gasped.

Jory slapped the reins on the backs of his team. "Get up! Haw!"

The cattle churned the water before struggling up the far bank.

Nicholas glanced at Matilda. "Looks like it's our turn."

She pursed her lips. Nodded.

"Henry, you and Bart ride Belle over to the other side," Nicholas ordered the older boys. He lifted Bart onto the mare's back as Henry hopped on. "Now you grab the saddle horn and don't panic if she starts swimming downstream, you hear?"

Both boys nodded.

Matilda gripped Johnny in her arms, Grundy beside her, and watched her two older boys on the horse's back. She whispered a silent prayer as Belle stepped onto the sandbar, splashed through the water between the two islands, and then trotted onto the third.

"Come on, Belle." Henry encouraged her in a loud voice as he leaned over the mare's neck. "Keep going."

Bart held tight to Henry's waist as the mare trotted into the water. Matilda held her breath as the mare scrambled and then began to swim.

Bart slipped to the side.

She screamed. "Bart!"

His legs pointed downstream, his grip on Henry's waist tugging the older boy askew off the saddle.

Was she going to stand here and watch her two oldest boys drown? Her stomach clenched in a contraction. Why? Why are they even risking their lives in this river?

The mare barreled up the slope on the far bank, and Bart slid to the ground. Matilda exhaled in relief.

"Mattie, climb into the wagon and hold tight. You too, Grundy." Nicholas urged their six oxen into the river and hopped onto the bench. The wagon lurched forward. Matilda laced one arm around Johnny's waist. Her other hand gripped the side of the wagon. Nicholas sat beside her with Grundy behind them.

"Relax." Nicholas kissed her cheek. "Just say one of those prayers. He'll see us across this river, just like He helped those folks cross the Jordan."

The wagon's wheels plunged into the water and jolted to a halt in the sand.

"Come on, Duke. Pet. Baul. Browny. Giddyup!"

The wagon jerked forward again, careening over the sandbar and into the water. After the second island, the animals plodded into deeper water that rose past their haunches. Praying, Matilda clutched the wagon's side and pursed her lips, tightening her grip on Johnny as her stomach clenched.

Only one more island to go. Why was she so afraid? After all they'd been through, they'd surely make the crossing here.

The current pushed the oxen downstream. Old Buck slid beneath the water.

"Uh, oh." Nicholas stood, slapping the reins as he cursed under his breath. She detected worry in his voice as he muttered, "Come on, Buck!"

When Old Buck scrambled to the surface, she heaved a sigh.

But the ox's horns caught in the guide rope. He plunged beneath the water again. Rising, the ox tossed his head, bucked, and twisted, trying to free his horns.

Nicholas groaned as he stripped off his shirt and boots. "I'm going to have to untangle him."

"Be careful!" Matilda squeezed Johnny tighter.

"Woman, if I was born …"

"I know, I know," she said. "Please … just … be safe."

"I will, sweet girl." He winked. "My angel is praying for me, right?"

He dove from the wagon seat into the water and swam with strong strokes toward where Old Buck thrashed against the current, bobbing beneath the water, struggling again to the surface. Whitewater foamed where the panicked ox reared his head and kicked his hooves while the rest of the team lurched forward, wild-eyed, trying not to be pulled under.

Nicholas dove beneath the water.

Matilda held her breath.

Seconds passed.

Where was he?

Her heart thudded as she counted the seconds.

A full minute now.

How long could someone survive under the water?

Her stomach twisted, like someone wringing a dish towel. Blood rushed to her temples, pounded in her ears.

She screamed. "Nicholas!"

"Pa!" Henry shouted from the shore. He raced to the water.

Matilda shifted her gaze to her son. "No! Henry!" She stood on the wobbling wagon seat. "Stop!"

Captain Magone whirled his stallion and rushed to the river. He slid off the horse's back and scooped Henry into one arm just as the boy tried to plunge into the Snake.

"Stay here." The captain dropped Henry onto the grass and dove into the water. He swam to where Old Buck floundered, tossing his head, horns somehow freed from the guide wire. Magone urged the animals forward. As they swam, the wagon jerked. Matilda fell to the seat and gripped the side.

She stared into the water.

Where was Nicholas? He was only joking about drowning. Just like he always did. "Where was he?" Magone shouted to Matilda.

She pointed to the once-frothy water, now placid. Tears streamed down her face.

Oh, dear God, no. Not Nicholas.

Magone dove beneath the water.

He surfaced. Hope swelled in Matilda but quickly fled when she realized he was empty-handed.

He dove again.

And again.

The oxen yanked the wagon toward the other bank. Matilda clutched Johnny tight.

"Mama, you're hurting me." Her youngest son squirmed in her arms. She loosened her grip, eyes scanning the water.

No. No. No.

She twisted her neck to watch the captain.

Please, Nicholas, come up for air.

The wagon rumbled onto the far shore. Matilda scrambled down with Johnny in her arms, Grundy on her heels, and ran to Bart and Henry. She held them both tight. Grundy clutched her skirts.

"Ma?" Bart asked. "What can we do?"

"Pray," she whispered.

Magone surfaced again, swam to the shore, and swung onto his horse. "I'll check downstream."

Other men ran along the river. Several dove into the water.

Matilda shook her head. Nicholas couldn't drown. He could swim circles around the strongest swimmer. Maybe the current pulled him downstream.

He'll surface.

He's a survivor.

Nothing can hold him back.

This journey was his idea. It's his dream. He'll be there at the end to see it through. This is all just a silly mistake.

Her legs trembled. Then her arms. She slid Johnny to the grass, lest she drop him.

Searing pain ripped through her abdomen, doubling her over. She tried to inhale but couldn't catch her breath. Warmth streamed down her inner thighs.

Dear Lord—help me! It's too soon for the baby to come!

"Nicholas," Matilda wailed.

"Mrs. Koontz." Sarah Jory wrapped an arm around her shoulders. "Come, sit down. Let me help."

"The boys—" Matilda sobbed. "Please. Take the boys. Don't let them see this."

She fell to her knees, arms clutching her stomach, teeth gritted in pain.

"Mama?" Johnny searched her eyes and grabbed her skirt. Then he howled. "Mama!"

Mrs. Jory picked up the toddler. "Boys, let's go set up camp."

"No," Henry barked. "I'm going to find Pa."

Bart and Grundy stood still, crying.

James Jory approached.

"Boys, let's go into camp." He put one arm around Bart and the other around Grundy. "We'll fix you something to eat while we wait for news."

Staring at the river, Henry darted downstream.

"Henry." Matilda's voice squeaked. "Come back!"

"I'm gonna find Pa." He raced away. "He swam downriver. I know he did. I'm gonna find him."

Matilda collapsed onto the ground as pain ripped through her. Then ... darkness.

◦◈◦

Snippets of conversation filtered through her mind, but Matilda couldn't open her eyes.

"How is she?" James Jory asked.

"Mrs. Knighten says the baby's coming—but it's too soon." Matilda recognized Sarah's voice.

Where was Nicholas? He should be beside her if the baby's coming. Where are the boys? Matilda tried to lift onto her elbows.

Her body refused to move. Her eyes gripped shut no matter how hard she tried to open them.

"She's lost a lot of blood," said Fannie Knighten, Lou's mother-in-law. "I don't know if she'll have the strength to push the baby out."

"Did they find him?" Sarah again. *Find who? What is she talking about?*

"Oh, James." A sob from Sarah Jory.

Who are they looking for? Not one of her boys. They were with Nicholas, weren't they? Nicholas? Where was he?

"I don't know what she's going to do. How—who—" James Jory again.

"Without her husband," Sarah whispered. "A widow with four young boys."

A widow? She wasn't a widow. Nicholas ... we were crossing the river. Memories flooded her. Nicholas kissing her lips. Stripping off his shirt and boots. Diving into the river. The water ... he never surfaced.

No. It's a mistake. A nightmare. She must be feverish. Because what would she do without Nicholas? He couldn't have drowned. Not her strong bear of a husband. He's invincible. He'll come strolling into camp at any moment, laughing about his swim downstream.

"I can't imagine he's gone," James Jory said. "He's so ... full of life." A sob choked his voice, cutting off his words.

"We'll do what we can to help." Sarah's voice. "I'll watch the boys."

"You're going to have your hands full pretty soon, dear. Magone will help with her wagon. The boys—" James choked on the words.

Nicholas cannot be dead. She's not a widow. The boys ... had they watched their father drown? Their hearts must be shattered. He was everything to their sons. They adored their father. She struggled again to sit up. Her body wouldn't move.

Sharp pain jolted through her again. Matilda groaned.

"The baby's coming." That was Mrs. Knighten.

A blanket lifted. Her body trembled. Pain. Agony. To ease her pain, she tried to roll over on the mattress inside the wagon. She couldn't move. Couldn't breathe. Was she dying too? Her boys. Silent sobs pierced her heart. She couldn't leave her boys without their mother too. Where are You, Lord? She moaned.

"I'll keep the boys occupied." James Jory's voice again. "Take care of her. She's all those boys have left."

A scream. *Who is screaming? Johnny?* No. It was her. *How could she scream when she couldn't open her eyes?*

"Is she gonna die too?" Oh, poor Henry. He sounded so brave … but the tremor in his voice betrayed his angst. *No, Henry, I won't die. God, please don't let me die.*

"I'm sure Mrs. Knighten knows how to care for your mother," James Jory said. *Thank God for the Jorys. They'd watch her boys until she was stronger.* "The Browns said you older boys can stay with them until your mother is feeling better. We'll keep Johnny here with us, close to his ma."

"Are they going to keep looking for Pa?" Henry asked.

"We'll have to ask the captain," Jory responded.

"Jory." The captain's voice. Matilda struggled to awaken. Why couldn't she? A sharp knife shot through her abdomen. Not a knife. A … argh! A moan escaped her lips as she struggled to awaken, to listen, to live.

"Boys." The captain cleared his throat. "I'm real sorry about your pa."

"You're still looking for him, aren't you?" Henry asked.

"I don't know, Henry. We've searched a couple of miles downstream. We saw no sign of him."

"We have to find him!" Henry's voice rose. "We just gotta find him."

"Son, I've got to tell you something. You're not going to want to hear this. But seeing as you're the man of the family now, I'm just going to say it."

"I'm not." Henry's voice choked. "Pa is."

"Henry …" Magone's voice.

"What?"

"When I was looking for your pa, swimming in that river, I found myself sucked down into a nasty whirlpool. I pert' near didn't have the strength to break away and make it back up to the surface."

Silence.

"Chances are your pa got caught in that whirlpool. I'm real sorry, Son. Might be Old Buck kicked him in the head while he was beneath the surface untangling the rope. If so, it probably knocked him unconscious. He wouldn't have known what happened."

No. Nicholas never would have... No! ... A scream.

"Ma?" Henry's voice again.

She tried to speak, to reassure him. She couldn't open her mouth. Her eyes. Darkness engulfed her. No! I need to stay awake. My boys...

A faint cry sounded. A baby's cry. My baby? Is... too early. A girl? A boy? Oblivion threatened her. Her baby...

Warmth on her chest. Her breast. The baby trying to suckle. Too weak to latch on.

Her baby... She inhaled and forced her eyes open. She needed to see her baby.

"It's a girl," Sarah told her, tears choking her voice. "A sweet girl."

A lantern light pierced the dimness inside the wagon. A tiny head, no larger than Nicholas' palm. Light hair like his. A petite nose like hers. Thin lips...like his. Blue eyes. All her babies had blue eyes.

What would they name her? She and Nicholas had talked of names if they had a girl. He wanted to name a daughter Mattie, after her. She lifted her hand, pressing the tiny mouth to her breast, but the baby wouldn't suckle. In fact, the frail wee one scarcely breathed. Would she live?... Her arm fell to her side. Tears rolled down her cheeks as blackness threatened to engulf her.

"Did I hear a baby?" Jory asked from outside the tent. "Did she have it?"

Sarah's voice answered. "A girl. But so tiny. Mrs. Knighten doesn't know if she'll live."

"How's Matilda?" James Jory asked.

"She woke up briefly when we put the baby to her breast," Sarah said. "Then she slipped back into sleep."

Matilda again struggled to respond, but she couldn't speak. Or even open her eyes.

"Poor thing. Such a shock," Jory said. "I can scarcely fathom it myself. He was only thirty-five. Such a strong man. I can't believe he's gone."

"James … are you going to tell the boys about the baby?" Sarah asked her husband.

"I'll tell them."

Silence. Her mind drifted …

"Boys." Jory's voice again. "Your mother has had her baby. You have a sister. But she's very small. And weak."

"Is she gonna die?" Bart asked.

"I can't say for sure," the British man said. "She might."

"What about Ma?" Grundy asked. "Is she … is she gonna die too?"

"I don't think so." Jory's voice again. "She's lost a lot of blood—too much. But your mother is a strong woman. She has a lot of inner strength—and faith in God."

Henry scoffed. "Pa did too."

TWENTY-SEVEN

September 1847, Three Island Crossing to the Whitman Mission

"MAMA!" JOHNNY CRIED. "I want Mama!" The sound of her son's shrill cries pierced the fog of darkness in Matilda's mind. She sat up but swayed and collapsed again.

"Johnny." Her parched throat burned. "Johnny."

She propped her elbows behind her and sat up again, slowly this time. She waited for the swaying to ease. Her head pounded as if her heart would explode through her ears. Rolling onto her hands and knees, she crawled to the opening of the jolting wagon and peered over the seat through the draped canvas. Why was she so weak? She glanced down. Her baby. She looked around inside the wagon. Where was her baby girl?

Henry led the oxen, and she spotted Bart ahead on the mare. She shifted forward to gaze right. Grundy held Johnny's hand, but her toddler screamed and pulled against his brother's grip, trying to yank free.

"Johnny."

"Whoa!" Henry stopped the oxen, ran to the wagon seat, and climbed up. "Ma? You awake?"

"Johnny can ride in here with me." Matilda whispered the words through her dry throat. "Where …?" She couldn't ask. She didn't want to know.

Henry dropped his eyes to the reins in his hands. "The baby?"

Matilda nodded.

Henry pursed his thin lips together, then thrust his head over his left shoulder. "Back there." He coughed. "She … she didn't make it."

Tears swam in her eyes. Her precious daughter. "Did they …?"

Henry nodded. "They buried her beside the trail. The captain … he made a cross."

"Your pa?"

Henry shook his head, shoulders shaking. "They never found him."

She reached a hand to touch Henry's shoulder. Nicholas was gone. Their father. Drowned in the Snake River. Their little sister … dead. Her boys had watched their precious father die. They couldn't even give him a proper burial.

Although tears flowed like blood from an open wound, she whispered, "How are you doing? All of you?"

Henry shifted his gaze to the side, his lips trembling. "I better get this wagon rolling again."

So strong for nine years old. He refused to cry.

"Where are we?"

"Grand Ronde Valley." Henry squinted his eyes. "You all right?"

"We passed Fort Boise?"

"Days ago." He tilted his head toward the back of the wagon. "You been sleeping a long time."

"I expect so."

"Mama!" Johnny wailed. "I want Mama!"

Henry climbed off the seat to the right. "Captain helped me haul the wagon back across the Snake again. Said Pa slapped enough pine tar over the bottom and sides to keep it dry. And it was."

"All the wagons get across?" Matilda asked.

"No mishaps." Henry kicked the dirt before picking up Johnny, who was whining to be lifted into the wagon.

"Thank God," she said, reaching out to grab Johnny as he scrambled through the opening into her arms.

"What's God got to do with it?" Henry asked, squinting at her. "If God cared, he wouldn't have let Pa die."

"Oh, Henry." She stretched out an arm to embrace him, but he stormed off to lead the team on foot.

Matilda pulled her youngest son to her breast and stroked trail dust from his blond hair. He clutched her tight, as if he'd never let go. Grundy hopped onto the moving wagon. "Ma?"

Matilda reached out with a free arm and pulled him into an embrace. "You ... We thought ..."

"Yes, I know." She squeezed him closer.

"The baby died." Grundy's lips trembled as he said the words. "Ma ... are you going to die too?"

"No, Honey." Matilda shook her head. "I'll be fine. Just a little weak right now." Sweat oozed from her brow. She might pass out. In truth, she yearned for the forgetfulness of oblivion.

But she needed to reassure her son. "Did you see your baby sister?"

Grundy nodded. "Mrs. Knighten let us tell her goodbye."

"I did too!" Johnny said. "I saw Baby."

Matilda forced herself to smile. "What did she look like?"

Johnny drew his brows together and thought a minute. "A potato with legs."

"Johnny!" Grundy shoved his little brother. "He even asked if he'd grow up to be a boy." He rolled his eyes. "The baby, she was ... she looked tiny ... just lying there. Mrs. Knighten wrapped her in one of the fleece blankets you made for her—the light green one."

Matilda thought back to her brief glimpse of the baby girl. Sandy hair. Thin lips. Petite nose. Her precious daughter.

"The captain kept us in camp a day so's you could regain your strength," Grundy continued. "He built her a box about the size of that." He nodded toward the Dutch oven. "The captain put her in a hole near the river. Near where ... Pa...."

Matilda nodded. "I hear he erected a cross."

"Nice one." Grundy took a shaky breath.

"Thank you for telling me." Matilda laid back. "Think I'll sleep a little. Johnny can cuddle with me."

Grundy shifted to climb down from the wagon.

"Grundy?"

He stopped and looked at her.

"Thank you for watching Johnny for me. You are such a good boy."

He beamed.

She snuggled into her bedroll again, Johnny still clinging to her. She inhaled his little boy smell and closed her eyes, picturing the angelic face of her baby girl who looked so much like her pa. She couldn't fathom what the future held for her and the boys with Nicholas gone.

Oh, God, why did You do this to me? Tears seeped from her closed eyelids before she plunged again into blackness.

That evening, when the wagon quit rolling, Matilda awoke again. She glanced at Johnny, who sat quietly beside her, stacking tin spoons and forks on her chest of goods. Utensils hung from the canvas. Gunpowder kegs beside her. All their worldly possessions packed in this wagon. She had grieved leaving her grandfather clock in Missouri. Grieved? She scoffed at her immaturity. What does a clock matter? What does any of it mean without Nicholas? Without her baby. She heard voices outside.

"Mrs. Koontz?" Captain Magone called. "Henry tells me you're awake."

"Yes, Captain." She shifted onto her elbows and knees and crawled to the opening. She thought about smoothing her hair. She must be a mess. But what did it matter?

"I'm real sorry about Nicholas." The captain stared at the ground and then looked her in the eyes. "We searched for him. Downstream several miles. We never found him."

Tears pricked her eyes. She couldn't speak, so she simply nodded.

Magone removed his hat and nodded at her. "I'm sorry about the baby, too."

She cleared her throat. "It's not your fault—any of it." She tried to comfort him, but words failed.

Magone shuffled his feet and gazed at the sky. "Be that as it may, I promise I'll do everything to see you and the boys safely to Oregon City."

Again, she nodded. But her mind raced ahead. And then what? A widow with four young boys. What would become of them? How would they find land? Build a cabin? Stake a claim? All without Nicholas?

The captain cleared his throat. "If you've a mind to, I'm sure you can find a company going east next spring to return home."

He nodded toward where the boys huddled around the fire.

"Henry's learned how to harness the oxen and drive the wagon." Magone glanced toward her eldest son. "Good strapping boy you have there. Hard to believe he's only nine."

Matilda followed his gaze. Nine, seven, five, and three. So young. Now fatherless. Tears pricked her eyes as she leaned back on the straw tick. Henry was a good boy but much too young to bear the responsibilities of a family. Oh, Nicholas. Why?

"The Browns will keep feeding your boys—and you too—until you regain your strength," the captain continued.

"When do you suppose we'll arrive in the Willamette Valley?"

"We're crossing the Blue Mountains soon and then we'll be into the Umatilla Valley." He looked at Johnny inside the wagon. "Mayhap you'll want to rest up a bit at the Whitman Mission, regain your strength."

"I'll consider it." Her limbs trembled with the effort to stay upright. "Thank you again, Captain Magone."

How could she care for her boys if she couldn't even sit upright?

The next morning, the captain helped nine-year-old Henry yoke the oxen and hook up the wagon. Matilda lay inside the wagon on the straw tick, peering through the canvas opening, Johnny by her side.

"We'll be leaving the Snake River today," Magone said to Henry. "It turns north, and we keep heading northwest toward the Blue Mountains and the mighty Columbia."

Her son nodded as he pulled down to cinch the harness to the yoke. "I'm not sorry to see the last of that river," Henry mumbled, then added with a growl, "I hate that river!"

Magone clapped him on the back. "Don't blame you a bit. I tend to agree."

Henry climbed into the wagon and Bart mounted Belle. The captain lifted Grundy to sit behind him on the mare.

Matilda raised herself enough to peer out the back opening in the canvas, watching the dusty trail fade behind them.

There it was, the slithering stretch of blue water snaking between rock outcroppings and canyons. The river they had followed for three hundred miles, the deceptively placid behemoth that had devoured her invincible husband.

The company halted briefly.

"Farewell Bend," Magone shouted. "Say goodbye to the Snake River."

Matilda crawled onto the seat for a last glimpse of the river, where she blew a kiss to bid a final farewell to her husband of ten years, her baby of ten hours. He had no cross to mark his death. She beckoned her boys to join her, embracing all four in her arms as they took a final glimpse of their father's watery grave.

Say goodbye to the Snake River? More like good riddance.

TWENTY-EIGHT

Mid-September 1847, Grand Ronde River

NEAR THE GRAND RONDE RIVER, the company saw longhouses constructed of wooden poles and covered with woven mats for the roof. The longhouses faced the river, with an opening in the top at the center where smoke curled into the sky. Black trees and the acrid stench of charred wood testified to recent forest fires in the region.

"Indians," Henry said from the wagon seat, jarring Matilda awake. "Captain Magone says they're Snake Indians."

She crawled forward to peer through the canvas opening. Both men and women in the Snake tribe wore their hair in long dark braids, most with beaded necklaces, the men shirtless with woven cloth from waist to just above the knees, the women in dresses of cloth or softened leather. Most welcomed the company, gesturing to blankets of beaded jewelry, moccasins, and food. Matilda returned to her mattress in the wagon and dressed.

Though still weak, she ventured out to trade shirts she had sewn for smoked salmon, squash, and camas bulbs. She listened to the conversation as she offered the shirts for food. A few white trappers with native wives shared tales of other wagon trains that had passed by earlier.

"One woman, she was so angry with her husband, she refused to leave camp one day," a mountain man said. "She wouldn't let her children leave either. Finally, the man drove off and left her there. His children rode with three other families in their company."

Another man took up the tale. "But she didn't stay put. She took a back trail and overtook her husband, who had sent their eldest son back for a horse he'd left at the camp. When he spotted his wife, he said, 'Did you meet John?' She said yes, but added, 'I picked up a stone and knocked out his brains.'"

Matilda gasped. A mother killed her own son?

The first man resumed telling the story. "He rode back to see if his son had indeed been killed, and while he was gone, his wife set fire to one of the wagons. Burned it all! When the man saw the flames, he rushed back. Then he mustered up spunk enough to give her a good flogging."

Matilda shook her head as she listened. She would never show her husband such disrespect. Then she took a deep trembling breath, remembering that she no longer had a husband.

She clenched her teeth and hurried back to her wagon, where she collapsed in exhaustion. How could she care for her children when she couldn't even stand for more than an hour? With her body so weak, she couldn't even care for herself, much less four boys.

She would still have a husband if they hadn't left Missouri. And a baby girl.

What was Nicholas thinking? He assured her over and over again that they'd be safe. But he lied. Of course, how could he know? But they never would have faced that river if only they'd stayed home. At least then she would have her mother's help. And her brothers and sisters.

Instead, she was thousands of miles from her family, with no future and no hope. What would she do? She lay on her bedroll and cried herself to sleep.

The trail rose into the Blue Mountains, weaving among tall pine and spruce trees. Matilda leaned against the wagon seat, watching

Henry guide the team. Bart sat astride Belle, while Grundy walked hand-in-hand with Johnny—beside the wagon but not too close.

Captain Magone rode up. "Henry, you're going to need to switch out your lead oxen a few times as we climb. Don't want to wear them out."

"Yes, sir." Henry jumped off the wagon seat and halted the team.

"Here, let me help." The captain dismounted and strode toward the head of the team.

"I can do it," Henry said, his voice faltering. "Pa showed me how."

Magone glanced at the boy. "I know you can, but I hope you'll let me help now and then. I need to make myself useful."

Matilda appreciated the captain's guidance of Henry, only nine years old but far more mature since the death of his father. He was fast becoming a man out of necessity.

Henry and the captain switched Old Buck and Jerry to the back and brought Browny and Duke forward.

"You'll probably need to do that at least two more times," Magone said. "This wagon's mighty heavy to haul uphill."

A wagon made heavier by Matilda's dead weight. She should try to walk. She dressed as the wagon lurched forward. When Henry stopped again to change out the oxen at Emigrant Springs, she crawled onto the bench.

"Ma?" Henry looked up. "What are you doing?"

"I'm going to try to walk a bit," she said. "Lighten the load."

"You sure?" Henry furrowed his brows. "You don't look like you can walk."

Grundy ran forward, Johnny in tow. "I'll help you, Ma. You can lean on me."

"I'll do that, Grundy," she said, reaching for his arm as she descended. With feet on the rocky trail, she exhaled. She could do this.

"Mama!" Johnny wailed, lifting his arms. "Carry me."

"Ma can't carry you, chuckaboo," Grundy said. "She's not strong enough."

Johnny started crying. Matilda held onto the wagon as she crouched to look him in the eye. "Can you be a big boy and hold my hand as we walk up this big mountain?"

Johnny's lower lip trembled, but he nodded.

Matilda lifted herself again. Could she walk up the mountain? Rather than a dozen or twenty miles a day, as they had covered on the prairie, with the uphill climb, the animals could make only four or five miles a day. If they could climb the hill lugging heavy wagons, she should certainly be able to haul herself uphill.

With Grundy's tiny arm wrapped around her waist and her hand holding Johnny's, she took a tentative step on shaky legs. One step. She exhaled. Two steps. The wagon lurched beside them as Henry led the oxen. Three steps. Four … Her vision blurred and she swayed. Five … Her knees buckled. She fell to the ground, face in the dirt.

"Mama!" Johnny screamed.

Grundy squatted beside her. "Ma?" He shook her shoulder.

Matilda forced herself to roll over. Why couldn't she walk? She pushed herself up on her elbows, gasping. "I'm fine. Give me a minute."

Galloping horse hooves drew closer. "Mrs. Koontz?" Captain Magone slid off his horse and rushed to her side. Turning to Grundy, he asked, "What happened?"

"She wanted to walk, but then she just fell."

Magone slipped an arm around her shoulders to lift her into a sitting position.

Matilda brushed dirt from her skirt but drew back her hand when she felt dampness. Blood tinged her hand.

"I'll carry you to the wagon and send Mrs. Knighten to help you."

Matilda tried to protest, but she couldn't even stand, much less walk back to the wagon. "Thanks…"

Magone settled her onto the straw tick and rode away.

"Matilda?" Fanny Knighten called. "It's me. Joe said you needed help."

She crawled into the wagon and looked at Matilda. "Why, you're white as a sheet." She placed a hand on her brow. "Not feverish." She lifted her skirt. "Oh, Lordy, you're bleeding." She pulled off her wet pantaloons. "You have clean rags?"

Matilda nodded and gestured to a basket.

"I'll clean you up and put on fresh underthings. You have some?"

"In the chest."

Fanny shuffled through a couple of drawers. "What's this?" She pulled out a bundle wrapped in paper.

"I don't know." Baffled, Matilda gazed at the packet. She had never seen it before.

"Well, you open it while I find your clothes." Fanny tossed the package onto Matilda's lap and continued rummaging in the chest.

Matilda held the paper in her hands. Was this something Nicholas had tucked away? Or one of the boys? No, they wouldn't have wrapped it. Nicholas then. She carefully removed the twine and unfolded the paper to find a cloth crimson bonnet with dancing blue and pink flowers.

"Oh, what a lovely cap!" Fanny said. "Where did you buy it?"

Matilda shook her head. "I didn't." As she lifted it, the smaller infant bonnet slipped onto her quilt. "Oh, Nicholas …"

Tears overflowed as she held both caps to her heart. He had bought these for her. He wanted to surprise her, maybe when the baby arrived. She rolled onto her side and sobbed.

❦

When Matilda awoke, the wagon was still. She glanced around. Fanny Knighten dozed in the corner. She was still here? How long had she slept? She struggled to sit up.

"Oh, you're awake," Fanny said, wiping a hand over her mouth as she knelt forward. "Must have dozed off."

"I'm so sorry to be such trouble," Matilda said. "You have your own family to tend."

"Nonsense," Fanny said. "Lou can take care of them."

"And the baby?"

"Of course." Fanny chuckled. "We're a hardy lot, we are."

Matilda offered a wavering smile. "The boys?"

"They're with the Browns for supper," Fanny said. "They left a bit of soup here for you." She stretched her arm for a tin. "Not warm anymore but…"

"It's fine." Matilda reached for the cup. "I'm so blessed to have people taking care of me and the boys. Thank you."

"You missed all the excitement though." Fanny ladled water into another cup and handed it to her.

Matilda sat up. "Did someone die?"

"No, no, nothing like that," Fanny said, waving her hands. "Henry Nelson nearly started a war with the Snakes."

"What?"

"When the Indians came by to trade, one hapless fellow made the mistake of peering inside Henry Nelson's tent, where Louisa was breastfeeding little George. Henry hollered at him something fierce, grabbed his ox-whip, and lashed the young man."

Matilda gasped. "No. What did the other Indians do?"

"They laughed." Fanny shook her head. "Could have turned out differently, though."

The next morning, Matilda realized the uphill climb had ended as they descended into the Umatilla Valley. They had beaten the snowfall in the Blue Mountains, although the downhill journey posed its own hazards. Despite Henry's insistence that he could do it, Magone led the oxen down the steep slope, pulling the beasts back to keep the wagon from careening off the trail and tumbling down the mountainside.

After reaching the valley floor, the company set up camp, where they were greeted by a priest who asked about his colleagues following with Bernier. They also met their first Cayuse, a man who stalked up to the black-robed priest with a crucifix hanging from his belt. The native gestured toward the crucifix and uttered words in a language they couldn't understand. He twisted his hands as if tearing the crucifix to pieces and then bellowed in rage as he tossed the imaginary pieces toward the ground. The only words Matilda understood were "black robe" and "Dr. Whitman."

When the captain stopped that night, Matilda asked him about the altercation.

"Seems Dr. Whitman's persuaded the Cayuse that the Catholic priests—black robes—are bad," he said. "At least this fellow thought so."

"Dr. Whitman?" Matilda asked. "He and his wife started a Presbyterian mission out here, didn't they?"

Magone nodded. "Eleven years ago. They call it Waiilatpu, which means People of the Rye Grass. Or people who sway like grass when they dance. Guess that's how the Nez Perce refer to the Cayuse."

"Are they friendly Indians?" Matilda asked.

"Seem to be, far as I can tell." Magone replaced his hat and tipped it to her. "Goodnight, ma'am. Rest well."

"Thank you, Captain—for everything."

A blush swept over his face. He again tipped his hat to her.

While he strode away, Matilda pondered the animosity shown by the Cayuse man.

As they camped along the Umatilla River, Sarah Jory visited … with her baby.

"Sarah, congratulations," Matilda said. "How was the birthing? I so wish I could have helped."

"Fanny Knighten took care of me fine. She said it was an easy birth—for a first baby." Sarah laughed. "It didn't feel at all easy to me." She glanced at the baby snuggly wrapped in a blanket. "But it was all worth it."

Matilda lifted her arms. "May I?"

Sarah nodded as she placed the infant into Matilda's arms.

"A girl?" Matilda asked, choking a bit on the words.

"Yes," Sarah said. "We named her Phoebe Ann. Born September 13…in Oregon Territory. Finally!"

Matilda lifted the baby quilt. "She's beautiful, Sarah." A plump, healthy baby, probably twice the size of her little girl, the one buried along the trail. Her vision blurred as liquid filled her eyes. "I'll bet Mr. Jory is popping the buttons off his shirt."

"He's certainly showing her off to everyone." She chuckled as she retrieved the baby from Matilda's arms. Her face sobered. "I'm so sorry about your daughter."

Matilda nodded, unable to speak.

"And Nicholas…"

Matilda's lips trembled. She didn't want to break down again, not in front of Sarah. She didn't want to taint the joy this first-time mother felt for her baby.

Sarah cleared her throat. "Riders from a train behind us said my husband's father and brothers will catch up soon." It was obvious to Matilda that Sarah wanted to change the subject, and she was happy to let her.

"That's wonderful news. It will be so nice to have family to help with Phoebe."

What Matilda wouldn't give to have her own family here. Even William and Jane lagged behind them … somewhere.

"But James ran into a little trouble with a Cayuse."

"What happened?" Matilda asked.

"A couple of oxen were missing, and he spotted a man driving them down the slope. When he confronted him, the man responded, 'Heap water.'"

Matilda repeated the words, baffled.

"That's precisely what I said." Sarah chuckled. "Apparently, this man said he was only watering the beasts and demanded a shirt in payment for his services. James refused, of course, and pointed out he was still missing an ox. He found it, but the next day, the same man appeared again, demanding a shirt in payment. I didn't have any shirts made to offer him. The Cayuse raised his fist and gestured toward his knife, so James, thinking quickly, offered him his powder horn."

"Gunpowder?" Matilda gasped. "Isn't that dangerous?"

Sarah shrugged. "It worked. He left, probably figuring he had left us defenseless, but James, of course, had plenty of powder in his keg inside the wagon."

"It sounds rather frightening," Matilda said.

"Oh, it was." Sarah nodded. "I lay inside the wagon with Phoebe, trying to keep her quiet."

"I wonder if every company has so many women birthing babies along the trail." Matilda absently swept her palm over her flattened abdomen.

"I doubt it." Sarah chuckled. "The men keep teasing the captain about being a bachelor and having to stop the train five times for the birthing of babies," Sarah said with a chuckle, counting off on her fingers. "Mrs. Watts, Mrs. Nelson, Mrs. Knighten, my Phoebe …" Her voice trailed off and her face flushed with embarrassment. "Oh, I'm sorry, Matilda."

Matilda glanced down a moment and then Sarah changed the subject. They chatted a bit longer, but after Sarah left, Matilda sank back onto the straw tick. *Why, God? Not that I'm jealous of Sarah; I'm not. I'm thrilled she and James have a healthy little one. But why my husband? My baby? What more will You take? What am I supposed to do now, a widow with four boys, so far from family? Return east to Missouri and risk losing the boys on the route? A woman alone can't own property. Henry can't file a land claim until he is twenty-one—a dozen years from now. What will I do?*

The wagon train reached the mighty Columbia River as they approached The Dalles Mission, which consisted of several rather dilapidated wooden buildings. But the majesty of the river brought tears to Matilda's eyes, the wide expanse of blue flowing through steep bluffs and rock outcroppings. Golden grass and verdant green shrubs, willows, and cottonwoods, fir trees and maples with leaves of red, yellow, and orange dotted the river's banks.

As their train of thirty-eight wagons camped near The Dalles Mission along the Columbia River in late September, Matilda climbed out of the wagon.

"Ma?" Henry asked. "You sure you should be up?"

"I can't sleep forever." Matilda smiled at her eldest son. "I appreciate you driving the team, Henry, taking over for your pa."

He simply nodded.

Captain Magone stopped by. "Mrs. Koontz, I'm glad to see you up," he said. "Might want to come hear what Dr. Whitman has to say." He offered her his arm. "I'll help you."

She leaned heavily on his arm as they walked slowly across the camp to where the company circled around a lean man with a long face covered with bushy sideburns. So this was the adventurous physician and missionary, Dr. Marcus Whitman. He looked to be a bit older than her, probably in his mid-forties.

"Welcome to Oregon Territory," he said. "You've survived the worst of the journey."

He gestured to a packhorse. "I've brought you fresh beef."

A cheer erupted. Steaks. Fresh beef sounded delicious after months of eating beans, bacon, and biscuits. He asked for men to step forward and divvy up the meat.

As they did, he gestured toward the river.

"Any and all of you are welcome to rest at our mission." He nodded toward a mountain peak in the distance. "You'll find snow in the mountains if you take the new Barlow Road."

"I heard tell it's a rough road for wagons." Henry Nelson stood with his hands on his hips. "Reckon we can get around that way?"

"I've seen people do it with wagons, even in the snow." Whitman shook his head. "Won't be easy, though. They follow the road to the Willamette River and then to Oregon City. The road's steep and rough in good weather. Snow's likely to leave it downright treacherous."

"What do we do then?" Henry asked.

"Most folks break up the wagons here at The Dalles Mission and float them with their goods down the Columbia to Fort Vancouver or Oregon City. They can take their cattle around the Barlow Road or hire others to do it."

"What's that toll road cost?" Solomon Brown asked.

"I believe they're charging five dollars a wagon and ten cents per head of stock," Whitman answered. "Best way to move the stock, that's for certain."

Matilda listened to the conversation, baffled about what to do. Should they take the Barlow Road? Could Henry manage the team over rough terrain? He was only nine.

Magone nodded toward the missionary. "As I mentioned before, you might want to consider staying at the Whitmans' for a bit to regain your strength. They have food, medicine, beds."

She gazed at the young man, so strong and caring. What would she and the boys have done without him? She nodded.

"People staying at here at the mission?" Nelson asked.

"Not now." Whitman shook his head. "We've just bought the Methodists' mission at The Dalles with its houses, schoolhouse, and barn. Quite dilapidated really. We'll be fixing it up. But those of you who need food, repairs, or provisions can swing by our mission, Waiilatpu, before going down the Columbia."

Most of the men shook their heads.

"Naw, we're eager to reach Oregon City," one man said.

So was Matilda, but she didn't think she could make it that far. She looked around. So many people, gaunt and pale with exhaustion, ready for their long journey to end. Leaving the wagons they had relied upon so heavily for months would be difficult, but if it meant they had finally arrived in the Willamette Valley, they could do it.

Dr. Whitman then preached a sermon to renew the spirits of the gathered group of weary travelers.

"The Lord Jesus Christ saw fit to bring you safely over the prairies and mountains." Dr. Whitman caught the eyes of the people surrounding him. "Yes, some of you have suffered tremendous losses along the way. But He brought you west for a reason, to help settle the land and bring His Holy Word to the natives living here, as my wife Narcissa and I have tried to do this past eleven years. We've taught the Indians to plant crops and worship God."

As the sermon continued, Matilda watched the men and women nod assent and bow their heads to pray. Afterward, Captain Magone drew her toward the missionary. She was exhausted but managed a slight smile.

"Doctor." He shifted the rim of his hat through his fingers. "This is Mrs. Koontz, who lost her husband crossing the Snake. She lost her baby, too, and ..." He gulped. "She's been bleeding. Think you could examine her?"

A flush rose to Matilda's face.

"Of course," Dr. Whitman replied.

Magone half-carried Matilda back to the camp. What energy she'd had faded quickly. Each step required tremendous effort. He set her on one of the boys' bedrolls in the tent and exited, holding the flap open for the doctor to stoop low and enter.

Matilda lay on a bedroll, exhausted, her eyes half closed, but she struggled to sit up.

The doctor placed a hand on her shoulder. "No need. Just rest while I do a quick examination."

Matilda sank back and breathed deeply. Her eyes drifted closed again.

"You've lost a lot of blood, haven't you?" he asked.

She nodded. "The baby ... She was early. After Nicholas..."

"Your husband?"

"When ... I watched ... my stomach ... the contractions. Blood...not water...poured out."

When the doctor pressed on her abdomen, she grimaced.

"Tender?"

"A bit."

"Do you have trouble breathing?" the doctor asked, listening to her heartbeat.

She nodded. "I don't understand why I'm so exhausted." She gestured to the tent flap, where she could hear her boys arguing. "I've had four boys. I was never so tired afterward."

"Headache?"

"Constantly." She pressed her hand to her forehead. "Sometimes my vision blurs too."

"Have you coughed up blood?" the doctor asked.

Matilda glanced at the tent opening and lowered her voice before answering. She didn't want to worry her boys. "A few times."

"Might be a clot." The doctor stood. "Happens sometimes after premature birth with a lot of bleeding."

"What do I do?" she asked.

"Rest." He packed away his medical equipment. "I recommend you stay at the mission with us until your strength returns. You don't want to exert yourself if it is a clot."

She emitted a weak laugh. "I couldn't exert myself if I tried."

"I'll let the captain know you'll be heading to the mission. Maybe others will too."

Shortly after he left, Sarah Jory called her name.

"Come in," she said.

"I heard you'll be going to the mission to rest up."

Matilda nodded. She didn't have much choice. She couldn't drive the team, care for the boys, even tend to herself.

"I'm sorry you're feeling so poorly, but on the other hand, I'm glad you'll be with us when we stop." As the baby cried, she shifted Phoebe into her other arm.

"You're going to the Whitmans' place too?"

"To wait for my husband's family," she said. "They're not far behind us. We'll stay there until everyone catches up. Then we'll go on to Oregon City."

Matilda smiled and reached for the baby … without tears, this time. "I'm glad you and James will be with us."

"In fact, you'll be riding with us," Sarah said. "The captain asked if we could haul you and your chest of goods with us. He can drive your rig to The Dalles for you."

Matilda frowned. "Do you have room for all of us? And my chest too?"

"It'll be a squeeze, but James said we can make it fit." As Phoebe started fussing, Sarah took the infant from Matilda's arms. "Besides, the boys walk most of the way, so it's just you and the chest we need to fit in."

"Johnny, too, sometimes," Matilda added.

"You can rest, and Captain Magone said he'll be back up to the mission to help you after seeing the rest of the folks safely to the Willamette Valley."

"Oh, that's good of him," she said. "Such a nice young man. He'll make someone a good husband someday."

Sarah smiled. "Yes, he will." She cleared her throat. "He might be willing to marry you."

"What?" Matilda scoffed. "I'm not marrying anyone. Besides, I'm more than a decade older than him. I'd never want to see him saddled with a widow and four boys." She shook her head and laughed weakly. "No, he deserves a sweet, young woman who will adore him. Someone like Mary Ann Thompkins. She nearly swoons whenever he passes by."

"Indeed she does." Sarah laughed. "And I think he may be sweet on her too."

No, Matilda didn't want to marry again. *Besides, who would want a jaded old widow, jilted by her first love, abandoned and left alone by her last?*

The next morning, Matilda struggled to her feet and stumbled to the wagon. Inside, she packed what she thought she and the boys would need for a rest at the mission. She fingered the tiny pouch of coins tucked beneath the clothing. She might need the money to return east … if she could bear to undertake the return journey and risk the lives of her sons.

She shook her head and collapsed onto a barrel. How could they start a new life out here? So far from family, with only a handful of coins left. *Oh, Nicholas! What am I to do now?*

"Ma?" Henry's voice shouted from outside. "You in the wagon?"

Matilda palmed her cheeks to hide her tears. "I'm here."

"Captain says we're to leave soon for the Whitmans' Mission. You ready?"

"Just a moment." She packed a few more clothes, her family Bible, and her sewing basket, then looked around the wagon. Would she ever see these things again?

Climbing out, Matilda turned to see Magone and James Jory waiting for her. "I've packed what we'll need into the chest, if you don't mind bringing it, Mr. Jory?" Tears swam in her eyes. "We are most grateful for your help."

Jory waved aside her thanks as he and Magone hopped onto the wagon and hefted out the wooden chest. They carried it to the Jory wagon, where he had cleared a spot.

Matilda climbed down and started following them. Her knees started to buckle.

Henry raced forward. "Here, Ma. Let me help you."

"Thank you." She wrapped an arm around his waist and leaned on him as he half-carried her to the wagon. "I'm sure I'll regain my strength soon. Johnny can sit here with me."

After she perched on the chest alongside Sarah and baby Phoebe, she lifted her youngest son onto her lap.

Rawlins strode by and stopped. "Mrs. Koontz." He tipped his hat. "Mrs. Jory."

The women tilted their heads slightly but remained silent.

"I was ... well, my condolences on the death of your husband, ma'am." He grunted the words.

Matilda pursed her lips, acknowledged the words with a nod, and looked away. She couldn't abide the man who had cursed her husband so many times.

Lou and Fanny Knighten reached inside the wagon to say goodbye. "We'll keep you in our prayers," Fanny said.

"Thank you ... for everything," Matilda said.

Sarah stood while holding her infant. "Thank you for helping me birth this little one."

Fanny kissed the baby's pink cheek, and Lou did the same before waving as they strode to their wagons, heading west.

TWENTY-NINE

October 1847, Whitman Mission

A S THE JORY WAGON HEADED NORTH, Henry rode Belle while Bart and Grundy walked alongside. They waved to the main company as the wagon train rolled west toward the Columbia River.

Four days later, the Jorys with the Koontzes, led by Dr. Whitman, arrived at Waiilatpu. Matilda sighed as she saw four wooden buildings nestled among dry grassland, fenced to keep in stock. Civilization after months of wilderness. Smoke curled from chimneys in a large T-shaped house. Wagons crowded the yard. Trees lined a meandering blue river. Tepees dotted the perimeter outside the wooden fence. The doctor called the river Walla Walla and said it led downstream six miles to a Hudson's Bay Company post.

After stopping near the largest building, Jory helped his wife and then Matilda down from the wagon. Henry rushed to his mother's side.

"Here, Ma." He wrapped his thin arm around her waist.

As they entered, a woman with a round face and blond hair twisted into a bun greeted them. She was about Matilda's age, late thirties.

"Welcome to Waiilatpu." She grasped their hands. "I'm Narcissa Whitman. Dr. Whitman and I are happy to have you at our home."

She lifted a corner of the blanket in Sarah's arms. "Oh, what a precious baby! A girl?"

Sarah nodded. "Yes, our darling Phoebe arrived just three weeks ago."

"Come on in and have a seat." Mrs. Whitman rushed to where Matilda leaned against Henry. "Oh, my dear! Let me help you inside."

Their hostess led her to a chair, where she plopped none too gracefully. Sweat beaded on her brow from the exertion. She lifted a palm to her forehead as her body swayed.

"Oh, dear lady. You need to lie down. Young man, help me get her to a bed."

Henry grasped his mother around the waist as Mrs. Whitman led them down a hallway. She opened a door to a room where a mattress lay on a wooden frame. Matilda's eyes watered. A real bed—after all these miles of walking?

Mrs. Whitman drew down the covers, and Matilda collapsed onto the bed. "Let me help you undress. You rest now and I'll bring you a bite to eat later."

"How can I thank you?" she whispered the words before snuggling under a heavy quilt.

"No thanks necessary," Narcissa Whitman whispered as she closed the door.

❦

Matilda's eyes fluttered open. She stretched in the warm bed. Oh, what a horrid nightmare she had been having!

Footsteps sounded in the hallway. She glanced at the door to see Mrs. Whitman enter with a tray. Mrs. Whitman? Does that mean— it wasn't a nightmare. Nicholas was truly dead. And her baby? She let her hand drift beneath the blanket to the flat stomach. Tears filled her eyes, and she looked toward a window. She had never cried so much in all her life. But then again, she had never lost so much.

"Dear Mrs. Koontz." Narcissa set the tray on a table beside the bed. "I've brought you some food. You've been asleep for two days."

"Please, call me Matilda." Tears flowed down her cheeks as she shook her head. "I'm not hungry."

"Now, you must eat to keep up your strength." Narcissa pulled the pillow from beneath her head and propped it against the wall. She grasped behind her shoulders and lifted her up. "You must be strong for your sons."

"But what am I—we can't—no."

"I realize you've suffered great losses on this journey, but you have four young boys out there relying on you to keep them safe and give them a home."

"How?" Matilda shook her head. "How can I do this alone? How could God do this to me?"

Narcissa sat on the bed and pursed her lips as she spooned broth from a bowl into Matilda's mouth.

"God?" She broke off a chunk of bread, dabbed it into the broth, and placed it into Matilda's mouth. "God isn't to blame. The Good Book says, 'Naked came I out of my mother's womb, and naked shall I return thither: the Lord gave, and the Lord hath taken away; blessed be the name of the Lord. In all this Job sinned not, nor charged God foolishly.'"

Matilda swallowed. "I know God's not to blame. I just—I just don't know what I'm going to do." Her shoulders shook. She bit her lip to choke back sobs as tears dribbled down her cheeks. "Oh, why did Nicholas bring us out here? We should have stayed in Missouri."

"Now, none of that!" Narcissa barked. "We've all suffered our share of troubles in the frontier. My own baby girl ..." Her voice trailed off.

"What happened to your daughter?" Matilda whispered.

"My little Alice drowned in the river out here. Seven years ago. She was only two." The missionary stiffened her back. "And the seven Sager children—two boys and five girls, the littlest one just a baby—orphaned when their parents died coming across the trail. Plenty of suffering to go around. But I've adopted them as my own, and they've become an unforeseen blessing in our lives. We don't anticipate tragedies, but when they happen, we adapt, we grow, we change because of them ... sometimes even for the better." She looked at Matilda.

"You lost your husband. Your boys lost their father." She nodded at Matilda. "They also thought they might become orphans when you took sick after losing your baby. But they still have you. Perhaps this is a test of your courage and fortitude. It's your job now to see that your husband's dream for his sons is fulfilled, no matter the cost."

"But how—what can I do, a woman alone?" Matilda's voice quaked at the enormity of the challenges ahead of her.

"A woman alone? Out here?" Mrs. Whitman scoffed and stood. "You won't be alone for long. Men far outnumber women in Oregon Territory. You'll have plenty of marriage offers."

"But I love Nicholas." Matilda's tears started again. "How can I go on without him?"

"Brace yourself, my dear. You have your boys to think about—their future." She cracked open the window. "After you're well, you go on to Oregon City and find a man who will take care of you and your boys. A good man. A Christian man. And create that future for your boys that your husband wanted. God will provide. Heed the words in Joshua 1:9: 'Have I not commanded thee? Be strong and of a good courage; be not afraid, neither be thou dismayed: for the Lord thy God is with thee whithersoever thou goest.'"

Matilda shifted onto her elbows. "My boys—Are they—?"

"Don't worry about your boys." Narcissa picked up the tray from beside the bed. "I've got my Helen and young Catherine Sager watching them. They'll be fine. Now you sleep some more and perhaps you'll be strong enough to join us for dinner tonight."

Matilda sank back into the soft mattress as her hostess left. Tears flowed as she wrestled with Mrs. Whitman's words. Marry again? She couldn't. *Oh, Nicholas! Why did you leave me?*

Seeking comfort, she reached for the Bible on the nightstand. It fell open to Jeremiah 1:17: "Gird up thy loins, and arise, and speak unto them all that I command thee: be not dismayed at their faces, lest I confound thee before them." Matilda curled up on her side, letting the book close. Faces didn't dismay her; the future did.

She drifted to sleep but awoke with a start, shuddering at the thought of anybody other than Nicholas sharing her bed.

Streaks of sunlight from the setting sun danced on the window as Matilda opened her eyes and peered at the crimson sky. Raising herself on her elbows and feeling stronger than she had in weeks, Matilda set her bare feet on the wooden floor and stood. Mrs. Whitman was right. If her family were to survive, she needed to be strong, courageous, and determined. Nicholas could no longer fulfill his dream, but she could. He wanted a future for their sons, and she would give it to them. Like Jeremiah, she was prepared for battle. As it said in Matthew 19:26: "With God all things are possible."

She grasped the bed and wall for support as she walked toward her chest of goods, which someone had placed in the bedroom. Kneeling, she pulled out a clean dress, put it on, and ran fingers through her hair to untangle the strands, then dug into the chest for a brush. Dressed, with her hair tied back, she shuffled to the door and followed the beefy aroma of a pot roast down the hallway to a large dining room, where more than a dozen people sat around a long table.

"Mama!" Johnny slid from his perch on a long wooden bench and ran toward her. She squatted down and scooped him into her arms.

"Mrs. Koontz." Dr. Whitman pushed back his chair and strode toward her. "Let me find you a chair."

She let him lead her to the table. "I can sit here beside Johnny. Thank you, Dr. Whitman."

An Indian woman in moccasins walked into the room with a plate filled with meat, potatoes, corn, and bread. She laid it before Matilda.

"Thank you." She smiled at the woman, but the Indian's features remained stoic.

Narcissa leaned toward her and touched her hand. "Never mind Alashanee. She's worried about her little boy who's taken sick."

Matilda followed the Indian woman with her eyes, her heart melting. She knew the fear of worrying about a sick child.

"Are you feeling better, Mrs. Koontz?" James Jory leaned forward from farther down the table to address her.

"Yes, much better. Thank you." She nibbled on her bread and then turned to his wife. "How is little Phoebe?"

"She's sleeping now." Sarah sighed. "Quiet. She's a darling, but ... I'm rather tired."

Matilda smiled as she lifted a knife to cut meat for Johnny. "Has your family joined you yet?"

"Not yet, but they should be here tomorrow, I believe." James Jory turned toward Sarah. "We look forward to introducing them to Phoebe."

"They'll be delighted with your daughter." Matilda smiled, although she felt her lips tremble as the shadow of her own daughter's fleeting life passed through her mind. She remembered the little light-haired infant wrapped in a blanket. So tiny. So frail. So weak. Tears pricked her eyes, and she dropped her gaze to her plate.

"Will you continue your journey when your family arrives?" Matilda glanced at James Jory.

"Yes, indeed. We're excited to find some good farmland in the Willamette Valley." He glanced at his wife. "By the way, Captain Magone said he still plans to come back here to help you and the boys down to Oregon City. He should be here in a few days, I imagine."

"The captain's coming back?" Henry spoke around a mouthful of potatoes.

"Henry." Matilda chided him. "Please do not speak with food in your mouth."

"Yes, Ma." He turned again to Jory. "Captain Magone's coming back?"

"He promised to return to see you boys and your mother to Oregon City, and he's most certainly a man of his word." A baby wailed and Jory pulled back his wife's chair as she rose to see to the infant. "Chances are good we'll all be traveling down the Columbia River together."

"That would be nice." Matilda smiled at him. "I don't know what I would have done without you and Sarah."

"The captain did most of the work. Sarah and I were happy to help."

When the meal ended, Matilda rose and gathered plates from the table. She carried them into the kitchen and set them beside Alashanee. She gestured toward the bucket of water and raised her hands.

Narcissa walked into the kitchen. "Don't worry about the dishes, Mrs. Koontz. Alashanee will wash them."

"I do want to help while I'm here." Matilda looked for a towel to dry the dishes. "I don't know how to thank you for your care and hospitality."

"We've been caring for emigrants here since they started coming across the mountains four years ago. You aren't the first who arrived sick, and you won't be the last."

Matilda nodded, then picked up a cloth and began drying dishes.

"You don't need to do that, Mrs. Koontz."

"I would like to." Matilda wiped a tin plate dry. "Keeping my hands busy prevents my thoughts from dwelling in darkness."

Mrs. Whitman gazed at her for a moment, lips pursed, then left the kitchen.

As Matilda dried more dishes, she wondered how to ask this native woman about her son. Just then Johnny flew through the kitchen door.

"Mama!" He wrapped his arms around Matilda's legs. "Henry won't let me play with the Indians!"

Matilda squatted, bracing herself against the washstand so she could keep her precarious balance. "Johnny. You need to do what your brother says. Henry's looking out for you." She stood again. "Now go along until I finish here," she said, panting from the simple effort of squatting. "We'll walk outside afterward."

Matilda glanced at the Indian woman beside her, smiled, and gestured toward Johnny. She pointed at herself and then at the woman. "You?"

Alashanee nodded and folded her arms as if cradling an infant.

"Sick?" Matilda put her hand on her brow and fluttered her eyelashes and then raised her eyebrows in question.

The Indian nodded.

Matilda frowned. She pointed to herself and then held out both arms in question. Could she help?

Alashanee shrugged and then shook her head. A tear trickled down her cheek.

THIRTY

THE NEXT MORNING, more than a dozen wagons rumbled into the fenced area before the mission's buildings. Matilda followed the Whitmans and the Jorys out the door to greet the newcomers.

"Father!" James Jory rushed forward and greeted an older man as he climbed down from his wagon. The two men embraced. "Mother!" He helped an older woman descend from the wagon. "I'd like you to meet the Whitmans and Mrs. Koontz."

Jory conducted the introductions, and his father did the same for his entourage.

"I'm James Jory Sr., and this is my wife, Mary." He swiveled to the left and gestured toward a young couple with a baby. "This is my son, John, and his wife, Caroline. She's Sarah's sister. And that's their baby, James." His grin stretched as he pointed toward his namesake.

He gestured behind him and rattled off the names of more people, leaving Matilda overwhelmed. "These here are my boys, Hugh, Thomas, and William." He tilted his head toward the back wagon. "Yonder is John Fenn, my son-in-law, and my daughter Elizabeth. He and my daughter Mary had three children—Nancy, Elizabeth, and James—before she passed away last year." He choked on his words, dropped his head, and swallowed. "Malaria. Then he and Elizabeth married in the spring, just before we left Illinois. So, he's still my son-in-law."

Dr. Whitman pointed to a dark-skinned man. "Who is that gentleman?" Matilda followed his gaze to see a scruffy-looking man on a horse.

James Jory Sr. raised his eyebrows. "I don't know if I'd exactly call him a gentleman. Name is Joe Lewis, I believe. He joined us just a few days ago after leaving another wagon train. Canadian, I believe, son of a black and an Indian." He dropped his voice. "But I hear tell he's a troublemaker. A couple of gents passing through warned us to steer clear of him, but I didn't see any harm letting him accompany us here."

Dr. Whitman gazed at Lewis before spreading his arms. "We welcome all emigrants. Come in. We'll provide you with cool water and something to eat."

Matilda started to return to the kitchen, but Narcissa grasped her arm. "Alashanee will prepare the food."

As the doctor turned toward the door, he spoke to the elder Jory. "How was the trip? Did you have any trouble?"

Jory nodded. "Indians stole a considerable amount of property from our camp."

"Where was this?" the doctor asked.

"Back up the trail a bit." The elder Jory shook his head. "We couldn't identify the thieves."

"Wait for a minute, will you?" Dr. Whitman strode toward the center of the yard and addressed the three dozen Cayuse who had gathered to see the newcomers. Many of the men and women wrapped themselves in blankets, their faces painted.

"How many times have I told you of God's commandments?" He opened his arms and waved in both directions at the assembled crowd. "Thou shalt not steal. Stealing is a sin in God's eyes. He will punish those who sin against Him."

He pursed his lips. "You there, Wild Oak, open that blanket!" The Indian he pointed toward dropped his head and slowly opened his blanket. A frying pan dropped to the ground. "The God of the heavens will punish those who break His laws."

As the missionary continued his harangue, more Cayuse opened their blankets and dropped utensils—knives, forks, pots. One man raised a skillet above his head and threw it toward the doctor. It scuffed the dry brown dirt, creating a cloud.

"They appear to be angry," John Fenn said to his daughter.

"But why?" His five-year-old girl looked up at him. "Why are they mad when we just want what's ours back?"

"I'm not entirely sure, Child. But they are."

He followed his father-in-law past Matilda and into the house.

Matilda held Johnny's hand as she and her boys walked the perimeter of the fence, gazing at the grist mill and the river in the distance. Each day she felt stronger, but only for an hour or two. Her stamina had disappeared somewhere along the trail. She didn't know how she could fend for herself and the boys if she couldn't stay awake more than an hour or two.

Johnny released her hand and raced ahead to where a handful of Cayuse boys played with a small, white woolly dog with pointed ears. He laughed as he reached the circle of boys. The dog turned to growl at him.

"Johnny!" Matilda strode over to her son. "Come back here."

"But I want to play!"

"That dog doesn't want to play with you." She grabbed his hand. "He doesn't know you yet. We'll have to give him time before you play with him."

One of the young Cayuse boys approached. He looked to be about five or six, wearing leather leggings and moccasins. His chest was bare, but a pink rash spread over his brown skin. He scratched at a red spot, coughed, and pointed to himself.

"Gray Wolf." Then he pointed toward Johnny.

Her three-year-old looked up at Matilda. "Ma?"

"I believe he wants to know your name. His is Gray Wolf."

Johnny looked at the Indian boy and pointed to himself. "Johnny." Then he pointed to the dog. "What's his name?"

The Cayuse boy's brows drew together before he uttered a sound like "Pancht."

"Pank!" Johnny ran toward the dog. "Pank!"

Gray Wolf followed on his heels. Soon all the boys started playing with the dog.

Matilda stood and put her hands on her hips. What was the rash on the boy's chest? She hoped it wasn't contagious. Perhaps this was the illness that Alashanee's son had.

"Johnny!" She shouted his name, but the word sounded hollow as it left her parched lips. Looking around, she spotted Bart and Henry leading Belle toward a water trough. "Henry!"

Her eldest son looked her way. "Ma?"

"Will you please bring Johnny inside the house?" Matilda felt faint as she grasped the fence post and dragged her body toward the T-shaped building. "I need to lie down."

"Sure thing, Ma."

She watched Henry jog toward the circle of boys. He tipped his hat, spoke to Johnny, and grabbed his little brother's hand. Johnny pulled back, but Henry scooped him into his arms and headed toward the house with his squirming bundle.

Matilda reached the door at the same time. "Thank you, Henry." She grabbed Johnny's hand. "Now, you're not to play with those boys."

"Why not?" He stomped his foot on the stoop.

"One of those boys looked sick, Johnny. I don't want you to catch whatever he has."

"I won't, Ma. I promise!"

She smiled slightly and drew him into the house, closing the door firmly behind her. She saw Grundy in the main room, sorting firewood. "Will you watch Johnny for a bit while I lie down? Please don't let him go outside."

Grundy nodded. As Matilda braced one hand against the wall, gasping for breath, she couldn't help thinking what a blessing her sons were to her. They were such good boys. What would she do—? *No. Don't think about it.*

By early November, Matilda had regained much of her strength over several weeks. She helped in the kitchen when she could or rested on a handmade, wool-stuffed sofa in the main room by the entryway. She didn't have the endurance she needed, but she could help around the mission. She also braced herself with the Word of God, trusting the Lord to guide her footsteps as she ventured into an uncertain future.

"Rider!" Francis Sager shouted the words.

Dr. Whitman and his wife strode to the door and opened it. A lone horseman dismounted from a stallion and removed his hat, twisting the rim in his hands. He looked familiar, but her vision was still a bit blurry.

"Greetings!" The doctor held out his hand. "What can we do for you?"

"Magone's the name. I understand Mrs. Koontz and her boys are here."

"Captain!" Matilda rushed forward at the sound of his familiar voice. She wanted to embrace him but knew that wouldn't be proper. Instead, she wrapped both hands around his. "I don't know how we can thank you for all you've done."

"No need," Magone said. "Thought I'd come back and check on you, see if you needed help down to Oregon City."

"Surely you'll stay through the winter here." Dr. Whitman let his glance slide over her body. "You're stronger, and the bleeding finally stopped, but you're still very weak. You can scarcely walk without wheezing. I'm thinking a blood clot might have settled in your lungs. I've given you willow bark in your tea to help improve your circulation, but you need rest. Honestly, I don't believe you're up to the journey downriver."

"But Doctor…" Matilda hesitated and pursed her lips. "I understand another Cayuse child died today from the measles. That makes six since Sunday." Turning to Magone, she continued. "I worry about the boys. I don't—I can't—I won't lose them too."

Narcissa Whitman wrapped an arm around Matilda's waist. "Indeed. You do need to pursue your husband's dream. Perhaps if you have the captain's help, the journey won't be too trying."

Matilda turned as James Jory Jr. walked into the yard. "Captain Magone! What a delight to see you again."

The two men shook hands.

"You planning to leave soon, Jory?" The captain gestured toward a wagon. "You ever connect with your family?"

"Indeed we did. We've all enjoyed the hospitality of the Whitmans these past two weeks, but we're anxious to reach the Willamette Valley before winter arrives. We've had beautiful weather this fall, but there's no point pushing our luck."

"That's why I thought I'd ride up here and see if Mrs. Koontz was up to traveling again." He dropped his gaze to his boots. "I promised..." He cleared his throat. "I promised to see everyone to Oregon Territory, and I haven't fulfilled that promise."

"Did the rest make it?" Matilda asked. "Have you seen William and Jane?"

"Yes, they arrived shortly after we did. I believe they settled south of the city a ways."

"What a relief! You've been a godsend to me and the boys, Captain." Matilda smiled. "We would like to join you for the trip to Oregon City."

"I doubt you're strong enough yet," the doctor cautioned her. "You're much improved over when you arrived, but you'll have to portage around Celilo Falls. That's a twelve-mile hike."

Matilda felt the blood drain from her face. Twelve miles! She was lucky to walk a mile, if that, during a day. "I can try to walk it. Or mightn't I ride in a boat down the river?"

"Those falls are treacherous. Just ask the Indians. Or a white man."

"That's quite true." Narcissa twisted her hands. "We've probably heard of five hundred men killed by those falls in the time we've been here."

Matilda paused. Five hundred dead? But how could she walk twelve miles? She couldn't. Maybe they should remain at the mission

… but Alashanee's baby boy had died, even though Dr. Whitman had tried to treat him. Whatever disease had killed him could threaten the lives of her boys. She couldn't lose them too. Not after Nicholas. The baby. No.

Even if it meant risking the falls, she must keep her boys safe, try to fulfill Nicholas' dream for their sons, take them to Oregon City. Head bowed, she whispered a prayer to God for guidance. She felt an inner peace. "I'll need to trust in the Lord's providence to see me over the falls then."

Both Dr. and Narcissa Whitman remained silent. So did the others.

Jory cleared his throat. "We were thinking of leaving in the morning, Joe. We can haul Matilda's chest in our wagon again. Will that work for you?"

"Sure will." Magone plopped his hat on his sweaty head. "I look forward to seeing you all to Oregon City. Fact is, I spoke with the chief factor there, or rather, former chief factor from Fort Vancouver. McLoughlin. He retired there and runs a store. Owns a mansion in the city, and he said you and the boys could stay there as long as you need."

Tears filled Matilda's eyes. She lifted her hands to her mouth to still her trembling lips.

"He's a doctor, too, so he can look after you."

"Why did he agree to help?" Matilda couldn't understand such generosity. "I don't have the money to pay him."

Magone shook his head. "It's taken care of. He's a man known for his generosity to Americans. He's been in trouble with his bosses at the Hudson's Bay Company for helping them. But now he's retired, he doesn't give a hoot what they think."

Matilda's brows drew together. "Did you—Captain, you didn't pay him?"

Magone shook his head and backed down the steps. "I need to take care of my horse. We'll leave at first light."

THIRTY-ONE

Early November 1847, Whitman Mission to Oregon City

ON THAT EARLY NOVEMBER MORNING, under cloudy skies, the Jorys prepared to haul their goods to flat-bottomed boats at the Walla Walla River, which they rented from Dr. Whitman for the trip down the Columbia River. Matilda offered James Jory Jr. the small pouch of coins Nicholas had tucked into her chest of goods.

"No, Mrs. Koontz. The Bible says to look out for widows and orphans." He gazed into her eyes. "You'll need what little you have once we reach Oregon City."

She smiled at him. "Your kindness to us has been tremendous. We can never repay you."

"No need for repayment." Jory dropped his gaze. "Your husband was a friend…"

"He respected you," Matilda said.

They left the mission and stood beside the loaded wagons. Matilda heard a squeal behind the building and glanced around to find her boys. *Henry, Bart, Grundy. Where was Johnny?*

She picked up her skirts and scurried around the side of the house as fast as her emaciated body would let her. As she drew near, words sounded from the far side of the house.

"He te-wat—medicine man," one Cayuse man said.

"Yes. Medicine man. But bad medicine. Poison. He will kill you all. His black magic makes your children sick. He's a bad man."

Matilda frowned as she peered around the corner. She spotted Joe Lewis speaking with several Cayuse men. She knew the doctor had hired Lewis to work around the mission during the coming winter. He had even given the man clothes, supplies, and food. Why was he saying such mean things about his employer?

"Black robes teach true. Not Whitman." He punched one hand into another and spit. "Bad religion. Bad medicine. Bad man."

When one of the Cayuse glanced at her, Matilda ducked back behind the building.

Heart beating fast, she rushed around another corner and spotted her son playing with the dog while Gray Wolf leaned against the wall, coughing, his face red and eyes watery. The boy's rash had spread from his chest to his arms and face. Measles! She hoped Johnny didn't catch the dreaded disease.

"Johnny." She held out her hand. "The captain's ready to lead us to the Willamette Valley."

"Wallmette Balley!" Johnny raised a hand in the air. "Whoopee!"

Matilda couldn't help smiling as she recalled the many times around the campfire when the boys let out such a yell whenever their father spoke about their new home.

Oh, Nicholas. You'll never see the Willamette Valley. She pulled back her shoulders. *But your boys will.*

"Say goodbye to Gray Wolf."

Johnny started toward his new friend, but Matilda gripped his shoulders, holding him back. "Just wave goodbye."

She and Johnny reached the gathered crowd just as they prepared to walk from the mission to the river. Leaving Belle proved the most heartbreaking for the boys. The mare couldn't travel on the river with them. The captain promised to retrieve the mare and bring her to them at Oregon City.

Matilda thanked the doctor and his wife for their care. "I wish I could repay you somehow."

Narcissa gave her a quick embrace. "Take care of your boys." She paused, then added, "And find a good husband."

Matilda and the boys waved goodbye to the doctor, his wife, and their adopted children—two Indians and the seven Sager children—as the wagons followed the dusty trail toward the Walla Walla River.

At the riverbank, the men rolled the wagons onto two flat-bottomed boats called bateaux and removed the wheels. Matilda's cedar chest rested among Sarah's belongings, her wagon somewhere near The Dalles Mission.

Dr. Whitman guided Matilda and the boys to an Indian canoe. At the far end sat an older man dressed in softened hide with fringe around the collar and beads adorning the sleeves.

"Mrs. Koontz, this is Heneme," the doctor said. "A Nez Perce. You can trust him with your life—and the lives of your sons."

Matilda gave the native a tentative smile. The Nez Perce were friendly, as she recalled. But the river … it appeared so placid, yet so had the Snake. What if one of the boys toppled out of the canoe? What if they capsized?

"Heneme." The man nodded and thumped his chest, drawing her attention away from the water.

Pointing to her sons, Matilda introduced each one. "Henry, Bart, Grundy, and Johnny."

"Sit. I paddle."

Matilda nodded and clutched Johnny tight onto her lap. She looked for Captain Magone and saw him speaking with the Jorys. He caught her eye and strode to the canoe.

"Are you settled well here?" The captain looked at the boys. "You all stay still while this canoe is floating. Heneme will do all the paddling and guiding of the canoe. From what I've been told, he's been floating on this river for years."

He glanced at Matilda. "I've loaded your goods onto the bateau. Jory's older boys will take the cattle downriver on the Indian trails." He gazed over her head.

Matilda followed his gaze and shivered at the menacing dark clouds toward the west.

"It's a hundred and fifty miles to the falls," Magone said, patting the side of the canoe. "Just enjoy the ride as we float. Heneme will pull the canoe to the shore when we need to make camp, and again when we must portage around the falls."

Despite the darkening sky, the day remained dry as they floated west down the Walla Walla River and past the sunbaked clay bricks of what must be the Hudson's Bay Company's trading fort Dr. Whitman had mentioned. Several other buildings and Indian camps clustered nearby.

Matilda's shoulders relaxed as she gazed at the hills rising from the river. The canoe floated downstream over the placid water, helped along by the current and occasionally by Heneme who directed their path by slicing his paddle into smooth green water like a knife cutting through cake.

As the much-smaller Walla Walla River entered the mighty Columbia, a fierce wind sprang up from the west, prompting Matilda to pull her wool blanket tighter over her shoulders and Heneme to plunge the paddle into the choppy water. "Boys, turn up your collars and hold those blankets tight."

Henry, busy gazing at first one shore and then the other, ignored her. Bart and Grundy lifted their coat collars over their ears.

"Henry." Matilda dropped her voice. "I don't want you taking sick. Please turn up your collar."

He did.

She snuggled closer to Johnny as the wind bit through her blanket. But then the dark clouds overhead let loose their load. Frigid raindrops pelted their faces, driving into their skin by the biting wind. Although she pulled the wool covering over their heads, Matilda and Johnny both wound up soaked to the skin within minutes. She glanced at Heneme, deep lines etched into his copper-colored skin, his expression impassive. He seemed oblivious to the storm. How could he not be frozen?

Then she looked at his leather leggings and saw frigid water roll off them into the belly of the canoe. His clothing was much better suited to the oncoming winter weather than her cotton and fleece.

As the sun dropped toward the west, Heneme angled the canoe toward a flat sandy area on the river's bank. The bateaux behind them also pulled up to the bank. Magone set up a tent and shepherded Matilda and her boys inside. He pulled a cloth from a saddlebag.

"Dry off with this," the captain said. "Try to warm up. We'll start a fire soon. Do you need dry clothes?"

"I'll go with you. I know where they are." Matilda watched Jory struggle to set up a tent as the wind howled, Sarah beside him, sheltering little Phoebe with her body. "Boys, stay inside and dry off."

She panted as she followed the captain to the bateaux. After he lifted her onto the flat-bottomed boat, she squeezed between furniture and boxes to her cedar chest and pulled clothes from a drawer. She tucked them near to her body as she trudged back to Magone. He helped her ashore, and she staggered through the drenching rain to the tent. Inside, gasping, she knelt for a minute before helping the boys change into dry clothes. Henry didn't want her help, of course, so neither did Bart.

She struggled to inhale, and a high-pitched wheeze rattled her chest. How could she walk twelve miles on a rough mountainous path when she couldn't breathe after walking two dozen steps? Enough! Whenever she finally found a new home, she'd never leave again. She'd had enough traveling in six months to last the rest of her life.

Day after day they floated downstream on the Columbia River, a deep wide river, the repository of so many tributaries. Smaller rivers emptied into this behemoth. The Snake River had joined the Columbia River upstream. Moisture filled Matilda's eyes as she envisioned her husband's body drifting underwater downriver in the Snake until caught by the current of the Columbia River. Was he below her now? Or had he already drifted to the Pacific Ocean?

"Ma?" Henry asked. "What are you thinking of?"

Matilda glanced at her eldest son, so much like his father in both looks and demeanor. She smiled, grateful he had pulled her depressive thoughts out of the water, into the sunshine. "How much you look like your pa."

He looked away.

"You look like him, and you act like him, and he'll always be with us," Matilda said.

He glanced back at her.

"Here." She crossed her arms over her chest. "In our hearts."

At last, after a week of floating downriver for sixteen hours a day and camping along the bank each night, they reached an Indian village of nearly two dozen lodges above Celilo Falls. The captain had told her that below the falls were a half dozen more longhouses. Natives in the villages fished at the falls for salmon.

That night, with the roar of waterfalls in the background, the adults nestled around a blazing fire to warm numb fingers and toes. The children had already gone to sleep.

"Tomorrow we'll be at Celilo Falls," Magone said. He glanced at Matilda. "That's where we need to portage around the river. It's a twelve-mile hike. James already said he'd help me carry your cedar box. Do you think you can make it?"

Matilda crossed both arms over her chest and gazed into the flickering flames. Blues danced between yellows and oranges. Twelve miles. She knew she couldn't walk that far. But what of the boys? Could she ride down the river, over the falls and through the rocks? What if she died? Her boys would be left alone, orphaned, without anyone to care for them. Oh, God, what should I do?

Trust Me.

As if she heard the words in her heart, a sudden peace warmed Matilda's chilled body, like soaking in a hot bath. She relaxed and looked up, holding the captain's gaze.

"I can't walk that far. But I can ride in the canoe."

"It's too dangerous." Magone stood and tossed the dregs of his coffee on the dying fire. "The river drops more than eighty feet in half a mile, pouring over three separate falls. The first waterfall drops twenty feet! Believe me, I saw it. The river shoots through narrow channels in a white froth." He paused. "The river there is ... deadly."

"What choice do I have?" Matilda asked.

"Maybe I can carry you."

"And my cedar chest? As well as Johnny?" Matilda smiled. "No, Captain." She lowered her voice. "Please keep my boys safe on the portage since I can't."

"Perhaps we could leave the chest here?" The captain offered the suggestion with raised eyebrows.

Matilda shook her head. "It's all I have left. We need clothes at the very least when we reach Oregon City." She sighed. "If you can carry the chest and keep my boys from slipping on the rock or sand as they portage around, I'll be forever indebted to you." She drew a deep, wheezing breath. "I can ride over the falls in the canoe."

"How?" Magone ran his fingers through his hair. He lowered his voice to a whisper. "How do you think you'll survive? Dr. Whitman said hundreds of people have died on those rapids."

Matilda nodded and looked at the fire again. Then she returned her eyes to his. "I trust the Lord to guide me through the waters, Captain."

He started to speak but pursed his lips instead.

"What is it, Captain?"

"Your husband … he trusted God, too, didn't he?"

Matilda blinked back tears and looked away. Nicholas had trusted God; so had she. Yet he died. But … somehow, inside, she knew God would be with her. In fact, so would Nicholas and her baby. She intended to wear the bonnet he'd bought for her and tuck the baby's into her pocket. God and his angel would watch over her.

"Heneme?" Magone turned toward the Indian and gestured with his hands. "Canoe over falls? With Mrs. Koontz?"

Heneme shook his head. "Non."

"Have you ever floated over the falls?" Matilda asked.

The large native man hesitated, nodded.

"See?" she told the captain. "I can do it."

"Non," Heneme repeated, shaking his head. He held one hand steady and gestured with his fingers as if flying free from the lower hand. "Fall out." Then he flailed his arms over his head. "Almost die."

Magone glanced at Matilda.

"What if you tied me inside the canoe?" She plucked a yellow weed from the grass and wove it around her flat hand to illustrate. "Then I won't fly out."

Heneme hesitated. He shrugged.

"All alone?" Magone asked. "Heneme? Go with her?"

"Non." He shook his head vehemently.

Matilda turned toward the captain. "I don't see any other option, Captain."

A short time later, Sarah Jory rushed to where Matilda sat on a Douglas fir log, watching the water. "I just heard you plan to canoe over the falls. Are you insane?" She shifted the bundled baby to her husband and put both hands on Matilda's shoulders. "Are you trying to kill yourself?"

"I don't plan to die, but I can't walk the distance around the falls."

"I'll help you walk it, the boys and I will."

Matilda arched a brow. "While carrying Phoebe?"

"Please, just let us try," Sarah pleaded. "If we can't do it, then you can ride the canoe."

"I'll try." Matilda smoothed her skirts and stood. "But if I can't walk, I believe God will carry me through those waters as he guided Moses through the Red Sea. I'd best go to sleep now—and pray."

She smiled as she walked to the tent and slipped inside. She gazed at her boys and saw Henry staring wide-eyed at her. She pressed a finger to her lips to indicate he needed to stay quiet. He pulled his lips together tight, but she saw a shimmer in his eyes.

"Pray for safety, Henry." She whispered the words as she bent over to kiss his forehead. "For all of us."

Thirty-Two

October 1847, Celilo Falls, Oregon Territory

THE NEXT MORNING, Matilda arose to see the sun shining overhead. Doubts assailed her. Would she drown in the Columbia River as her husband had in the Snake? She learned to swim as a child in a placid pond, but if she capsized in the river's wild rapids, could she keep her head above the roiling water long enough to reach the shore? Would she have the strength to swim? How long could she hold her breath?

She tugged on the crimson bonnet with blue and pink flowers from Nicholas and tucked her daughter's matching cap into a pocket of her pantalets. She inhaled a deep breath but coughed, covering her mouth with a handkerchief. Blood. She glanced around, folded the handkerchief quickly, and tucked it inside her sleeve. She promised she would try to walk.

The Jorys and others in the party divided up the belongings they needed to carry around the waterfall and the sets of lower rapids, called the Short Narrows and the Long Narrows. They offered cotton shirts to a couple of Indians to help them carry their goods.

The captain and James Jory hefted Matilda's chest of goods. Sarah, one arm holding Phoebe, slipped her free arm around Matilda's waist.

271

Henry draped his little arm around her waist from the other side. Bart and Grundy held Johnny's hands between them.

They started walking. Once again, Matilda counted the steps. One, two, three, four…

Phoebe wailed. Sarah let go of Matilda and placed the baby over her shoulder, patting her back. "She probably just needs to burp."

Matilda panted, trying to catch a deep breath. Her vision blurred. She swayed slightly.

"Ma?" Henry gripped her waist tighter.

"I'm …" A rattling cough erupted from her chest, doubling her over as she struggled to breathe.

"Ma!"

Drops of blood sprayed the worn rock at their feet. She pitched forward, dragging Henry with her. Sarah screamed.

"Henry …"

He scrambled to his knees beside her. "I'm not hurt, Ma."

Captain Magone lifted her in his arms.

As Sarah wiped blood from her face with the corner of Phoebe's blanket, Matilda offered a tremulous smile. "I … tried."

"Oh, Matilda." Sarah cried, almost as loud as her baby. "I'm sorry I made you promise to try."

She nodded and knew what had to be done. She would put all her trust in God, for both her safety and that of her sons. As Magone set her on the fir log, Matilda reached for her boys.

"Henry, it's a steep hike around the falls," she said. "You hold Johnny's hand the entire time." She gazed into her eldest son's eyes. "Promise me."

He nodded his blond head, his face solemn. "Ma?"

She looked him in the eye. "What is it?"

"Nothin'." He dropped his gaze, then stepped forward and clutched her tight around her waist.

She hugged him until he drew back. "I'll see you in a bit. I know you'll watch over your brothers."

"Bart, Grundy." She turned to her middle boys. "You two stay together and hold hands the entire time."

"Do we have to?" Bart asked with a bit of a whine in his voice.

"Yes, you do," Matilda said.

"Why can't I hold your hand?" Grundy asked.

"I'll be coming a bit later." She dropped her gaze to the ground. "You just do as I said. Promise me?"

"Yes, Ma." They both mumbled the words.

She hugged them. "There's my good boys." She reached down to pick up Johnny. "Now, Johnny, you heed Henry. Don't run off, you hear?"

He nodded but started squirming, so she let him slide down her body to the ground. She watched as the boys followed the elder Jorys down a narrow trail along the river.

"Mrs. Koontz?" Captain Magone sidled up beside her. "Ma'am?"

Matilda swiped her hands down her skirts and blinked away her tears. "Yes, Captain. I'm ready." She shuffled to the western red cedar canoe, where Heneme stood holding a rope.

"Heneme?" She glanced at the Indian, then at the canoe. "Where—how do you want me to lie?"

"Mrs. Koontz." The captain's voice sounded in her ear as he slid the brim of his hat through his fingers. "I want to say—I want you to know—if anything happens, I'll make sure your boys get to William and Jane."

"Thank you." Matilda's breath caught in her throat. She couldn't contain the surge of emotion she felt for the young man as she found herself suddenly throwing her arms around him in a grateful embrace. How could they have survived without the captain's friendship? A sob caught on her whispered words. "For everything."

The younger man stiffly returned her hug before releasing her and clearing his throat. He nodded, his cheeks slightly pinker than they were a moment earlier. "Good luck."

Lifting her skirts, she stepped over the rim into the canoe. She looked again at Heneme and then over his shoulder at white water spewing above the rocks.

"Down." He gestured with his hand. "Flat."

She tucked her skirts beneath her legs as she lowered herself to the bottom of the canoe and slid beneath the wooden slats used as seats toward the bow. She tugged on her bonnet from Nicholas and caressed her side where the matching cap nestled. Her angels…

Heneme tossed the end of the rope to Magone and indicated he should wind it through the bottom slat and bring it back. Heneme wove the rope between the slats until Matilda was cocooned underneath the crisscrossed weave. If the canoe tipped over, she would stretch her arms against the rope to maintain an air pocket … as long as she could, anyway.

Her heart pounded in her chest as she stared at the overhanging branches of a pine tree. This could be her coffin. Her tomb. They might never find her body if white water dashed the canoe against the rocks and it broke apart. *Oh, God! What am I doing?*

"Mrs. Koontz. Heneme said Indians by The Dalles Mission will retrieve the canoe," Magone said. "They wait below the rapids and gather everything they can that floats downriver."

Matilda clenched her lips together. She raised her hands to grasp the rope in front of her face. "Will you pray, Joseph? Please?"

The captain nodded. "Indeed I will, the entire time I'm walking. You are a remarkable woman, Mrs. Koontz."

She tried to smile, but her teeth wouldn't let loose of her lips.

Heneme looked her in the eye and raised his eyebrows. She tipped her head slightly in assent. He pushed the canoe into the river.

Oh, Lord, I trust in You. I trust in Your promises. I trust You to keep me and my boys safe. "When thou passest through the waters, I will be with thee; and through the rivers, they shall not overflow thee." She prayed God's promise in Isaiah 43 would hold true for her too. She clenched her eyes shut tight as the canoe spun around. She was floating headfirst toward the waterfalls. *Oh, dear God!*

She opened her eyes again. Steep cliffs towered above the river. The wood bumped against a rock. She screamed and grasped the rope even tighter. Matilda glimpsed the blue sky overhead. White water churned and gurgled beside her. Frigid water sloshed inside the canoe, soaking her skirts.

Her head bumped the end of the canoe. Her legs flew forward toward her face, stopped only by the rope crisscrossing the canoe.

She was flying!

She braced herself for the landing. She tightened her neck, tucked her head into her shoulders, wove her arms through the rope above to increase her grip.

Soaring.

Plunging.

The deafening roar pounded her ears like a war party's drums, louder and louder.

Frigid water engulfed her. She opened her eyes to darkness. She held her breath. *Please, God, let this canoe resurface.* Deeper it plunged. Down. Down. As if propelled by a giant, crushed beneath his foot.

Turning.

Twisting.

The faces of her boys flashed through her mind. She promised Henry. All of them.

Just as Matilda thought she must open her mouth to inhale water, the canoe bobbed to the surface—upright. She breathed deeply. Water dripped from the rope into her mouth, and she sputtered.

She was alive!

Oh, dear Lord, thank You!

The captain had said the first waterfall plunged the farthest—nearly twenty feet—and she had survived. But the lower rapids posed great dangers too. The entire river spewed through a narrow channel and whirled and swelled into huge waves. The rigid piece of hardwood, carved into a canoe, tossed and spun, like a galloping horse whirling in a fast polka.

Bam!

The canoe hit a rock. But at least she was floating feet first now, rather than headfirst.

Thank You, Lord, for small mercies.

Bang!

A huge black rock loomed overhead on the right. Water sloshed into the canoe as it tipped sideways. Matilda thrust her weight to the opposite side, hoping to keep from capsizing.

The canoe plummeted downriver and, battered by another rock, fishtailed one hundred eighty degrees. She was headfirst again. Whitewater foamed in the narrow channel, sloshing into the canoe. She shut her eyes as her stomach somersaulted.

The canoe soared into the air, then plunged into the water.

And a third time.

Finally, the craft slowed its frenetic headlong plunge.

Matilda opened her eyes. Was it over? Had she indeed survived? She felt a lurch to the left of the canoe and then a tug as it traveled toward shore. Pine tree branches loomed overhead.

She tried to lift her head but couldn't, every part of her body numbed by fear and cold. She heard the canoe scrape against sand. She closed her eyes as her body trembled in relief.

Thank You, God. Thank You!

Someone shouted above her, but she didn't understand the words. She opened her eyes to see a native gesturing as he shouted. Another man bent over the canoe to work out the knots in the rope.

She lay there, staring at the men, trying to calm her frantic heart. Breathe in. Breathe out. Her diaphragm didn't cooperate. She shook. Everything trembled. Her fingers. Her legs. Her arms. Her chest.

She couldn't breathe. Mouth open, she gasped for air.

The first man reached into the canoe, pulled under her arms, and slid her out. Water dripped from her sodden dress. He set her on her feet, but her legs folded, and she collapsed to the ground.

The man shouted something to a woman and lifted her again, hefting her over his shoulder. As he trudged toward one of dozens of longhouses facing the river, Matilda glimpsed the woman's feet in leather moccasins trailing behind him.

After the man set her on the dirt before a fire and left, the woman draped a fur over her shoulders. She sat beside her, eyes wide.

"You—over water?" The woman gestured with her hands, fingers wiggling as she imitated the rapids. "Yes?"

Matilda nodded. "Yes."

The woman eyed her with respect and pointed skyward. "God?"

Matilda nodded, knowing full well God had carried her safely over the falls. She prayed He would keep the others safe on the portage around the falls.

Silence reigned. As warmth from the fire penetrated the chill in her bones, chasing it away like a dog pursuing a cat, Matilda's eyelids fluttered and closed. She curled onto her side and slept.

Laughter warmed her heart as Nicholas lifted their little girl in his arms, swaying first one way, then the other, swooping up and down. Then light shone on Matilda's face, awakening her. She blinked at a crimson sky and stretched out an arm for her husband.

Nothing. She raised herself on the elbows. Nicholas? Reality pummeled her as she recalled the Snake River, her husband disappearing underwater, never surfacing. Oh, Nicholas. She rubbed a palm over her flat stomach. Her precious daughter.

Her angels.

Her body trembled of its own accord like an autumn leaf in the wind. Icy cold. Foaming water. The falls. The plunge. She couldn't breathe. She panted.

"Mama!" Johnny's distant wail pierced her ears.

Matilda sat upright, every muscle in her body objecting to the movement, and looked around the longhouse. She tried to stand but her legs shuddered, flopping like wet noodles. Her head throbbed as blood pulsed in her temples, her neck stiff from wrenching this way and that at the river's whim. A chill raced through her, mimicking the frozen stiffness of her body when the native pulled her from the canoe, soaked and frigid.

"Here." The words slipped through her tongue in a hoarse whisper.

Johnny raced through the opening of the longhouse and barreled into her arms. She nearly toppled. "Johnny." She hugged him. "Bart. Henry. Grundy. Boys, come here."

She embraced each of her sons in turn. The captain entered the longhouse, a grin spreading across his face.

"You seem none the worse for your adventure."

She strained to smile. "I wouldn't precisely say so, but I survived, thanks to God." She looked at her sons. "And so did they. Thank you."

"We'll ride the flat-bottomed boats downstream and then travel up the Willamette River to Oregon City." James Jory Jr. entered the longhouse, followed by Sarah, holding little Phoebe. She hurried over to Matilda's side.

"Thank God you're safe." Sarah sat beside her on the ground. "My legs ache so!"

"Let me take little Phoebe." Matilda reached for the infant, despite her aching muscles. "I've just awoken from the most refreshing sleep. I'll watch her while you rest."

Sarah handed her the cooing baby. Matilda tilted her head toward the fur behind her. "Use that to warm up. It's toasty by the fire."

Matilda rocked the baby to sleep and later, after returning the infant to her mother, rose to her knees and then stood, her legs aching but stronger than earlier. She limped outside the longhouse, her boys trailing behind.

"I've set up your tent over yonder." Magone pointed to the canvas pitched beneath a canopy of fir trees.

"Thank you again." Matilda led the boys to the tent. "It's time you slept. You must be exhausted."

Henry spread out a bedroll. "Here, Johnny. You crawl in."

"You sleep with me?" Johnny tugged his brother's sleeve.

"Yeah, yeah. I'll sleep with you." Henry crawled into the bedroll beside the toddler as Bart and Grundy did the same.

"Was it scary, Ma?" Bart asked his mother. "Going down the river?"

"Yes." Matilda paused. "Terrifying, in fact. But God carried me through it."

"Why didn't God carry Pa through the Snake?" Grundy asked.

Matilda blinked back sudden tears. She bent before him. "I don't know the answer to that question, Grundy. Maybe someday we can ask God."

"We passed Wascopam Mission," Bart said. "The Methodist one at The Dalles. Dr. Whitman said his nephew's there, but we didn't stop. Saw lots of other folks there who were building rafts. The captain and Mr. Jory, they carried our chest on poles."

Matilda smiled. "You can tell me more about it tomorrow. Let's get to sleep now."

Bart grinned at her. "I'm sure glad you're fine, Ma."

"Me too, Bart." She sighed. "Me too."

The next morning, as the boys chattered about their adventures during the portage, they boarded the bateaux and floated downriver.

"I asked Mr. Hinman to take care of your rig and oxen when I was down here earlier," Captain Magone told Matilda. "I tried to check with him now, but he said he was too busy to talk."

"You've done more than anyone could ask."

"I'll track down your cattle and let you know when I do." Magone gazed toward the riverbank. "We'll be in Oregon City soon. I'll introduce you to John McLoughlin, and he'll take care of you from there."

"I don't know how we can repay your kindness."

"No need." Magone's face flushed red. "I only wish Nicholas hadn't … well, I wish he had made it too."

Matilda remained quiet. This was her husband's dream, building a house in the green fertile farmland of the Northwest. Raising the boys in Oregon Territory. Farming and raising cattle. His dream. And now hers.

The captain cleared his throat. "Do you know what you'll do next? I spoke with William when I brought the others earlier. He promised to send word east to let the family know what happened. He said he might be able to take you back to Missouri in the spring."

"And leave Jane alone out here?" Matilda shook her head. "No, I don't think going back is the answer. Besides, we're lucky five of us arrived safely. I can't take the chance of losing one of my boys on the journey home."

She sighed. "Truth be told, I can't fathom retracing that arduous trek. It was horrid enough once." She gazed at the riverbank, the towering Douglas fir trees, the green grass swooping like velvet toward the river. "No. I believe whenever I find a home out here, I'll stay put. Forever."

"You'll probably be looking for a husband?" He glanced sideways at her. "I know I'm a mite young…"

"Oh, Joseph!" She smiled. "I've seen the way you look at Mary Ann Thompkins. She adores you. You deserve a pretty, young woman who will give you many children. I'm old enough to be her mother."

"You're not old." Magone let his gaze sweep over her body, and he flushed again. "I mean, you're older than me, but you're not old."

Matilda arched an eyebrow. "I am more than a dozen years older than you. And probably a score older than Mary Ann." She placed a hand on his arm. "You need to marry a beautiful young woman who deserves a goodhearted, strong man like you." She tucked one of her auburn curls back into her bun. "I may marry again, although I can't imagine a husband other than Nicholas."

"He was one of a kind, that's for sure." Magone chuckled. "Never met a man so jovial. What a keen sense of humor he had. And his laugh!"

Matilda smiled at the memory of her husband's boisterous laughter. Yes, he was one of a kind. But Mrs. Whitman was right. She had no time for foolish or romantic notions, not when her family's survival depended entirely on her. Who knew what tomorrow would bring? Words from the gospel of Matthew echoed in her mind. "Take therefore no thought for the morrow: for the morrow shall take thought for the things of itself."

Matilda heard the thunderous roar and jerked to her feet. Her eyes skittered ahead, flashing left and right. Fear pounded in her heart. Her body trembled as she panted.

"It's the falls—Willamette Falls." Magone shifted on his feet beside her on the flat-bottomed boat. "Don't worry. They'll stop the bateaux before we reach them."

Matilda's hand pressed against her pounding chest. She inhaled deeply and coughed. "We're almost to Oregon City?"

"Just ahead. You can't miss it."

"The end of the Oregon Trail," Matilda whispered. Dozens of wooden buildings nestled along the east side of the river, some with whitewashed walls, others with bare wood planks. A main street ran through the town's center, a church with a belfry towered over the shorter buildings. The forty-foot-high Willamette Falls served as a dramatic backdrop to the city, which had about seventy-five buildings.

"What's that, Ma?" Grundy pointed to a large wooden structure along the riverbank.

"I'm not certain." She looked toward the captain.

"Believe that's a grist mill, grinding wheat into flour." The captain pointed down the shore. "That there's a lumber mill."

"It's larger than I imagined." Matilda surveyed the shoreline. "How many people are here?"

"Heard tell about a thousand," Magone said. "Growing all the time, with each wagon train that rolls west. It's the capital of the provisional government."

The guides navigated the boat to the shore. The captain assisted her to the shore.

"I'll take you to Dr. McLoughlin's place straightaway." Magone replaced his hat on his head. "It's just up the hill a bit."

Matilda turned to the Jorys.

"James, Sarah." She blinked back tears. "Thank you so much for all you've done for our family."

Sarah embraced Matilda. "You would have done as much for us."

James Jory shook her hand. "Mrs. Koontz, we'll probably see you again soon. We'll make a point to stop by the doctor's when we're in town."

He turned to Captain Magone. "Thank you again for your help, Joseph. We could never have asked for a better captain."

Magone shook his hand. He glanced at the dark clouds overhead. "I'd better get Mrs. Koontz and the boys to the big house."

As they walked along Main Street, the captain pointed out commercial stores, two blacksmith shops, and two flour mills in the bustling community of Oregon City. Matilda followed him up the hill, her right hand grasping Johnny's. She pulled her little son along at times as he swiveled his head right and left, trying to take in all the sights.

Standing before the large two-story white house, Matilda glanced at Magone. "Are you sure we're welcome here?"

"I assure you. He asked me to bring you here. He's a most hospitable man."

At his knock, a large older woman with brown skin answered.

"Captain Magone, isn't it?" She opened the door wider. "And is this the poor widow you spoke of?"

"Good afternoon, Mrs. McLoughlin." Magone removed his hat and tipped his head. "Yes, this is Mrs. Koontz, and these are her sons—Henry, Bart, Grundy, and Johnny."

"Come in. Come in." She led the way inside. "You must be hungry after your journey. Eloisa! We have guests."

A younger woman hurried from another room, wiping her hands on a cloth.

"This is the Widow Koontz." Mrs. McLoughlin introduced Matilda to her daughter, Eloisa. "We have a room ready for you."

Matilda couldn't speak around the lump that formed in her throat as the words "Widow Koontz" pierced her soul. Taking a deep, steadying breath, she replied, "We are so grateful for your hospitality." She followed the older woman, herding her boys before her. "We can never thank you enough."

"My husband likes to help people—British, Americans, Indians." She smiled. "We welcome you to our home and to Oregon Territory."

Oregon Territory. We made it, Nicholas. She blinked back tears.

After freshening up in the room they shared, they walked to the dining room for a feast of fried chicken, potatoes, corn, and bread. When the meal ended, Captain Magone rose. "I'll be saying goodbye now."

"Will you be seeking land in the valley?" Matilda asked.

"I'm heading back to The Dalles Mission to see if I can round up any of your missing cattle. I'll be in touch."

"Thank you again. You are truly the best of friends."

She bid him goodbye and realized she and her boys were now living in a strange house in a strange land at the mercy of strangers.

Come what may, they would survive.

Thirty-Three

November 1847, Oregon City

D R. JOHN MCLOUGHLIN towered over Matilda by a foot. As she entered the dining room that evening carrying a bowl filled with mashed potatoes, she saw the legendary doctor seated at the head of the table. She had heard much about the former chief factor of the Hudson's Bay Company at Fort Vancouver, but she never imagined meeting him in person, much less staying in his Oregon City home with his wife, daughter, and grandchildren.

He stood and grasped her hand, gazing at her with steely blue-gray eyes. Shoulder-length bushy white hair framed his ruddy face. He was probably in his sixties.

She thanked him for his hospitality and scurried back to the kitchen for more platters of food. As they sat for dinner, she spoke again to her host.

"We'd like to repay you." From her pocket, Matilda brought out the pouch containing a few coins and handed it to him. "It isn't much, but it's all we have. And the boys and I are hard workers."

He gave her back the money pouch. "I'm sure Marguerite will appreciate your continued assistance in the kitchen."

"I surely would," Marguerite McLoughlin said to her husband. "You're a talented cook, my dear. Eloisa and I can both learn from you."

Warmth flooded Matilda's cheeks as she looked down at the table. "I enjoy cooking."

The doctor's deep voice boomed when he spoke. "Your older boys might be able to work at the store."

"Can we, Ma?" Henry sat up straighter in his chair.

"Yes, Ma. Can we?" Bart shifted his gaze between his mother and the older man.

"As long as you don't believe they'll be a hindrance." She looked at her sons in turn. "They're good boys."

"How long have you lived here, Dr. McLoughlin?" Henry asked the question before shoveling a chunk of roast beef into his mouth.

He stared ahead for a moment. "Marguerite, when did we move here?" He winked at Henry. "We've been married almost forty years, and she remembers details better than I do—even though she's a decade older than me."

Matilda stopped with her fork halfway to her mouth. He had married an older woman? They seemed so well matched, the doctor and his wife. Perhaps … No, Captain Magone deserved a young woman like Mary Ann Thompkins, not a widow with four boys.

"It was 1825, because David was only four," Marguerite said. "So going on twenty-three years." She dished a helping of roast beef onto her plate. "Eloisa, you were what? Eleven?"

Eloisa nodded, her mouth full.

"I started as chief factor at Fort Vancouver," the doctor continued. "Built three houses here in '29. Ran fur-trading posts both places."

"Why's it called Oregon City now?" Bart asked.

"When the Americans moved in and settled south of the Columbia River, I gave them land for a Methodist church and a store—Abernethy's Store down the street." McLoughlin shook his head. "I changed the name from Willamette Falls when I platted the town. I decided to call it Oregon City, since it's the end of the Oregon Trail. The place just keeps growing."

McLoughlin waved his hand over his plate. "You cook this, Mrs. Koontz?"

Heat flushed her cheeks. She nodded.

"You are a good cook." He leaned back and scrutinized her face. "You're a handsome woman, too, and men outnumber women here twenty to one."

"She don't need a husband!" Henry interrupted. "She has one—our pa."

"Henry!" Matilda's face flushed even more. "Your manners. Dr. McLoughlin is our host."

"But Ma—ain't no one going to take Pa's place."

"You're right, Henry. Nobody could ever take your father's place." She bit her lower lip. "But, chances are, I'll need to marry again to provide a good home for you boys."

"I don't want a new pa." Henry pushed back his chair and stormed from the room.

Matilda's heart broke at her son's anguish. She didn't want any husband but Nicholas, yet she might need to marry again. Henry was too young to understand. She wanted to comfort him, but leaving the dinner table would be rude.

"Now, Mrs. Koontz, there's no need to rush to marry again." The chief factor strode to a sideboard and poured liquid from a decanter into a glass.

"We're happy to have you here," Marguerite said. "We don't want you marrying the first man who comes courting. Believe me, you'll have your pick with so many men here looking for a wife."

Matilda shook her head. Marcus had rejected her, calling off their engagement and leaving her devastated. Nicholas had pursued her for years before she finally relented and married him. Their love had flourished, growing deeper and stronger with each passing year. No wonder her heart felt shattered, leaving only a hollow void. Now, instead of love, she would marry for a roof over her head and security for her sons. Necessity outweighed romance for a widow alone with four boys on the Northwest frontier.

"In the meantime, I'd better make myself useful and wash these dishes." Matilda stacked the plates and strode toward the kitchen. "Grundy, Bart. Will you bring in the rest?"

"Yes, Ma." Bart pushed back his chair, loaded his arms, and followed her. Grundy trailed behind him.

As she lowered dishes into the sink, Matilda spoke to Grundy. "Please watch Johnny while I'm busy here." Gazing at Bart, she added, "You want to find Henry? Please tell him I need to speak with him after I clean up."

Bart nodded and ran down the hallway. Eloisa entered the kitchen and picked up a dish towel.

After helping her finish cleaning up, Matilda folded the wet cloth and draped it over a rack to dry. She walked down the hall and peered into the rooms. She found Henry sitting on their bedroom floor, his back to a wall, tossing a marble into the air and catching it. Bart was nowhere to be seen, so evidently Henry had chased him off.

She stepped into the room and sat on the narrow bed. "Would you like to talk?"

"What's there to talk about?" Henry glared at her. "You might be able to forget Pa, but I can't. I won't!"

Matilda crossed her arms over her chest and bit back the tears that threatened. "I haven't forgotten your father. I'll never forget your father. I loved him. I still do." She paused and cast her eyes upward, as if the words she needed were written on the ceiling.

Her mind returned to her conversation with Mrs. Whitman several weeks earlier, when the older woman talked about trusting God and preparing for her family's future. The doctor's wife didn't know the effect of her words. Narcissa had helped Matilda realize her family could still achieve her husband's dream, but it was up to her to see it through.

She must be wise in her decision, though. All their lives depended on it. She would continue to ask the Lord for guidance navigating their unknown future … and even this conversation with her sons. "Mrs. Whitman made a good point when she explained that I'll likely need to marry again in order to achieve your father's dreams."

"What does that old lady know?" Henry blurted out.

"Henry!" she chastised. "She and her husband were kind to us and nursed me back to health."

"Yeah." Henry glowered. "I suppose so."

Matilda sighed. "Nobody will ever take your father's place, but we do need a roof over our heads. We can't impose forever on the McLoughlins."

She looked at her eldest son, love filling her heart. She recalled Nicholas strutting around their house, filled with pride as he held his firstborn son. She blinked back tears. "You remember the dream your father shared, about building a cabin in the woods, farming hundreds of acres, raising cattle and horses?"

Henry nodded.

"I want us to achieve his dream. For him. For you. For me. But… I can't do it without a husband."

"Why not?" Henry demanded. "Why can't you do it without a husband?"

"Only men can own property." She clasped her hands in her lap. "The law won't let me claim the land as a woman."

"But I'm a man," Henry inserted. "I helped get the wagon across the trail. I drove the team. Got us here to Oregon City."

"Yes, you did. And a fine job you did, too, Henry." She hugged him briefly. "The captain told me how respectful and diligent you were, how good you were with your brothers. I'm proud of you."

Matilda swallowed. She loved this boy. He was so like his father. Strong, determined, stubborn. "But you're nine, Henry. Only men over eighteen can hold land. It's the law."

"It's a stupid law," Henry said.

"If your father had died after he filed for the land, I could have kept the property," she said. "At least that's what the doctor told me. But a woman alone with four boys … without a husband…" She sighed.

Henry remained quiet. She could almost see his brain sifting through options, trying to find an alternative where there was none. She should know. She'd reviewed her limited options time and again.

She bent to look him in the eye. "The Bible tells us an important truth, Henry, and I'm holding on to Jeremiah's promises: 'For I know the thoughts that I think toward you, saith the Lord, thoughts of peace and not of evil, to give you an expected end.' Our lives, Henry, our futures, are all in God's hands." She paused. "Well, we might be able to live with William and Jane for a time." Matilda leaned toward her son. "I'm certain he'll invite us when he knows we've arrived. So … that's one option." She stood. "Meanwhile, we'll do our best to help Dr. and Mrs. McLoughlin in gratitude for their hospitality."

She walked to the door and turned. "Dr. McLoughlin said he'll take you to the store with him in the morning. You will help him, won't you?"

Henry nodded, still clutching the marble in his palm, eyes to the floor.

A constant drizzle from gray and cloudy skies soaked the grass. The days settled into a routine as Henry and Bart helped Dr. McLoughlin in his store each day. They'd lived with the McLoughlins for nearly three weeks.

Matilda found work helping a tailor in town after she showed him samples of her stitchery. She insisted on giving most of what she earned to the McLoughlins for their room and board.

She rose early one morning to leave for the tailor's but checked on her younger boys first. Grundy was awake and dressed, but Johnny lay in the bed, tossing and kicking at his covers, his face flushed. Matilda placed her hand on his sweaty brow. His skin was burning.

Dropping to her knees beside the bed, she pulled back the covers to examine her three-year-old's body. She inhaled a deep breath. Just as she had feared. A red rash spread across his stomach and up his chest.

Measles!

Her hands and legs trembled as she ran to the kitchen and dipped a clean cloth in cool water. *I can't lose Johnny, too.* She knelt by his bedside and placed the wet cloth on his brow.

"Grundy." She tried to keep panic from her voice. "Please can you go to the tailor's and tell Mr. Wirt I won't be in today. If he has sewing for me to do, please bring it back, and I'll work on it here. Tell him … tell him Johnny has the measles."

"Measles?" Grundy scratched his head. "Isn't that what killed all those Cayuse kids?"

"Yes, it is. But …" she paused. "Johnny will be fine." *God willing.* She stroked Grundy's shoulder and propelled him toward the doorway. "Go on, now. Be quick about it."

Grundy's footsteps raced down the hallway and pattered down the stairs.

Matilda tried to think back to when the older boys had the disease four years ago—before Johnny was born. They coughed frequently and their noses ran constantly. She'd tried to keep them from scratching the pustules on their skin so they wouldn't scar. Beyond cooling her youngest son's fever and feeding him broth, she couldn't think how else to treat her son. Perhaps she could ask Dr. McLoughlin when he returned home tonight. She prayed. Fervently.

"Mama?" Johnny coughed and sat up. "I don't feel good."

"I know, honey. You just lie there. I'll bring you some soup."

He fell back against the pillow. Matilda brought a bowl of broth from the kitchen. She nudged him awake again. "Here, Johnny. Wake up and eat some soup."

He twisted his head away, but as she brought the spoon to his mouth, he opened his lips and swallowed. After only a few sips, he turned away, fast asleep.

Matilda dampened the cloth and cooled his forehead. She heard the downstairs door open and close, then footsteps on the steps.

Grundy opened the bedroom door, his arms full of cloth. "Here, Ma. He said he hopes Johnny gets better soon." He handed her the material, dropped to the floor, and crossed his legs under him. "He said you could sew those here. And don't come back till Johnny's better."

Matilda grimaced. Nobody wanted to be near anyone who had been exposed to the measles. She didn't blame Mr. Wirt. They often heard reports of deaths from measles, especially among the Native Americans.

As she sewed a shirt and watched Johnny, a loud pounding sounded on the door downstairs.

"Mrs. Koontz?" Marguerite McLoughlin hollered.

"Grundy, you stay with Johnny." Matilda set down the shirt and skittered to the hallway. "Stay here."

She ran down the stairs to the door, where Mrs. McLoughlin stood beside two bedraggled men whose clothes were caked with dirt and mud.

"Mrs. Koontz, do you suppose your son could fetch John?" Although Marguerite's face remained stoic, her voice wavered slightly, catching on her husband's name.

Matilda nodded and raced back up the stairs. "Grundy. Will you run to the store and ask Dr. McLoughlin to return home? Tell him it's important."

"What is it, Ma?"

"I don't know, Son. Please hurry."

Grundy rushed down the stairs and out the door. After checking on Johnny, who slept fitfully, Matilda returned to the parlor, where Mrs. McLoughlin had seated the two men. After glancing at her hostess, Matilda said, "I'll bring coffee."

Marguerite nodded her thanks.

Matilda returned with three mugs and a pot of hot coffee. She would wait until the men left before asking the doctor if he would examine Johnny.

The front door opened, and Dr. McLoughlin barreled inside, Grundy at his heels.

Matilda motioned to her son. "Please go on up and sit with Johnny."

"But, Ma, do I have to?" He looked at the two men seated at the table. "Something exciting's happened."

"Never you mind. Please do as I told you." She patted his bottom. "Up the stairs."

As she stacked cookies she had baked yesterday onto a plate to serve in the dining room, Matilda considered what news the men brought. She didn't want Grundy to hear anything horrible. He and her other sons had already suffered enough. When she carried the cookies into the sitting room, Dr. McLoughlin nodded at her. "Pull up a chair, Mrs. Koontz. This concerns you, too, since you know the Whitmans."

"What is it?" Matilda glanced at each man in turn as she sat. "Has something happened to them?"

McLoughlin gestured toward the stockier of the two men.

"Sixty Cayuse and Umatilla attacked the mission. Killed the doctor and his wife."

Matilda gasped. "Oh, no!" Tears welled in her eyes.

"They pounded on the door and demanded milk and medicine," the stockier man continued. "When the doctor brought medicine, a Cayuse struck him in the head from behind with a tomahawk. Another shot him in the neck." The man dropped his eyes to the table. "Mrs. Whitman tried to help her husband, but they made her leave the house. Then they shot her. Killed the Sager boys—John and Francis—along with nine other men."

"When did it happen?" The doctor's voice was low.

"Monday night, November 29th. They hacked the doctor's face so bad we couldn't hardly recognize him." The stocky man pounded his fist on the table. "Heard that cussed devil Joe Lewis stirred up the Indians, talking bad about the Whitmans."

"Oh, no." Matilda whispered the words again.

"What is it, Mrs. Koontz?" the doctor asked.

"I heard him, before we left the mission, talking with a group of men." She recounted what she remembered. "I should have told someone, but we were leaving and…" Truth be told, she'd forgotten, plain and simple. And now the Whitmans were dead.

Marguerite McLoughlin patted her hand. "You couldn't have known, dear."

The thinner man added, "They took the others hostage."

"How many?" McLoughlin rubbed a hand over his chin.

"More than fifty, mostly women and children," said the stocky fellow. "Joe Meek's daughter. Jim Bridger's, too. And the Sager girls."

"They're demanding a ransom," the other man said.

"What do they want?" McLoughlin asked.

"Blankets. Shirts. Rifles. Ammunition. Tobacco." The stocky man continued the story. "Peter Skene Ogden's gone to Vancouver to talk with the chief factor."

McLoughlin nodded. "This bloodshed is likely to continue. And it's the Cayuse who will pay the price."

"As well they should." The stocky man again pounded the table. "If I could get my hands on them, I'd string them up sooner—"

McLoughlin coughed, and the man stopped midsentence.

"Sorry, Mrs. McLoughlin. Ma'am."

"Please excuse me." Matilda stood. "I need to check on my son."

She swept from the room before she could burst into tears. Those precious people! Slaughtered by the same Indians she had met at the mission only a few weeks ago. She trembled as she bent over Johnny and then pulled Grundy onto her lap, even though she knew he considered himself too old at five for snuggling. But she needed the comfort of holding him close.

She recalled Mrs. Whitman's words to her in the kitchen: "We've been caring for emigrants here since they started coming across the mountains four years ago. You aren't the first who arrived sick, and you won't be the last."

A shudder rolled through Matilda, the fine hairs prickling at the back of her neck. Her family very well could have been the last.

THIRTY-FOUR

AFTER FOLLOWING DR. MCLOUGHLIN'S recommended bed rest, fluids, and sponge baths, Johnny's measle spots faded. Matilda's heart broke for all the Cayuse mothers whose children had died from the disease, but she thanked God for sparing Johnny's life.

Tasking Grundy with watching his younger brother, Matilda left for work at Mr. Wirt's. The sun wouldn't rise for another half hour, but she needed to finish her sewing before the shop opened at eight.

As she neared the tailor's shop, a hand grasped her elbow. She turned. Nicholas' nemesis, Jim Rawlins, leered at her. Matilda's heart pounded. She glanced around the deserted street.

"Mrs. Koontz, isn't it?" the familiar high-pitched voice said. "It's me, Jim Rawlins."

Matilda looked pointedly at his hand on her arm.

Rawlins laughed and dropped it before tipping his hat. "I meant no offense, Mrs. Koontz," he said. "I only wanted to offer my condolences again on the death of your husband."

"Once was enough, Mr. Rawlins." Matilda pursed her lips, recalling how Nicholas had chuckled when he told her Rawlins had cursed him, saying he hoped her husband would die at the hands of a hostile Indian or a ravenous bear. She swallowed the lump in her throat. "You got what you wanted. Nicholas is dead."

And she wanted nothing to do with Rawlins. Pulling her skirts away from his muddy boots, she resumed her stride toward the tailor's shop.

"Now, please don't be like that, Mrs. Koontz." Rawlins grabbed her upper arm and jerked her to a halt. "I'm just trying to see if I can help in any way."

Matilda yanked her arm loose. Her skin tingled like dozens of filthy spiders crawled over it. "I have nothing to say to you."

"Why, Mrs. Koontz, you're a widow alone out here." He strutted beside her as she hurried. "You need a man to claim your land. To farm. To help raise those boys."

Matilda's face flamed in fury at the unfair truth in his words.

"How dare you!" She shouted, glaring into his squinty eyes. "How dare you even speak to me after setting fire to our wagon and cursing Nicholas. I never want to see you again."

As she reached for the doorknob of the tailor's shop, Rawlins grabbed her arms and spun her to face him, lifting her feet from the ground. She struggled, kicking her legs, pounding her fists.

"Put me down!" Matilda raised the volume of her voice. "Now!"

"Don't be so high-and-mighty, *Matilda*!" He hissed her name as if speaking with a serpent's tongue. "What makes you think I set fire to your wagon? Nobody saw what happened, so nobody knows what happened." He stepped back and released her. "Without your husband, you'll need a man out here. I can help."

She wanted to spit in his face, but she had never spit in her life. Instead, she yanked one arm free and slapped him. "I'd never marry you, not if you were the last man on earth!"

As red spread across his cheek, Rawlins grabbed her by the arms again. "You struck me! You vicious wench!"

Footsteps pounded on the makeshift boardwalk.

"What's going on?" A deep voice boomed the question in a British accent. "Unhand the lady, you miscreant!"

Matilda shifted her gaze from Rawlins to a gentleman in a suit, his raised arm holding a riding crop. Bushy brown sideburns flanked the man's cheeks, and one eye appeared completely white.

Rawlins released Matilda's arms and whipped around. "Who do you think you are? This doesn't involve you."

"Any time an animal paws a lady in public, it's my business." He snapped the riding crop against his shiny boot, glaring at the taller man. "I'll thank you to go on about your business and leave this lovely lady alone."

Rawlins stood a moment and glared at the newcomer. He started to open his mouth, but the stockier man once again raised his riding crop.

"Would you prefer that I bring this down on your head?" The gentleman spoke the words softly, yet his furrowed brows and one-eyed glare indicated he meant what he said.

Rawlins winked and leered. "I'll see you soon, Mrs. Koontz."

Shivers slid down her spine as Rawlins sauntered down the muddy road. She released her breath. Her body trembled, and she leaned against the shop door. Tears swam in her eyes as she shifted her gaze to her rescuer.

"Tha—Than ..." The words caught. She tried again. "Thank you."

The British gentleman shook his head and pulled down his waistcoat before looking at her. "My dear lady, you've had quite a shock." He removed his tall top hat, lowered it to his waist, and bowed. "May I introduce myself? John Robinson Jackson, at your service."

Matilda tried to smile, but her lips quivered. "Mrs. Nicholas Koontz," she said, adding after a moment. "Matilda Koontz."

"I'm sorry your husband wasn't with you this morning to kick that scoundrel down the road." Mr. Jackson shook his head. "What kind of manners do these wild men possess? To accost a lady!"

"I'm unharmed, Mr. Jackson." Matilda smoothed her skirts, wiping sweat from her palms. "Only a bit shaken."

"Do you know that cad?"

Matilda nodded. "He accompanied us west in Captain Magone's train, but he and my husband didn't get along."

"I can see your husband possesses outstanding discernment, madam." Mr. Jackson smiled.

Matilda dropped her eyes. She cleared her throat, then gazed toward the gray January clouds masking the rising sun. "Late husband."

"Oh, I am so sorry." Jackson stepped back. "May I ask what happened?"

"He drowned in the Snake River … at Three Island Crossing."

"Was that last summer?" Jackson asked.

Matilda nodded. She didn't trust her voice to speak.

He cleared his throat. "I know how hard it can be to lose your spouse. My sweet Rachel died in childbirth—back in '38. Can't believe she's been gone a decade." He dropped his eyes to the ground. "Our wee babe died in my arms."

Matilda's eyes watered, knowing full well the heartache of losing both a spouse and a baby. But she remained silent.

Jackson cleared his throat again. "Do you have children, ma'am?"

"Yes, four sons. We've been fortunate that Dr. and Mrs. McLoughlin opened their home to us until we decide what to do next."

"You couldn't be in better hands." Jackson glanced down the road toward the large white house. "He and Marguerite are wonderful people."

"Indeed they are." Matilda glanced at the door behind her. "I should be going—Mr. Wirt is expecting me to open the shop."

"Oh, by all means." Jackson bowed again. "I'm sorry to delay you. I imagine I'll see you while I'm in town for supplies. John has already invited me to dinner before I leave for the north again next week."

Matilda offered a tentative smile as she opened the shop door. "It's nice to meet you, Mr. Jackson. I look forward to seeing you later. And, again, thank you."

Thirty-Five

THAT NIGHT, EXHAUSTED, Matilda collapsed onto the bed. Sleep eluded her as she fretted over the encounter with Rawlins, grateful again for the intervention of the fine British gentleman. He was a curious man, handsome despite his blinded eye, of medium build with dark hair and long sideburns. Matilda chastised herself. How could she even think of a man as handsome? And what did looks matter? Nicholas was the finest man she'd ever met, but nobody would call him handsome. Jovial, yes. Practical. Hardworking. Oh, how she loved him!

Was it wrong to think of another?

She probed the hole in her heart left by the death of her husband, the loss of her daughter, the pain in Jackson's voice when he spoke of the deaths of his wife and baby. So much pain. When would it end? Tears dampened her pillow as she sobbed.

Matilda woke up groggy and forced herself to rise. She had responsibilities. Her sons depended on her, especially Johnny, although he was healing well. In the kitchen, she tied on an apron before baking a pie and preparing sandwiches for Captain Magone, who had been so kind to her and the boys.

Mr. McMillan, who was in their wagon train, said the captain was still at The Dalles Mission, searching for her cattle. She wanted to send food in gratitude for his efforts on her behalf, and Mr. McMillan was heading to the mission today, so he could give her package to him. She hoped the young man wed Mary Ann Thompkins and found land to claim. She also heard the captain had joined the volunteer Oregon militia chasing Cayuse warriors into the mountains.

She carried the food to the tailor's shop, where Mr. McMillan said he'd pick it up. With so many single men in Oregon City, the shop stayed busy with mending, laundering, and sewing new trousers, shirts, coats, and warm cloth hats. Matilda counted herself fortunate to find a job to help offset the expenses incurred by her hosts. Dr. McLoughlin didn't want to accept her money, but she had pleaded with him. She didn't want to be a burden. Nicholas wouldn't want her to be one either.

"Federal troops are here to hunt down the Indians who killed Dr. Whitman and his wife." Mr. Wirt glanced out the shop window as a dozen men on horses passed. "I hope they find them." The tailor gave her a quick look. "You're fortunate you left when you did."

"Indeed, we are." Matilda folded the shirt she had finished mending and joined her employer at the window. "They were so kind to us, tending to me until I gained strength."

"Those Indians knew the Whitmans." Mr. Wirt shook his head. "I don't know why they turned on them."

"The measles, I think." Matilda whispered the words as she returned to the counter and picked up a pair of trousers to patch. She knew how frightened the Indians had been, watching helplessly as their children suffered from measles and died. Joe Lewis had fueled their anger. Even so, she couldn't countenance violence. How could bloodshed help those who had perished? And now, with the arrival of the soldiers, even more people were likely to die.

Matilda thought of the Sager boys who had already suffered the deaths of both parents ... and now themselves. Their sisters must be devastated. She recalled the Whitmans with immense gratitude. True, the doctor could be abrupt in dealing with the natives, perhaps even harsh. And his wife largely ignored them, almost like slave owners in Missouri who viewed people as property based on their skin color. But both of the Whitmans had shown nothing but kindness to her and the boys.

While she sewed later that afternoon, the bell above the door jangled. Matilda bit the end of the thread, tied off the stitch, then stood and walked to the counter.

"May I help you?" Something about the well-dressed man in front of her struck a familiar chord, but she couldn't place him.

"Matilda?" The man removed his hat. "Is that you?"

She tilted her head and looked again at the man—blond hair curling at his shoulders, a trimmed mustache, blue eyes. Why did he seem familiar?

The man laughed. "It's not good for a man's pride when his former fiancée can't remember him."

"Marcus?" Shocked, she dropped the shirt in her hands. "Is that you? I'm sorry, but it's been nearly twenty years. What are you doing in Oregon Territory?"

He laughed again. "Same as most everyone else, I expect. Looking for free land and a new life."

"But your family. Did you bring your wife and children?"

Pink rose to his cheeks as he shook his head. "Mmmm ... no. She—We ... " He glanced around the shop. "I'm alone out here."

"I'm so sorry, Marcus." Matilda bit her lip. "Did she pass away?"

He shrugged noncommittally, looking away from her, both hands in his front pockets. "Oregon Territory offers everyone a new start, doesn't it?"

"I thought you'd settled in St. Louis. That's what Philip said he'd heard."

"Your brother? I remember him. How is he?" Marcus leaned an elbow on the counter and gazed at Matilda. "Did he come west too?"

She shook her head. "Not yet. He plans to come in a year or two with his family. But his eldest son traveled with us."

"Us? Is your husband here with you? I heard you'd married."

Matilda flushed as Marcus roved his eyes over her body. "Yes, I did marry. Nicholas Koontz."

"Nicholas?" Marcus chuckled. "Wasn't he the fellow always hanging around your place whenever I came courting?"

"He wasn't overly fond of you." Matilda smiled.

"Probably not, since I was moving in on his girl." Marcus laughed again. "Where is the big old coot?"

Matilda sighed. "He—he didn't make it."

"What do you mean, he didn't make it?"

Matilda folded a cloth on the counter and tucked it into a cubbyhole. "He drowned. Crossing the Snake River."

"Oh, I see." Marcus coughed. "I'm sorry to hear that. So you're alone out here?"

"Not alone, no. I'm here with our four boys."

"Four sons?" Marcus gently tossed his head. "My, you have been busy!"

"I'm still busy, Marcus." She placed both palms on the counter and looked him in the eye. "I'm working for Mr. Wirt. What can we do for you?"

"Oh, yes. I did come in here for a reason, didn't I?" He rubbed his palm over his forehead. Reaching into a saddlebag slung over his shoulder, he pulled out a wad of clothes. "I need to have these washed and mended. Won't do for me to run around with holes in my shirts and pants."

Matilda spread out three shirts and two pairs of pants. She ran her fingers over the material to find the holes.

"I need buttons on those shirts, too."

"I can see that." Matilda mentally counted the number of patches she'd need to sew on the shirts and pants, the buttons, and estimated the cost. "We can have these for you by the end of the week."

He lifted his hat off his head and ran his fingers through his curls. "Matilda, do you reckon—" He replaced his hat. "Do you think we could have dinner one night?"

Matilda swallowed. She would have given anything when she was eighteen to rekindle their flagging romance. But that was before he had broken her heart, before she'd married Nicholas at twenty-six. Now she was a woman alone, far from home. She enjoyed seeing a familiar face. But Marcus? He had hurt her deeply.

"What do you say?" He leaned again on the counter. "Please? Just two old friends enjoying dinner together?"

"I don't know." She knelt below the counter to rearrange material in a cubby and escape his jaunty gaze. "I don't think it would be appropriate."

The door rattled and Mr. Wirt entered the store and glanced at her. "Is everything in hand here?"

"Yes, it's fine. This gentleman just dropped off clothing for us to mend."

"I'll be back tomorrow." Marcus dropped his voice. "And the next day. Until you say yes."

He pivoted on his foot and bowed briefly to Mr. Wirt on his way out of the store.

"What does he mean, he'll be back tomorrow?" Mr. Wirt harrumphed. "We have other customers ahead of him. Didn't you tell him that?"

"Yes, Mr. Wirt. I told him we could have his clothes mended and ready for pickup at the end of the week."

"That's right." He shuffled behind the counter. "You go on in back and sew for a while. I'll watch for customers."

Matilda welcomed the chance to escape with her needle, thread, and turbulent thoughts.

THIRTY-SIX

ONLY TWO DAYS AFTER SHE MET HIM on the street, John R. Jackson joined them for dinner as he said he would.

Dr. McLoughlin introduced her and the boys to the British gentleman.

"I had the pleasure of meeting Mrs. Koontz a few days ago." Mr. Jackson bowed at the waist. "It's nice to see you again, madam."

Blood rushed to Matilda's face as she recalled the way he had interceded on her behalf with that oaf Rawlins. She murmured a greeting.

As they gathered around the table, Dr. McLoughlin addressed his guest. "How does the construction go, John?"

"The cabin is finished. I hope to expand it later." He glanced at Matilda and her sons. "I've been here more than three years, so I've had time to stake out my land and build."

"Where have you settled then?" Matilda asked.

"Up north," Jackson said. "The doctor here didn't want Americans settling north of Fort Vancouver, but he didn't mind letting a Brit live there. After all, the French-Canadians have been at Cowlitz Farm for more than a decade."

"Cowlitz Farm?"

"The Hudson's Bay Company has two farms up north—one at Fort Nisqually, the other on a prairie at Cowlitz Farm," Dr. McLoughlin explained. "The prairie yields a fine harvest of crops—wheat, oats, peas, and potatoes. They supply Vancouver in winter."

"You live at this Cowlitz Farm, Mr. Jackson?" Henry mumbled around the food in his mouth.

"Henry." Matilda leaned toward him. "You know better than to speak with your mouth full."

Her son gulped. "Do you?"

Jackson chuckled. "No, young man. I don't live at the farm. But I do have land just north of there on what I call Highland Prairie."

"Is it good farmland?" Henry asked.

"Indeed it is."

"Then how come you're here in Oregon City?"

"Henry," Matilda admonished her son. "You don't need to interrogate the McLoughlins' guest."

"No need to worry, Mrs. Koontz." Jackson gave all his attention to Henry. "Fact is, I come down here at least twice a year for supplies. And I always stop to see my friends." He nodded to the doctor and Marguerite.

"It's nice to have friends, especially in these uncertain times," the doctor said as he set down his fork and reached for the platter filled with pot roast, potatoes, and carrots.

"What's happened at the Whitman Mission since..." Jackson cleared his throat and paused as he glanced at Matilda's boys.

"Joe Meek left for Washington City," the doctor said. "He's pleading for a military presence in Oregon Territory to curtail Indian uprisings."

"Meek?" Jackson looked toward the ceiling. "The name sounds familiar, but I can't place him."

"His daughter, Helen, was captured by the Cayuse," Dr. McLoughlin said.

"She was only ten." Tears filled Marguerite's eyes. "She died of measles while in captivity. So did Louise Sager." She swallowed. "Only six."

"Measles?" Johnny's head lifted from his plate. "Like I had?"

Matilda nodded as she glanced at her youngest son, thankful he had survived the illness that had killed those little girls.

Jackson dabbed his mouth with a napkin. "Excellent meal, as usual, Mrs. McLoughlin."

"Actually, Mrs. Koontz prepared most of our dinner." Marguerite smiled at Matilda. "It's been a joy to have someone share the burden of cooking."

"And she's a fine cook too." Dr. McLoughlin placed his napkin beside his empty plate. "Would you care for a cordial, John?"

"Indeed, I would." Jackson stood and bowed to the ladies. "Thank you for a fine dinner." He then followed his host to the library.

The next morning, a rider brought Matilda a letter from Captain Magone. She glanced at the date—January 20, 1848—before she broke the seal. She smiled when she read his greeting, addressing her as "respected friend." He thanked her for the items she had sent his way, but her smile faded as she read the rest of his missive. The man charged with delivering her rig to Park Rose northeast of Portland, a Mr. Alanson Hinman, failed to do so.

The words blurred before her. This Mr. Hinman had stolen her rig? With all their belongings inside? Their clothing, cooking utensils, rifles, gunpowder? Their mattress, quilts, blankets? Everything they had carefully packed in Missouri and hauled more than two thousand miles west save for the few items in her chest of goods. Matilda felt tears stream down her cheeks. They had nothing! She swiped at her damp face so she could continue reading. The captain said he hoped Johnny had recovered from the measles and noted some of Matilda's cattle had been found but not Browny or Old Buck. Or their mare, Belle.

The captain promised to do his best to find and return their animals.

She tucked away the letter, retrieved her handbag, and kissed Grundy and Johnny goodbye before walking toward the tailor shop.

The older boys were already at McLoughlin's store. Marcus had indeed stopped by Mr. Wirt's tailor shop every day, asking her to join him for dinner. To be honest, she was flattered by his attention. She could still lose herself in those crystal blue eyes that twinkled with humor more often than not. She shook herself. "A dandy." That's what Nicholas had called Marcus. Of course, Nicholas was anything but a dandy—and proud of it, too. They couldn't have been more different.

As Matilda entered the shop, she spied Marcus at the counter. He swiveled on his heel and bowed.

Matilda smiled. A dandy, indeed. Nicholas would have laughed at his flirtatious manner.

"I'm hoping to persuade you to enjoy dinner with your old friend from Missouri."

Mr. Wirt lifted a bolt of fabric onto a shelf. "I had wondered why such a fine-looking gentleman would stop every day at a tailor's shop, especially since Mrs. Koontz gave you your clothes on Friday."

Marcus laughed. "I once courted your delightful employee, Mr. Wirt. In fact, we were engaged to marry."

Mr. Wirt's brows drew together as he looked at Matilda. "Is that true, Mrs. Koontz?"

Matilda nodded but kept quiet. She'd just as soon forget the fact that Marcus had jilted her all those years ago.

"Whatever happened?" Mr. Wirt lifted another fabric bolt.

Marcus raised one eyebrow as if daring her to contradict him and then winked. "I believe the lady's attentions were drawn elsewhere, to one Nicholas Koontz, if I'm not mistaken."

Matilda dropped her gaze. "It was all so long ago. And as I've told Mr. Springer already, I prefer to eat dinner with my sons."

"Nonsense." Mr. Wirt hurried around the counter and lowered his voice, though not enough to prevent the words from reaching Marcus. "Mrs. Koontz. You are a widow; you must think of your boys. If you know this fellow, let him take you to dinner."

"Mr. Wirt, I—" Matilda drew a breath and dropped her voice. "Nicholas has been gone only four months."

"In normal circumstances, it might be too soon to court anyone." Mr. Wirt tipped his head to look into Matilda's eyes. "But these are not normal circumstances. You need to think of your future."

Matilda turned away, striding toward the back room. She brought her palms up to cover her face and shook her head. "I don't know ..."

"Mr. Springer seems like a nice man." Mr. Wirt had followed and now prodded her toward the shop's main room. "Dinner isn't a marriage commitment. Just see how it goes."

While Mr. Wirt's interference irritated her, she appreciated his willingness to give her a job when she most needed one. Perhaps he was right. She might need to remarry. But could she trust Marcus after he'd broken her heart once? And what happened to his wife? He never answered her question when she asked about her. Could Matilda marry someone she didn't love? She smiled slightly. She and Nicholas had grown up together, annoying friends who fought and played, but she had grown to love and admire him during their decade of marriage. Maybe she could chance it again.

Resigned, Matilda shuffled into the room and stood behind the counter.

"Well?" Marcus raised both eyebrows. "Dinner tonight? At the hotel?"

"Yes, Marcus." She drew her hands over her hair and patted her bun. "We're staying with Dr. McLoughlin."

He tipped his hat toward her. "I'll stop by for you at dusk."

Matilda had only two dresses in the chest the young captain and Mr. Jory had carried around the falls, so she picked her Sunday best. As she twisted her auburn hair into a bun, a knock sounded on the bedroom door.

"Just a moment." She tucked in a loose strand and opened the door. "Henry. What is it, Son?"

"Bart says you're going to dinner with a man tonight."

Matilda sat on the foot of her bed. "Marcus is a friend from back east."

"Was he a friend of Pa's, too?" Henry glared at her.

"Not exactly." Matilda pulled her eldest son toward her. "I knew him before your father and I started courting."

"So now Pa's gone, you're courting him again?"

Matilda stood. "No, Henry. I'm not courting." She pulled a shawl from a drawer and draped it over her shoulders. "We are going to dinner. That's all."

Henry snorted and stormed out.

Matilda sighed. She walked downstairs to the parlor, where she found Dr. and Mrs. McLoughlin.

"I understand a man is taking you to dinner tonight." Dr. McLoughlin puffed on a pipe. "Marcus Springer. Do you know much about him?"

"I knew Marcus in Missouri, Doctor. We were ... friends."

"I see." McLoughlin puffed again. "John Jackson's coming for dinner again tomorrow." He dumped ash from his pipe into the fire. "He's a good man, Mrs. Koontz. Well off. He could take good care of you and your sons."

"He hasn't—" Matilda stopped. "Mr. Jackson hasn't indicated any desire to court me, Doctor."

"Oh, no?" McLoughlin chuckled. "He's certainly admired you from afar then. He's enamored of your cooking and your looks. He likes your boys, too."

A knock sounded.

"I'll answer that." The doctor strode forward. "I want to meet this fellow."

He opened the door to find Marcus, a small bouquet in hand.

"Um ... Dr. McLoughlin?" Marcus seemed taken aback. "I—these are for Mrs. Koontz."

"I see." Dr. McLoughlin opened the door a bit wider. "Marguerite!" He turned toward his wife. "Would you put these in water? It looks like Mrs. Koontz is ready to leave."

"Thank you." Matilda smiled at Marguerite, then repeated the words to Marcus.

He reached out and cupped her elbow in his palm. "We'll be eating at the hotel. We won't be late."

"See that you aren't." Dr. McLoughlin growled the words. Matilda hid a smile. She imagined the old bear testing the mettle of this young cub. She wondered how much it would take to scare off Marcus once again.

The evening ended at the front porch. When Marcus leaned forward to kiss her, Matilda stepped back.

"Thank you for a pleasant time." As she reached for the doorknob, she stopped and turned. "I do have a question, though. Why did you leave me when we were engaged to be married?"

Marcus backed away as if too close to a fire. "I, um, well..." He cleared his throat. "We were both so young, Matilda, and the distance between our places was so far."

She arched a brow. "I was nearly twenty, and you were even older."

Marcus dropped his gaze to the stone steps. "The truth is, I was scared." He glanced at her face and then away. "I didn't know if I would make a good husband. And when you talked about having children, I panicked."

Matilda chuckled. "Perhaps you were right to leave." She shrugged. "Nicholas was a wonderful husband and father." She grasped the knob and twisted it. "Did you have children?"

Marcus let his gaze drift over her head. He nodded slightly. "I don't want to talk about it."

Had something happened to his children? And his wife? Why wouldn't he talk to her about them?

He placed a hand on her shoulder.

At her look, he let it drop.

"I'm not the same man I was then. I've changed," he said. "Will you have dinner with me again tomorrow night?" Marcus lifted her chin to look into her eyes.

She recalled her teenage years and how giddy he had made her feel when he gazed at her with that sultry look. Now the half-closed lids simply looked ridiculous.

"I can't tomorrow night, Marcus." Mr. Jackson was coming to dinner. She opened the door. "Perhaps another time."

"Friday then?" He held her arm.

Eager to check on her boys, she nodded and entered the house. As she tiptoed up the stairs, she heard the scamper of feet from her room. Of course the boys had waited up for her. She opened the door. All four of her boys lay in their beds, eyes closed. She smiled and kissed each on the forehead.

Thirty-Seven

MATILDA HUNG HER CLOAK on a peg as voices wafted from the living room. What were her boys doing? She hurried to shoo them outside but stopped at sight of the circle on the floor.

Mr. Jackson sat on the rug with Johnny on his lap. "Now you pick one of my cards, Henry."

Henry squinted his eyes as he reached for a card. "I don't want that Old Maid!"

"It's a chancy draw, my boy." Jackson held his cards in a loose grip. "You never know when that little lady will appear."

"Mama!" Johnny scrambled from Jackson's lap and rushed to her, gripping her around the legs. "Play cards."

She bent to lift her youngest son into her arms and smiled. "Good afternoon, Mr. Jackson."

"Mrs. Koontz." He scrambled to stand. "It's always a pleasure to see you."

"I hope my boys haven't been bothering you."

He waved a hand dismissively. "Not at all." He grinned at her sons. "The fact is, I hoodwinked them into playing cards. They took pity on me."

Matilda laughed. Such a kind and gracious gentleman.

"Come on, Ma," Grundy said. "Play with us."

"Why don't Johnny and I sit and watch for a bit so we can learn how it's played?" She settled into a rocking chair.

Henry selected his card and exhaled loudly. "Whew! That was a close one. I thought for sure I'd get her. Your turn, Bart."

As the game progressed, the boys laughed and teased each other, almost like they had with their pa. Matilda relaxed, cradling Johnny as she gently rocked him. He snuggled deeper, nestling his nose into the crook of her neck, his rhythmic breath puffing against her skin. Her eyes widened as she realized what she was feeling: Contentment. A slow smile spread as she closed her eyes. Not long ago, she never imagined feeling content about anything in life. But here she was, surrounded by her laughing sons, snuggling the youngest, listening to the banter among her boys and … Jackson.

"A penny for your thoughts?"

Her eyes flew open at the words, so similar to Nicholas' common phrase but spoken in a soft and lilting English accent. "I so enjoy hearing my sons laugh, Mr. Jackson." She smiled. "Thank you."

"You're raising fine young lads." He glanced at Henry, Bart, and Grundy before looking toward Johnny, sound asleep in her arms. "They're grand fellows. Your husband must have been quite a jolly cove."

"A cove?"

"Fellow. Man." Jackson smiled. "Sometimes I forget myself and throw in English phrases nobody here understands."

"I think of a cove as a small bay." She chuckled as she rocked. "But yes, Nicholas was a jolly man. A hard worker. He loved to regale the boys with stories."

"You should hear the one about his grandpa and the bear!" Henry said.

"And the one about the Indians," Grundy added.

"Well, I hope to hear all those stories." Jackson ruffled the hair of both boys. "Now who has that Old Maid?"

When Marguerite walked into the living room, Matilda laid a sleeping Johnny on the sofa. "Here, let me help you with dinner," she whispered.

"It's fine if you'd prefer to stay with your boys."

"No, they're enjoying a game with Mr. Jackson." She followed Marguerite into the kitchen and tied an apron around her waist.

"John's a good man." Marguerite handed her a basket of potatoes to peel and winked. "He'd make someone a fine husband."

Matilda offered a noncommittal assent as she cut the peeled potatoes and put them into a pan of water to boil.

Marguerite heated lard in a skillet on the stovetop, then salted and pounded flanks of beef before lifting them into the pan, where fat sizzled around the meat.

"As I said, he'd make a good husband." Marguerite looked her in the eye. "He's already built a cabin, and he's planting crops, raising cattle, establishing a fine farm." She shifted back to the stove and flipped the meat. "You could do a lot worse."

Matilda chuckled. "For one thing, he hasn't expressed the slightest interest in marrying me. Besides, I don't know that I'm ready."

"He has, though," Marguerite said.

"Has what?"

"Expressed interest." She laughed. "I heard him asking John all about you and the boys the other evening in the library. He definitely expressed interest."

Matilda kept silent as she worked, pondering the words of her hostess and the surprising but welcome contentment she'd experienced earlier. Not love, like what she'd shared with Nicholas. But perhaps …

On Friday afternoon, a knock sounded at the front door. Before Matilda reached the bottom of the stairs, Marguerite McLoughlin had opened the door. "Mrs. Koontz?" she called. "Marcus Springer is here to see you."

Matilda walked to the door.

"I thought perhaps we could walk near the falls today." Marcus grinned. "I know a perfect spot. I've brought a bit of food."

"What about the boys?" Matilda glanced behind her. "They're anxious to see the falls."

"Um ... I thought it could be just the two of us."

Matilda shook her head.

"But then again, I'm sure your sons would enjoy the outing." He stepped into the house. "What do you say, boys? Would you like to join us for a picnic?"

Her sons shouted their agreement.

Matilda glanced at the basket hanging over Marcus' arm. "I don't imagine you have enough food for all of us." She took the basket. "I'll collect more." Turning to her sons, she said, "Find your jackets. The weather can change quickly."

She hurried to the kitchen, sliced bread, added meat and cheese, then tucked cookies into the basket. Reentering the foyer, she lifted her shawl from a peg.

Marcus took it and draped it over her. As his hands lingered on her shoulders, he leaned forward to whisper, "You look lovely today, as usual. Whatever was I thinking when I let you go?"

Heat rushed to Matilda's cheeks. Marcus hadn't exactly let her go. He had simply forgotten about his fiancée in Saint Charles when his interests were drawn elsewhere. Nicholas had described Marcus back then as a dandy and a flirt. From the looks of it, he still was. She fastened Johnny's coat while Marcus picked up the basket and handed it to Henry.

As they left the house, Matilda smiled as the boys scampered ahead toward the falls. Her former fiancé strolled beside her. "I was hoping to speak with you today. About our future."

"Our future?" Matilda frowned. "What future?"

"That's what I wanted to talk about. I'd like you to marry me, Matilda. We could start fresh here in Oregon Territory. Just you and me."

"What?" Matilda stopped. "What do you mean—just you and me? What about my boys?"

"Oh …" He cleared his throat. "You told me William was worried about Jane's sadness over being unable to conceive." He looked at the ground and kicked a stone. "I thought they might want to raise the boys, seeing as they don't have any children of their own." He leaned close to whisper in her ear. "We could start our own family here."

Matilda pushed away from him. "I will never abandon my sons. Ever." She strode ahead of him and grasped Johnny's hand. The nerve of him! How could he even suggest such a thing? They had just lost their father, and now he wanted her to abandon them too? Only a selfish cad would consider such a thing.

"Matilda." Marcus ran to catch up. "I was only jesting. Of course I want to be a father to your sons."

She doubted he was joking. "My boys and I will be staying together with William and Jane."

"But Matilda—I love you." The words sounded hollow.

Matilda turned toward him. "You scarcely know me. I am not the naïve girl you proposed marriage to in Saint Charles. I'm a grown woman, a widow with four children whom I love. I have responsibilities." She inhaled deeply and blinked away tears. "My romantic notions drowned in the Snake River with Nicholas." She scooped Johnny into her arms as she scurried forward to catch up with her older boys. Marcus lagged behind.

A tall man moved into her path. She stopped and drew back.

"Excuse me, ma'am." Jim Rawlins doffed his hat. "Thought those were your boys passing by. Figured maybe I could join you."

"Mr. Rawlins." Matilda gripped Johnny tighter. "I'll thank you to move out of my way."

"I'm happy to accompany you, Mrs. Koontz." Menace glinted from his eyes.

"No, thank you." Matilda glanced over her shoulder. Marcus had stopped several yards behind her. "We have an escort. Marcus!"

Her former beau shuffled forward.

"Mr. Rawlins, this is Mr. Springer. Marcus, Mr. Rawlins." Matilda skirted away from Nicholas' nemesis. "We must be going."

Rawlins reached out a hand to grasp her elbow, but she shook it off and stormed away. Marcus scurried to keep up.

Behind her, Matilda heard Rawlins' guffaw. She shivered and then sighed. How many other unwanted attentions would she need to fend off as a widow alone in the west?

I miss Nicholas.

When they arrived back at the McLoughlins' home, Matilda urged the boys to wash up for dinner while she said goodbye to Marcus.

"Thank you for the afternoon. The boys and I enjoyed the falls." She swallowed. "But I believe your time would be better spent courting someone else."

"Matilda. Don't be like that." He leaned close and lifted her chin. "There aren't any other women out here as handsome as you."

She recoiled, recalling his timidity when he met Rawlins. She thought of the way Nicholas had stood up to the belligerent oaf. And another man had done so too—Mr. Jackson. The contrast couldn't have been starker. Nicholas was right. Marcus truly was a dandy, all fancy clothes and fine words but little substance.

"I'm sure you'll find someone to woo here in the west." She closed and locked the door.

⚜

Matilda stifled tears as she stared at the blank page. She dreaded having to write the long overdue words to her mother, explaining how both Nicholas and their baby had died. Although her nephew had sent the news east with a traveler more than six months ago, she still had heard nothing from Missouri. Her mother would say she had warned them, time and again, not to go west.

She had. But it didn't matter now.

"How much for postage to St. Louis?" Matilda handed the one-page folded letter to the postmaster.

"Feels like four-pound paper." He weighed the letter in his hand. "A dime will cover it."

Matilda dug into her reticule to retrieve the silver Seated Liberty and handed him the coin.

The man glanced at her name on the letter. "Koontz?" He furrowed his brow. "I believe I have something here for you." He disappeared into a back room and returned to the counter with a letter in hand. "Yes, I thought so. Matilda Koontz?"

"Yes." She inhaled a deep breath. Who could have written to her?

"Here you go." He gave her the letter.

Leaving the small post office, she fingered the paper, looking first at her name and then the return address—William Glover, Champoeg. Her nephew. He and Jane had settled in a French community, judging by the name. She'd heard of the settlement, halfway between Oregon City and Salem. She scurried home to read the letter.

"Boys," she called as she entered the McLoughlins' home. "We have a letter from William and Jane. Gather close."

She sat on a sofa with her sons beside her, scanned the letter's contents, and began to read.

"Dear Aunt,

"I have neglected writing to you thinking I would come down soon but matters and things have made it difficult. I would have been down some time ago had it not been for the Indian trouble."

"Does he mean with the Whitmans?" Henry asked.

She scanned the words and shook her head. "No, not the Cayuse War. I believe he's referring to that battle at Abiqua in February— only two months ago."

"What happened?" Grundy asked. "Was William fighting Indians?"

"I don't know." Matilda glanced at the letter and then closed her eyes, trying to remember what she'd heard from the doctor. "I believe after the men traveled east to fight the Cayuse at Waiilatpu, women left unprotected in the valley were forced to give blankets, food, and livestock to Indians whenever they demanded them. They had to cook for them too."

"Cayuse Indians?" Grundy's eyes opened wide. "The ones who killed …"

"No, no." Matilda leaned forward to reassure her third son. "It wasn't Cayuse. I think Dr. McLoughlin called them Klamath who were visiting the Molallas …. Not all of them. Just some troublemakers."

"What did they want?" Bart asked.

"They might not like white settlers building homes on what they consider their land." She sighed. "But I don't know for sure. All I recall is that white men and Indians exchanged bullets and arrows for two days. Then it was over."

"Who won?" Grundy asked.

"I'm not certain. Let's read the rest of what William wrote." She held up the letter.

"I was in the battle if it deserves to be named. We killed some seven or eight of them and drove the balance off. A good many of the people up here are pretty badly scared, thinking that the Klamath will come on in the summer, but as to my own part, I apprehend no danger."

He discussed plans for a large garden, filled her in on the happenings of mutual friends, and repeated his offer to help.

"I am ready and willing at any time to do anything in my power that I can without money. Money is a thing I can't get. It is my calculation for you to live with me and I want you to. I will do everything to make you comfortable and it will be my delight to do so.

"Jane sends her best love to you and children and wants to see you all very bad."

"That's the end." Matilda smiled at the boys and refolded the letter. "Wash up before dinner."

As she tucked away the letter in their bedroom, she wondered how Jane fared in her new home. Did she still grieve her inability to conceive? She whispered a prayer that God would fill Jane's womb with a little one. Then she brushed her hand over her abdomen, tears springing to her eyes at the thought of her daughter. She wiped them away. No time for self-pity. William and Jane were gracious to offer her and the boys a place to live, but was it realistic?

Unbelievably, she had options. A home with William and Jane. Life with Marcus the dandy. According to Marguerite, John R. Jackson had shown interest before leaving for his cabin up north. But the good Lord knew she'd rather live in a tent alone with her boys than spend another minute in the presence of Jim Rawlins.

THIRTY-EIGHT

THE BELL OVER THE DOOR jangled. Matilda set aside her stitching and stood to greet the customer entering the tailor's shop, then halted. She bit her lower lip and drew a deep breath.

"Widow Koontz." Jim Rawlins sauntered to the counter, towering over her, his spectacles reflecting light from the lamp. He pulled his hand from behind his back. "I brought these for you."

Matilda stared a moment longer into the eyes of the thin man her husband detested. Then she lowered her gaze to his fistful of flowers.

"Thank you, but no." She backed away from the counter. "I don't … don't want anything from you, Mr. Rawlins."

He slapped the flowers onto the counter and leaned forward. "You do need something from me, Mrs. Koontz. You still need a husband. You'll never survive out here—a widow alone with four boys."

She shook her head, wishing with all her heart Mr. Wirt would return from the post office. "I'll be fine."

Rawlins chuckled. "Not likely." He stepped behind the counter.

She shuffled back and bumped against the wall.

"Who's going to prove up land for your claim? Build your cabin? Discipline those boys of yours?" He scoffed. "I can make you a good husband. I'd treat you well. I'll stop by McLoughlin's so he can help you see sense."

"Please don't bother the McLoughlins." Matilda hated the way her voice pleaded. "They've been nothing but gracious to me and the boys."

"They're probably mighty tired of having a houseful of ragamuffins." He sneered. "I imagine he'll be only too happy to plead my case."

Matilda gulped. He gave voice to doubts plaguing her mind each day she remained under the McLoughlin roof. She cooked and cleaned to ease the burden of housing them, and she gave the doctor every extra penny she earned. But the truth was, it couldn't be easy feeding five extra people for months. What could she do?

Rawlins laughed again. "I see you're beginning to heed my words." He tipped the brim of his hat and winked. "Perhaps I'll see you when I stop by tonight."

The bell jingled as Mr. Wirt entered. He looked up from the post in his hand. "Good day, sir. Can I do anything for you?"

Rawlins chortled. "No. I'm just on my way out."

Matilda sank into the chair. She grabbed the sewing, hoping to dissuade the older man from questioning her.

"What did the gentleman want?" He laid the mail on the counter. "Does he need clothes mended?"

Matilda inhaled deeply to steady her voice before she spoke. "No, he didn't need anything mended."

Her employer picked up the crumpled bouquet. "Did he bring these for you?"

Matilda nodded. "I don't—"

"Mrs. Koontz, you're quite pale." Mr. Wirt lifted a folded letter from the pile and waved it before her face, fanning her. "Do you know that man?"

"He traveled west with us in Captain Magone's company."

"What does he want?" The tailor tipped his head to the side. "Is he courting you?"

Matilda pursed her lips. "He wants to." She stood. "But my husband had no use for the man—and neither do I."

He returned to the pile of mail. "I understand ... and that other young man seems quite enamored of you. But ... you probably don't want to wait too long to decide."

Tears threatened to flood her eyes. Bowing her head, she folded the suit she'd been sewing. "Sir, I hope you don't mind. I'm not feeling well. May I leave early?"

He eyed the pile of work he'd left earlier. She had mended and neatly folded each shirt, jacket, and pair of pants, stacking them behind the counter with tags listing the owners. "Of course. Thank you for finishing your work for the day. I hope you feel better soon."

Matilda clutched her bag and darted outside. She needed fresh air. Time to think. She ducked her head and trudged north up Main Street but veered toward the river to gather her thoughts. Nobody was expecting her yet anyway at the McLoughlin home.

Sauntering toward the Willamette, Matilda hoped the deafening roar of the terraced falls would stifle the conflicting emotions swirling inside her. *Oh, Lord, please no.* Mr. Wirt had given her an option beyond living with William and Jane. He was old enough to be her father, true, but a good man, nonetheless.

What should she do? How could a widow provide for her boys? Would circumstances force her to spend a lifetime with a husband she despised?

She kicked a stone in her path. *Nicholas ... why? Why, oh, why?*

Just then a scream pierced her consciousness over the echo of the falls. Matilda shook herself from her reflections and looked around.

A mother holding an infant in her arms gestured wildly on the other side of the city's main street. A toddler with dark curls—a little girl—darted into the road. A team of horses pulling a wagon bore down on her.

Oh, dear God! She lifted her skirts and ran, knowing she would never arrive in time.

A tall man in black coat and pants rushed forward and scooped up the youngster, scarcely halting before reaching the other side.

Matilda released her breath, not realizing she'd been holding it in horror.

When the wagon passed, the child unharmed, she sank onto a stone.

The toddler's rescuer lifted the girl and crossed the road to the frantic mother. The figure looked familiar, but his face was shadowed. After he bent to retrieve a black top hat and riding crop from the boardwalk, Matilda recognized John R. Jackson.

He caught her gaze and tipped his hat to her.

She smiled. First, he'd saved her from Rawlins, and now he'd rescued a little lass. He was not only a gentleman but a protector too.

As she tossed in bed, sweat drenched her body. Rawlins grabbed her. No, let me go! She yanked against the strong fingers gripping her upper arm, cringing at his rough skin on her soft flesh. She screamed.

"Mama?" Grundy shook her shoulder. "Mama. Wake up."

Matilda rolled onto her side and gazed into the brown eyes of her third son. Such a kindhearted boy. Johnny whimpered in his sleep from the other side of the bed.

"Are you okay?" Grundy's brows drew together in a frown. "Are you—are you dying?"

Matilda sat up and pulled her son onto the bed beside her. "No, Grundy. Just a nightmare."

"Were you dreaming about Pa again?"

Matilda bit her lower lip. In the early months, her poor boys often awakened in the wee hours of the morning, reliving that horrible moment when their father plunged beneath the deep waters of the Snake, never to resurface. Could they ever shake the horrendous sight from their memories? She doubted it. She never would.

"No, honey. I don't quite remember my nightmare. But as we both know, the best cure for a frightening dream is to wake up, so it's faded away now." She squeezed him tightly. "Now crawl back into bed and sleep."

Grundy scurried across the room to the bed he shared with Bart and Henry and slipped beneath the covers. His rhythmic breathing soon followed.

Matilda lay back in the bed, staring at the ceiling. Tears seeped from the corners of her eyes, dampening the sweat-drenched pillow even more. Would she be stuck with Rawlins? Her skin crawled at the thought of his touch. No. She had options.

Tugging her Touching Stars friendship quilt over her shoulder, she closed her eyes. How she yearned for a trusted friend's advice. If she needed to marry again, perhaps Marcus … But could she trust him? He'd broken her heart once, but maybe he'd matured since then. Ten years and marriage to Nicholas had certainly changed her.

Matilda rolled over and kicked off the red and green quilt. She'd spoken about Nicholas, but Marcus hadn't said much about his wife. What was her name? Ida. How and when had she died? Did they have children? Her thoughts flitted over their recent walk and his reticence. *I talk about Nicholas all the time. I wonder why he doesn't speak of Ida.*

❧

The following evening, Matilda kissed her boys goodnight as she heard a knock on the door downstairs. She hurried to greet Marcus before he disturbed the McLoughlins.

"You going out again tonight with that young man?" The doctor's growl halted her footsteps.

"Yes, Doctor. Mr. Springer has invited me to dinner."

"Has he made his intentions known?"

Another knock resounded.

"Um … yes, I mean … sort of." Matilda looked between the doctor and the foyer. "He … he wants to marry me, if that's what you mean."

The doctor hefted his large frame from the chair and set down the pipe he'd been puffing. "That's exactly what I mean." He strode toward the entryway. "Mrs. Koontz, you need a husband, not a suitor."

Matilda dropped her head. "I know."

The doctor yanked open the door, and Marcus flashed a look at the older man, grinned, then peered into the house. "Matilda? Are you ready?"

"What exactly are you planning to do with Mrs. Koontz this evening, young man?" The doctor's voice boomed.

Heat rushed to Matilda's cheeks as if she were a young girl rather than a widow with four boys.

"We're enjoying supper at the café," Marcus explained. "Then perhaps a walk by the falls."

"What are your intentions toward Mrs. Koontz?"

Matilda wanted the floor to open and swallow her.

"I'm hoping ... I would like to marry her, sir."

"Good." McLoughlin draped an arm over his shoulder. "That's what I wanted to hear."

Marcus grinned at the doctor and then at Matilda. "Are you ready to leave?"

Matilda nodded and grabbed her jacket from a peg. Perhaps the good doctor truly was tired of his unexpected houseguests.

Marcus pulled the jacket from her hands and draped it over her shoulders. "Might be a bit chilly at that."

As they walked toward the café, Marcus filled the silence with banter. "I thought the old man would pummel me if I gave him the wrong answer."

"He wouldn't." Matilda smiled. "Dr. McLoughlin is the most gracious of men."

"He's a grizzly bear. And a mountain of a man who could rip this slim body to shreds with his teeth."

Matilda chuckled. Definitely a dandy. Nicholas would have enjoyed teasing Marcus—that is, if he hadn't been courting her.

He opened the café door and bowed at the waist, ushering her inside. He pulled out her chair and sat beside her. An attractive woman stepped to the table and rattled off the supper fare—pot roast or broiled salmon with mashed potatoes, huckleberry pie or bread pudding for dessert. Marcus ordered the pot roast and pie for both of them and winked at the serving woman who blushed.

A draft filled the room as the door opened again. Matilda glanced up to see Rawlins storm toward their table. Oh, dear, what now? She dropped her gaze to her hands, hoping he'd pass by.

"You two together again. Ain't that pretty." He guffawed, hands on his hips as he cleared his throat and looked around for a spittoon. Seeing none, he spewed into the corner.

Marcus gazed around the room. People stared at the two men. "I say—"

"Ha!" Rawlins bellowed. "You popinjay." He bent at the waist, both hands splayed on the table, and stared into Marcus' eyes. "I've been asking around about you, seeing as you're taking up with Mrs. Koontz here."

"What has Mrs. Koontz to do with you?"

Rawlins laughed. "Promised old Nick I'd look after her if anything happened." He curled his lip as he grinned at Matilda.

She cringed.

"So I took it upon myself to learn more about you." He cleared his throat. "Ran into an old acquaintance of yours from St. Louis."

Marcus hissed, "Sir, do you mind lowering your voice? You're drawing attention."

"I'll bet you don't want any attention, you reprobate." Rawlins raised his voice. "You're nothing but a scallywag." He sneered as he drew out the last word.

"Sir ..." Marcus flushed.

"Mr. Rawlins." Matilda cleared her voice. "Do you mind? We hoped to enjoy supper in peace."

"You'll thank me when you hear what I have to say, Widow Koontz." Rawlins glared at Marcus. "What do you know about this fellow?"

"Marcus and I knew each other in Missouri years ago."

"And did you know he's married?"

Marcus paled.

Matilda glanced between the two men. "Yes ... I knew he was married. His wife ... like Nicholas, he lost his wife."

"Ha!" Rawlins slapped his palm on the table as he lowered himself into a chair across from them. "That's rich. Yes, he lost her all right—lost her in Missouri. Heard tell he left her and three children back in St. Louis."

"What?" Matilda's heart stopped. "No ..." She turned to her dinner companion. "Marcus? You told me she died ... cholera..."

Marcus, jaw clenched, glared at Rawlins. But when he looked Matilda's way, he dropped his gaze. "I divorced her before I left." He reached for Matilda's hand. "She didn't want to come west. I know you understand how important that is."

Oh, no. She'd stepped out with a married man? *Oh, God, forgive me.* He may have divorced his wife, but they were still married in the eyes of God—and in her mind as well. Matilda's hands trembled as she reached for her reticule. "I'm not feeling well."

"I don't imagine you are." Rawlins laughed. "What would Nicholas say about his widow being courted by a married man?"

Her eyes swam as she stood, her legs shaky. She grasped the back of the chair. "I believe I'll return to the McLoughlins."

"I'll go with you." Rawlins grasped her arm.

Her skin crawled. Marcus had duped her again. She let Rawlins lead her from the table where Marcus sat, head down, a hand at his brow.

"I said you'd be glad to hear what I had to say." Rawlins' eyes exuded satisfaction and something else. Triumph. "Now you know I'm the best choice for you. He's a liar and good-for-nothing slacker, clearly not the choice for a fine woman like you. I, on the other hand, have money and a homestead. I could help your boys secure property when the time comes. It would be a marriage of sensibility."

Matilda, still shaken, wavered as she looked at the hard lines creasing his face. He couldn't really be the smart solution to her hardships, could he?

Matilda trudged silently beside him. She didn't like his hand on her arm. She didn't like the man at all. She looked up the street. How far were they from the McLoughlin home?

Rawlins stopped, swirling her toward him. His breath smelled of sour whiskey. Her stomach roiled. "You think you're too good for me."

Matilda yanked her arm, but Rawlins tightened his grip.

"I'd make a good husband," Rawlins spewed the words, his stale breath hot in her face. "A widow with four young'uns. That's a lot for any man to take on, but I'm game. I want to marry you, Mrs. Koontz, and help raise your boys."

"Mr. Rawlins. Please." Matilda gave him a pleading look. "Please. Just escort me back to the McLoughlins' home. I … I need time to think."

Rawlins scoffed. "What's to think about?" He loosened his grip on her arm as he sauntered forward. "You need a home. I need a wife, someone to cook and clean and …" His gaze roved over her body. "Keep me warm at night."

Spiders skittered over her skin at his words. She gasped and dropped her eyes to the ground. She glanced at the empty street. Would anyone hear her if she screamed?

A hand swept over her back and settled on the bustle of her skirt. Nicholas, why aren't you here? She dipped her hand through the drawstring of her reticule, seeking anything to protect her. A needle wouldn't offer much help.

Rawlins laughed. "Calm down, Matilda."

Her name on his lips licked like a serpent slithering down her back.

"I'll wait a bit." He stopped before the McLoughlin home. "Not long, mind you. But I do intend to marry you."

Matilda wrenched away from him and raced to the door. Mercifully, it opened to her grasp. She slid inside, shut the door, and bolted it. Her body trembled as her legs gave out. She slid to the floor in the foyer, arms wrapped around bent knees, head lowered into her arms, and sobbed.

Matilda thrashed around in bed most of the night, her mind reliving the heartbreak from her teenage years, then worrying about the wife and children Marcus left behind in Missouri. What if Nicholas had gone west without her? She rejected the thought as soon as it entered her mind. He never would have left her.

But he had. She bit back a sob. *Nicholas. Why did you die? We need you.*

The next morning, she arrived early at the tailor's shop and sewed, but questions plagued her mind. Why was Marcus so deceitful? Why couldn't Jim Rawlins accept she had no interest in him? Would William and Jane tire quickly of them if they crowded into their new cabin?

"Mrs. Koontz." Mr. Wirt's voice interrupted her morose thoughts. "You seem distracted today."

"I'm sorry, Mr. Wirt." Matilda folded the shirt she had finished stitching and handed it to her boss. "I didn't sleep well."

He examined her stitches. "Your work is admirable, Mrs. Koontz." He looked into her eyes before continuing. "Is it—I mean, you've had several young men vying for your attentions. Are you having difficulty deciding?"

Matilda scoffed, then lifted a hand to her mouth as she feigned a cough. No reason to burden Mr. Wirt with her woes. "No. Well, I mean, I don't have—that is, Mr. Springer isn't an option. Neither is Mr. Rawlins."

Mr. Wirt shook his head. "That Rawlins fellow struck me as a bit abrasive, but the other man—Mr. Springer? He seemed like a charmer."

"Indeed, he is a charmer." Matilda stood to retrieve a new bolt of flannel. "He charmed me into believing he wanted to marry me—but he left a wife and three children in Missouri."

Mr. Wirt gasped. "No. That scalawag." He pulled out a paper with an order and handed it to her. "You are welcome here as long as you'd like, Mrs. Koontz. You do commendable work." He cleared his throat. "If I were twenty-five years younger …" His face flushed. "I mean, not that you'd have me, but … I would …"

His voice trailed off. Matilda glanced at the older gentleman who had treated her with nothing but kindness since her arrival in this city—a widow with four boys, looking for a way to earn a living. She smiled at him.

"You would probably never consider me as a prospect for a husband." Mr. Wirt rubbed a palm over his clean-shaven chin and smoothed down a few wisps of hair. "A handsome woman such as yourself, but if—I mean, I'd be honored… that is, if you need a home for your boys…"

Matilda placed a hand on his forearm. "Mr. Wirt, you honor me." She sighed. "My boys are right, you know. Nicholas died only seven months ago, and we all miss him dearly. It's difficult to think of marrying anyone, but I am honored by your offer." She chuckled. "Imagine the chaos a wife and four children would bring into your calm and organized life."

He smiled a bit tremulously. "Yes, I'll admit I'm set in my ways." His eyes crinkled at the corners as he widened his grin. "You would be quite a catch, though, for this old bachelor."

"Thank you. I'll keep your generous offer in mind." Matilda seated herself again behind the table to cut out a shirt. She could do far worse than spend the rest of her life with a man as kind as Mr. Wirt.

Indeed, she never considered herself a beauty or any kind of catch; rather, practically a spinster when she married Nicholas at twenty-six. Although he always called her his "beauty" and "pretty filly," his ardor colored his perception. But out here, men flocked to her, even though she had four sons. Or perhaps it was because she had four sons? Hmmm … Do they want her boys as field hands on their homesteads? Not Mr. Wirt, though. As a shopkeeper, he didn't own a homestead. Maybe she should consider his offer more seriously.

THIRTY-NINE

A S MATILDA OPENED THE DOOR after another long day working for Mr. Wirt, boisterous laughter erupted from the sitting room. The McLoughlins must have company. She hung up her shawl and brushed back her hair, tucking a stray strand into her bun. Perhaps she could help in the kitchen.

"Mrs. Koontz? Is that you?" The doctor's deep voice reverberated as he bellowed the words.

Matilda stepped around the corner. "Yes, Dr. McLoughlin."

"You remember John Jackson, don't you?"

"Of course." Matilda dipped her head and then gazed at the British gentleman she'd seen rescue a child a few days earlier. "How are you, sir?"

"Grand," he said, stroking his thick dark sideburns. "It's wonderful to see you again, Mrs. Koontz."

"Nice to see you too." Matilda smiled, her cheeks warm, then turned toward the doctor. "Perhaps I should help Marguerite in the kitchen." As she left the room, she heard footsteps above. She detoured upstairs to check on her sons.

"Mama!" Johnny spied her first and surged forward, nearly toppling her. "You're home."

She gripped the door frame to steady herself. Then she bent to pick up her littlest son. "Have you been good for your brothers?"

Johnny nodded before popping his thumb into his mouth.

"Boys, you'll need to be quiet." She glanced at Henry, Bart, and Grundy. Such precious children. "The McLoughlins have company. I'm going to help with supper."

"We'll be quiet, Ma." Bart reached for Johnny.

She raced down to the kitchen, where Marguerite was already working. Grabbing an apron, she wrapped it around her waist. "How can I help?"

The next hour passed in a whirlwind of chopping, peeling, boiling, and baking. She and Marguerite filled the serving bowls and platters with venison, potatoes, and carrots that Eloisa carried to the table. Then Matilda and Eloisa called their children to the meal. With everyone seated, the doctor offered a brief prayer and then passed the food platters and bowls.

"I understand Joseph Meek is in Washington City." John Jackson placed a piece of venison on his plate.

"Indeed, nine other men joined him to deliver the petition for official territorial status." The doctor poured gravy over his mashed potatoes. "I hope they succeed. We need a military presence here."

"Seems all Congress can discuss is the Mexican War and slavery," Jackson offered.

"I doubt Joseph will let them ignore him, especially not after his daughter died of measles as a captive." Dr. McLoughlin eyed his dinner guests and changed the subject. "John, why don't you tell Mrs. Koontz a bit more about your farm?"

Jackson wiped his mouth with his napkin. "The land north of the Columbia River toward Puget Sound is abundant with timber and prime farmland." He pulled a parchment from his inside pocket. "In fact, the editor of the *Oregon Spectator* asked me to write a piece about the region for his newspaper."

"Why don't you read it?" McLoughlin nodded toward his guest.

Jackson laughed. "I'm sure it would bore the other dinner guests to no end."

"Not at all, Mr. Jackson." Matilda leaned forward. "We are eager to learn about this land."

"I'll just mention a few of the highlights." Jackson unfolded the paper. "The Cowlitz settlement is in a prairie district on the Cowlitz River, about thirty miles upstream from its mouth. The settlement is small, composed principally of Canadians. The soil is extremely rich and covered with timber. Strong signs of lead and iron ore appear as you proceed up the river. Stone coal is found in great abundance. The river—"

"What's stone coal?" Grundy asked, the words garbled as he chewed.

"Grundy, you know better than to interrupt—and with a full mouth, too." Heat filled Matilda's cheeks. "I apologize, Mr. Jackson."

"Think nothing of it, ma'am." Jackson set down his fork and faced Grundy. "As to your question, stone coal is also called anthracite or hard coal. It's the highest quality coal with the fewest impurities. Best coal you can find anywhere."

Grundy swallowed and flashed a look at his mother. "Thank you for explaining, sir. I'm sorry I interrupted."

Jackson smiled and glanced at Dr. McLoughlin who nodded at him to proceed.

"The river is navigated by bateaux," he said. "More experienced watermen than myself say it may be navigated by steamboat. The settlement has a saw and flouring mill. The plains are small but beautiful. North of the settlement are the waters of the Chehalis River, which is about one hundred fifty miles long, a safe and easy stream for navigation. The country and soil are admirably adapted to agriculture and grazing purposes."

He paused again.

"Go on, please, Mr. Jackson," Marguerite said. "I've seldom ventured north of Fort Vancouver. What else did you write?"

Jackson continued. "There is a small American settlement at the head of the Sound, which also has a saw and flouring mill. The settlement is called New Market, and I have seen as good vegetables growing there as I ever saw on the continent of America. Ten miles from New Market is another small American settlement, on the Nisqually bottom, formed in 1847. The soil here is equal to the soil in the Cowlitz settlement, and three miles beyond is Fort Nisqually."

"They grow wheat up there, don't they?" the doctor asked.

"I've seen it produce twenty bushels to the acre, as good a quality as any in the territory," Jackson said. "The land east toward the mountain is a beautiful landscape."

"What's the Puget Sound like?" Henry asked.

"I've mentioned it in this piece, young man." Lifting the paper again, Jackson continued reading. "Puget Sound is a beautiful sheet of water, more than one hundred miles in length, which, with its numberless bays and harbors, will admit of the settlement of one thousand families, on a section each, and each having ship navigation at their own door."

"Do you know any Indians?" Henry asked.

Jackson laughed. "Many. They're helpful. Fact is, the first white man in the region married an Indian."

"Who's that?"

"Simon Plamondon, a trapper for the Northwest Fur Company." Jackson tousled Henry's hair. "A giant of a man."

"Taller than you?" Bart asked.

"Oh, yes, by about half a head over my six feet." Jackson chuckled, then glanced at Matilda. "Perhaps someday I'll be able to show the region to you."

Matilda smiled briefly as her face flushed. She dropped her gaze.

"Mama. Mama." Johnny pulled Matilda's arm. She bent closer to the youngster. "What's wrong with his eye?"

Heat seared her face as she whispered, "Hush now." She couldn't blame Johnny for asking about Jackson's blinded white eye, but she prayed the gentleman hadn't heard her son's question.

Jackson winked and flashed her a slight grin, then bent in his chair to look her youngest son in the eye. "Well, young man, I wasn't much older than you when I was thrown from a horse and landed in a hawthorn bush."

"A haw...what's a haw bush?"

"Hawthorn, a bush with white flowers and spiky thorns. The thorns scraped my eye, and one pierced the eyeball."

"Eww!" Henry said. "That must have hurt!"

"Indeed it did." Jackson turned toward Henry. "But it hurt like the dickens, but even more when the doctor pulled out the thorn. My eye turned white, and I couldn't see a thing—then or now."

Matilda stood to clear the dishes, head down. Dr. McLoughlin and John Jackson retired to the library for their cordials while the women cleaned up.

"Mrs. Koontz?" John Jackson stood at the door to the kitchen. "Might I please have a word with you?"

"Of course." Matilda wiped her hands on a dish towel and then ran her palms over her auburn hair to tuck in any loose strands.

Jackson cleared his throat. "Would you like to take a stroll with me?"

Matilda smiled, removing her apron. "Thank you, Mr. Jackson. I'd enjoy that."

She walked with him to the foyer and lifted her shawl. He took it from her, draped it over her shoulders, and opened the door. "After you, ma'am."

She glanced at her escort. "I apologize for Johnny's impertinence in asking about your eye."

Jackson laughed softly. "I'd wonder too if I was a lad."

"You seem good with children." Matilda waved toward the street. "I saw you save that little girl from the horse and carriage."

Jackson shrugged. "I certainly couldn't stand by and do nothing. I'm glad I saw her in time."

"I'm sure her mother is grateful." She swallowed. "I know I would be."

They strolled in silence. Frogs croaked in the distance. Small white trilliums bloomed among green leaves in nearby forests. Splendid purple flowers covered a large bush, shimmering in the setting sun.

"What are those blossoms?" Matilda lifted one of the tender blooms to her nose and inhaled.

"Rhododendrons." Jackson leaned forward to sniff the flower. "Nice fragrance. They grow throughout the Northwest. I have plenty on my property."

Matilda sighed. "It truly is a beautiful land. I only wish …"

"I'm certain you must miss your husband dearly."

"He was so eager for his sons to grow up here." Matilda sighed. "Now they will … but without their father."

"Your sons look to be fine healthy boys." Jackson pulled a pipe from his pocket. "They appear to have adjusted well, despite their loss."

"We don't have much choice, do we?" Matilda gazed at the orange glow spreading across the sky to the west. "They're strong boys, much like their father."

"Have you thought about what you'll do?" Jackson lit his pipe and inhaled. "The doctor told me your nephew offered you a home with him."

"He did." She didn't mention that Mr. Wirt had proposed marriage.

"I'd like to offer you another option."

Matilda glanced at him, then returned her gaze to the sky.

"I have a fine little cabin at the Highlands. The house is small, but it's large enough for you and me and your boys." He chuckled. "I built it for myself without much thought for the niceties, such as windows. I never imagined …" He cleared his throat. "I didn't anticipate I'd marry again … until I met you, Mrs. Koontz."

She drew in a quick breath.

"I'd like to offer you and your sons a home at the Highlands." He stopped walking and gazed at her. "If you'll marry me."

Matilda remained silent for a moment. "That's a kind offer, Mr. Jackson. I just—I don't believe I know you well enough to marry you."

"What is it you would like to know? Please, ask me anything." He spread his arms wide, his pipe in one hand, smoke curling upward. "I have nothing to hide."

She chuckled. "Oh, my! Where to begin?"

"I'll make it easy for you. I'll tell you a bit about myself. I was born in England, Durham County to be exact, on January 13, 1800. That makes me what—ten or fifteen years older than you?"

Matilda did the math in her head—forty-eight. "Ten."

"My father was a farmer near Raby Castle, owned by the sixth earl of Westmoreland. I have two brothers and four sisters. Parents are Michael Jackson and Mary Robinson. I can read and write, learned to farm, and practiced the butcher trade for a while."

Matilda changed the subject. "Why did you leave England?"

"Same reason your Nicholas wanted to move west. Better life. More opportunity." Jackson puffed his pipe. "I arrived in New York in September of '33 and figured I'd stay there. Even applied for citizenship."

"Are you an American then?" Matilda asked.

"I filed all the paperwork for citizenship in the Court of Common Pleas in Dutchess County, back in '34, but I moved to Illinois before they approved it." He winked at her. "I'd prefer you didn't let Dr. McLoughlin know that, though. The good doctor always figured me for a British citizen, and I never dissuaded him. Elsewise, as a good British subject and chief factor of Fort Vancouver, he might have ordered me to go south to the American side of the Columbia instead of letting me travel north."

"Oh, that's right—Polk's famous battle cry, fifty-four-forty or fight." She chuckled.

"The president didn't keep all the land to Alaska, but he forced the British north from the Columbia," Jackson said. "They had to give up Fort Vancouver, the Cowlitz Farm, Nisqually."

"You're quite familiar with this land, aren't you?"

"I've learned quickly, I'd say." Jackson puffed a circle of smoke from his pipe. "Met a lot of French-Canadian trappers. Friendly lot. Not too happy to see the British forced out. But … they'll make good Americans too." When he grinned, his mutton-chop sideburns on his otherwise clean-shaven face expanded.

She smiled. "What did you do in Illinois?"

"Worked on farms near Briggsville and Pittsfield in Pike County," he said. "Plowed their fields and saved money until I could buy my own land. Had to take some folks to court to recover what they owed me."

"Oh, dear. That sounds difficult."

"I kept meticulous records." Jackson guided her across the road. "Sometimes the judge made them pay; sometimes he didn't. I bought and sold land. Livestock too—cattle, pigs, horses. Sawed fences for folks and broke land."

He sounded like an industrious worker. A lot like Nicholas. A bit more refined though. "What was your wife like, Mr. Jackson?"

He nodded. "Rachel …" His eyes lifted to the sky. "She was so young when she died, not quite twenty, in fact. A sweet girl. Lovely." He swallowed. "She wanted a child so much, and then…"

Tears pricked Matilda's eyes. "I'm so sorry." She placed her hands over her stomach. "I … I lost a baby on the trail. After Nicholas …"

"Oh, dear lady!" Jackson reached a hand to hers in a comforting gesture. "I didn't know the extent of your heartache."

Matilda appreciated his kindness. "Thank you."

He cleared his throat and tucked a hand into his trouser pocket. "After Rachel, I figured I'd just remain a bachelor." He glanced at Matilda. "Then I met you." A flush crept up his face around the sideburns. "I'll admit I've taken quite a fancy to you, Mrs. Koontz. You're a beautiful woman, and it's easy enough to see you've got a good heart, too."

He lifted his eyes to the road before looking back at her. "It's mighty lonely up north, and I could use the company of you and your boys."

"Do you want more children?"

Jackson chuckled. "I'm not a spring chicken, but I'd like to have children, yes." He shrugged. "But if I didn't have any, we'd have four fine young boys already."

At least he included her sons in his marriage proposal. He didn't plan to ship them off as Marcus had suggested.

"What about you?" he asked. "Do you want more children?"

Matilda thought about her sons, her daughter, the future. "I love children." As moisture threatened to fill her eyes, she changed the subject to safer ground. "When did you come to Oregon, Mr. Jackson?"

"I moved to Missouri first in '40 and farmed for three years. Raised cattle. But the flood of '44 destroyed my crops. I shifted the livestock to higher ground but lost all that work." He threw up both arms. "Decided then I'd had enough. Stories I'd heard about Oregon with its mild climate sounded better than what I faced in Missouri. So I left that spring. Brought my cattle west with me."

"You herded the cattle?" Matilda was surprised. He looked like such a gentleman; she couldn't imagine him as a cowhand.

"Sure did. Brought wheat, peas, oats, and pork with me on pack mules. Joined Colonel Nathaniel Ford's company. Had about a hundred wagons and five hundred people."

"Was the crossing difficult with such a large group?"

"Other than the mud?" Jackson chuckled. "We had a wet spring. Bolts of lightning threatened to stampede the cattle every time it stormed." He shook his head. "Two solid months of rain. Only eight dry days."

"We enjoyed better weather on our journey."

"Most everyone probably did. We couldn't imagine so much rain. Folks started wondering if it was worth it, but turning back meant more of the same. At least the west offered a new climate." He turned toward her. "Tell me about your journey—I mean, that is, if it's not too painful."

Matilda spoke about their journey, their stay with the Whitmans, and her tumultuous trip over the falls. She didn't mention the Three Island Crossing.

By that point in their walk, they had returned to the McLoughlin home, but Jackson guided her to a bench. "On our trip, I and another gent by my same name—John H.P. Jackson—had horses and mules stolen by Indians, and we each had to pay a chief more than three dollars for their return." Jackson scoffed. "Quite a racket they have there." He sobered. "We did lose some people in the wagon train—Mr. Barnett died of typhus. He was a good man."

"Did you stop at the Whitmans' mission?"

"No." Jackson shook his head. "We were too eager to settle the land. Rode through to The Dalles Mission and herded those cattle down a narrow path to Fort Vancouver. That's where I met the doctor. Like I said, he let me settle up north, since I was from England."

Matilda drew her shawl tighter.

"It's growing late—and chilly." Jackson helped her to her feet. "Thank you for the walk, Mrs. Koontz. I hope we can do it again. I'll be returning home next week, so I hope you'll consider my offer. I'd make you a good husband. I can provide for you and your boys. I already have a cabin, and I'll build you a larger house. Sawmills are scarce, so it'll probably be a log cabin, but I'll install plenty of paned windows so you can enjoy the glory of the majestic mountains and deep forests." He lifted her hands and looked into her eyes. "You'd make me a happy man if you would agree to be my wife."

"Thank you, Mr. Jackson." Matilda smiled. "I am honored. I do have one more question, though."

"By all means, ask anything."

"Are you a praying man?" Matilda gazed at the twinkling stars in the night sky and drew a deep breath. "I mean, are you a Christian?"

Jackson chuckled. "Spent my early years attending the Anglican church every Sunday with my parents. Yes, I'm a Christian." His brows drew together. "Although, to be honest, I haven't been as diligent about church attendance in recent years." He chuckled. "Of course, we don't have many churches up north, but I've been to the Catholic mission a time or two at the request of Simon Plamondon, a French-Canadian who urged the bishop in Quebec to start the mission."

"So are you Catholic?" Matilda asked.

"No, I'm Protestant, but the only church around is the Catholic mission—at least at present." He breathed deeply. "Truth is, I see God all around my place. In the mountains, the vast prairies, the tall trees and rushing rivers, even the stars above." He shrugged. "He's everywhere. Seems to me that's what it says in the Bible somewhere: 'The heavens declare the glory of God; and the firmament sheweth his handywork.'"

"Psalm 19," Matilda said without thinking. "I love that verse." She stood. "I enjoyed our talk, and I thank you for the kind offer. I need to pray about it."

"By all means, yes." Jackson led her to the door.

Mr. Jackson appeared to be a good man. Dr. McLoughlin certainly seemed to think so. And Mr. Wirt—he was so kind to offer, but she knew a wife and four children at his age could only bring him misery.

If she accepted his proposal, she hoped her new home would be everything John had promised. When she'd prayed, it seemed God wanted her to accept his proposal. But would she and her boys grow to love this man?

❧

The next afternoon, Matilda called her boys to the sitting room. She sat in the rocker, her sons gathered on the floor at her feet. "We need to discuss our future."

"Aren't we going to live with William and Jane?" Henry asked.

"Jane doesn't like us." Grundy nudged his older brother. "Why would we want to live with them?"

"Of course, Jane likes you." Matilda leaned forward and pulled Johnny onto her lap. "William did offer to let us live with them." She drew a deep breath. "We also have other options."

"Like what?" Henry leaned back on his elbows. "You're not going to marry that Mr. Springer, are you?"

"No, Henry, I'm not going to marry Mr. Springer." Matilda looked at each boy in turn. "However, Mr. Jackson has asked me to be his wife."

"What?" Henry jumped to his feet. "Ma, you can't marry him—or anyone. You're Pa's wife. He's … Pa's …" He trailed off, his eyes watery.

Matilda swallowed the lump in her throat and forced back tears. "I realize your father has been gone only seven months." She sighed. "But we must look forward, not backward. We must think of our future—where we're going to live and how we'll manage."

"We can make it on our own!" Henry shouted.

She reached forward, pulling Henry toward her, and held his thin shoulders. "I don't believe we can live alone and provide you with the future your father wanted. But Mr. Jackson can give you that future. He has the land. A home. Cattle."

Henry yanked away. "He's not going to be my pa!"

"Nobody can ever take the place of your father." Matilda pleaded with her eldest son. "He won't be your father, not like Nicholas. He'd be your Oregon pa."

"Are we going to have to call him pa?" Henry demanded.

"No. You can call him Mr. Jackson for now. Perhaps after we've been together for a time, you'll find a name you can call him."

"I'd call him a wife-stealer." Henry scowled.

"Or Mr. White-Eye," Grundy muttered.

"Grundy!" Matilda furrowed her brows.

He mumbled an apology.

"Do you love him, Ma?" Bart asked her.

Matilda let her gaze fall on his gentle face. "Not yet. But I imagine … in time I will."

"How do you know?" Henry asked. "You don't hardly even know him. None of us do. He could be as bad as that Mr. Rawlins."

"You've met him several times." Matilda looked him in the eye. "Do you think he's a bad man?"

Henry stuffed his hands into his pockets. "Naw. I s'pose not."

"You know he's a gentleman." Matilda sighed. "You like Dr. McLoughlin, don't you? He speaks very highly of Mr. Jackson."

Henry's voice dropped to a whisper. "It's too soon."

Matilda saw liquid in his eyes. Tears filled hers too. But she couldn't cry. She needed to be strong. For her sons. For herself. For their future.

"Mr. Jackson is leaving for his home in a week." She stood. "He wants us to marry before he leaves, so we can go with him."

"But…" Henry jumped to his feet and stormed from the room.

Matilda sighed.

"Will you have a fancy wedding?" Grundy asked.

"We'll just have a simple ceremony." She looked at her boys. "You'll all be there with me. This marriage will unite all six of us as a family."

Bart nodded. Grundy shrugged. Johnny continued playing with sticks on the floor. She left the room in search of her eldest son. She found him outside on the bench.

"Henry?" She spoke softly. "Do you mind if I sit with you?"

He shook his head and wiped his face with the sleeve of his shirt. "I miss Pa."

"So do I." Matilda tried to still the quiver in her voice. She inhaled a shaky breath. "I will always miss your father. I loved him dearly." She pulled Henry close. "Just like I know you did."

"Will it ... will it ever quit hurting?"

Her heart broke for Henry, the son most like her husband, his father's shadow from as soon as he could walk. "I believe the pain will ease, but he'll always hold a part of our hearts." She sighed. "And he's still here."

"What do you mean?"

"I see him in you." She gazed into his eyes, so like his father's. "And in Bart. Grundy. Johnny. And I know someday we'll all be together again."

Henry nodded. "Ma?"

"Yes?"

"If you need to marry Mr. Jackson, you can."

Matilda bit her lip to keep it from trembling. She dabbed at tears. "Thank you, Henry."

So much had happened since they left Missouri a year ago. The long trek. Friendships formed. The heartache and loss.

Nicholas hadn't survived the journey, but she and the boys would fulfill his dream.

Nicholas, we have reached the promised land!

The boys had a bright future ahead, and so did she, with a good and faithful man at her side.

Epilogue

MATILDA SIPPED HER LUKEWARM TEA, fatigued from recounting her experience.

"So, to answer your question, Colonel Hobart, yes, the Oregon Trail was as dangerous as people say it was."

The reporter gawked at the crumpled woman before him, perhaps trying to reconcile her frailty with the image of the strong and determined woman of her story.

"Your house now has plenty of windows, doesn't it?" He glanced through the glass facing east. "And beautiful flowers, a huge vegetable garden, and is that an orchard?"

"Yes, it is." Matilda rocked slowly in her chair. "Thank you."

"Did you ever see your mother again?"

Matilda shook her head. "We wrote letters. Mother lived with my sister and her husband and then with a brother. She died in 1856. But Philip and Sarah settled in Oregon. Philip visited us a time or two."

"What about Captain Magone? Did he find your cattle?"

A frown creased Matilda's wrinkled face. "No, I didn't see the captain again. He never tracked down the folks who stole my cattle.

He wrote to me when he and Mary Ann Thompkins married. They had several children, I believe."

"Is he still living?"

"Indeed, he is." Matilda chuckled. "Last year you may have read in the newspapers about a man who walked from Canyon City in Oregon all the way across the country to the World's Fair in Chicago. That was Captain Magone. Took him seventy days. He averaged thirty miles a day, twice what our oxen could do."

Colonel Charles W. Hobart shifted in his seat. "What has your life looked like since your arrival? Was the promise of this fertile land worth the journey?"

She gazed out the window at the lavender lilacs encircling the entrance, the rhododendrons blooming beside them. She ran her palm across the black leather cover of the Bible in her lap. "My boys helped build this place. Did you know it was the first courthouse in Washington Territory?"

"I did." Hobart cleared his throat. "I met your son, Bart. Are your other boys living nearby?"

Matilda fingered the ties of her crimson bonnet, remembering how she found the surprise gift from Nicholas so many decades ago. She drew a deep breath. "John lives on Drews Prairie, not far from here."

"And the others?"

She lapsed into silence.

Colonel Hobart cleared his throat. "Did you and Mr. Jackson have children together?"

Matilda nodded. "Mary, who lives just down the road. And Louisa; she and her husband live in Chehalis."

He leaned back in his chair. "I understand Mr. Jackson passed in 1873."

"Yes, he did. May 23. We had just celebrated our twenty-fifth wedding anniversary." She rocked in her chair, caressing the Bible in her lap. "We shared many good years together." Her eyes glistened as a slight smile lifted her cheeks. "He helped form Washington Territory, you know. He voted at both the Cowlitz and Monticello conventions to carve out this state. He was the first sheriff, clerk, justice of the peace, and census taker. We operated a hotel here for a number of years."

Again, she grew quiet.

"If you don't mind my asking, how ... how did you handle so much grief?"

"I find hope in here." She lifted her Bible and looked him in the eye. "Because of God's promises, I know I'll see them all again in heaven."

AUTHOR'S NOTE

Matilda Koontz and John R. Jackson married on May 4, 1848, in the Baptist Church of Oregon City and left with her four boys for the Highlands. The boys helped build the first courthouse in Washington Territory, which still stands today south of Chehalis. On clear days, majestic Mount Rainier towers in the distance.

The Jacksons operated a hotel at their place on the Highlands. Matilda became known for her hospitality throughout the region and even in the nation's capital. Among those enjoying her hospitality were Washington Territorial Governor Isaac Stevens and generals Ulysses S. Grant, Philip Sheridan, and George McClelland.

John and Matilda had three children together—Mary, Louisa, and Andrew.

But Matilda's grief didn't end.

Grundy died of white swelling of the knee on December 7, 1855, during the Indian Wars. He was fourteen, and Matilda refused to leave the cabin for the protection of a fort, insisting she would stay by his side.

Henry was eighteen when he drowned in the Cowlitz River on June 1, 1857.

And her youngest child, Andrew Jackson, succumbed to diphtheria on February 27, 1861.

William and Jane, who lived near present-day Mount Angel, Oregon, never had children.

Although inspired by the life of Matilda Koontz Jackson, this novel is a work of fiction.

Readers today may find the word Indian objectionable when referring to Native Americans, but in a novel about a nineteenth-century pioneer, using modern, inclusive terms would be distracting and historically inaccurate, suggesting a racial tolerance not practiced at the time.

The incident with the priest refusing to conduct the funeral for little Sara Brown (whose first name I changed to Sadie to avoid confusion with Sarah Jory) actually happened. It was shared in the Archbishop Augustin Magloire Alexandre Blanchet's journal.

If you enjoyed *The Reluctant Pioneer*, please consider leaving a review on Amazon, Barnes and Noble, or Goodreads.

If you're interested in Matilda's nonfiction story, check out *Washington Territory's Grand Lady: The Story of Matilda (Glover) Koontz Jackson*, which was a finalist for the Western Writers of America Spur Award and the Will Rogers Medallion. It can be found at Barnes & Noble, Amazon, Walmart, and other retailers.

As a thank you for reading my debut novel, receive a free color pictorial booklet of the Oregon Trail along with special tidbits from Matilda's life including the short diary Nicholas wrote as they embarked on their journey. Just type in this link: https://Book Hip.com/KLDXDSS

Visit me at maczander.com or on Facebook at Julie McDonald Zander, Author, or on Goodreads.

Acknowledgments

So many wonderful writers contributed to helping me write this debut novel of Matilda Koontz Jackson's life. I appreciate the kindness of critique group members who taught me to leave the reporter behind and focus on the story.

I'm indebted to my critique group members in the Portland area—Melanie Dobson, Nicole Miller, Tracie Heskett, and Dawn Hill Shipman. I also appreciate the members of the Inklings who meet weekly in Centralia, Washington—Kyle Pratt, Carolyn Bickel, Debby Lee, Barbara Tifft Blakey, Heather Alexander, and Kristie Kandoll.

I'm grateful to my good and talented friend Paula Slavens, who invites me to run away once a year with her to Newport, Oregon, where we work on our writing projects and catch up on each other's lives.

Special thanks to the people who read an early copy of this novel and provided insights to improve it—my husband, Larry, and daughter, Nora, as well as Barbara, Heather, Sandra Crowell, Jana Kaye, Linda Kann (my walking partner), Joyce Scott, and Robin Montgomery.

I appreciate the endorsements of Barbara, Melanie, Dawn, Marilyn Rhoads, and Leslie Gould.

Editor and proofreader Katie Heister offered wonderful suggestions to improve the story. I also appreciate the final proofreading by Sue Miholer of Picky, Picky Ink.

I am grateful to my personal history clients who have taught me so much throughout my career.

Special appreciation and love goes to my husband, Larry Zander, my first and last in-house editor who has saved me from so many errors. Thanks to my parents who encouraged me in all my endeavors and to my precious children, Paul and Nora, and stepchildren, Amanda and Andrew.

ABOUT THE AUTHOR

Julie McDonald Zander, an avid fan of history, earned a bachelor's in communications and political science from the University of Washington. After working two decades as a newspaper reporter and editor, she launched a personal history business to capture and preserve life stories. Her company, Chapters of Life, has published more than seventy-five books. She and her husband live in the Pacific Northwest, where they raised two children.

Nonfiction Books
by Julie McDonald Zander

Retracing the Oregon Trail in Pictures:
Following the Journey of Matilda Koontz Jackson

Don Buswell: Going Strong at 101

James Stafford: Advocate for the Arts

Carol Ponder and the History of Salzer Valley

Washington Territory's Grand Lady:
The Story of Matilda (Glover) Koontz Jackson

Escape from Communism:
The Life & Loves of Anna (Strods) Melkers

Centralia College: Its People and Their Stories

Chapters of Life at the Southwest Washington Fair

These Walls Talk: Lewis County's Historic 1927 Courthouse

Chehalis: A 'Can-Do' Community, A History of Industrial
Development in Lewis County, Founders Edition

A History of the Chehalis Industrial Commission: A Community-
Owned Not-for-Profit 501(c)3 Group of Friends!

Herman Klaber 'King of Hops'

Chapters of Life in Chehalis 1915 (edited and republished)

Bucoda: The Little Town with a Million Memories

Chapters of Life in Bucoda

Winning a War: Stories of Those Who Fought, Served, and Sacrificed during World War II

Anatomy of a Miracle: Centralia Christian School: The First Thirty Years with Jess Daniels

Legacy of Two Lumbermen: The Hemphill-O'Neill Company History

Life on the Home Front: Stories of those who worked, waited, and worried during WWII

Made in the USA
Columbia, SC
03 December 2024

48128149R00212